PENGUIN CLASSICS

THE DUEL
AND OTHER STORIES

ANTON PAVLOVICH CHEKHOV, the son of a former serf, was born in 1860 in Taganrog, a port on the Sea of Azov. He received a classical education at the Taganrog Secondary School, then in 1879 he went to Moscow, where he entered the medical faculty of the university, graduating in 1884. During his university years he supported his family by contributing humorous stories and sketches to magazines. He published his first volume of stories, *Motley Stories*, in 1886 and a year later his second volume, *In the Twilight*, for which he was awarded the Pushkin Prize by the Russian Academy. His most famous stories were written after his return from the convict island of Sakhalin, which he visited in 1890. For five years he lived on his small country estate near Moscow, but when his health began to fail he moved to the Crimea. After 1900, the rest of his life was spent at Yalta, where he met Tolstoy and Gorky. He wrote very few stories during the last years of his life, devoting most of his time to a thorough revision of his stories for a collected edition of his works, published in 1901, and to the writing of his great plays. In 1901 Chekhov married Olga Knipper, an actress of the Moscow Art Theatre. He died of consumption in 1904.

RONALD WILKS studied Russian language and literature at Trinity College, Cambridge, and later Russian literature at London University, where he received his Ph.D. in 1972. He has also translated 'The Little Demon' by Sologub and, for the Penguin Classics, *My Childhood*, *My Apprenticeship* and *My Universities* by Gorky, *Diary of a Madman* by Gogol, *The Golovly Family* by Saltykov-Shchedrin and *The Kiss and Other Stories*, *The Party and Other Stories* and *The Fiancée and Other Stories* by Chekhov.

CHEKHOV

THE DUEL

AND OTHER STORIES

TRANSLATED WITH AN INTRODUCTION BY
RONALD WILKS

PENGUIN BOOKS

PENGUIN BOOKS

Published by the Penguin Group
Penguin Books Ltd, 27 Wrights Lane, London w8 5tz, England
Viking Penguin, a division of Penguin Books USA Inc.
375 Hudson Street, New York, New York 10014, USA
Penguin Books Australia Ltd, Ringwood, Victoria, Australia
Penguin Books Canada Ltd, 2801 John Street, Markham, Ontario, Canada l3r 1b4
Penguin Books (NZ) Ltd, 182–190 Wairau Road, Auckland 10, New Zealand

Penguin Books Ltd, Registered Offices: Harmondsworth, Middlesex, England

This translation first published 1984
7 9 10 8 6

Translation and Introduction copyright © Ronald Wilks, 1984
All rights reserved

Printed in England by Clays Ltd, St Ives plc
Filmset in Monophoto Bembo

Contents

To my son, Alexander
                    R.W.

Introduction

The six stories in this selection were written between 1891 and 1895, before the period of the great plays, but when Chekhov was at the height of his powers as short-story writer. They deal with a variety of themes — religious sectarianism, megalomania, scientific controversies of the day, provincial life in all its tedium and philistinism — and in all of them we see the hand of a master.

The title story, *The Duel*, was written after Chekhov's return from the convict settlement on Sakhalin, where he had travelled to gather material for a detailed survey, the fruits of which appeared in his remarkable *Sakhalin Island*. It was first published in Suvorin's *New Times* in 1891 and can perhaps be viewed as the last in the line (together with Tolstoy's *Hadji Murat*) of that great tradition of nineteenth-century Russian literature with the Caucasus as its setting, that stemmed from Pushkin and Lermontov. It is one of his longest works of fiction (it could rightly be termed a short novel) and, as he himself admitted, cost him much trouble, with a great deal of revision. *The Duel* differs from most of his other stories in its firm narrative line and tautly constructed plot and sub-plot; and in the strong use of dialogue to advance the story it has close affinities with his plays — the confrontations between the main characters clearly resembling those in *Uncle Vanya*.

At the time of writing *The Duel* Chekhov was having frequent arguments with the leading Moscow zoologist V. A. Wagner. As his brother Michael writes in his memoirs, 'there were frequent quarrels about the then fashionable "degeneration", the rights of the strong, which became the basis of von Koren's philosophy ... Anton always supported the opinion that strength of spirit in men can always conquer inherited defects.'

In this story Ivan Layevsky, a self-styled 'St Petersburg Hamlet', has escaped to the Caucasus with distinctly Tolstoyan ideas of the noble life of toil on the land. Having run away with another man's wife (distinctly un-Tolstoyan), instead of putting these ideas into motion Layevsky lapses into complete idleness, neglecting his very undemanding work as a civil servant and spending his time drinking and playing cards. In turn, Nadezhda his mistress, with whom he had hoped to enjoy his idyllic visions, sleeps with the local chief of police and prostitutes herself to the son of a shopkeeper to whom she is in debt. The zoologist von Koren, who has come to the small seaside town on the Black Sea to study 'the embryology of the jelly-fish', symbolizes the Nietzschean strong man of action (his name bears witness to the fact that most leading zoologists in Russia were of German extraction) and he bitterly attacks Layevsky for his laziness and pernicious, demoralizing influence on the local populace. In von Koren's advocacy of the 'extermination' of Layevsky – the logical conclusion, in his eyes, of his scientific theories – Chekhov vigorously examines the application of zoology and neo-Darwinism to ethics and politics in vogue at the time. Darwinism was seen by extreme thinkers as a justification for war and suffering and Chekhov attacks this faith in the perfectibility of the human species that condoned the extermination of the weak and ineffectual. A searching analysis of these theories is seen also in *A Dreary Story* and in *Gusev*. Contrary to the zoologist Wagner's belief that the weak must be eliminated from society in the interest of the progress of humanity, Chekhov always held that the human spirit can triumph over inherited defects by effort and education and thus von Koren, the intellectual *Übermensch*, is treated satirically. Chekhov had no blind faith in nineteenth-century positivism nor belief in the inevitability of progress: although a man of science himself, he did believe in the ultimately civilizing powers of knowledge and education, however.

Besides the major characters – von Koren, Layevsky, Nadezhda, the good-natured, ever-helpful Dr Samoylenko and the self-righteous, effusive Mrs Bityugov – the minor characters are treated with the sure touch of the future master dramatist. Kerbalay, the smiling, shifty Tartar innkeeper, the morose Dr Ustimovich, and Govorovsky and Boyko, the young officers who are present at the duel – all are vividly portrayed.

As Lermontov had done so superbly before him, Chekhov brilliantly captures the atmosphere of a small, dull Black Sea resort with the looming mountains all around, and his life in that region surely afforded much material. The descriptions of the mountain scenery are poetic and highly evocative and recall passages in *A Hero of Our Time*:

Here and there that gloomy, magnificent mountain was intersected by narrow defiles and clefts, from which dampness and a sense of mystery came wafting towards the travellers. Through the defiles they caught sight of other mountains – brown, pink, lilac, smoky or suffused with light.

Wherever they looked, the mountains loomed on all sides and seemed to be bearing down on them; the evening shadows swiftly closed in from the direction of the inn and the dark cypress, making the narrow, sinuous Yellow River valley look even narrower and the mountains higher. The river gurgled and cicadas chirped incessantly.

Turgenev was perhaps in Chekhov's mind in the duel scene, which has clear affinities with the scene in *Fathers and Sons*. In the story there are frequent references to Bazarov, of whom von Koren is a clear descendant, while Layevsky has much in common with Lermontov's 'superfluous man', Pechorin.

Although the final moral regeneration of Layevsky and his reconciliation with Nadezhda may appear rather forced, the story presents a harmonious novelistic structure. Typically of its author, *The Duel* closes on a fine note of subdued optimism regarding the human lot:

'The boat's tossed back,' he thought; 'it makes two movements forward and one back, but the oarsmen don't give up, they swing the oars tirelessly ... Life is like that ... As they search for truth, people take two paces forward and one back. Suffering, mistakes and life's tedium throw them back, but thirst for the truth and stubborn willpower drive then on and on. And who knows? Perhaps they'll arrive at the real truth in the end.'

My Wife was published in 1892 and Chekhov at one time had wished to change the title to *In the Country*, but on editorial advice retained the original one. The story subsequently underwent some important revision in the face of critical opinion. *My Wife* deals with the gradual spiritual impoverishment of a self-centred man who is indifferent to the problems and sufferings of others, and who has no real interest in normal social life. In the first edition of the story, Asorin, the main character, by whom the story is told in the first person, had made a strong defence of his cult of indifference, the only way he could attain peace of mind, but Chekhov later cut out the passages where this indifference was shown as a positive quality. In his implied criticism of the self-pity of this priggish character, with his pompous speeches and pedantic language, Chekhov, in this story, is primarily attacking the current modish cult of pessimism and that section of the Russian intelligentsia that had a fondness for high-flown theorizing but was aloof to positive action.

At the time of writing My Wife – the so-called 'hungry year' – Chekhov was taking an active part in organizing famine relief in the Nizhny-Novgorod and Voronezh districts and worked hard to raise subscriptions; he described My Wife as a topical story about famine victims and sharply takes to task the ineffectiveness and inaction of the local would-be philanthropic gentry, with their idle committee meetings that are in reality nothing but disguised social events. In view of the fact that peasants are starving, the outrageously sumptuous meal that is eaten at Bragin's house – comparable with the gargantuan repasts in Dead Souls – very clearly shows Chekhov's feelings on the matter. The long inventory of dishes carries with it a strong indictment not only of over-indulgence, but moral indifference to those who are in need:

For the cold dish, white sucking-pig with horse-radish and sour cream was served; then a rich, boiling-hot cabbage soup with pork and buckwheat gruel ... Pie was served and then (with long intervals for imbibing fruit liqueurs) we had pigeon stew, a kind of fried giblets, roast sucking-pig, duck, partridge, cauliflower, fruit dumplings, curds and whey, jelly – and pancakes and jam to round it all off.

After this it is not surprising the participants lapse into a postprandial coma.

Asorin, the 'hero', who is insufferable to all, his wife in particular, has no social interests or love of people, is complacent, and indulges in self-pity which towards the end of the story becomes decidedly mawkish. The 'escape' motif, so common in Chekhov's stories and plays, is prominent here and Asorin is too weak-willed, too bogged down in his snug domesticity to make a break – although he does go through the motions, actually getting as far as the railway-station. But he considers himself too old to go back to a lonely bachelor-style life in St Petersburg and fails to make a new start.

Murder, a sombre story portraying life among religious sectarians in the north of Russia, was first published in 1895, but, for maximum effect, Chekhov significantly condensed it for the final version, for inclusion in his collected works. It was written shortly after the death of Leskov, who had given the most powerful and intimately knowledgeable portraits of sectarianism and religious fanaticism in Russian literature. Chekhov too, as seen in *The Bishop* and the peasant stories, such as *In the Ravine*, had a profound knowledge of Russian religious life, and in *Murder* paints a powerful picture of its darker side. Here rival interpretations of the complex Greek Orthodox ritual clash, leading to the murder of one cousin by another. In the end, the murderer undergoes moral regeneration in Siberia, having come to the realization that his own intolerance and vanity of spirit, his impatience with the religious beliefs of others, have ruined him. And constantly voiced in this story is the message that the rich cannot enter the kingdom of God – the murderer Yakov's illicit trade in vodka being in flagrant contradiction to Christ's teaching.

The violence of the act of murder (described in the most clinical manner and all the more effective for that) is paralleled in the blizzards that rage from the beginning of the story; dark, elemental forces appear to be at work:

It was not freezing – it was thawing on the roofs – yet it was snowing hard. The snow swiftly whirled through the air and white clouds chased each other along the railway track. Dimly lit by a moon that lay hidden high up in the clouds, the oak-grove lining both sides of the track kept up a constant roar. How terrifying trees can be when they are shaken by a violent storm!

The descriptions of railway lamps dimly glimpsed, snow whirling 'like witches at a sabbath', the sinister moaning of the wind in the deserted upper storey of the old coaching-inn, Yakov's picturing of himself as a huge and terrifying wild beast out in the fields, all add to the drama and mystery.

Drawing on his impressions of his stay on Sakhalin Island, Chekhov describes to superb effect the scene at the grim penal settlement to which Yakov has been sent:

Turned out of bed only a short time before, the convicts went along the shore half asleep, stumbling in the dark and clanking their chains. To the left they could barely make out a high, incredibly gloomy cliff, while to the right was pitch-black, unrelieved darkness and the long, drawn-out, monotonous moaning of the sea. Only when a warder lit his pipe, casting a brief light on a guard with a rifle and two or three rough-looking convicts standing nearby, or when he went close to the water with his lantern, could the white crests of the nearest waves be seen.

All is unrelieved gloom, mirroring Yakov's spiritual darkness. But there is hope yet: as he peers through this gloom, Yakov feels he has found faith at last – in love for his fellow-beings, however wretched and evil they may be and he offers prayers to God, in the manner he had been seeking for so long, unfettered by the dogmas of hidebound ritual.

The Black Monk was first published in 1894 in the journal *The Artist*. Replying to Suvorin's statement that he had depicted his own spiritual state in the story, Chekhov wrote: 'If an author describes someone who is mentally ill, it does not mean that he himself is. I wrote *The Black Monk* without any melancholy thoughts, in cold reflection. I simply had the urge to depict megalomania. I dreamt of the monk who floats over the field and when I woke up I wrote about him to Misha [Chekhov's brother].' Major critics of the time looked upon the story as a psychiatric case-study, but it is far more than this, raising philosophical and existential questions of the greatest importance.

The Black Monk concerns an academic, Kovrin, who goes one spring to his former guardian's estate to rest his shattered nerves. This guardian, Pesotsky, is a celebrated, fanatical horticulturalist, and for the finely detailed descriptions of the garden and orchard Chekhov drew material from his own life on his estate of Melikhovo, where he experimented, planted fruit trees, built hot-houses, and so on. However, in the character of Pesotsky, Chekhov is making fun of horticulturalists, especially in the highly amusing description of the ornamental sections of the garden with its 'oddities, elaborate monstrosities and travesties of nature'. After a short period of recuperation, Kovrin begins to have hallucinations in the form of a mysterious black monk, clearly a projection of his own consciousness. In this fine study of the progress of megalomania, Chekhov drew on his medical experience. Kovrin engages the monk in conversation and is praised by him for his devotion to the rational and the beautiful instead of remaining one of the 'common herd', the message being that thinking men are neurotic and suffer, while the unthinking masses are healthy and sane:

Heightened awareness, excitement, ecstasy – everything that distinguishes prophets, poets, martyrs to an idea, from ordinary people is hostile to man's animal side – I mean, his physical health. I repeat: if you want to be healthy and normal, go and join the herd.

There is a certain similarity between Kovrin and Poprishchin, the 'hero' of Gogol's *Diary of a Madman*, where idealism and noble motives are punished with insanity. Kovrin's individuality is stifled by the course of treatment prescribed for his illness by the smothering solicitude of his wife Tanya. Here it is interesting to note that, as in *The Russian Master*, milk, which Kovrin now has to drink as part of a strict diet instead of the wine he used to enjoy, serves as a symbol of the stifling domestic ministerings that Kovrin has to endure. After some weeks of this ordeal Kovrin rises up in protest against what he considers attempts to restore him to 'normality':

'Why, why did you try to cure me? All those bromides, idleness, warm baths, supervision, the cowardly fear with every mouthful, every step. All this will finally turn me into a complete idiot. I was going out of my mind, I had megalomania, but I was bright and cheerful , even happy . . . Now I've grown more rational and stable, but I'm just like everyone else, a nobody.'

And later he adds,

'How fortunate Buddha, Muhammad or Shakespeare were in not being treated by kind-hearted relatives for ecstasy and inspiration! If Muhammad had taken potassium bromide for his nerves, had worked only two hours a day and drunk milk, then that remarkable man would have left as much to posterity as his dog. In the long run doctors and kind relatives will turn humanity into a lot of morons.'

However, the central irony of the story lies in the fact that Kovrin really is a nobody, as he finally comes to admit, and he tries to accept that 'every man should be content with what he is'. None the less, he dies happy, after the final visitation by the monk – happy in the blissful delusion that he was 'one of God's Chosen, and a genius', in the thought that he was 'dying only because his weak human body had lost its balance and could no longer serve to house a genius'.

Terror was written on Christmas Eve 1892, and published in Suvorin's *New Times* the very next day. This was Chekhov's last contribution to the journal in which so many of his stories had been published.

Consistent with his belief that ordinary, commonplace objects give the writer the best material for fiction and that real life, however seemingly prosaic, is far more interesting that any invented world of the imagination, Chekhov demonstrates the truth of this in the case of Dmitry Silin, a small landowner. Silin, highly valuing the friendship of the narrator of the story, finds everyday life with a wife who does not love him and who finally betrays him with the narrator–friend far more frightening than any possible world of preternatural visions and apparitions from beyond the grave: for him, reality holds horrors in plenty.

In *Terror* Chekhov creates a most uncanny, ominous atmosphere, with the mysterious character called Forty Martyrs lurking in the background, while wraith-like swirls of mist rise from the river – an image twice repeated in the story. When Silin's friend tries to allay his doubts and fears by stating that we fear only that which we do not understand, Silin immediately counters with the assertion: 'But we don't really understand life, do we? Tell me if we understand this life any better than the world beyond.' And Silin's incomprehension is underscored by his wife's betrayal (with his own best friend who had come to stay with him) despite her having vowed never to deceive him, although she did not love him. Thus Silin is betrayed on two counts, which gives point and substance to his horror of life.

The final story in this selection, *The Two Volodyas*, was published in 1893 in the *Russian Gazette* and severely censored, much to Chekhov's anger. In an amusing letter he accused the censors of 'really infantile chastity', 'astounding cowardice' and of generally cutting the story to pieces. The excised passages were not reinstated in later editions. This story concerns the archetypal Chekhovian frivolous, flighty, dissatisfied young woman, married to an older man and frustrated in her attempt to have a lasting affair with someone much younger. At the beginning she is shown returning rather tipsy from a restaurant and trying to convince herself that, despite his years, her husband is most attractive. But when she approaches a convent the turning-point in the story comes as she suddenly remembers her friend who became a nun and decides to pay her a visit. The austere, rather funereal surroundings in the convent and her friend's virginal pallor give her a jolt. She recognizes the hollowness of her existence and begins to think about the meaning of life, the inevitability of death.

But she can find no outlet in religion and is condemned to a life of spiritual and sexual frustration with the husband she married for his money. In this story the severe, ascetic convent with its solemnly tolling bells is shown in sharp contrast with the meaningless existence of the 'heroine', in which she will never find fulfilment. As she comes to admit, 'there was no escape for girls and women in her circle, except perpetual troika-rides or entering a convent to mortify the flesh.' Hers is a wasted life and it hardly attracts sympathy from the author; the case is fully stated.

The Duel

I

It was eight in the morning, a time when officers, civil servants and visitors usually took a dip in the sea after the hot, stuffy night, proceeding to the Pavilion afterwards for tea or coffee. When Ivan Layevsky, a thin, fair-haired young man of about twenty-eight, came down for his bathe in slippers and with his Ministry of Finance peaked cap, he met many of his friends on the beach, including Samoylenko, an army doctor.

The stout, red-faced, flabby Samoylenko, with his large, close-cropped head, big nose, black bushy eyebrows, grey side-whiskers and no neck to speak of, with a hoarse soldier's voice as well, struck all newcomers as an unpleasant army upstart. But about two or three days after the first meeting his face began to strike them as exceptionally kind, amiable, handsome even. Although a rude-mannered, clumsy person, he was docile, infinitely kind, good-humoured and obliging. He called everyone in town by their Christian names, lent money to everyone, gave medical treatment to all, arranged marriages, patched up quarrels and organized picnics, where he grilled kebabs and made a very tasty grey mullet soup. He was always helping people and interceding for them, and there was always something that made him happy. He was generally regarded as a saint, with just two weaknesses: firstly, he was ashamed of his own kindness and tried to conceal it behind a forbidding expression and an affected rudeness; secondly, he liked to be called 'General' by the medical orderlies and soldiers, although he was only a colonel.

'Just answer one question for me, Alexander,' Layevsky began when he and Samoylenko were right up to their shoulders in the water. 'Suppose you fell in love and had an affair with the woman. Suppose you lived with her for more than two years and then, as happens so often, you stopped loving her and felt she was no more than a stranger. What would you have done in that event?'

'Very simple. I would say "Get out, my dear" – and that would be that.'

'That's easy enough to say! But supposing she had nowhere to go? Supposing she was all on her own, with no family, not a penny to her name, no job . . .'

'What of it? Five hundred roubles down, to keep her quiet, or twenty-five a month and no arguments. Very simple.'

'Let's assume you could pay her the five hundred or twenty-five a month, but the woman I'm talking about is educated and has her pride. Could you really offer someone like that *money*? How would you pay her?'

Samoylenko wanted to give him an answer, but at that moment a large wave broke over them both, crashed onto the beach and roared back over the shingle. The two friends came out of the water and started dressing.

'Of course it's difficult living with a woman if you don't love her,' Samoylenko said shaking the sand out of his boot. 'But you must consider, Ivan, would it be humane? If it were me, I wouldn't let her see I didn't love her any more and I'd stay with her until my dying day.' Suddenly he felt ashamed of these words and thought again. 'In my opinion we'd be better off if there weren't any women at all, damn them!'

The friends dressed and went into the Pavilion where Samoylenko was one of the regulars, and even had his own cups, saucers and glasses reserved for him. Every morning he was served a cup of coffee, a tall, cut-glass tumbler of iced water and a glass of brandy on a tray. First he would drink the brandy, then the hot coffee, then the iced water, all of which obviously gave him great enjoyment, as afterwards his eyes would gleam and he would gaze at the sea, stroking his side-whiskers with both hands, and say: 'A remarkably beautiful view!'

Layevsky was feeling jaded and lifeless after a long night of gloomy, empty thoughts which had disturbed his sleep and only intensified the humidity and darkness, it seemed. Nor did the swim and the coffee make him feel any better. 'Alexander, may we carry on this conversation?' he said. 'I shan't hide anything and I'm telling you quite candidly, as a friend: things with Nadezhda are bad . . . very bad! Forgive me for letting you into my secrets, but I must tell *someone*.'

Samoylenko had anticipated that he was going to tell him this; he lowered his eyes and drummed his fingers on the table.

'I've lived with her for two years and now I don't love her any more . . .' Layevsky said. 'To be more precise, I've come to realize I never *did* love her. These two years have been sheer delusion.'

Layevsky had the habit of closely studying his pink palms, biting his nails or crumpling his shirt cuffs during a conversation. And this is what he did now. 'I know only too well you can't help,' he said, 'but I'm telling you, talking things over is the only salvation for failures, or Superfluous Men like yours truly. I always feel I have to start generalizing after anything I do, I have to find an explanation and justification for my absurd existence in some sort of theory or other, in literary types – for example in the fact that we gentlefolk are becoming degenerate, and so on . . . All last night, for example, I consoled myself by thinking how right Tolstoy is, how ruthlessly right! And it made me feel better. A really great writer, my friend, say what you like!'

Samoylenko, who had never read Tolstoy and had been meaning to read him every day, was taken aback and said: 'Yes, all writers draw on their imagination, but he writes directly from nature . . .'

'Good Lord!' Layevsky sighed, 'how civilization has crippled us! I fell in love with a married woman, and she with me. At first there was kissing, and quiet evenings, and promises, and Spencer, and ideals, and mutual interests . . . What a sham! Essentially, we were just running away from her husband, but we deluded ourselves into thinking we were running away from the emptiness of our lives. We imagined our future like this: first, until we got to know the Caucasus and the people here, I would wear my civil service uniform and work in a government office; then, out in the wide open spaces, we would buy a little plot of land, work by the sweat of our brows, cultivate a vineyard, fields, and so on. If you yourself or that zoologist friend of yours, von Koren, had been in my place, perhaps you would have lived with Nadezhda for thirty years and left your heirs a thriving vineyard and three thousand acres or so of maize. But I felt a complete failure, from the very first day. It's insufferably hot and boring in this town, no one you can make friends with, and out in the country, under every bush and stone you think you're seeing poisonous spiders, scorpions and snakes. Beyond the fields there's nothing but mountains and the wilderness. Foreign people, foreign landscape, pathetic cultural standards – all this, my friend, is a different proposition from strolling along the Nevsky in your fur coat, arm-in-arm with Nadezhda and dreaming of sunny climes. Here you have to go at it hammer and tongs – and I'm no fighter. Just a wretched bag of nerves, an old softy ... I realized from the very first day that my ideas about the life of labour and vineyards aren't worth a tinker's cuss. And as for love, I must inform you that life with a woman who's read Spencer and gone to the ends of the earth for you is just about as boring as living with any village girl. There's that same old smell of ironing, face powder and medicine, the same curling-papers every morning, the same self-deception ...'

'You can't run a household without ironing,' Samoylenko said, blushing because Layevsky was speaking so frankly about a woman he knew. 'Ivan, I can see you're feeling a bit low this morning, aren't you? Nadezhda is a beautiful, cultured woman and you're a highly intelligent man ... Of course, you're not married,' Samoylenko continued, looking round at the neighbouring tables, 'but after all, that's not your fault ... What's more, one has to cast aside one's prejudices and keep up with modern ideas on the subject. I'm all for civil marriage myself, yes ... But I do think that once you've started living with someone you must stay that way till your dying day.'

'But without loving her?'

'I'll tell you why, here and now,' Samoylenko said. 'About eight years ago there was an old shipping-agent living here, a very intelligent man. This is what he used to say: the most important thing in family life is patience. Are you listening, Ivan? Not love, but patience. Love can't last very long. You've been in love for two years but now your domestic life has entered that stage when you have to bring all your patience into play to maintain your equilibrium, so to speak ...'

'You can believe that old agent of yours if you like, but his advice makes no sense at all to me. Your old gentleman could have been fooling his partner, testing his stamina, at the same time using the unloved woman as something essential for his exercises. But *I* haven't fallen that low yet. If I wanted to put my powers of endurance to the test, I'd buy dumb-bells or a lively horse, but I'd leave human beings alone.'

Samoylenko ordered some chilled wine. After they had drunk a glass each Layevsky suddenly asked, 'Can you please explain what softening of the brain is?'

'It's ... how can I best explain it to you? It's an illness where the brain gets softer, as if it were decomposing ...'

'Is it curable?'

'Yes, if it hasn't gone too far. Cold showers, plasters ... and some sort of medicine you have to drink.'

'Oh. Well, so you see the state I'm in. I can't live with her, it's more than I can cope with. While I'm sitting here with you I can philosophize and smile all right, but the moment I'm home I really get very down in the dumps. I feel so bad, so absolutely awful, that if someone told me I must live with her, let's say just one more month, I think I'd put a bullet through my brains. And at the same time I just can't leave her. She's got no one else, she can't work, neither of us has any money ... Where could she go? And to whom? I just can't think ... Well now, tell me what to do.'

'Hm ... yes ...' Samoylenko mumbled, at a loss for a reply. 'Does she love you?'

'Yes, as much as anyone of her age and temperament needs a man. She'd find it as difficult to part with me as with her powder and curling-papers ... I'm an indispensable component of her boudoir.'

Samoylenko was taken aback by this. 'You're really in a foul mood today, Ivan,' he said. 'Probably it's lack of sleep.'

'Yes, I had a bad night ... And I feel generally pretty rough, old chap. It all seems so futile, I feel so nervy, so weak ... I must get away from here!'

'But where to?'

'Up north. To pines, mushrooms, people, ideas ... I'd give half my life to be somewhere near Moscow or Tula now, to have a swim in a river, then cool down, then wander around for about three hours, with the most wretched student even, and talk, talk, talk ... You remember the scent of that hay! And those evening walks in the garden when you can hear the piano in the house, the sound of a passing train ...'

Layevsky smiled with pleasure, his eyes filled with tears and in an effort to hide them he leant over to the next table for a box of matches without getting up.

'It's eighteen years since I was up north,' Samoylenko said. 'I've forgotten what it's like there. If you ask me, nowhere's as magnificent as the Caucasus.'

'There's a painting by Vereshchagin in which some prisoners condemned to death are languishing at the bottom of a terribly deep well. Your magnificent Caucasus strikes me as exactly the same kind of bottomless pit. If you offered me two choices – being a chimney-sweep in St Petersburg or a prince in this place – I'd opt for the chimney-sweep.'

Layevsky thought for a moment. As he looked at that stooping figure, those staring eyes, that pale sweaty face with its sunken temples, the gnawed finger nails and the slipper hanging down from Layevsky's heel, revealing a badly darned sock, Samoylenko felt a surge of pity. Then, probably because Layevsky reminded him of a helpless child, he asked:

'Is your mother still alive?'

'Yes, but we never see each other. She never forgave me for this affair.'

Samoylenko was very fond of his friend. In his eyes Layevsky was a thoroughly decent 'hail-fellow-well-met' type, a genuine student, the kind of person with whom one could have a good laugh over a drink and a real heart-to-heart chat. What he understood about him he disliked intensely. Layevsky drank a great deal, and at the wrong time, played cards, despised his work, lived beyond his means, often used bad language, wore slippers in the street and quarrelled with Nadezhda in public. Samoylenko liked none of this.

But the fact that Layevsky was once a university student, in the arts faculty, that he now subscribed to two literary reviews and often spoke so cleverly that only few could understand him, that he was living with a woman of culture – all this was beyond Samoylenko's understanding and it pleased him; he considered Layevsky his superior and respected him.

'Just one more thing,' Layevsky said, shaking his head. 'Just between ourselves. I'm not telling Nadezhda for the moment, so don't let the cat out of the bag when you see her. The day before yesterday I received a letter saying her husband had died of softening of the brain.'

'May he rest in peace!' Samoylenko sighed. 'But why are you hiding it from her?'

'Showing her that letter would mean "Off to the altar, please!" Things between us have to be cleared up first. When she's convinced that we can't go on living together I'll show her the letter. There'll be no danger then.'

'Do you know what, Ivan?' Samoylenko said and his face took on a sad, pleading expression, as if he was about to beg for something very nice and was afraid of being refused. 'Get married, my dear chap!'

'Why?'

'Do your duty by this beautiful woman! Her husband has died – this is the way Providence has of showing you what to do!'

'But please try and understand, you silly man! That's impossible. Marrying someone you don't love is just as vile and dishonourable as celebrating Mass and not believing in God.'

'But it's your duty!'

'Why is it my duty?' Layevsky asked irritably.

'Because you took her away from her husband and therefore you assumed responsibility.'

'Well, I'm telling you in plain language, I don't love her!'

'Then if you don't love her, show her some respect, spoil her a little.'

'Respect, spoil?' Layevsky said, mimicking him. 'Do you think she's a Mother Superior? ... You're not much of a psychologist or physiologist if you think that respect and honour on their own will do you much good when you live with a woman. What women need most is bed.'

'Ivan, Ivan!' Samoylenko said, embarrassed.

'You're a big baby, all theories. As for me, I'm old before my time and a pragmatist, so we shall never see eye to eye. Let's change the subject.' Layevsky called out to one of the waiters, 'Mustafa, how much do we owe you?'

'No, no,' the doctor said, grasping Layevsky's arm anxiously. 'I'll do the honours. I ordered.' And he called out to Mustafa. 'Charge it to me.'

The friends got up and walked in silence along the front. They stopped at the main boulevard to say good-bye and shook hands.

'You gentlemen are too spoilt!' Samoylenko sighed. 'Fate has sent you a young, beautiful, educated woman and you don't want her. If only God would send me some hunch-backed old crone, how happy I should be – as long as she was affectionate and kind. I'd live in my vineyard with her and ...' Samoylenko suddenly pulled himself up. 'As long as the old witch could keep my samovar on the boil!'

After bidding Layevsky farewell he went off down the boulevard. Whenever that ponderous, majestic, stern-faced man strolled along the boulevard in his snow-white tunic and impeccably polished boots, thrusting his chest out and flaunting his splendid Order of Vladimir (with ribbon) he was very pleased with himself and thought the whole world was looking at him in delight. Without turning his head, he looked from side to side and concluded that the boulevard had been beautifully planned, that the young cypresses, the eucalyptus and those unsightly, anaemic-looking palm-trees were very beautiful in fact and, given time, would cast a broad shade, and that the Circassians were a decent, hospitable people. 'Strange that Layevsky doesn't like the Caucasus,' he thought. 'Most strange.' Five soldiers with rifles saluted as they passed him. On the pavement, on the other side of the boulevard, a civil servant's wife was walking along with her schoolboy son.

'Good morning, Mrs Bityugov!' Samoylenko called out, smiling pleasantly. 'Have you been for a bathe? Ha, ha, ha ... My regards to Mr Bityugov.'

He walked on further, still smiling pleasantly, but when he spotted a medical orderly coming towards him he suddenly frowned, stopped him and asked, 'Is there anyone at the hospital?'

'No one, General.'

'What?'

'No one, General.'

'Very good . . . Carry on.'

Swaying majestically, he went over to a soft drinks kiosk, where an old, full-bosomed Jewess who pretended to be a Georgian was sitting behind the counter.

'Please give me a glass of soda water!' he said, so loud, he might have been giving orders to a regiment.

II

The main reason for Layevsky's dislike of Nadezhda was the falsity – or the apparent falsity – of everything she did. All he had read attacking women and love, it seemed, couldn't have been more applicable to himself, Nadezhda and her husband. When he arrived home she was already dressed and had done her hair, and she was sitting at the window drinking coffee, looking through a literary review with an anxious look on her face. He reflected that simply drinking coffee hardly warranted such a worried look and that her fashionable hair-do had been a sheer waste of time, since there was no one around worth pleasing in this kind of place and no point in the exercise anyway. And reading that review was only another pretence. He thought that she had only dressed up and had done her hair to look pretty, and in the same way the reading was just to make herself look clever.

'Do you mind if I go for a bathe today?' she asked.

'Why not? I don't suppose the mountains will cave in if you do or if you don't.'

'I only asked because the doctor might be annoyed.'

'Well, go and ask him. I'm not qualified to speak on the subject.'

What Layevsky disliked most about Nadezhda on this occasion was her bare white neck and the little curls around the back, and he remembered that when Anna Karenina stopped loving her husband, she had conceived a particular loathing for his ears. 'How true, how true!' he thought. Feeling weak and despondent, he went to his study, lay down on the couch and covered his face with a handkerchief to keep the flies away. Dull, lazy, monotonous thoughts lumbered through his mind like a long train of peasant carts on a foul autumn evening and he lapsed into a drowsy, depressed state of mind. He thought he was guilty as far as Nadezhda and her husband were concerned and that her husband's death was his fault. He felt he was to blame for ruining his own life, for betraying the wonderful world of noble ideas, learning, work, which did not seem to exist or be capable of realization in this seaside resort with its hungry, prowling Turks and lazy Abkhazians, but only in the north with its opera, theatres, newspapers and great diversity of intellectual life. Only there could one be honourable, clever, noble-minded and pure – not in this sort of place. He accused himself of being without ideals or guiding principles in life, although he only had a vague idea what that meant. Two years before, when he had fallen in love with Nadezhda, he thought all he had to do to escape the nastiness and futility of life was to become her lover and go away with her to the Caucasus. Similarly, he was convinced that he only had to abandon Nadezhda and go to St Petersburg to achieve his every desire.

'Escape!' he muttered as he sat biting his nails. 'Escape!'

He imagined himself going on board ship, having lunch, drinking cold beer, chatting with the ladies on deck, then catching a train at Sevastopol – and away! Hail, Freedom! Stations flash past one after the other, the air grows cooler and sharper. Now he can see birches and firs, that's Kursk, now Moscow ... Cabbage soup, mutton with buckwheat, sturgeon, beer at station buffets – in brief, no more of this barbarity, but *Russia*, the real Russia. The passengers discuss trade, new singers, Franco-Prussian accord. Everywhere life is vigorous, cultured, intelligent, brimming with energy. Faster, faster! Here at last is the Nevsky Avenue, Great Morskoy Street, then Kovensky Lane, where once he had lived with students. Here is that dear grey sky, drizzle, those drenched cab-drivers ...

'Mr Layevsky!' someone called from the next room. 'Are you in?'

'I'm here!' Layevsky answered. 'What is it?'

'I've got some papers.'

As Layevsky lazily got to his feet, his head was reeling and he went into the next room yawning and shuffling his slippers. One of his young colleagues was standing by the window that over-looked the street and laying out government papers along the sill.

'Won't be a second, old man,' Layevsky said softly and went off to find an ink-pot. He returned to the window, signed the papers without reading them and remarked, 'It's hot!'

'Yes, sir. Are you coming to the office today?'

'I don't think so ... I'm not feeling too good. My dear chap, please tell Sheshkovsky I'll look in after dinner.'

The clerk left. Layevsky lay down on his couch again and thought, 'So, I must carefully weigh up the pros and cons and come to a decision. Before I leave this place I must settle my debts. I owe about two thousand roubles. I've no money ... Of course, that's not important. I could pay part of it now, somehow or other and I'll send some later from St Petersburg. The main problem's Nadezhda ... I must get things straight between us, before I do anything else ... Yes.'

A little later he was wondering if it might be best to go to Samoylenko for advice. 'I *could* go and see him,' he thought, 'but what's the use? I'd only say the wrong thing again, about boudoirs, women, what's honourable or not. And how the hell can I discuss what's honourable or not when the most urgent thing is to save my own skin, when I'm suffocating in this damned slavery and killing myself ... It's time I realized that carrying on living as I am is shameful and an act of cruelty before which all else pales into insignificance!'

'Escape!' he murmured, sitting down. 'Escape!'

The deserted beach, the merciless heat and the monotony of the eternally silent, hazy, pinkish-violet mountains saddened him and seemed to be lulling him to sleep and robbing him of something. Perhaps he *was* very clever in fact, talented and remarkably honest; perhaps he might have made an excellent district official, public servant, orator, commentator on current affairs, champion of causes, had he not been shut in on all sides by sea and mountains. Who knows? And if this were true, wasn't it stupid to argue whether it was the right thing or not if a talented and useful man – a musician or artist, for example – tore walls down and fooled his jailers to escape from prison? For any man in that situation, everything was honourable.

At two o'clock Layevsky and Nadezhda sat down to lunch. When the cook served rice soup with tomatoes Layevsky said, 'The same old thing every day. Can't she make cabbage soup?'

'We haven't any cabbage.'

'That's strange, Samoylenko has cabbage soup, Marya Bityugov has cabbage soup, only *I* am obliged to eat these sickly slops. It's no good, my dear.'

Like most married couples, at one time Layevsky and Nadezhda could not finish lunch without some scene or tantrums. But since Layevsky decided he did not love her any more, he tried to let Nadezhda have everything her own way, spoke gently and politely to her, smiled and called her darling.

'This soup's like liquorice,' he said, smiling. He was making a great effort to be friendly, but it was too much for him and he told her, 'No one looks after things in this house. If you're really so ill, or if you're too busy reading, I could see to the cooking, if you like.'

Earlier she would have replied, 'See to it, then,' or 'It's obvious you want to turn me into a cook,' but all she did now was give him a timid look and blush.

'Well, how do you feel today?' he asked affectionately.

'I'm all right today, just a little weak.'

'You must look after yourself, my dear. I'm terribly worried about you.'

In fact there *was* something wrong with Nadezhda. Samoylenko said she was suffering from intermittent fever and was giving her quinine. But another doctor, Ustimovich – a tall, skinny, unsociable person who stayed in during the day and strolled slowly along the front in the evenings, coughing away, his walking-stick pressed to his back with his hands – found she had some woman's complaint and prescribed hot compresses. Before, when Layevsky was in love with Nadezhda, her illness had made him feel sorry for her and worried, but now he could see it was mere pretence. That sallow, sleepy face and sluggish look, those yawning fits she had after attacks of fever and the way she lay under a rug during them, making herself look more like a little child than a grown woman, the stuffiness and unpleasant smell in her room – to his mind all this served to destroy any romantic illusions and were enough to throw cold water on any ideas of love and marriage.

For a second course he was served spinach and hard-boiled eggs, while Nadezhda had jelly and milk, as she wasn't well. At first, when she anxiously touched the jelly with her spoon and then lazily started eating it, washing it down with milk, the gulping noise aroused such violent hatred that it made his head itch. The way he felt, he knew very well, would have insulted a dog even, but he was not angry with himself, but with Nadezhda for stirring such feelings in him and he understood why lovers sometimes murder their mistresses. Of course, he could never have committed murder himself, but if he had happened to be on a jury at that moment he would have found for the accused.

'*Merci*, my dear,' he said after dinner, and kissed Nadezhda on the forehead.

Back in his study he paced up and down for five minutes, squinting at his boots, after which he sat on the couch and muttered, 'Escape! Escape! Just get things straight and then escape!'

As he lay on the couch he remembered that he was possibly to blame for the death of Nadezhda's husband. 'It's stupid blaming someone for falling in or out of love,' he said, trying to convince himself as he lay there lifting his legs up to put his boots on. 'Love and hatred are beyond our control. As for her husband, I was possibly one of the causes of his death, indirectly. But there again, is it my fault that I fell in love with his wife, and his wife with me?'

As he walked along Layevsky thought, 'I'm just like Hamlet in my indecision! How truly Shakespeare observed it! Oh, how truly!'

III

To ward off boredom and to cater for the desperate needs of new arrivals and bachelors who had nowhere to eat, owing to the complete absence of hotels in the town, Dr Samoylenko maintained a kind of *table d'hôte*. At the time in question only two of these gentlemen were taking meals with him, von Koren, a young zoologist who had arrived in the summer to study the embryology of the jellyfish in the Black Sea; and Deacon Pobedov, who had left theological college not long before and had been dispatched to this small town to stand in for the old deacon, who was away taking the cure. Each paid twelve roubles a month for lunch and dinner, and Samoylenko had made them promise faithfully to be there for lunch at two o'clock on the dot.

Von Koren was usually first to arrive. He would silently sit down in the drawing-room, pick up an album from the table and examine faded photographs of certain strange gentlemen in wide trousers and toppers, and ladies in crinolines and lace caps. Samoylenko could remember the names of only just a few and would comment with a sigh on those he had forgotten, 'A very fine person, of the highest intellect!'

When he had finished with the album, von Koren would take a pistol from the shelf, screw up his left eye and keep it pointed for a long time at Prince Vorontsov's portrait; or he would stand in front of the mirror surveying his swarthy face, large forehead and hair that was as black and curly as a Negro's, then his faded cotton print shirt with its large floral pattern resembling a Persian carpet, then the broad leather belt he wore as a waistcoat. This self-contemplation gave him almost greater enjoyment than inspecting those photographs or that expensively mounted pistol. He was satisfied with his face and with his beautifully trimmed beard and broad shoulders that were clear proof of his good health and strong build. He was satisfied too with his terribly smart outfit – from the tie, which matched his shirt, right down to his yellow shoes.

While he was standing before the mirror looking through the album, Samoylenko was rushing bare-chested around the kitchen and pantry, without jacket or waistcoat. He sweated profusely as he excitedly fussed around the tables, preparing the salad, or some sort of sauce, or the meat, or cucumbers and onions for the soup, glaring furiously and alternately brandishing a knife and a spoon at the batman who was helping him.

'Vinegar!' he commanded. 'No, not the vinegar, I meant salad-oil!' he shouted, stamping his foot. 'And where are *you* going, you swine?'

'To get the oil, General,' replied the stunned batman in a high-pitched voice.

'Hurry up! It's in the cupboard. And tell Darya to put some more dill into the cucumber jar. Dill! Cover up that sour cream, you moron, or the flies will get to it!'

The whole house seemed to echo with his shouts. At about ten or fifteen minutes to two the deacon arrived — a thin young man of about twenty-two, long-haired, beardless and with a barely visible moustache. After he entered the drawing-room he crossed himself before the icon, smiled and held out his hand to von Koren.

'Hallo,' the zoologist said coldly. 'Where have you been?'

'Fishing for gobies in the harbour.'

'Why of course. It's quite evident, deacon, you'll never put your mind to doing some work.'

'Why ever not?' the deacon said smiling, shoving his hands into the cavernous pockets of his white hassock. 'Time enough for work tomorrow!'

'You always win,' the zoologist sighed.

Another fifteen or twenty minutes passed and still they weren't summoned to the table; and they could still hear the clatter of boots as the batman scurried from pantry to kitchen and back again, while Samoylenko shouted, 'Put it on the table! What *are* you doing? Wash it first!'

The deacon and von Koren, who were starving by now, showed their impatience by tapping their heels on the floor, like a theatre audience. At last the door opened and the harassed batman announced, 'Lunch is ready!'

In the dining-room they were confronted by an angry, crimson-faced Samoylenko, who looked as if he had been boiled in that hot kitchen. He glanced at them malignantly and there was a horrified look on his face as he lifted the lid of the soup tureen and filled their plates. Only when he was convinced that they were enjoying the food, that it was to their taste, did he heave a gentle sigh and sink into his deep armchair. His face took on a languid, unctuous expression.

Leisurely, he poured himself a glass of vodka and said, 'To the younger generation!'

After his talk with Layevsky, Samoylenko had passed the entire morning until lunch feeling rather heavy at heart, despite his generally excellent mood. He felt sorry for Layevsky and wanted to help him. Drinking his vodka before starting the soup he sighed and said, 'I saw Ivan Layevsky today. The poor devil's having a rough time of it. Materially, he's in a bad way, but the main problems are psychological. I do feel sorry for the young man.'

'Of all people I'm not sorry for *him*!' von Koren said. 'If that nice young gentleman were drowning I'd help him down with a stick and tell him, "Drown, my dear chap, please drown."'

'That's not true, you wouldn't do it.'

'And why not?' the zoologist said with a shrug of the shoulders. 'I'm just as capable of a good deed as you are.'

'Is making someone drown a good deed?' the deacon asked, laughing.

'If it's Layevsky – yes.'

'There's something missing in the soup,' Samoylenko said, trying to change the subject.

'There's no question about it, Layevsky's as harmful and dangerous to society as a cholera microbe,' von Koren went on. 'Drowning him would be rendering it a service.'

'It does you no credit speaking like that about your fellow human being. Tell me, why do you hate him?'

'Don't talk such nonsense, doctor. It's stupid hating and despising a microbe. But to think that any passing stranger just has to be thought of as your fellow human being, without discrimination – that's not rational at all, but a refusal to take any reasonable attitude towards people, if you don't mind my saying so. In short, it's the same as washing your hands of the matter. That Layevsky is a swine – I won't conceal the fact – and I regard him as such with the clearest conscience. But if *you* consider him your fellow, then go and drool over him as much as you like. If you consider *him* your neighbour that means you have the same attitude towards him as to the deacon and myself, and that means any old attitude. You're equally indifferent to everyone.'

'Calling the man a *swine*!' Samoylenko muttered, frowning with disgust. 'That's so awful, words just fail me!'

'People are judged by their actions,' von Koren went on. 'So now you can judge for yourself, deacon. There's something I'd like to tell you. Mr Layevsky's activities lie wide open before you, like a Chinese scroll, and you can read about them from beginning to end. What has he achieved in the two years he's been here? Let's count it on our fingers. Firstly, he's taught the people in this town to play whist. This game was unknown here two years ago, but now everyone's playing it from morning to night, even women and teenagers. Secondly, he's taught the people to drink beer, which was also unknown in this place. And the people are indebted to him for information regarding different brands of vodka, with the result that now they can tell Koshelyov from Smirnov No. 21 blindfold. Thirdly, when men used to sleep with other men's wives in this place before, they kept it a secret, for the same reasons that motivate burglars, who go about their business in secret and don't tell the whole world about it. Adultery used to be looked on as too shameful for the public eye. But Layevsky has shown himself to be a pioneer in this field, he's living quite openly with another man's wife. Fourthly ...'

Von Koren quickly finished his soup and handed the batman his bowl. 'I saw through Layevsky the very first month we met,' he went on, turning to the deacon. 'We both came here at the same time. People of his sort love friendship, togetherness, unity and so on, because they always need partners for whist, for drinking and eating. What's more, they're great talkers and need an audience. We became friends – by that I mean he came over to my place every day and loafed around, interrupted my work and told me all about his mistress. At first he startled me by his extraordinary mendacity, which simply made me feel sick. As one friend to another, I told him off, asked him why he drank so much, why he lived beyond his means and ran up so many debts, why he neglected his work, why he read nothing, why he was so uncultured, why he was so ignorant – and his sole reply to all my questions was to smile bitterly and say, "I'm a failure, a Superfluous Man," or "What do you want from us, old man, we're just left-overs from the serf system?" or

"We're *all* going to pot." Or he'd spin me a whole yarn about Onegin, Pechorin, Byron's *Cain*, Bazarov, calling them "our fathers in the spirit and in the flesh". You must understand that *he*'s not to blame if official parcels lie around unopened for weeks, or if he drinks and sees that others get drunk with him. Onegin, Pechorin and Turgenev, who invented failures and the Superfluous Man – they're to blame. The reason for his outrageous depravity and disgraceful carryings-on can't be found in him at all, but somewhere outside, in space. What's more – and this is a cunning stroke – he's not alone in being dissipated, lying, and vile, but *we* too – we "men of the eighties", we, "the lifeless, neurotic offspring of serfdom", we "cripples of civilization". The long and short of it is, we must realize that a man of Layevsky's calibre is great, even in decline; that his debauchery, ignorance and filthy ways are a quite normal evolutionary phenomenon, sanctified by the laws of necessity, that the reasons for all this are elemental, of world-shattering importance, and that we must cringe before Layevsky, since he's a doomed victim of the epoch, of trends of opinion, or heredity and all the rest of it. Whenever civil servants and their wives listened to him there would be sighs and gasps and for a long time I did not realize the kind of person I was dealing with – a cynic or a cunning rogue? People like him with a modicum of education, who appear to be intellectuals and with a lot to say about their own noble qualities, are dab hands at passing themselves off as highly complex characters.'

'Be quiet!' Samoylenko said, flaring up. 'I won't have you maligning the noblest of men in my presence!'

'Don't interrupt, Alexander,' von Koren said icily. 'I've nearly finished now. Layevsky is a fairly uncomplicated organism. This is his moral framework: slippers, bathing and coffee early in the morning, then slippers, exercise and conversation; at two – slippers, lunch and booze; bathing, tea and drinks at five, followed by whist and telling lies; supper and booze at ten; after midnight – sleep and *la femme*. His existence is bounded by this strict routine, like an egg by its shell. Whether he's walking, losing his temper, writing or having a good time, in the end everything boils down to drink, cards, slippers and women. Women play a fateful, overwhelming role in his life. He'll tell you he was already in love at the age of thirteen.

When he was a first-year student, he lived with a woman who had a good influence on him and to whom he owes his musical education. In his second year he redeemed a prostitute from a brothel and raised her to his level – that's to say, made her his mistress. She stayed with him for six months and then fled back to Madame, an escape that caused him no end of spiritual distress. Alas, he suffered so much he was compelled to leave university and live at home for two years without doing a thing. But it was for the best. At home he started an affair with a widow who advised him to drop law and take up modern languages. And that's precisely what he did. The moment he finished the course he fell madly in love with this married woman he's with now – what's her name? – and had to run away with her to the Caucasus, presumably for the sake of his ideals ... Any day now he'll tire of her and fly back to St Petersburg – and that will be because of his ideals too.'

'How do you know?' growled Samoylenko, looking daggers at the zoologist. 'Come on, better have something to eat.'

Boiled grey mullet *à la polonaise* was served. Samoylenko laid a whole fish on each of his guests' plates, pouring the sauce himself. Two minutes passed in silence.

'Women play an essential part in every man's life,' the deacon observed. 'There's no getting away from it.'

'Yes, but how great? For each one of us a woman is mother, sister, wife, friend. But to Layevsky she's everything – and at the same time she's only someone to go to bed with. Women – I mean living with one – are his whole purpose in life, his whole happiness. If he's cheerful, sad, bored, disenchanted it's always because of a woman. If his life has turned sour, then a woman's to blame. If a new life has brightly dawned, if new ideals have been unearthed, you only have to look for the woman. Only books or paintings featuring women satisfy him. According to him, the age we live in is rotten, worse than the forties and sixties, just because we cannot completely surrender ourselves to love's ecstasy and passion. These sensualists must have some sort of tumour-like growth which, by exerting pressure on the brain, has taken complete control of their minds. Just watch Layevsky when he's with people. You'll see, if you raise some general topic – cells, or the instincts, for example – he'll sit on one side, not listening or saying a word, lifeless and bored: none of it interests him, everything is trivial and second-rate. But just mention male and female, talk about female spiders devouring the male after mating, say, his face will light up, his eyes will burn with curiosity – in brief, he will come to life. However noble, elevated or unbiased his ideas may seem, they invariably centre around the same point of departure. You might be walking down the street with him and meet a she-ass, for example. He'll ask, "Tell me what you get, please, if you mate a she-ass with a camel?" And as for his dreams! Has he told you about his dreams? They are superb! First he'll dream he's getting married to the moon, then that he's been summoned to a police station and ordered to live with a guitar ...'

The deacon broke into loud peals of laughter. Samoylenko frowned and angrily wrinkled his face to stop laughing, but he couldn't control himself and burst out laughing.

'And he never stops talking nonsense. Good Lord, the rubbish he talks!'

IV

The deacon was very easily amused – any little trifle was enough to send him into stitches and laugh until he dropped. It seemed he only liked company because people had their funny side and he could give them all comical nicknames. He called Samoylenko 'Tarantula', his orderly 'the Drake', and went into raptures when von Koren once called Layevsky and Nadezhda 'macaques'. He would hungrily peer into faces, listen without blinking and one could see his eyes fill with laughter and his face grow tense as he waited for a chance to let himself go and roar with laughter.

'He's a dissipated, perverted type,' the zoologist continued, while the deacon, expecting something funny, stared at him. 'You'll have to go a long way to find such a nobody. Physically, he's flabby, feeble and senile, while intellectually he's no different from any old merchant's fat wife who does nothing but guzzle, drink, sleep on a feather bed and have sex with her coachman.' Again the deacon burst out laughing. 'Now don't laugh, deacon,' von Koren said; 'that's stupid, after all.' Waiting until the deacon stopped, he went on, 'If this nonentity weren't so harmful and dangerous I wouldn't give him another moment's thought. His capacity for doing harm stems from his success with women, which means there's the danger he might have offspring and in this way he could present the world with a dozen Layevsky's, all as sickly and perverted as himself. Secondly, he's highly contagious – I've already told you about the whist and the beer. Give him another year or two and he'll have the whole Caucasian coastline at his feet. You know how much the masses, especially the middle strata, believe in things of the mind, in university education, refinement of manners and polished self-expression. Whatever abomination he may perpetrate, everyone believes there's nothing at all wrong, that this is how it should be, since he's a cultured, liberally minded man with a university education. And the fact that he's a failure, a Superfluous Man, a neurotic, a victim of the times means that he's allowed to do whatever he likes. He's a nice young fellow, a good sort, so genuinely tolerant of human frailty. He's obliging, easygoing, undemanding, not in the least high and mighty. One can have a nice little drink with him and swap dirty jokes, or have a chat about the latest gossip. The masses, who have always tended towards anthropomorphism in religion and morals, like those idols most who have the same weaknesses as themselves. Judge for yourselves the wide field he has for spreading infection! What's more, he's not a bad actor, a clever impostor, there are no flies on *him*. Just take his little tricks and dodges, for example his attitude to civilization. He hasn't a clue about it, yet you can hear him say, "Oh, how civilization has crippled us! Oh, how I envy savages, those children of nature, ignorant of civilization!" You must understand that, at one time, in the old days, he was devoted to civilization heart and soul. He was its servant, he knew its innermost secrets, but it exhausted, disillusioned and cheated him. Can't you see that he's a Faust, a second Tolstoy? And he shrugs off Schopenhauer and Spencer as schoolboys, gives them a paternal pat on the shoulder as if to say, "Well, Spencer, what have you got to say, old pal?" Of course, he's never read Spencer, but how charming he seems when he tells us – with mild, casual irony – that his lady friend "has read her Spencer".

And people listen to him and no one wants to know that not only does this charlatan have no right to talk about Spencer in that tone, but that he isn't even fit to kiss his feet! Only a highly selfish, vile, disgusting animal would ever go about undermining civilization, authority and other people's gods, slinging mud at them with a playful wink, merely to justify and conceal its own impotence and moral bankruptcy.'

'I don't know what you expect of him, Kolya,' Samoylenko said, eyeing the zoologist more guiltily than hatefully. 'He's like everyone else. Of course, he has his weaknesses, but he keeps abreast of current ideas, does his work and is useful to his country. Ten years ago there was an old shipping-agent here, a man of the greatest intellect. What he used to say was . . .'

'Enough of that, enough!' the zoologist interrupted. 'You tell me he's working for the government. But what has he done? Have things improved here, are the clerks any more conscientious, honest, courteous, since *he* arrived on the scene? On the contrary, with the authority of a cultured, university man he's only sanctioned slackness. He's punctual only on the twentieth of the month, when he gets paid, the rest of the time he shuffles around at home in his slippers and tries to give the impression he's doing the Russian government a great favour by living in the Caucasus. No, Alexander, you shouldn't stand up for him. You're completely lacking in sincerity. If you were really so very fond of him and considered him your neighbour, then, before anything else, you wouldn't be so blind to his weaknesses, you wouldn't be so tolerant. Instead, you'd try to render him harmless, for his own good.'

'Which means?'

'Neutralizing him. Since he's incorrigible, there's only one way to do it . . .' Von Koren ran his fingers along his neck. 'Either by drowning him or . . .' he added, 'in the interests of humanity, in his *own* interest, such people should be exterminated. No doubt about it.'

'What are you saying?' Samoylenko muttered as he stood up and looked in amazement at the zoologist's calm, cool face. 'Deacon, what is he saying? Have you gone out of your mind?'

'I wouldn't insist on the death penalty,' von Koren said. 'If that's

THE DUEL

been proven harmful, then think of something else. If Layevsky can't be exterminated, then isolate him, strip him of his individuality, make him do community work.'

'What are you saying?' Samoylenko said, aghast. 'With pepper, with pepper!' he cried out in despair when he saw the deacon eating stuffed marrows without any. 'You're an extremely intelligent man, but what are you saying? Forcing our friend, such a proud, intelligent man, to do community work!'

'But if he's proud and tries to resist, then clap him in irons!'

Samoylenko was speechless and could only twiddle his fingers. The deacon peered into his stunned face, which really did look funny, and burst out laughing.

'Let's change the subject,' the zoologist said. 'Remember one thing, Alexander, primitive man was protected from men like Layevsky by the struggle for survival and natural selection. But nowadays, since civilization has significantly weakened this struggle and the process of natural selection too, the extermination of the weak and worthless has become our worry. Otherwise, if people like Layevsky were to multiply, civilization would perish and humanity would degenerate completely. We'd be the guilty ones.'

'If we're going to drown and hang people,' Samoylenko said, 'then to hell with your civilization, to hell with humanity! To hell with them! Now, let me tell you. You're a deeply learned man, highly intelligent, the pride of your country. But the Germans have ruined you. Yes, the Germans, the Germans!'

Since leaving Dorpat, where he studied medicine, Samoylenko rarely saw any Germans and had not read one German book. But in his opinion the Germans were to blame for all the evil in politics and science. Even he could not say how he had arrived at this opinion, but he stuck firmly to it.

'Yes, the Germans!' he repeated. 'Now come and have some tea.'

All three stood up, put their hats on and went out into the small garden, where they sat in the shade of pale maple, pear and chestnut trees. The zoologist and the deacon sat on a bench near a small table, while Samoylenko sank into a wicker armchair with a broad, sloping back. The orderly brought them tea, preserves and a bottle of syrup.

It was very hot, about ninety in the shade. The burning air had become listless, inert; a long cobweb stretching down to the ground from the chestnut hung limp and motionless.

The deacon took his guitar — it was always lying on the ground near the table — tuned it and began to sing in a soft, thin voice, 'Oh, the young college boys were standing by the tavern ...', but immediately stopped, as it was so hot, wiped the sweat from his brow and looked up at the deep blue, blazing sky. Samoylenko dozed off; he felt weak, intoxicated by the heat, the silence and that sweet afternoon drowsiness which swiftly took control of his limbs. His arms drooped, his eyes grew small, his head nodded on his chest. He gave von Koren and the deacon a sickly, sentimental look and murmured, 'The young generation ... A great man of science and luminary of the church ... You'll see, that long-skirted pro-pounder of sacred mysteries will probably end up as a Metropolitan ... and we'll all have to kiss his hand ... Well, good luck to him.'

The sound of snoring soon followed. Von Koren and the deacon finished their tea and went out into the street.

'Going to catch gobies in the harbour again?' the zoologist asked.

'No, it's a bit too hot.'

'Let's go to my place. You can do up a parcel for me and copy something out. At the same time we can discuss what you are going to do. You must do some work, deacon, you can't go on like this.'

'What you say is fair and logical,' the deacon said, 'but my present circumstances do provide some excuse for my idleness. You know yourself that uncertainty as to one's position significantly increases apathy. The Lord alone knows if I'm here temporarily or for the duration. Here I am living in uncertainty, while the deaconess is vegetating at her father's and feeling lonely. I must confess this heat has fuddled my brains.'

'Nonsense,' the zoologist said. 'You should be able to get used to this heat and being without the deaconess. You shouldn't pamper yourself, take a firm grip.'

V

In the morning Nadezhda went for a bathe, followed by Olga her cook with jug, copper basin, towels and a sponge. Out in the roads two strange ships (obviously foreign freighters) with dirty white funnels lay at anchor. Some men in white, with white shoes, were strolling up and down the quayside shouting out loud in French, and they were answered by people on the ships. A lively peal of bells came from the little town church.

'It's Sunday!' Nadezhda remembered with great pleasure.

She was feeling quite well and her mood was gay and festive. She thought she looked very sweet in her new, loose dress of coarse tussore, in her large straw hat with its broad brim pressed down so tightly over her ears that her face seemed to be looking out of a box. She thought that there was only one young, pretty, cultured woman in the town – herself. Only she knew how to dress inexpensively, elegantly and tastefully. Her dress, for example, had cost only twenty-two roubles, yet it was so charming! She was the only woman who could please the men in a town that was full of them and so they just could not help envying Layevsky, whether they liked it or not.

She was glad Layevsky had been cool and grudgingly polite towards her lately – at times he had been impertinent and even downright rude. Once she would have answered his outbursts and his contemptuous and cold, or strange and inscrutable, glances with reproaches, would have threatened to leave him or starve herself to death; but now she only replied with blushes, looked guilty, and rejoiced in the fact that he did not show any affection. It would have been even better and more pleasant if he had told her off or threatened her, since she felt entirely to blame. She thought she was the guilty one – firstly, for not showing any sympathy for his dreams of a life of toil, on account of which he had given up St Petersburg and come out here to the Caucasus. She was convinced that this was the true reason for his recent anger with her. When she was on her way to the Caucasus she thought that on the very first day she would find herself a quiet little place near the sea, with a cosy, shady little garden with birds and streams where she could plant flowers and vegetables, keep ducks and hens, entertain the neighbours, dole out medicine to the poor peasants and give them books. However, as it turned out, the Caucasus offered nothing but bare mountains, forests, enormous valleys – it was a place where one always had to be choosing, making a fuss, building. There just weren't any neighbours around, it was terribly hot, and one could easily be burgled. Layevsky was in no hurry to acquire a building-plot. Of that she was glad and it seemed they had both tacitly agreed never to mention that 'life of toil' again. His silence on the subject meant he was angry with *her* for not saying anything about it, so she thought.

Secondly, without his knowledge, she had spent about three hundred roubles over these two years on various trifles at Achmianov's shop. Buying cloth, silk, a parasol, little by little, she had run up a sizeable bill without even noticing it.

'I'll tell him today,' she decided, but immediately realized that it was hardly the best time to talk to Layevsky about bills in his present frame of mind.

In the third place she had already entertained Kirilin, an inspector in the local police, twice in Layevsky's absence – one morning when Layevsky had gone for a swim, and then at midnight, when he was playing cards. Nadezhda flushed as she recalled this and she looked at her cook as though she was frightened she might read her thoughts. These long, insufferably hot, tedious days; these beautiful, languorous evenings; these stifling nights; her whole life there, when from morning to night time hung heavily; the obsessive thought that she was the youngest and most beautiful woman in the town and that she was squandering her youth; and Layevsky himself, so honest, idealistic, but so set in his ways, perpetually shuffling about in his slippers, biting his nails and plaguing her with his moods – all these things gradually made her a victim of desire, so that, like a woman insane, she could think only of one thing, day and night. In her breathing, her glances, her tone of voice, the way she walked, she was ruled by desire. The roar of the waves told her how she must love, so did the darkness of evening, and the mountains too . . . And when Kirilin had begun courting her, she was neither able nor willing to resist, and she had given herself to him.

Now those foreign ships and men in white somehow put her in mind of a huge ballroom: the sounds of a waltz rang in her ears, mingling with French, and her breast trembled with inexplicable joy. She wanted to dance and to speak French.

Joyfully she thought that there was nothing so terrible in being unfaithful to him and her heart had played no part in that betrayal: she still loved Layevsky and this was plain from her jealousy of him, from feeling sorry for him and bored when he was out. As for Kirilin, he was just ordinary and a little on the coarse side, despite his good looks. She had already broken off with him and there would never be anything between them again. It was all over, finished, and it was no one's business – if Layevsky chanced to find out he would never believe it.

There was only one bathing-house on the beach – for ladies; the men swam out in the open. As she entered the bathing-house, Nadezhda met Marya Bityugov, the middle-aged wife of a civil servant, together with her fifteen-year-old schoolgirl daughter Katya. Both of them were sitting on a bench undressing. Marya Bityugov was a kindly, emotional, refined lady who spoke with a drawl and over-dramatically. Up to the age of thirty-two she had been a governess, then she married Bityugov, a short, bald, extremely docile man who combed his hair over his temples. She was still in love with him, jealous of other women, blushed every time the word 'love' was mentioned, and assured everyone she was very happy.

'My dear!' she said, enraptured at seeing Nadezhda and assuming that expression all her friends called 'sugary'. 'My dear, I'm so pleased you've come! We shall bathe together – how delightful!'

Olga quickly threw off her dress and blouse and began undressing her mistress.

'Not quite so hot today, is it?' Nadezhda said, shrinking at her naked cook's rough hands. 'Yesterday I nearly died from the heat!'

'Oh yes, my dear! I almost suffocated. Can you believe it, I bathed three times yesterday, just imagine my dear, three times! Even my Nikodim was worried.'

'Well, how can people be so ugly?' Nadezhda thought as she looked at Olga and the civil servant's wife. She glanced at Katya and thought, 'Quite a good figure for a young girl!'

'Your Nikodim is very, very nice!' she said. 'I'm just mad about him.'

Marya Bityugov replied, forcing a laugh, 'Ha, ha, ha! How delightful!'

Free of her clothes, Nadezhda had a sudden urge to fly and she felt that she had only to flap her arms to soar up into the sky. As she sat there undressed she saw Olga was looking at her white body rather disgustedly. The wife of a young soldier, Olga was living with her lawful husband and for this reason considered herself superior. Nadezhda also felt that Marya Bityugov and Katya despised and feared her. This was unpleasant, so she tried to raise herself in their opinion and said, 'At home in St Petersburg the holiday season is in full swing right now. My husband and I have so many friends! We should go and see them.'

'Your husband's an engineer, I believe?' Marya Bityugov asked timidly.

'I'm talking about Layevsky. He knows a lot of people. Unfortunately his mother's a terrible snob, and she's a little soft in the head ...'

Nadezhda did not finish and plunged into the water; Marya Bityugov and Katya followed her in.

'Society is so riddled with prejudices,' Nadezhda said. 'It's harder to get on with people than you think.'

Marya Bityugov, who had worked as a governess with aristocratic families and who knew about high society, said, 'Oh, yes! Would you believe it, my dear, you had to dress for lunch *and* dinner at the Garatynskys', no question, so they gave me a dress allowance, apart from my salary, just as if I were an actress.'

She stood between Nadezhda and Katya as though shielding her daughter from the water that was washing over Nadezhda. Through the open doorway which led out to the sea they could see someone swimming about a hundred yards from the bathing enclosure.

'Mama, it's Kostya!' Katya said.

'Oh, oh!' Marya Bityugov clucked in horror. 'Kostya, come back!' she shouted. 'Kostya, come back!'

Kostya, a boy of fourteen, dived and swam further away to show off to his mother and sister, but he tired and hurried back. It was plain from his serious, tense expression that he did not trust his own strength.

'Boys are so much trouble, my dear!' Marya Bityugov said, feeling relieved now. 'It always seems that he's about to break his neck. Oh, my dear, how lovely to be a mother – but at the same time, it's a real worry! Everything scares you.'

Nadezhda put on her straw hat and struck out to sea. She swam ten yards or so and then floated on her back. She could see as far as the horizon, ships, people on the beach, the town, and all these sights, together with the heat and the translucent, caressing waves, excited her and whispered that she needed to live ... live ... A sailing-boat rushed swiftly past, vigorously cutting through the waves and air. The man at the rudder was looking at her and she felt how pleasant it was to be looked at.

After their bathe the ladies dressed and went off together. 'I'm usually running a temperature every other day, but I don't lose any weight, despite this,' Nadezhda said, licking her lips that were salty after the bathe, and smiling at bowing acquaintances. 'I've always been plump and now I seem to have put on even more weight.'

'My dear, it all depends on one's disposition. If you're not inclined to put on weight, like myself for example, then it makes no difference how much food you eat. But my dear, your hat's dripping wet.'

'It doesn't matter, it will soon dry.'

Nadezhda caught another glimpse of those French-speaking men in white strolling along the front. And once again, for some strange reason, she felt the joy rise up within her and she dimly remembered some great ballroom where she had once danced – or was it only a dream? And from deep down inside her came muffled, hollow whispers, telling her she was a petty-minded, vulgar, worthless, insignificant woman.

Marya Bityugov stopped by her front gate and invited her to come in and sit down. 'Please do come in, my dear,' she said imploringly, and at the same time she looked anxiously at Nadezhda, half hoping she would refuse.

'Delighted,' Nadezhda agreed. 'You know how I love visiting

you.' And she went into the house. Marya Bityugov asked her to sit down, gave her coffee and rolls. Then she showed her photographs of her former charges – the Garatynsky girls, who were married now; and she showed her Katya and Kostya's examination marks. They were very good, but to make them appear even better she sighed and complained how difficult schoolwork was these days. She looked after her guest, but at the same time felt sorry for her and was worried in case her presence might have a bad effect on Kostya and Katya's morals. She was pleased Nikodim was out. Convinced that all men fell for *her sort*, she felt Nadezhda might have a bad influence on Mr Bityugov as well.

As she chatted with her guest, Marya could not forget that there was going to be a picnic later that afternoon and that von Koren had particularly requested her not to tell the 'macaques' about it – that is, Layevsky and Nadezhda. But she accidentally let it slip, blushed deeply and told her in an embarrassed voice, 'I do hope you'll join us!'

VI

The arrangements were to drive about five miles out of town along the southbound road, to stop near the inn at the junction of the Black and Yellow Rivers, where they would make some fish soup. Samoylenko and Layevsky led the way in a cabriolet, followed by Marya Bityugov, Nadezhda, Katya and Kostya in a carriage drawn by three horses; in this carriage were the hamper and the crockery. In the next carriage sat Inspector Kirilin and young Achmianov – the son of the merchant whom Nadezhda owed three hundred roubles. Huddled up on a bench opposite them, legs crossed, was Nikodim Bityugov, a smart little man with his hair brushed over his temples. Last of all came von Koren, and the deacon, who had a basket of fish at his feet.

'Keep to the r-r-ight!' Samoylenko shouted at the top of his voice whenever they met a bullock cart or an Abkhazian on his donkey.

'Two years from now,' von Koren was telling the deacon, 'when I have the funds and staff, I'll be off on my expedition. I'm going up the coast from Vladivostok to the Bering Straits, then to the mouth of the Yenisey. We're going to make a map, study the fauna and flora and carry out detailed geological, anthropological and ethnographic surveys. It's up to you whether you come or not.'

'That's impossible,' said the deacon.

'Why?'

'I'm a family man, I'm tied down.'

'The deaconess will let you go. We'll see she has nothing to worry about. Even better, you might try to persuade her, for the good of society, to become a nun. That would enable you to become a monk yourself and come on the expedition as a regular priest. I can fix it.' The deacon remained silent. 'Is your theology up to scratch?'

'Pretty weak.'

'Hm . . . can't advise you there, because I don't know much about it myself. Give me a list of the books you need and I'll send them to you this winter from St Petersburg. You'll also have to read the memoirs of missionaries. There you'll find excellent ethnologists and experts in oriental languages. When you're familiar with their approach you'll find you can tackle the work more easily. Well, don't waste your time while you're waiting for books, come and see me and we'll study the compass and do some meteorology. All that's essential.'

'Well now . . .' muttered the deacon and he burst out laughing. 'I've applied for a post in Middle Russia and my archpriest uncle promised to help. If I join you I'll have troubled him for nothing.'

'I don't understand why you can't make your mind up. If you go on as you are, just an ordinary deacon, your only duty conducting services on Sundays and high holidays, and taking it easy the rest of the time, in ten years you'll be just the same – although you might have acquired whiskers and a beard. Whereas if you come on the expedition you'll be a different man in ten years' time, you'll be rich in the knowledge that you've achieved something.'

Cries of horror and delight came from the ladies' carriage. They were travelling along a road carved out of a sheer cliff and everyone felt they were racing along a shelf attached to a high wall and that at any moment they would all go hurtling over into the abyss. On the right stretched the sea, while on the left was a rugged brown wall covered in black patches, red veins and creeping roots, while up above bushy conifers seemed to be leaning down towards them and gazing in fear and curiosity. A minute later there was laughter and more shrieks – they had to pass under an enormous, overhanging rock.

'I don't know why the hell I've come with you,' Layevsky said. 'It's so stupid and trivial! I should be on my way north, running away, escaping, but for some reason here I am on this ridiculous picnic.'

'But look at that view!' Samoylenko told him when the horses had turned to the left and the Yellow River valley opened out before them, with the glinting river itself flowing yellow, turbid, insane . . .

'I can't see anything nice about it,' Layevsky answered. 'Always going into raptures over nature is to betray poverty of imagination. Compared with what my imagination can offer me all those streams and cliffs are absolute rubbish, nothing else.'

The carriages were travelling along the river bank now. The lofty, precipitous banks gradually closed in, the valley narrowed, confronting them now in the form of a gorge. The great crag which they were passing had been constructed by nature from huge rocks that were exerting such pressure on each other that Samoylenko had to grunt every time he looked at it. Here and there that gloomy, magnificent mountain was intersected by narrow defiles and clefts, from which dampness and a sense of mystery came wafting towards the travellers. Through the defiles they caught sight of other mountains – brown, pink, lilac, smoky, or suffused with light. Every now and then, as they passed the defiles, they could hear water pouring down from above, splashing over the rocks.

'Blasted mountains,' Layevsky sighed; 'they bore me stiff!'

At the point where the Black River flowed into the Yellow, where its ink-black waters stained the yellow as they did battle with them, stood Kerbalay the Tartar's inn, just off the road. The Russian flag flew over it and the name *Pleasant Inn* was chalked on the signboard. Nearby was a small garden, enclosed by a wattle fence, with tables and benches, and from a miserable looking thorny bush rose a solitary cypress, beautiful and dark. Kerbalay, a small sprightly Tartar in dark blue shirt and white apron, was standing in the road. Clasping his stomach he bowed low to the approaching carriages and smiled to reveal his brilliant white teeth.

'Hallo, my dear old Kerbalay!' Samoylenko shouted. 'We're just going on a little bit further, so bring us a samovar and chairs. Look lively now!'

Kerbalay nodded his close-cropped head and muttered something which only the occupants of the last carriage could make out, 'We've got trout today, General.'

'Bring it then, bring it!' von Koren told him.

About five hundred yards past the inn the carriages stopped. Samoylenko chose a small meadow strewn with rocks that made good seats. Here there was a tree felled in a storm, lying with bared, shaggy roots and dried-up yellow needles. A rickety plank bridge spanned the river and right opposite, on the far bank, was a little shed used as a drying-room for maize; with its four low piles it reminded one of the fairy-tale hut that stood on chicken's legs. A short ladder led down from the door.

Their first impression was that they would never get out of the place. Wherever they looked, the mountains loomed on all sides and seemed to be bearing down on them; the evening shadows swiftly closed in from the direction of the inn and the dark cypress, making the narrow, sinuous Yellow River valley look even narrower and the mountains higher. The river gurgled and cicadas chirped incessantly.

'Enchanting!' Marya Bityugov said with deep sighs of delight. 'My dears, look how beautiful it is! So very quiet!'

'Yes, it really is nice,' agreed Layevsky, who liked this view. For some reason he felt suddenly sad when he gazed at the sky and then at the blue wisp of smoke curling out of the inn's chimney. 'Yes, very nice!' he repeated.

'Mr Layevsky, please describe the view for us!' Marya Bityugov said.

'What for?' Layevsky asked. 'First-hand impressions are better than any description. The wealth of colour and sound that we all receive from nature through our senses is turned into an ugly, unrecognizable mishmash by writers.'

49

'Is that so?' von Koren asked coldly, selecting the largest rock near the water and trying to climb up it and sit down. 'Is that so?' he repeated and stared at Layevsky. 'What about *Romeo and Juliet*? Or Pushkin's Ukrainian Night*? Nature should prostrate herself before them.'

'That may be so,' Layevsky agreed, too lazy to offer any considered reply. 'However,' he said a little later, 'what exactly is *Romeo and Juliet*? Beautiful, poetic, divine love is only roses covering up the rottenness beneath. Romeo's an animal, like anyone else.'

'No matter what anyone tells you, you always turn it into . . .'

Von Koren glanced at Katya and did not finish.

'And *what* do I turn it into?' Layevsky asked.

'Well, for instance, if someone says, "What a lovely bunch of grapes," you reply, "Yes, but how ugly when they've been chewed and then digested in the stomach." Why say things like that? It's nothing very original and it's really a strange way of expressing yourself.'

Layevsky knew that von Koren did not like him and therefore was scared of him. When von Koren was around, he thought, people felt very awkward, as if someone were standing guard behind their backs. Ignoring this last remark he walked away and regretted having come.

'Ladies and gentlemen, quick march! Get some wood for the fire!' Samoylenko commanded.

Everyone wandered off at random, leaving only Kirilin, Achmianov and Bityugov behind. Kerbalay brought some chairs, spread a carpet and stood several bottles of wine on the ground. Inspector Kirilin, a tall, distinguished-looking man who wore a raincoat over his tunic in all weathers, put one in mind of those young provincial police chiefs with his proud bearing, solemn walk and deep, rather hoarse voice. He had a sad, sleepy look, as if he had just been woken against his will.

'What's *that* you've brought, you scum?' Kirilin asked Kerbalay, slowly enunciating every word. 'I asked you to serve Kvarel, but what have you brought, you Tartar pig? Eh? What?'

---

* A celebrated passage from the narrative poem *Poltava* (1828).

'We have plenty of our own wine, Inspector Kirilin,' Bityugov observed timidly and politely.

'So what? But I want you to have some of my wine as well. I'm on this picnic and I assume I've a perfect right to contribute my share. That's what I ass-ume! Bring ten bottles of Kvarel.'

'Why so many?' Bityugov asked in surprise, knowing full well that Kirilin had no money.

'Twenty bottles! Thirty!' shouted Kirilin.

'Don't worry,' Achmianov whispered to Bityugov, 'I'll pay.'

Nadezhda was in a gay, playful mood. She felt like skipping, laughing, shouting, teasing, flirting. In her cheap cotton dress with its pattern of blue dots, her little red shoes and that same straw hat, she felt as tiny, natural, light and ethereal as a butterfly. She ran across the rickety bridge and looked down at the water for a minute to make her head go round; then she cried out and ran laughing towards the shed, conscious that all the men – even Kerbalay – were feasting their eyes on her. In the swiftly approaching dusk, when the trees, mountains, horses and carriages had all merged together and a light gleamed in the windows of the inn, she climbed a mountain path that threaded its way up the hillside between boulders and prickly bushes, and sat on a rock. Down below, the bonfire was already burning. With sleeves rolled up, the deacon was walking about and his long black shadow moved in a radius around the fire. He was piling on wood and stirring the pot with a spoon tied to a long stick. Samoylenko, his handsome face coppery-red, was fussing around the fire as though at home in his own kitchen.

'But where's the salt, gentlemen?' he shouted fiercely. 'I bet you've forgotten it. And why are you all lounging about like country squires while I'm left to do all the work?'

Layevsky and Bityugov were sitting side by side on the uprooted tree, gazing pensively at the fire. Marya, Katya and Kostya were taking teacups, saucers and plates out of the baskets. Von Koren stood wondering at the water's edge, his arms folded and with one foot on a rock. Red patches of light cast by the bonfire wandered with the shadows over the ground near dark human shapes, trembled on the mountains, trees, bridge and drying-room. The steep, hollowed-out far bank was lit up all over and its reflection flickered in the river, to be torn to shreds by the fast-flowing, turbulent water.

The deacon went to fetch the trout which Kerbalay was cleaning and washing on the bank, but he stopped half-way to look around. 'Heavens, how beautiful!' he thought. 'Just people, rocks, a bonfire, twilight, a twisted tree – nothing more than that, but how beautiful!'

Near the drying-room on the far bank some strangers came into view. It was impossible to make them all out straight away in the flickering light and bonfire smoke drifting over the river, but one could make out some details – first a shaggy fur cap and a grey beard, then a dark blue shirt, rags hanging from shoulder to knee and a dagger across a stomach, then a swarthy young face with black eyebrows, thick and sharp as if drawn in charcoal. About five of these people were squatting in a circle, while another five or so went into the shed. One of them stood in the doorway, hands thrust behind him, with his back to the fire, and started telling what was undoubtedly a most interesting story because, after Samoylenko had put some more wood on the fire, making it flare up, scattering sparks and brightly illuminating the shed, two calm, deeply attentive faces could be seen looking through the doorway, while others in the circle had turned round to listen as well. Shortly afterwards the men in the circle struck up a slow-moving song, rather like those sung in church during Lent. As he listened the deacon pictured himself ten years from then, after he had returned from the expedition: he is a young monk and missionary, a celebrated writer with a glittering past; he is ordained Archimandrite, then Bishop. He celebrates mass in the cathedral. With his golden mitre and image hanging round his neck, he steps up into the pulpit and proclaims as he makes the sign of the cross over the congregation with his three- and two-branched candelabrum, 'Look down from heaven, oh Lord. Behold and visit this vineyard, which Thy right hand hath planted!' And the children would respond, singing 'Holy God' in angelic voices.

'Deacon, where's that fish?' he heard Samoylenko say.

Returning to the bonfire, the deacon imagined a religious procession moving along a dusty road on a hot day in July. Leading the way are men with banners and women and girls carry the icons. They are followed by choirboys and a lay reader with a bandaged cheek and straw in his hair. Then (in the correct order) follow the deacon, then the parish priest with calotte and cross, and after them a crowd of peasant men, women and boys raising clouds of dust. And there in the crowd are the priest's wife and the deaconess in kerchiefs. Choirboys sing, children howl, quails call and a lark bursts into song. Now they stop to sprinkle the cattle with holy water. They move on and kneel to pray for rain. Then food, conversation ...

'All that would be very nice too,' thought the deacon.

VII

Kirilin and Achmianov clambered up the mountain path. Achmianov lagged behind and stopped, while Kirilin went over to Nadezhda.

'Good evening!' he said, saluting.

'Good evening.'

'Oh, yes!' Kirilin said, gazing pensively at the sky.

'What does *that* mean?' Nadezhda asked after a short silence, noticing that they were both being watched by Achmianov.

'Well now, it means,' the police-officer said, articulating every syllable, 'our love has withered without having time to blossom, in a manner of speaking. How else can I take it? Is this some special kind of flirtatiousness on your part or do you take me for some ruffian whom you can treat as you like?'

'It was a mistake! Leave me!' snapped Nadezhda looking at him in terror on that wonderful evening and asking herself in bewilderment if there actually had been a time when this man had attracted her and was close to her.

'Well then!' Kirilin said. He stood silently pondering for a moment, then he asked, 'What now? Let's wait until you're in a better mood. In the mean time, may I make so bold as to assure you I'm a respectable man and I forbid anyone to doubt it. No one plays games with me! *Adieu!*'

He saluted and made off through the bushes. A little later Achmianov hesitantly approached. 'A fine evening!' he said with a slight Armenian accent.

He was quite good-looking, dressed smartly and had the easy-going manner of a well-bred young man. But Nadezhda did not

ANTON CHEKHOV

like him, as she owed his father three hundred roubles. What was
more, she did not like the fact that a shopkeeper had been invited
to the picnic, and she did not like being approached by him on an
evening just when she felt so pure at heart.

'On the whole, the picnic's been a success,' he said after a pause.

'Yes,' she agreed, casually adding as though she had just remembered
that debt, 'Yes, tell them in your shop that Mr Layevsky will call soon
to pay the three hundred ... I don't remember exactly how much.'

'I'd lend you another three hundred just to stop you reminding
me of that debt every single day. Why do you have to be so prosaic?'

Nadezhda burst out laughing. The funny thought occurred to her,
that if she were sufficiently immoral and were so inclined, she could
have settled that debt in one minute. What if she were to turn that
handsome young idiot's head? How comical, absurd, how insane
that would be! And suddenly she had the urge to make him fall
in love with her, to take what she could, drop him and then sit
back to see what happened.

'Allow me to give you a piece of advice,' Achmianov said timidly.
'I beg you to steer clear of Kirilin. He's been saying terrible things
about you everywhere.'

'I'm not interested in hearing what any fool has to say about me,'
Nadezhda said coldly and she became dreadfully worried; that
amusing idea of having a game with young, handsome Achmianov
suddenly lost its charm.

'I must go down now,' she said; 'they're calling.'

Down below the soup was ready. They poured it into the bowls
and drank it with that air of ritual solemnity exclusive to picnics.
They all found the soup delicious and declared they had never tasted
anything so appetizing at home.

As usually happens on picnics, in all that jumble of napkins, packets,
useless scraps of greasy paper floating around in the wind, no one
knew where anyone else's glass or bread was, they spilt wine on
carpet and knees, they scattered salt all over the place. All around
it was dark now and the bonfire was dying out. Everyone felt too
lazy to get up and put more wood on; everyone drank wine and
Kostya and Katya were allowed half a glass each. Nadezhda drank
one glass after another, became drunk and forgot Kirilin.

'A splendid picnic and an enchanting evening,' Layevsky said, exhilarated by the wine, 'but I prefer a good winter to all of this. "His beaver collar sparkles silver with frosty dust"*.'

'Each to his taste,' von Koren observed.

Layevsky felt awkward: his back was hot from the fire, while von Koren's loathing was directed at his chest and face. This decent, clever man's hatred of him, which most probably was founded on some sound, underlying reason, humiliated him and made him feel weak. Lacking the strength to combat it he said in a cringing voice,

'I'm passionately fond of nature and I'm sorry I'm not a scientist. I envy you.'

'Well, I don't feel envious or sorry,' Nadezhda said. 'I don't understand how anyone can seriously study small beetles and bugs when the common people are suffering.'

Layevsky shared this opinion. He knew nothing whatsoever about the natural sciences and therefore he could not stand that authoritarian tone of voice and show of erudition and profound wisdom affected by students of ants' antennae and cockroaches' legs. It always annoyed him to think that these people presumed to solve questions embracing the origin and life of man on the evidence of these antennae, legs and something called protoplasm – for some reason he always imagined this as an oyster. But he saw that what Nadezhda had said was false and retorted (merely for the sake of contradicting her), 'It's not the bugs that are important, but the deductions you make from them!'

VIII

It was late – past ten – when they climbed back into the carriages. Everyone was seated, with the exception of Nadezhda and Achmianov, who were chasing each other along the opposite bank and laughing.

'Ladies and gentlemen, hurry up!' Samoylenko shouted at them.

'We shouldn't have served wine to the ladies,' von Koren said softly.

* From the first chapter of Pushkin's *Eugene Onegin*.

Exhausted by the picnic, by von Koren's hatred of him and by his own thoughts, Layevsky went to meet Nadezhda. She was in high spirits, radiant and she felt as light as a feather; when she seized him by both hands and laid her head on his chest, breathlessly laughing out loud, he took a step backwards and said sternly, 'You're behaving like a . . . tart.'

This was so very nasty that he even felt sorry for her. On his tired, angry face she read hatred, pity, self-annoyance, and suddenly she lost heart. She realized she had gone too far, had behaved far too irresponsibly, and sadly she climbed into the first empty carriage with Achmianov, feeling ponderous, fat, coarse and drunk. Layevsky got in with Kirilin, the zoologist with Samoylenko, the deacon with the ladies and the convoy moved off.

'That's typical of macaques,' von Koren began, wrapping himself in his cape and closing his eyes. 'You heard her say it, how she wouldn't want to study bugs and beetles, because the common people are suffering. That's how all macaques judge people like me. They're a servile, crafty breed, intimidated by ten generations of the knout and fist; they tremble, show feeling and cringe only when they're forced to. But just let your macaque loose where he can be free, where there's no one to grasp him by the scruff of the neck, and he will display himself and make his presence felt. Just look how brazenly he behaves at painting exhibitions, museums, theatres, or when he passes judgement, puffs himself up, gets on his hind legs, lashes out, criticizes . . . And he never fails to criticize – this shows how much of a slave he is! Just listen: professional people come in for more abuse than crooks and this is because three quarters of society consists of slaves, of these same macaques. You'll never find one of these slaves holding his hand out and offering you his sincere thanks for working.'

'I don't know what you expect!' Samoylenko said, yawning. 'That poor woman, in her simplicity of mind, wanted to have a serious talk with you and here you are jumping to conclusions. You're annoyed with him over something or other, so you have to drag *her* into it as well. But she's a fine woman!'

'Hey, that's enough! She's just an ordinary kept woman, dissolute and vulgar. Listen to me, Alexander, if you met a simple peasant woman who wasn't living with her husband, who did no work and could only giggle all the time, then you would tell her to go and do some work. So why are you so timid, so frightened of speaking the truth? Just because Nadezhda's living with a civil servant, not a sailor?'

'So what should I do with her then?' Samoylenko said angrily. 'Beat her?'

'Don't flatter vice. We only condemn vice behind its back, but that's the same as poking your tongue out when no one's there. I'm a zoologist or sociologist, which comes to the same thing. You're a doctor. Society trusts us and it's our duty to point out the dreadful damage that the existence of women like Nadezhda Ivanovna might inflict on it and generations to come.'

'Fyodorovna,' corrected Samoylenko. 'But what must society do?'

'Do? That's its own affair. In my opinion the most straight-forward and the safest way is by force: she should be returned to her husband *manu militari* and if he won't take her back then she should be sentenced to hard labour or some house of correction.'

'Ugh!' Samoylenko sighed. He was silent for a moment, then he quietly asked, 'Only a short time ago you were saying people like Layevsky should be exterminated ... Tell me, if the state or society gave *you* the job, could you do it?'

'I wouldn't hesitate.'

IX

When they arrived home Layevsky and Nadezhda went into their dark, stuffy, dreary rooms. Neither said a word. Layevsky lit a candle while Nadezhda sat down and, without taking off her cloak or hat, looked at him with sad, guilty eyes.

He realized she was waiting for an explanation. But that would have been so boring and futile, so exhausting, and he felt depressed at having lost his temper and spoken rudely to her. He happened to touch the letter in his pocket that he had intended reading to her for days now and thought that by showing it to her this would help to distract her attention.

'It's high time things were sorted out,' he thought. 'I'll give her the letter and what will be, will be.'

He took the letter out and gave it to her. 'Read this. It concerns you.'

Then he went into his study and lay down in the dark on his couch without a cushion. Nadezhda read the letter and felt the ceiling had fallen down, that the walls had closed in on her. Suddenly everything seemed cramped, dark and frightening. Quickly she crossed herself three times and murmured, 'May he rest in peace ... May he rest in peace.' And she burst into tears.

'Ivan!' she called. 'Ivan!'

There was no reply. Thinking Layevsky had come into the room and was standing behind her chair she sobbed like a child and asked, 'Why didn't you tell me before that he'd died? I wouldn't have gone on the picnic and I wouldn't have laughed in that dreadful way ... The men said such vulgar things to me ... What a disgrace, what a disgrace! Save me, Ivan, save me ... I'm out of my mind ... I'm ruined!'

Layevsky heard her sobs. He felt he was nearly suffocating and his heart was pounding. In his despair he got up, stood in the middle of the room, groped for the armchair near the table and sat down.

'This is a prison,' he thought. 'I must get away ... I can't go on like this.'

It was too late now for cards and there were no restaurants in the town. He lay down again, stuffed his fingers in his ears to shut out the sobs and suddenly he remembered that he could call on Samoylenko. To avoid Nadezhda, he climbed into the garden through a window, over a fence and went down the street.

It was dark. A ship had just docked – a large liner judging by her lights. The anchor-chain rattled away. A small red light swiftly moved from shore to ship – this was the Customs boat.

'The passengers are snugly asleep in their cabins,' Layevsky thought and envied others their rest.

The windows in Samoylenko's house were open. Layevsky peered through one of them, then another. Inside it was dark and quiet.

'Are you asleep, Alexander?' he called. 'Alexander!'

He heard some coughing and then a cry of alarm. 'Who in the devil's name is that?'

'It's me, Alexander. Please forgive me.'

A few moments later the door opened, a lamp cast its soft light and the massive figure of Samoylenko appeared, all in white and with a white night-cap.

'What do you want?' he asked, breathing heavily and scratching himself as he stood there half asleep. 'Just a moment, I'll open up.'

'Don't bother, I can get through the window.'

Layevsky climbed through a small window, went up to Samoylenko and gripped his arm.

'Alexander,' he said in a trembling voice, 'save me! I beg you, I implore you! Try and understand! I'm in absolute agony. Another couple of days of this and I'll hang myself like ... like a dog!'

'Wait a minute ... What exactly are you on about?'

'Light a candle.'

'Oh, oh,' Samoylenko sighed, lighting a candle. 'Good heavens, it's already past one, my dear chap.'

'Forgive me, but I can't stay at home,' Layevsky said, greatly relieved at the candle-light and Samoylenko's presence. 'You, Alexander, are my best, my only friend. You are my only hope. Whether you want to or not, please save me, for God's sake! I must escape from here at all costs. Lend me some money!'

'Oh, good Lord, good Lord!' Samoylenko sighed, scratching himself. 'I was just falling asleep when I heard the ship's siren ... and now you ... Do you need much?'

'At least three hundred roubles. I must leave her a hundred and I need two hundred for the journey ... I already owe you about four hundred, but I'll send you everything in the post ... everything ...'

Samoylenko grasped both side-whiskers in one hand, stood with legs apart and pondered. 'Well now,' he murmured pensively. 'Three hundred ... All right. But I don't have that much. I'll have to borrow it from someone.'

'Please borrow it then, for God's sake!' Layevsky said and he could tell from Samoylenko's face that he wanted to lend him the money and that he would not let him down. 'Borrow it, I'll pay you back without fail. I'll send it from St Petersburg the moment I arrive, don't worry about that.' Brightening up he added, 'I'll tell you what, Sasha, let's have some wine.'

'All right, let's drink some wine.'

They both went into the dining-room.

'But what about Nadezhda?' Samoylenko asked, putting three bottles and a bowl of peaches on the table. 'She's not staying on, surely?'

'I'll arrange everything, everything,' Layevsky said, with a sudden surge of joy in his heart. 'Later on I'll send her money and then she'll come and join me. We'll sort things out all right once we're there. Your health, my friend.'

'Wait a moment!' Samoylenko said. 'Try this first ... it's from my own vineyard. That one's from Navaridze's and this is an Akhatulov ... Try them all and tell me quite frankly what you think ... Mine's a little sharp, eh? Do you think so?'

'Yes. You've really cheered me up, Alexander. Thanks. I'm a new man.'

'Rather sharp?'

'Damn it, I don't know. But you're a wonderful, marvellous person.'

As he looked at his pale, excited, kind face Samoylenko remembered von Koren's opinion, that such people should be exterminated, and Layevsky struck him as a weak, defenceless child whom anyone could harm or exterminate.

'Be sure you make your peace with your mother when you go,' he said. 'This sort of thing's not very nice.'

'Yes, yes. Without fail.'

For a moment neither said a word. When the first bottle was finished Samoylenko said, 'You ought to make it up with von Koren too. You're always quarrelling.'

'Yes, he's a very fine, very clever man,' Layevsky agreed, now ready to praise and forgive everyone. 'He's a remarkable man, but I find him impossible to get on with. No! Our temperaments are too far apart. I'm a sluggish, feeble, servile sort of person. I might offer to shake hands with him when the time's right, but he'd turn away in contempt . . .' Layevsky sipped his wine, paced up and down and then continued, from the middle of the room, 'I understand von Koren perfectly. He's the firm, strong type, a despot. You've heard him always going on about expeditions and these are no idle words. He needs a desert, a moonlit night. All around, sleeping in tents and under the open sky, are his hungry, sick Cossacks, guides, bearers, doctor, priest, worn out by killing treks. He's alone, doesn't sleep and he sits like Stanley on his camp-stool, feeling lord of the desert and master of these people. He's always going somewhere and his men groan and die, one after the other, but on and on he goes, until he himself perishes in the end. None the less he's still tyrant, still lord and master, since the cross over his grave can be seen by caravans thirty or forty miles off and it rules the desert. I'm only sorry this man isn't in the army. He would have made an excellent, brilliant commander. He would have known how to drown his cavalry in a river and build bridges from the corpses, and such daring is more necessary in war than any fortifications or tactics. Oh, I understand him perfectly! But tell me why is he hanging about here? What's he after?'

'He's studying marine animals.'

'No, my friend. No, no!' Layevsky sighed. 'A scientist on board ship told me the Black Sea is poor in fauna and that the excess of sulphuretted hydrogen in its depths makes organic life impossible. All serious zoologists work at the marine biological stations in Naples or Villefranche. But von Koren is stubborn and independent. He's working on the Black Sea because no one else is. He's severed all links with the university, he won't have anything to do with scientists or colleagues, as he's first and foremost a tyrant, and then a zoologist. He'll go far, you see. And now he's dreaming that when he gets back from his expedition he'll root out intrigues and mediocrity from our universities and make the professors crawl like worms. Despotism is just as powerful in the academic world as in war. But he's spending a second summer in this stinking little dump, as it's better to be boss in a village than underdog in town. Here he's lord and master. He rules everyone here with a rod of iron, crushes them with his authority. He's taken everyone in hand, pokes his nose into other people's business, gets involved in everything and everyone is scared of him. He senses I'm slipping through his fingers and he hates me for it. Didn't he tell you I should be exterminated and made to do community work?'

'Yes,' Samoylenko laughed.

Layevsky laughed too and drank some wine. 'He's even despotic in his ideals,' he said, laughing and nibbling a peach. 'Ordinary mortals working for the common good think of their fellow men – me, you, human beings in brief. But for von Koren people are amateurs and nonentities, too insignificant to serve any purpose in life. He does his work and he'll go on his expedition where he'll break his neck, not out of love for his fellow men, but in the name of some abstraction such as humanity, future generations, the ideal race. He's striving to improve the human race and in this respect we're nothing but slaves for him, just cannon fodder or beasts of burden. Some he would exterminate or pack off to labour camps, while others he would subject to strict discipline, making them get up and go to bed to the sound of the drum, like Arakcheyev★. Or he'd bring in eunuchs to mount guard over our chastity and morals, he'd order anyone stepping outside the bounds of our narrow, conservative morality to be shot. And all this to improve the human race. But what *is* the human race? An illusion, a mirage ... Despots have always been illusionists. I understand him perfectly, my dear chap. I appreciate him and don't deny his importance: men like him provide a firm foundation for the world and if it were left to us alone we'd make as big a mess of it as those flies are making of that picture, for all our kindness and good intentions.'

Layevsky sat down by Samoylenko and said with genuine conviction, 'I'm a superficial, insignificant wreck of a man! The air I breathe, this wine, love – all in all, I've paid for everything in my life up to now with lies, idleness and cowardice. Up to now I've been deceiving others and myself and have suffered as a result. And even my sufferings have been cheap and vulgar. I bow humbly before von Koren's hatred, since I loathe and despise myself at times.' Highly excited, Layevsky once again paced the room. 'I'm glad I can see my own shortcomings so clearly and I admit them,' he said. 'That

★ Count A. A. Arakcheyev (1769–1834), fanatical disciplinarian and founder of the notorious military colonies in the reign of Alexander I.

will help me to rise from the dead, become a new man. My dear fellow, if you only knew how passionately, with what yearning I long for this regeneration! I will be a real person, I promise you! I will be a man! I don't know whether it's the wine or if it's really happening, but it seems ages since I knew such bright, pure moments as I'm experiencing right now with you.'

'Time for bed, my dear chap,' Samoylenko said.

'Yes, yes ... Forgive me. I'm going right now.'

Layevsky fussed around the furniture and windows in search of his cap.

'Thank you,' he muttered, sighing. 'Thank you ... Kindness and a friendly word are better than any charity. You've given me a new lease of life.'

He found his cap, stopped for a moment and gave Samoylenko a guilty look.

'Alexander!' he begged.

'What?'

'My dear friend, please let me stay the night.'

'Be my guest ... Why not?'

Layevsky lay down on the couch and went on talking to the doctor for a long time.

X

Three days after the picnic Marya Bityugov unexpectedly called on Nadezhda. Without a word of greeting or taking her hat off she seized both her hands, pressed them to her breast and said in extreme agitation, 'My dear, I'm so upset, absolutely stunned. Yesterday, it seems, our dear, charming doctor told my Nikodim that your husband has died. Tell me, my dear, is it true?'

'Yes, it's true. He's dead,' Nadezhda replied.

'That's terrible, just terrible, my dear! But every cloud has a silver lining. Your husband was probably a wonderful, extraordinary, saintly person, but men like him are needed more in heaven than in this world.'

Every little feature and spot on Marya Bityugov's face trembled, as though tiny little needles were jumping about under her skin;

she produced that sugary smile and said breathlessly, ecstatically, 'So, my dear, you're free! You can hold your head high now and not be afraid to look people in the face. From now on God, and everyone here, will bless your union with Layevsky. It's so enchanting it makes me tremble for joy! I'm lost for words. I'll see to the wedding arrangements, my dear. Nikodim and I have always been so fond of you, you must allow us to give our blessing to your lawful, unsullied union. When, when is the day?'

'I haven't given it any thought,' Nadezhda said, freeing her hands.

'But that's not possible, my dear. You *must* have thought about it!'

'Really, I haven't!' Nadezhda said laughing. 'What's the point of our marrying? I don't see the need for it. We'll carry on as before.'

'What are you saying!' Marya Bityugov said, horrified. 'For God's sake, what are you saying?'

'Marrying won't improve anything. On the contrary, it would even make things worse. We would lose our freedom.'

'My dear! My dear, what are you saying!' Marya Bityugov cried, stepping back and wringing her hands. 'You're quite outrageous! Come to your senses! Calm down!'

'What do you mean, *calm down*? I haven't lived yet and you tell me to calm down!'

Nadezhda recalled that she actually hadn't had much of a life up to now. After boarding-school she married someone she did not love. Then she went away with Layevsky and stayed the whole time with him on this boring, deserted coast, hoping for better things. Was that any kind of life?

'We ought to get married,' she thought, but then she remembered Kirilin and Achmianov, and she blushed.

'No, it's impossible,' she said. 'Even if Ivan Layevsky went down on his knees and begged me, I'd still refuse.'

Marya Bityugov sat silently for a minute on the couch, sad and serious, and staring at one point. Then she stood up and said coldly, 'Good-bye, my dear! Forgive me for disturbing you. Although it's not easy for me to say this, I must tell you that from now on it's all over between us and despite my deep regard for Mr Layevsky the doors of my house are closed to you.'

She pronounced this with great solemnity and seemed overcome by her own seriousness. Her face trembled again and assumed that mild, sugary expression. Holding out both her hands to a frightened, bewildered Nadezhda she pleaded, 'My dear, please allow me to be your mother or elder sister – for one minute! I'll speak to you frankly, just like a mother.'

Nadezhda felt such warmth, joy and self-pity deep down inside, it was as if her mother had in fact risen from the dead and was standing before her. Impulsively she embraced Marya Bityugov and buried her face in her shoulder. Both burst into tears and sat sobbing on the couch for several minutes, without looking at each other, unable to speak one word.

'My dear, my little child!' Marya Bityugov began. 'I'm going to tell you a few home truths and I shan't spare you!'

'Please do, for goodness' sake! Please do!'

'Trust me, my dear. You will remember that I was the only lady here who invited you home. You horrified me from the very first day, but unlike the rest, I just couldn't give you the cold shoulder. I suffered for that dear, kind Mr Layevsky as though he were my own son. He was a young man in a foreign country, inexperienced, weak, without his mother – and how I suffered! My husband was against making friends with him but I managed to win him over ... We began inviting him home and of course that meant you as well, otherwise he would have taken offence. I have a daughter, a son ... You understand. A child's tender mind and pure heart – you know the passage, "Whoever should offend one of the little ones". When I had you home I trembled for my children. Oh, when you're a mother you'll understand my fears. Everyone was amazed that I received you – please forgive me – like a respectable person and they kept dropping hints. And of course there was gossip and speculation. In my heart of hearts I condemned you, but you were so unhappy, pathetic, so outrageous in your behaviour that I wept for pity!'

'But why, why?' Nadezhda asked, shaking all over. 'What harm have I ever done anyone?'

'You've committed a terrible sin. You've broken the vow you made to your husband at the altar. You've seduced a young man who, if he had never met you, might have taken a lawful wife from a good family, someone of his own class, and might have been leading a proper life now, like everyone else. You've ruined his youth. Don't say anything, my dear, don't say anything! I just can't believe that men are to blame for our sins, the woman's always the guilty party. When it comes to family life men are so thoughtless, they live by their minds and not their hearts, they understand very little, but a woman understands everything. Everything depends on her. Much has been given to women, but much will be required of them. Oh, my dear, if women were sillier or weaker than men in this respect, God would never have entrusted them with bringing up boys and girls. And then, my dear, you trod the path of vice and left all sense of shame behind you. In your position another woman would have hidden herself, locked the doors and stayed at home, and you would only have appeared in God's temple, pale, all dressed in black, weeping. And everyone would have really been saddened and said "Oh Lord, this fallen angel returns to Thee ..." But you cast all modesty aside, my dear, you lived quite brazenly, outrageously, as if you prided yourself on your sins. You behaved wantonly and laughed as I watched you. I shuddered in horror, afraid that heaven's thunder might strike our house when you were there.

'My dear, don't speak, don't speak!' Marya Bityugov shrieked, seeing that Nadezhda wanted to say something. 'Trust me, I won't deceive you, I won't hide a single truth from your inner eye. Listen to me, my dear. God puts his mark on great sinners and this is what you bear. Remember, your dresses always were shocking!'

Nadezhda, who had always greatly admired her own dresses, stopped crying and looked at her in amazement.

'Yes, shocking!' Marya Bityugov continued. 'Anyone can tell what your behaviour's like from the pretentious, gaudy dresses you wear. Whenever people looked at you they all had a good laugh to themselves, but I suffered terribly. And if you'll forgive me for saying so, my dear, you're not very clean! You gave me a fright when we met in the bathing-house. Your top dress isn't too bad, but what you wear *underneath*, your petticoat and slip ... well my dear, it makes me blush! And poor Mr Layevsky's no one to knot his tie properly for him and one look at his linen and boots shows no one looks after the poor man at home. And he never has enough to eat, my dear. In fact, if there's no one at home to see to the tea and coffee you'll have to spend half your salary in the Pavilion. And your house is awful, just awful! No one in the whole town has flies, but your place is swarming with them, all the saucers and plates are black with them. And as for the window-sills and tables, there's dust, dead flies, glasses ... Why keep glasses there? And you never clear the table, my dear. It makes one ashamed going into your bedroom, underwear just thrown anywhere, all those rubber things of yours hanging on the wall and that china *object*, whatever that may be, standing there ... My dear! A husband should know nothing of these things and his wife should keep herself as pure as an angel for him. Every morning, as soon as it's light, I wake up and wash my face with cold water so that my Nikodim won't see me looking sleepy.'

'But those are trivial little things,' Nadezhda sobbed. 'If only I were happy, but I'm so miserable!'

'Yes, you're dreadfully unhappy!' Marya Bityugov sighed, barely able to stop crying herself. 'And great sorrow awaits you in the future. A lonely old age, illnesses, then you will have to answer at the Day of Judgement. It's terrible, terrible! And now that fate is lending you a helping hand you stupidly turn your back on it. You must get married, there's not a moment to lose!'

'Yes, I should, I should,' Nadezhda said, 'but it's impossible!'

'But why?'

'It's impossible! Oh, if only you knew!'

Nadezhda wanted to tell her about Kirilin, about yesterday evening's meeting with young, handsome Achmianov on the quayside, and about her crazy, ridiculous idea of getting rid of that debt of three hundred roubles, about how amusing it had all been, about how she had returned home very late that evening feeling irrevocably ruined – like a prostitute. She herself did not know how it had all come about. And now she wanted to make an oath, with Marya Bityugov as witness, that she would settle that debt, without fail. But she could not speak for sobbing and shame.

'I shall go away from here,' she said, 'Ivan can stay if he likes, but I'm going.'

'But where?'

'Back to central Russia.'

'And what will you live on there? You haven't a penny, surely?'

'I'll do some translating ... or open a little lending library.'

'Stop day-dreaming, my dear. You need money to start a library. Well, I'll leave you now, so please calm yourself, think it over and tomorrow you'll come and see me, all nice and cheerful. That will be delightful! Well, good-bye, my little angel. Let me give you a kiss.'

Marya Bityugov kissed Nadezhda on the forehead, made the sign of the cross over her and quietly left. It was already growing dark and Olga had lit the lamp in the kitchen. Nadezhda went into the bedroom and lay down on the bed. She began to run a high fever. She undressed as she lay there, crumpling her dress down to her feet, then she rolled herself into a ball under the blanket. She felt thirsty, but no one was there to bring her a drink. 'I'll settle that debt!' she told herself and in her delirium she imagined she was sitting beside some sick woman whom she recognized as herself. 'I'll settle it! How stupid to think that just for some money I'd ... I'll leave and send him the money from St Petersburg. First a hundred roubles ... then another hundred ... then another ...'

Late that night Layevsky returned.

'A hundred to begin with, then another ...' Nadezhda told him.

'You should take some quinine,' he said and thought to himself, 'It's Wednesday tomorrow, that ship will sail and I won't be on it. That means I'm stuck here till Saturday.'

Nadezhda knelt up in bed.

'I didn't say anything just now, did I?' she asked, smiling and screwing up her eyes in the candle-light.

'No. We'll have to send for the doctor tomorrow morning. Get some sleep now.'

He took a pillow and went towards the door. Ever since he finally made up his mind to go away and abandon Nadezhda she began to arouse pity and guilt in him. He felt rather shamefaced when he was with her, as though she were an old or sick horse that was going to be put down. He stopped in the doorway and looked back at her. 'I was feeling irritable at the picnic and I said something very rude to you. Please forgive me, for God's sake.'

With these words he went to his study and lay down, but it was a long time before he fell asleep.

The next morning, Samoylenko, in full ceremonial uniform (today was an official holiday), parading his epaulettes and medals, took Nadezhda's pulse and examined her tongue. As he came out of the bedroom, Layevsky, who was standing in the doorway, worriedly asked, 'Well, is it all right? Is everything all right then?' Fear, extreme anxiety and hope were written all over his face.

'Relax, it's nothing dangerous,' Samoylenko said. 'Just an ordinary fever.'

'That's not what I meant,' Layevsky said, impatiently frowning. 'Did you get the money?'

'My dear chap, do forgive me,' Samoylenko whispered, glancing back at the door in embarrassment. 'Please forgive me, for heaven's sake! No one has any spare cash and up to now I've managed to collect only five or ten roubles here and there – all in all, a hundred and ten. I'll be speaking to some other people today. Please be patient.'

'But Saturday's the last day!' Layevsky whispered, trembling with impatience. 'In the name of all that's holy, by Saturday! If I can't get away on Saturday, then I won't need anything ... anything! I don't understand how a doctor can be short of money!'

'Good God, all right then. As you like,' Samoylenko whispered so rapidly and impatiently his throat squeaked. 'I've been stripped bare. I'm owed seven thousand and I'm up to my eyes in debt. Is that *my* fault?'

'Do you mean you'll have it by Saturday? Yes?'

'I'll try.'

'I *beg* you, my dear chap! You *must* see I have the money by Friday morning.'

Samoylenko sat down and wrote out a prescription for quinine solution with *kalium bromatum*, rhubarb infusion, tincture of gentian and *aqua foeniculi* – all in the same mixture, with rose syrup to take the bitterness away – and then he left.

XI

'You look as if you've come to arrest me,' von Koren said when he saw Samoylenko entering in full regalia.

'I was passing by and thought, why don't I drop in and have a taste of zoology?' Samoylenko said as he sat at the large table that the zoologist had knocked together himself from some simple boards. 'Good day, Your Grace!' he said, nodding to the deacon who was sitting by the window copying something out. 'I'll just stay for a few minutes, then I must rush home to see to lunch. It's time already ... I'm not disturbing you, I hope?'

'Not at all,' the zoologist answered, laying out some papers covered with fine handwriting over the table. 'We're busy copying up some notes.'

'Oh ... my God, my God ...' Samoylenko sighed. From the table he gingerly picked up a dusty book, on top of which was a dry, dead insect, like a spider, and said, 'Really! Just imagine some little green beetle going about its business when along comes this frightful object. I can imagine how horrified it would be!'

'Yes, I suppose so.'

'Is it equipped with poison to defend itself from its enemies?'

'Yes, for protection and for attacking as well.'

'Well, well, well ... And everything in nature, my dear gentlemen, has its function and reason,' Samoylenko sighed. 'But there's one thing I don't understand. You're a terribly clever man, so please explain this. You know, there are some small animals, no larger than rats, quite pretty to look at but extremely vicious and immoral. Let's suppose one of these tiny creatures is making its way through a forest. It sees a bird, catches it and eats it. It moves on and sees a small nest in the grass with eggs in it. It's not hungry any more as it's eaten its fill, but it bites into one of the eggs and pushes the others out of the nest with its paw. Then it meets a frog, has a little game with it. After tormenting it, off it goes licking its lips and then along comes a beetle. It crushes it with its paw. And so it harms and destroys everything in its path. And it clambers into other animals' lairs, ruins ant-hills just for the fun of it, cracks snails open with its teeth ... If it comes across a rat, it starts a fight. If it sees a small snake or a baby mouse it just has to throttle them. And so it goes on, all day long. Tell me then, what's the use of such an animal? Why was it created?'

'I don't know what animal you're talking about,' von Koren said, 'most likely an insectivore. Well now, the bird was caught because it was careless. It destroyed the nest of eggs because the bird was stupid, built its nest badly and did not succeed in camouflaging it. And there was most likely some defect in the frog's colouring, otherwise your animal wouldn't have spotted it, and so on. Your animal destroys only weak, stupid, careless creatures – briefly, creatures with defects that nature doesn't consider necessary to hand down to posterity. Only the most artful, cautious, strong and developed animals survive. Therefore, quite unaware of the fact, your little animal serves a magnificent end – progress towards perfection.'

'Yes, yes ... By the way, old boy,' Samoylenko said casually, 'lend me a hundred roubles, will you?'

'All right. Among the insectivores there's some very interesting examples. Take the mole. It's said to be useful because it destroys harmful insects. There's a story about some German who sent Kaiser Wilhelm I a moleskin coat, but it seems the Kaiser ordered him to be reprimanded for destroying so many useful animals. However, the mole can be just as cruel as your little beast and it's also a very great nuisance, as it wreaks havoc in the fields.'

Von Koren opened a money-box and took out a hundred-rouble note.

'Moles have a powerful thorax, like bats,' he went on, shutting the box, 'tremendously developed bones and muscles and unusually well-armed mouths. If they were as big as elephants they would be invincible, capable of annihilating everything. It's interesting – when two moles meet underground they both start digging a little platform for themselves, as if they'd agreed on it beforehand. They need this platform to make it easier to fight. When it's finished they battle away furiously and fight until the weaker drops.' Von Koren lowered his voice as he added, 'Now, take your hundred roubles, but on condition it's not for Layevsky.'

'And supposing it is for Layevsky!' Samoylenko said, flaring up. 'Is that any of your business?'

'I can't let you have money if it's to help Layevsky. I know your fondness for lending people money. You'd lend any old bandit money if he asked you. I'm sorry, I can't help you in that direction.'

'Yes, it *is* for Layevsky!' Samoylenko said, standing up and brandishing his right arm. 'Yes, for Layevsky! What the hell, no one has the right to damned well try and teach *me* what to do with my money! You don't want to lend me it, eh?'

The deacon burst out laughing.

'Don't get so excited, just think a minute,' the zoologist said. 'Doing Mr Layevsky a good turn is just as silly in my opinion, as watering weeds or feeding locusts.'

'I think it's our duty to help our neighbours,' Samoylenko shouted.

'In that case, help that starving Turk lying beneath the fence! He's a labourer and he's more valuable, more useful than your Layevsky. Let *him* have the hundred roubles. Or contribute a hundred towards my expedition!'

'I'm asking you, are you going to let me have it or not?'

'Tell me frankly, what does he need the money for?'

'It's no secret. He has to travel to St Petersburg on Saturday.'

'Oh, so that's it!' von Koren drawled. 'Aha ... we understand. And is she going with him, or what?'

'She's staying on for the time being. He's going to straighten his affairs out in St Petersburg and send her money, and then she'll go as well.'

'Very neat!' the zoologist said with a short, high-pitched laugh. 'Very neat. A brilliant idea.'

He rushed over to Samoylenko, faced up to him and stared him right in the eye. 'Tell me honestly, now,' he asked; 'he doesn't love her any more, does he? No?'

'No,' Samoylenko said, breaking into a sweat.

'How revolting!' von Koren said and his face clearly showed his disgust. 'There are two alternatives, Alexander: either you've both hatched this plot together or – pardon me for saying so – you're a stupid ass. Can't you see he's making a fool of you, in the most shameless fashion, as though you were a little boy? Surely it's clear as daylight that he wants to get rid of her and abandon her here. She'll be hanging round your neck and it's also clear as anything that you'll have to send her to St Petersburg at your own expense. Surely that fine friend of yours can't have dazzled you so much with his virtues that you're blind to what's patently obvious?'

'These are mere conjectures,' Samoylenko said, sitting down.

'Conjectures? But why is he travelling alone and not with her? And ask him why *she* shouldn't go on ahead, with him following afterwards? The crafty devil!'

Overcome by sudden doubts and misgivings about his friend, Samoylenko's spirits fell, and he lowered his voice.

'But that's impossible!' he said, recalling the night when Layevsky had stayed with him. 'He's going through so much!'

'What of it? Thieves and arsonists also suffer!'

'Let's suppose you're right,' Samoylenko said reflectively. 'Granted ... On the other hand, he's a young man in a strange country ... a student ... we're students as well and he had no one to turn to here for help besides us.'

'Help him perpetrate his filthy tricks just because you were both at university at different times and neither of you did a stroke of work there! What nonsense!'

'Hold on, let's consider it calmly.' Shaking his fingers, Samoylenko worked it all out. 'Perhaps we could manage it like this ... I'll give him the money, but I'll insist he gives me his word of honour to send Nadezhda the money for her fare within one week.'

'And he'll give you his word, he'll even shed a tear or two and convince himself it's all genuine. But what is his word worth? He won't keep it, and when you meet him a year or so from now, on Nevsky Avenue, with his new lady-love on his arm, he'll start defending himself, saying civilization has crippled him and that he's a chip off the same block as Rudin.* Give him up, for God's sake! Steer clear of this muck, don't go raking around in it!'

Samoylenko pondered for a moment and then said in a determined voice, 'I'm going to lend him the money all the same. You do as you like, but I'm in no position to refuse someone on the basis of mere suppositions.'

'That's excellent. So go and embrace him if you like.'

'Well, give me the hundred roubles, then,' Samoylenko timidly asked.

'No, I won't.'

Silence followed. Samoylenko felt quite weak. His face took on

* Turgenev's 'Superfluous Man'.

a guilty, ashamed, ingratiating expression and somehow it was strange to see a huge man like him, with epaulettes and medals, looking so pathetic and bewildered, just like a child.

As he laid down his pen the deacon said, 'The local bishop doesn't do his parish rounds in a carriage, but on horseback. He makes a terribly moving sight, sitting on his little horse. His simplicity and humility are permeated with biblical grandeur.'

'Is he a good man?' von Koren asked, glad of a change of subject.

'Well what do you think? If he weren't how come that he's a bishop?'

'There are some very fine and talented bishops about,' von Koren said. 'The only pity is, though, many of them have this weakness – they imagine they're state dignitaries. One tries to Russianize everything, another criticizes science. It's not their business. They'd do better if they looked in at the consistory more often.'

'Laymen aren't qualified to judge bishops.'

'But why not, deacon? A bishop is a man, like myself.'

'He is and yet he isn't,' the deacon replied in an injured voice, picking up his pen. 'If you *were* the same, then divine grace would have descended on you, and you yourself would be a bishop. But as you're not a bishop that means you can't be such a man.'

'Don't talk rot, deacon!' Samoylenko said, becoming very upset. 'Listen, I have an idea,' he added, turning to von Koren. 'Don't lend me the hundred roubles. As you'll be eating here for another three months before winter's here, you can pay a quarter in advance.'

'I won't do it.'

Samoylenko blinked and turned crimson. Mechanically, he drew the book with the spider on it over towards him and inspected it. Then he stood up and reached for his hat.

Von Koren felt sorry for him. 'Living and working with a man like that!' the zoologist said, and indignantly kicked a piece of paper into the corner. 'Please try and understand that this is not goodness of heart or love, but cowardice, poison! Whatever reason achieves, it's wrecked by your ineffectual, half-baked emotions! When I had typhoid as a schoolboy, my aunt was so sorry she stuffed me with pickled mushrooms and I nearly died. Both my aunt and yourself should see that love for one's neighbour should not be in the heart or the pit of the stomach or the small of the back, but *here*!' von

Koren tapped his forehead. 'Take it!' he said and flung a hundred-rouble note in front of him.

'Now don't upset yourself, Nicholas,' Samoylenko said meekly as he folded the bank-note. 'I understand you very well, but ... put yourself in my position.'

'You're an old woman, that's what!'

The deacon burst out laughing.

'Listen, Alexander, a last request!' von Koren said heatedly. 'You should make one condition when you give that swindler the money: either he takes his lady friend with him or he sends her on ahead. Otherwise don't let him have it. You can't stand on ceremony with him. Tell him that, but if you don't, then on my word of honour, I'll go to his office and throw him down the stairs. And I won't have anything more to do with you! So there!'

'All right. If he travels with her or sends her on ahead, that will suit him all the more,' Samoylenko said. 'He'll even be glad. Well, good-bye.'

He made a fond farewell and left, but before shutting the door behind him he looked round at von Koren, pulled a terrible face and said:

'It's the Germans who've corrupted you, my friend. Yes, the Germans!'

XII

Next day, a Thursday, Marya Bityugov was celebrating her son Kostya's birthday. Everyone had been invited for pies at midday and for chocolate in the evening. When Layevsky and Nadezhda arrived in the evening, the zoologist was already sitting in the drawing-room drinking chocolate.

'Have you spoken to him?' he asked Samoylenko.

'Not yet.'

'Now be careful, don't stand on ceremony with him. The check of these people really defeats me! Surely they know very well what the Bityugovs think of their liaison, yet still they sneak their way in.'

'If you let yourself be ruled by every little prejudice, then you shouldn't go anywhere,' Samoylenko said.

'Is the mass's revulsion for extra-marital love and dissipation a prejudice then?'

'Of course. Prejudice and the readiness to hate. When soldiers spot a girl of easy virtue they guffaw and whistle. But just ask them how *they* carry on.'

'They don't whistle for nothing. Young girls strangle their illegitimate babies and go off to hard labour, Anna Karenina threw herself under a train, in villages gates are smeared with tar. Both of us – I don't know why – admire Katya's purity, everyone has a vague need for pure love, although he knows that such love doesn't exist. Surely all of *that* can't be prejudice? My dear fellow, all that's survived from natural selection. And if it weren't for that mysterious force that regulates sexual relationships, people like Layevsky would have shown you what's what and humanity would have gone to the dogs within two years.'

Layevsky came into the drawing-room. He greeted everyone and smiled an oily smile as he shook von Koren's hand. He waited for the right moment and told Samoylenko, 'Excuse me, Alexander, I have something to say to you.'

Samoylenko stood up, put his arm around his waist and they both went into Nikodim Bityugov's study.

'It's Friday tomorrow,' Layevsky said, biting his nails. 'Did you get me what you promised?'

'Only two hundred and ten. I'll have the rest today or tomorrow. Don't worry.'

'Thank God!' Layevsky sighed and his hands shook with joy. 'You're my salvation, Alexander, and I swear by God, by my own happiness and by anything else you care to name that I'll send you the money the moment I arrive. And I'll settle my old debt as well.'

'Look here, Ivan,' Samoylenko said, turning red in the face as he took hold of one of his buttons. 'Forgive me for meddling in your private affairs but . . . why don't you take Nadezhda with you?'

'You're so silly, how could I! One of us has to stay behind, or the creditors will start kicking up a fuss. After all, I owe the shops seven hundred roubles, perhaps more. You wait, I'll send them the money and keep them quiet, then she can leave as well.'

'Oh . . . But why can't you send her on ahead?'

'Good Lord, how could I do that?' Layevsky asked, horrified. 'After all, she's a woman, what could she do there on her own? What does she understand? It would only hold things up and be a waste of money.'

'That makes sense,' Samoylenko thought, but he remembered his conversation with von Koren, looked down and said gloomily, 'I can't agree with you. Either travel with her or send her on ahead ... or ... or ... I shan't lend you the money. That's my last word on the subject.'

As he retreated he banged his back on the door and went into the drawing-room red-faced and dreadfully embarrassed.

'Friday ... Friday,' Layevsky thought as he went back to the drawing-room. 'Friday ...'

He was served a cup of chocolate; the hot liquid burnt his lips and tongue as he kept thinking, 'Friday ... Friday ...' For some reason he could not get the word Friday out of his mind; he could think of nothing else and all he knew (his heart, not his head, told him) was that he would not be leaving on Saturday.

Looking very neat and tidy, his hair brushed down over his temples, Nikodim Bityugov stood before him and asked, 'Please have something to eat ... Please.'

Marya Bityugov was showing her guests Katya's school marks, remarking in her drawling voice, 'They make things so terribly, terribly hard for students these days! They ask so much of them!'

'Mama!' groaned Katya, not knowing where to put herself for embarrassment.

Layevsky also looked at the marks and complimented her. Scripture, Russian Language, Conduct – 'excellents' and 'very goods' danced before his eyes: all this and the perpetually nagging thought of that Friday, Nikodim's hair brushed down over his temples and Katya's red cheeks, struck him as such an immense, crushing bore that he was ready to cry out loud in despair. 'Will it, will it really be impossible for me to escape from this place?' he asked himself.

Two card-tables were placed side by side and they sat down to play Post Office.

'Friday ... Friday ...' he thought, smiling as he took a pencil from his pocket. 'Friday ...'

He wanted to weigh his position up carefully, but he was too frightened to think. The realization that the doctor had found him out in that deception he had so long and so carefully concealed from himself, terrified him. Whenever he contemplated the future he did not let his thoughts run away with him. He would just enter a railway carriage and leave – in that way he would solve the problem of his life, and he would not allow his thoughts to wander any further. Like a dim light in distant fields, now and then the thought flashed through his mind that somewhere (in a St Petersburg back street, in the remote future) he would have to resort to some little lie in order to get rid of Nadezhda and settle his debts. Only once would he have to lie and then he would experience a completely new lease of life. That would be a good thing: at the price of some trivial little lie he would be able to purchase absolute respectability.

But now that the doctor had, in his refusal, crudely brought his duplicity to light, he realized that he would need to lie not only in the remote future, but today, in a month's time, and until the day he died perhaps. In fact, in order to make his escape, he would have to lie to Nadezhda, his creditors and his superiors at the office, and afterwards, to obtain money in St Petersburg, he would have to lie to his mother and tell her that he'd already broken with Nadezhda. His mother wouldn't let him have more than five hundred roubles, which meant he had already cheated the doctor, as he wouldn't be able to send him any money in the near future. And then, when Nadezhda arrived in St Petersburg, he would have to resort to a whole series of petty and major lies to get rid of her. Once again there would be more tears, boredom, that wretched existence again, remorse and consequently no new lease of life. It was all a great sham, nothing more. An enormous mountain of lies loomed up in Layevsky's mind, and he would have to take drastic measures to leap over it in one bound without lying in instalments. For example, he would have to get up from his seat, put his cap on and leave straight away without the money and without a word to anyone. But Layevsky felt he was not equal to that. 'Friday, Friday,' he thought. 'Friday.'

The guests wrote little notes, folded them in two and dropped them into Nikodim Bityugov's old top hat. When it was full Kostya pretended to be a postman and walked round the table handing them out. The deacon, Katya and Kostya were in raptures as they received comical messages and tried to reply with even funnier ones.

'We must have a talk,' Nadezhda read in her note. She exchanged glances with Marya Bityugov, who produced one of her sugary smiles and nodded.

'What is there to talk about?' Nadezhda thought. 'If the whole thing can't be discussed then there's no point in saying anything.'

Before coming to the party she had knotted Layevsky's tie and this insignificant act had filled her heart with tenderness and sorrow. His anxious expression, his distraught glances, his pale face and the incomprehensible change that had recently come over him, the fact that she was harbouring a terrible, loathsome secret from him, the way her hands had trembled when she tried to tie the knot – all this told her that their days together were numbered. She looked at him fearfully and penitently, as if he were an icon. 'Forgive me, forgive me ...' she thought. Achmianov could not keep his black, amorous eyes off her from across the table. Desires troubled her, she was ashamed of herself, afraid that one day even her anguish and sorrow would not prevent her from yielding to lust, afraid that, like a confirmed drunkard, she was powerless to control herself.

Unwilling to carry on an existence which was shameful for her and insulting to Layevsky, she decided that she would leave. Tearfully she would beg him to let her go, and if he offered opposition, she would leave secretly. She would not tell him what had happened: at least let him have pure memories of her to cherish.

'I'm in love, I'm in love, I'm in love,' she read. 'That's from Achmianov.'

She would go and live in some backwater, work, and send Layevsky money, embroidered shirts and tobacco anonymously, and only when he was old – or if he were dangerously ill and needed a nurse – would she return to him. In his old age he would find out the reason why she had refused to be his wife, why she had left him – then he would appreciate the sacrifice she had made and he would forgive her.

'You've got a long nose.' That must be the deacon or Kostya.

Nadezhda imagined firmly embracing Layevsky as she said

good-bye, kissing his hand and vowing to love him forever. And later, among strangers in her backwater, she would think every single day that she had a friend somewhere, a man she loved, pure, noble, highly idealistic, who held unsullied memories of her.

'If you won't meet me today, then I shall take steps, I swear it. Please understand, one doesn't behave like this with respectable people.' That was from Kirilin.

XIII

Layevsky received two notes. He unfolded one of them and read, 'Don't leave, my dear chap.' 'Who could have written that?' he wondered. 'Not Samoylenko of course ... And it's not the deacon, he doesn't know I want to go away. Von Koren perhaps?'

The zoologist bent over the table and drew a pyramid. Layevsky thought he could detect a smile in his eyes.

'Samoylenko's let the cat out the bag, most likely,' Layevsky thought.

The next note was in the same rough handwriting, with long tails and flourishes: 'Someone won't be leaving on Saturday.'

'What stupid insults,' Layevsky thought. 'Friday, Friday ...'

Something stuck in his throat. He touched his collar and tried to cough, but broke into loud laughter instead.

'Ha, ha, ha!' he guffawed. 'Ha, ha, ha!' 'What am I laughing at?' he asked himself. 'Ha, ha, ha!'

He tried to control himself by covering his face with one hand, but his chest and neck were choking with laughter and he did not succeed. 'How stupid, though!' he thought, roaring with laughter. 'Have I gone out of my mind?'

His guffaws became shriller and shriller until they sounded like a small spaniel yapping. He tried to get up from the table, but his legs would not obey him and strangely, as though it were pleasing itself, his right arm started jumping about on the table, convulsively trying to grab hold of the notes and crumple them up. The astonished glances, Samoylenko's serious, frightened face, the zoologist's coldly contemptuous sneers, told him he was having hysterics. 'How scandalous, how disgraceful,' he thought, feeling warm tears on his face. 'Oh, oh, what a disgrace! Nothing like this has ever happened to me.'

They supported him under the arms and led him off somewhere, holding his head from behind; a glass sparkled before his eyes and knocked against his teeth. Water spilled onto his chest; then he saw a small room with two beds standing in the middle, covered with clean, snow-white bedspreads. He slumped onto one of them and burst out sobbing.

'It's nothing, nothing ...' Samoylenko was saying. 'It's quite common, quite common.'

At the bedside stood Nadezhda, frightened out of her wits, trembling all over and expecting something terrible.

'What's the matter?' she asked. 'What's wrong? For God's sake, tell me.' 'Did Kirilin write to him?' she thought.

'It's nothing,' Layevsky said, laughing and crying. 'Leave me, dear ...'

His face expressed neither hatred nor disgust – this meant he knew nothing. Nadezhda calmed down a little and went back to the drawing-room.

'Don't upset yourself, my dear!' Marya Bityugov said, sitting down beside her and taking her hand. 'It will pass. Men are just as weak as we sinful women. You're both going through a crisis at the moment, it's so understandable! Well, my dear, I'm waiting for an answer. Let's have a talk.'

'No, let's not,' Nadezhda said, listening to Layevsky's sobs. 'I'm so depressed ... Please let me leave now.'

'What are you saying my dear!' Marya said, taking fright. 'Surely you don't think I would let you go without any supper? Let's have something to eat, then you can go.'

'I feel so depressed,' Nadezhda whispered, clutching the back of her chair to stop herself falling.

'He's had a fit!' von Koren said gaily as he came into the drawing-room, but the sight of Nadezhda embarrassed him and he left.

When the fit was over Layevsky sat on the strange bed thinking: 'What a disgrace, howling like a silly schoolgirl! I must look so stupid and disgusting. I'll leave by the back door. No, that would mean I'm taking the fit seriously. I should try and make a joke of it.'

He had a look in the mirror, sat for a little while and then went into the drawing-room.

'Here I am!' he said, smiling. He suffered torments of shame and felt that his presence made the others feel ashamed too. 'Things like that happen,' he said, taking a seat. 'I was just sitting there when suddenly I had a terrible stabbing pain in my side ... absolutely unbearable, my nerves couldn't take it and ... what happened was so stupid! Ours is a neurotic age, can't be helped!'

He drank wine at supper, chatted and now and then – to the accompaniment of convulsive sighs – kept stroking his side as if to show he still had pain. And no one – except Nadezhda – believed him and he saw it. After nine o'clock everyone went walking along the boulevard. Fearing that Kirilin might attempt to talk to her, Nadezhda tried to stay close by Marya Bityugov and her children. Fear and dejection weakened her and she felt a fever was coming on; she was very weary and could hardly move her legs. But she did not go home, since she was convinced she would be followed by Kirilin or Achmianov, or both of them. Kirilin was walking behind, with Nikodim Bityugov, softly chanting, 'I wo-on't allow myself to be tri-fled with! I wo-n't allow it!'

They turned off the boulevard towards the Pavilion and walked along the beach. For a long time they watched the phosphorescent glow of the sea. Von Koren started explaining the reason for the phosphorescence.

XIV

'But it's time I was off to whist ... They're waiting,' Layevsky said. 'Good-bye, everyone.'

'Wait, I'm coming with you,' Nadezhda said, taking his arm. They said good-bye to the others and left. Kirilin also made his farewell, saying he was going the same way and walked along with them.

'Whatever will be, will be,' Nadezhda thought. 'Let it be ...' She felt that all the nasty memories had left her mind and were walking by her side, breathing heavily in the dark, while she was like a fly that has fallen into an ink-pot, crawling along the road and staining Layevsky's side and arm black. If Kirilin does something horrible, she thought, then she would be to blame, not he. After all, there was a time when no man would talk to her like Kirilin and it was she who had severed this period like a thread, destroying it for ever. But who was to blame? Stupefied by her desires, she had begun to smile at a complete stranger, most probably because he was tall and well-built. After two meetings he bored her, and she dropped him – surely that entitled him to behave as he liked to her, she thought.

'I must say good-bye here, my dear,' Layevsky said, stopping. 'Mr Kirilin will see you home.' He bowed to Kirilin, quickly crossed the boulevard, went across the street to Sheshkovsky's house, where the lights were burning in the windows. Then he could be heard banging the gate.

'I want to have a little talk with you,' Kirilin began. 'I'm not a street urchin, not a mere nobody ... I demand serious attention!'

Nadezhda's heart pounded away. She did not answer.

'At first I ascribed the sharp change in your attitude to flirtatiousness,' Kirilin continued, 'but now I see that you simply don't know how to behave towards respectable people. You simply wanted a little game with me, like that Armenian boy, but I'm a respectable man and demand to be treated as such. And so, I'm at your service.'

'I feel so depressed,' Nadezhda said, and burst into tears. To hide them she turned away.

'I'm depressed as well, what of it?' Kirilin paused for a moment and then said distinctly and deliberately, 'I repeat, my dear lady. If you don't grant me a rendezvous today, I shall make a scene this evening.'

'Just let me off for today,' Nadezhda said in such a plaintive, thin voice, she did not recognize it.

'I must teach you a lesson. Excuse my bad manners, but I have to teach you a lesson. Yes, Madam, you must be taught a lesson. I demand two meetings – tonight and tomorrow. The day after you'll be quite free to go where the hell you like, with whoever you like. Tonight and tomorrow.'

Nadezhda went over to her gate and stopped. 'Let me go!' she whispered, trembling all over and unable to see anything in front of her in the dark except a white tunic. 'You're right, I'm a dreadful woman ... I'm to blame, but let me go, I beg you.' She touched his cold hand and shuddered. 'I beg you.'

'Unfortunately, no!' Kirilin sighed. 'No! It's not my intention to let you go. I only want to teach you a lesson, to make you understand. Besides, Madam, I really don't trust women.'

'I feel *so* depressed.'

Nadezhda listened hard to the steady roar of the sea, glanced up at the star-strewn sky and felt she wanted to finish with everything there and then, to rid herself of the wretched sensation of a life of sea, stars, men, fevers.

'But not in my house,' she said coldly. 'Take me somewhere else.'

'Let's go to Myuridov's, that's the best place.'

'Where is it?'

'Near the old rampart.'

She walked rapidly down the street and then turned up a side-street leading to the mountains. It was dark. Pale patches of light from illuminated windows lay here and there on the road and she felt like a fly, perpetually falling into an ink-pot and then crawling out again into the light. Kirilin was following her. At one spot he stumbled, nearly fell and burst out laughing.

'He's drunk,' Nadezhda thought. 'So what ... So what ... So be it.'

Achmianov had also quickly taken leave of the company and had followed Nadezhda to invite her to go boating with him. He went up to her house and peered across the fence. The windows were wide open and there were no lights. 'Nadezhda!' he called. A minute passed. He called out again.

'Who's there?' – it was Olga.

'Is Nadezhda home?'

'No, hasn't come back yet.'

'Strange ... very strange,' Achmianov thought, beginning to feel terribly anxious. 'She *was* on her way home ...'

He went along the boulevard, down the street and then he looked into Sheshkovsky's windows. Layevsky was sitting at the table, without a frock-coat, staring at his cards.

'That's strange, most strange ...' Achmianov muttered and he felt ashamed when he remembered Layevsky's fit. 'If she's not at home, then where is she?'

Again he went over to Nadezhda's house and looked at the dark windows. 'I've been tricked,' he thought, remembering that when they had met at midday at the Bityugovs she had promised to go boating with him in the evening.

The windows in Kirilin's house were dark and a policeman sat fast asleep on the bench by the gate. One glance at the windows and the policeman and everything became clear to Achmianov. He decided to go home and started off, but once again found he was near Nadezhda's flat. He sat down on a bench there and took his hat off; his head seemed to be burning with jealousy and injured pride.

The parish church clock struck only twice every twenty-four hours: at noon and midnight. Soon after it had struck midnight there came the sound of hurried footsteps.

'So it's at Myuridov's again, tomorrow evening,' Achmianov heard and he recognized Kirilin's voice. 'Eight o'clock. Until then, Madam.'

Nadezhda came into sight near the garden fence. Not noticing Achmianov on the bench, she flitted past like a ghost, opened the gate and entered the house, leaving the gate open. In her room she lit a candle and quickly undressed. But she did not lie on her bed, but fell on her knees in front of a chair, embraced it and pressed her forehead to it.

Layevsky came home after two in the morning.

XV

Layevsky had decided not to tell her the pack of lies all at once, but gradually, and the next day, after one o'clock, he went to Samoylenko's to ask for the money that would enable him to travel that Saturday, without fail. After yesterday's fit, which had added a further sharp feeling of shame to his already deeply depressed state of mind, staying any longer in that town was out of the question. If Samoylenko insisted on his conditions, he thought, then he might possibly agree to them and take the money. Tomorrow he could tell him at the very last moment, just when he was about to leave, that Nadezhda had refused to go with him. That evening he could try and persuade her that it was all in her best interests. But if

Samoylenko, obviously under von Koren's influence, refused point-blank to give him the money or stipulated new conditions, then he could possibly leave for New Athos or Novorossiisk that same day on some cargo ship, or even a sailing-boat. From there he would have to swallow his pride and send his mother a telegram and stay there until she sent him his fare.

When he called at Samoylenko's he found von Koren in the drawing-room. The zoologist had just arrived for lunch and as usual he had opened the album and was studying pictures of men in top hats and ladies in lace caps.

'What a nuisance,' Layevsky thought on seeing him. 'He might get in my way.'

'Good morning,' he said.

'Good morning,' von Koren replied, without looking up.

'Is Samoylenko home?'

'Yes, he's in the kitchen.'

Layevsky went towards the kitchen, but as he looked through the doorway he saw Samoylenko was busy making a salad; he went back to the drawing-room and sat down. He had always felt ill at ease with the zoologist and now he was afraid of having to talk about the fit. More than a minute passed in silence. Suddenly von Koren looked up at Layevsky and asked, 'How do you feel after what happened yesterday?'

'Excellent,' Layevsky replied, turning red. 'It was really nothing very much.'

'Before yesterday I'd always thought that only ladies had hysterics, that's why I supposed at first you had St Vitus's dance.'

Layevsky smiled obsequiously and thought, 'How tactless of him. He knows only too well how bad I'm feeling.'

'Yes, strange thing to happen,' he said, still smiling. 'I've been laughing about it all morning. The curious thing about hysterics is that you know they're ridiculous, you laugh deep down about them, yet they still make you cry. In this neurotic age we're slaves of our nerves. They are our masters and do what they like with us. Civilization has double-crossed us there!'

As Layevsky went on he was not pleased that von Koren was listening to him seriously and attentively, watching him intently, without blinking an eyelid, as if he were an object for study. And he was annoyed with himself for being totally unable to drive that obsequious smile from his face, despite his dislike for von Koren.

'However, I must confess,' he went on, 'there were some more immediate reasons for the hysterics, and fairly substantial ones at that. My health has recently had a severe shake-up. Add to that, boredom, eternal poverty, lack of congenial company with mutual interests ... My position is worse than a governor's.'

'Yes, your position is hopeless,' von Koren said.

These calm, cold words, partly mocking, partly prophetic, were insulting for Layevsky. As he recalled the contemptuous, disgusted way the zoologist had looked at him the day before, he paused for a moment and then asked, no longer smiling, 'And how did you find out about my position?'

'You mentioned it yourself only just now, and your friends take such a burning interest in you it's all one hears about all day long.'

'Which friends? Do you mean Samoylenko?'

'Yes, he's one.'

'I'd prefer it if Samoylenko and all the rest didn't worry about me so much.'

'Here's Samoylenko now; ask him to stop worrying about you so much.'

'I don't like your tone of voice,' Layevsky muttered, as if he realized only now that the zoologist hated and despised him, was taunting him and that he was his most deadly, most implacable enemy. 'Please reserve that tone of voice for someone else,' he said softly, without the strength to speak out loud for the hatred that was already choking his heart and chest – just like yesterday's urge to laugh.

In came Samoylenko, without his frock-coat, sweaty and crimson-faced from the hot kitchen. 'Oh, so you're here,' he said. 'Hallo, my dear chap. Had lunch? Now don't be shy, tell me if you've eaten.'

'Alexander,' Layevsky said, standing up, 'if I came to you with an intimate request, it doesn't mean I've freed you from your obligation to be discreet and respect other people's secrets.'

'What's wrong, then?' Samoylenko said in astonishment.

'If you don't have the money,' Layevsky went on, raising his voice and excitedly shifting from one foot to the other, 'then don't lend me any, refuse me. But why do you have to spread it all over town that my position's hopeless and so on? I cannot bear these acts of charity, good turns from people who talk big and in the end give you nothing! You can boast to your heart's content about your good deeds, but no one ever gave you the right to reveal my secrets!'

'What secrets?' Samoylenko asked in bewilderment, losing his temper. 'If you've come here for a slanging-match then you'd better leave now. Why don't you come back later?'

He remembered the rule, that when one is angry with a close friend, counting mentally up to a hundred has a calming effect. And he started counting, quickly.

'I beg you not to concern yourself about me!' Layevsky went on. 'Don't take any notice. And what business is it of anyone's who I am and what kind of life I lead? Yes, I want to get away! Yes, I run up debts, drink, live with another man's wife. I have fits, I'm a vulgar person, and I'm not as profound as some other people. But whose business is that? You should respect individuals!'

'Forgive me, my friend,' Samoylenko said when he had counted to thirty-five, 'but . . .'

'Respect individuals!' Layevsky interrupted. 'To hell with all this bitchiness, all these "oohs" and "ahs", this constant hounding, eaves-dropping, this friendly sympathizing! They lend me money and then subject me to conditions as if I were a child! I'm treated like God knows what! I don't want *anything*!'

Layevsky started shouting and he staggered from agitation, afraid he might have another fit. The thought, 'So I shan't be leaving this Saturday', flashed through his mind. 'I don't want *anything*! All I ask, if it's all the same with you, is to be spared this supervision. I'm not a child, I'm not insane and I ask you to end this surveillance!'

The deacon entered and when he saw pale-faced Layevsky waving his arms and addressing these strange words to Prince Vorontsov's portrait, he stood by the door, as if rooted to the spot.

'This continual prying into my soul,' Layevsky went on, 'offends my dignity as a human being and I ask these volunteer sleuths to stop spying! It's enough!'

'What . . . what did you say?' Samoylenko asked – having counted to a hundred he grew crimson-faced as he walked over to Layevsky.

'It's enough!' Layevsky repeated, gasping for breath as he picked his cap up.

'I'm a Russian gentleman, doctor and colonel,' Samoylenko said slowly and deliberately. 'I have never spied on anyone and I won't allow myself to be *insulted*!' he shouted in a broken voice, laying particular stress on the last word. 'So will you shut up!'

The deacon, who had never seen the doctor look so magnificent, proud, crimson-faced and fearsome, put his hand over his mouth, ran out into the hall and stood roaring with laughter. As though he were peering through a mist, Layevsky saw von Koren stand up, put his hands in his trouser pockets and stay in that position, as if waiting to see what would happen next. The calmness of his posture struck Layevsky as provocative and insulting in the extreme.

'Please take back what you just said!' Samoylenko shouted.

Layevsky, who could no longer remember *what* he had said, replied, 'Leave me in peace! I want nothing! All I want is for you and these German–Jewish immigrants to leave me in peace! If not, I shall take steps! I will fight!'

'Now I understand,' von Koren said as he rose from the table. 'Before he departs, Mr Layevsky wishes to amuse himself with a little duelling. I can accord him that pleasure. Mr Layevsky, I accept your challenge.'

'Challenge?' Layevsky softly enunciated as he went over to the zoologist and looked hatefully at his dark forehead and curly hair. 'Challenge? If that's what you want. I hate you! I hate you!'

'Absolutely delighted. First thing tomorrow morning, near Kerbalay's, please yourself about the details. And now beat it!'

'I hate you!' Layevsky said softly, breathing heavily. 'I've hated you for a long time. A duel? Yes!'

'Get him out of here, Alexander, or I shall have to leave,' von Koren said. 'He might bite me.'

Von Koren's cool tone calmed the doctor. Suddenly he recovered his senses and he gripped Layevsky around the waist, muttering in an affectionate voice that shook with emotion as he led him away from the zoologist. 'My friends ... my good, kind friends ... You've just got a little excited, let's call it a day ... it's enough. My friends ...'

When he heard that soft, friendly voice Layevsky felt that something quite unprecedented and monstrous had happened to him, as if he'd nearly been run over by a train. He was close to tears, waved his arm in capitulation and ran out of the room.

'God, how dreadful to be the target of someone's hatred and to make the most pathetic, despicable, helpless spectacle of oneself in front of him!' he thought soon after as he sat in the Pavilion. And he felt as if the feeling of hatred that this man had just stirred in him had left a deposit of rust on his body. 'God, how idiotic!'

Some brandy with cold water cheered him up. He clearly pictured von Koren's calm, arrogant face, the expression he had worn the day before, his carpet-like shirt, his voice, his white hands, and an intense, passionate, all-consuming hatred welled up inside him and sought gratification. He imagined knocking von Koren to the ground and stamping on him. Down to the very last details, he recalled everything that had happened and was amazed how he could have smiled so obsequiously at that nonentity, how he could have valued the opinions of those obscure little nobodies living in a wretched dump that apparently was not even on the map and which no self-respecting Petersburger had ever heard of. If that nasty little town were suddenly to vanish or burn down, the telegram bearing this news would have been read in Central Russia with the same boredom as any advert for second-hand furniture. Killing von Koren tomorrow, sparing his life, did not matter a damn, it was equally pointless and boring. He would wound him in the leg or arm, then have a good laugh at him; just as an insect with a torn-off leg loses its way in the grass, so he would be lost with his mute suffering in that sea of nonentities, all as insignificant as himself.

Layevsky went to Sheshkovsky's, told him everything and invited him to act as second. Then they both went off to the local postmaster's, invited him to be a second and stayed for lunch, over which they cracked a great deal of jokes and had a good laugh together. Layevsky poked fun at himself, saying he hardly knew how to fire a pistol and dubbing himself 'Royal Marksman' and 'William Tell'.

'That man must be taught a lesson,' he said.

After lunch they sat down to cards. Layevsky joined in, drank wine, and reflected how stupid and senseless duels were, all things considered, as they never solved any problem, but only aggravated them; all the same, at times there was no other course of action. For example, he couldn't report von Koren to the Justice of the Peace for that kind of thing! And the impending duel seemed all the more attractive, as after it he could not possibly stay any longer in that town. He grew slightly tipsy, amused himself at cards and felt everything was fine.

But when the sun set and it became dark, he was overcome by uneasiness. This was not fear of death, since while he was lunching and playing cards he felt confident somehow that the duel would come to nothing. It was fear of the unknown, of what was bound to happen the following morning for the first time in his life, and fear of the approaching night ... He knew the night would be long and sleepless, and that not only would he have to think of von Koren and his hatred, but about that mountain of lies he would have to surmount and which he had neither the skill nor strength to avoid. It was as though he had suddenly been taken ill. All at once he lost interest in the cards and the other players, fidgeted and asked if he could go home. He wanted to be in bed as soon as possible, to lie quite still and to prepare his thoughts for the night that lay ahead. Sheshkovsky and the postmaster saw him home, then went to von Koren's to discuss the duel.

Layevsky met Achmianov near his flat. The young man was out of breath and excited.

'I've been looking for you, Mr Layevsky!' he said. 'Please come quickly.'

'Where?'

'A gentleman you don't know has some very urgent business with you. He begs you to drop in for just a minute, there's something he wants to discuss with you ... It's a matter of life and death to him ...'

In his excitement Achmianov pronounced these words with a strong Armenian accent, making two syllables out of 'life'.

'Who is he?' Layevsky asked.

'He told me not to reveal his name.'

'Say I'm too busy at the moment. I'll come tomorrow, if that suits him.'

'But that's impossible,' Achmianov said, horrified. 'He wants to tell you something that is so very important to you ... *very* important! It will be disastrous if you don't go.'

'That's strange,' Layevsky muttered, unable to understand why Achmianov should be so worked up and what manner of secrets could be lurking in that dull, nasty little town that no one wanted. 'That's strange,' he repeated thoughtfully. 'All right, let's go. It's all the same to me.'

Achmianov quickly went on ahead and Layevsky followed. They went down the main street, then an alley.

'What a bore,' Layevsky said.

'Any moment now, we're nearly there.'

Near the old rampart they went along a narrow alley between two fenced patches of waste ground; then they entered a kind of large courtyard and went over to a small house.

'That's Myuridov's, isn't it?' Layevsky asked.

'Yes.'

'But why are we going in the back way? I don't understand. We could have come in from the street, it's quicker.'

'It doesn't matter.'

Layevsky found it odd too when Achmianov led him round to the back door and waved his hand at him, as if asking him to step softly and not make a sound.

'In here, in here,' Achmianov said, cautiously opening a door and tiptoeing into the hall. 'Quietly please, I beg you ... they might hear.'

He listened hard, took a deep breath and whispered, 'Open this door and go in ... Don't be scared.'

Bewildered, Layevsky opened the door and entered a room with a low ceiling and curtained windows. A candle stood on the table.

'Who do you want?' someone asked in the next room. 'Is that you, Myuridov?'

Layevsky went into the room and saw Kirilin, with Nadezhda beside him. He didn't hear what was said to him, moved backwards and didn't realize when he was back in the street again. His hatred for von Koren and his anxiety had completely disappeared. On his way home he clumsily waved his right arm and carefully inspected the ground under his feet, trying to walk where it was smooth. Back in his study he paced up and down, rubbing his hands together and awkwardly jerking his shoulders and neck, as if his waistcoat and shirt were too tight. Then he lit a candle and sat down at the table.

XVI

'The humane studies you're talking about will only satisfy men's thinking when they converge with the exact sciences as they advance and go along arm in arm with them. Whether they'll meet under the microscope or in the soliloquies of a new Hamlet, or in some new religion, I can't say But I do think that another ice age will be upon us before that comes about. The most stable and vital part of all humane studies is the teaching of Christ, of course, but just look at the diversity of interpretations! Some scholars teach us to love our neighbours, but make an exception for soldiers, criminals and the insane. They make it legal for the first to be killed in war, the second to be locked up or executed, and the last to be prohibited from marrying. Other commentators teach us to love our neighbours without exception, irrespective of the pros and cons. According to them, if a consumptive or murderer or epileptic comes up to you and proposes to your daughter, you must give your consent. If cretins wage war on the sound in body and mind, the healthy must lay their heads on the block. If this advocacy of love for love's sake, like art for art's sake, were to grow strong, it would lead in the end to the total extinction of mankind and as a result one of the most enormous crimes ever to be seen on this earth would have been committed. There are countless different teachings and if this is so, then no serious mind can ever be satisfied with any one of them and would hasten to add its own commentary to the sum total. So, you should never base a question on philosophical or so-called Christian premises, as you call them, or you'll only stray further from the correct solution.'

The deacon listened attentively to the zoologist's words and inquired after a moment's thought, 'Is the moral law, that is inherent in everyone, an invention of the philosophers, or did God create it together with the body?'

'I don't know. But this law is so common to all nations and epochs it strikes me it has to be recognized as an organic part of man. It is not an invention, it exists and will continue to do so. I wouldn't go so far as to say that one day we'll be able to see it under the microscope, but there's already evidence that proves its organic links. Serious illness of the brain and all the so-called mental illnesses manifest themselves first and foremost in violations of the moral law, as far as I know.

'Very well. So, just as the stomach wants food, the moral sense requires us to love our neighbours. Right? But our natural self resists the voice of conscience and reason out of sheer selfishness and many ticklish questions arise as a result. And to whom should we turn for the solution of these problems if you don't want us to deal with them from a philosophical standpoint?

'Take note of the small store of precise knowledge that we in fact do possess. Trust what you can see, and the logic of facts. True, it's not much to go on, but on the other hand it's not as shaky and vague as philosophy. Let's suppose the moral law demands that you should love people. What then? Love should lie in the elimination of everything that in any way harms people and threatens them with present or future danger. Knowledge and what we can observe tell us that humanity is threatened by the morally and physically abnormal. If that is correct, then you must do battle with these freaks of nature. If you can't raise them to the norm, you'll at least have the strength and ability to render them harmless – by that I mean exterminate them.'

'That's to say, love is when the strong conquer the weak?'

'Without any doubt.'

'But it was the strong who crucified our Lord Jesus Christ!' the deacon retorted heatedly.

'That's just the point, it wasn't the strong who crucified him, but the weak. Civilization has weakened the struggle for existence and natural selection, which it is trying to annihilate. That gives rise to the rapid multiplication of the weak and their superiority over the strong. Just imagine if you succeeded in instilling bees with crude, raw human ideals. Where would it lead? The drones, who should be killed, would survive, eat all the honey, and corrupt and smother the others, and as a result we'd have the weak holding sway over the strong, so that the latter became extinct. Exactly the same is happening to humanity now, the weak oppress the strong. The savage who is strongest, wisest and who has the highest moral standards, who is as yet untouched by culture – he's the one who makes the most progress; he is the leader and master. But we civilized men crucified Christ and keep on crucifying him. That's to say, we are lacking in something ... And this "something" must be restored or there'll be no end to this folly.'

'But what's your criterion for distinguishing between the strong and the weak?'

'Knowledge and the evidence of my senses. Consumptives and the scrofulous are known by their symptoms and the immoral and insane are judged by their actions.'

'But surely mistakes can happen!'

'Yes, but there's no point in worrying about getting your feet wet when a flood is threatening.'

'That's philosophy,' the deacon laughed.

'Not at all. You've been so spoiled by seminary philosophy that you see fog just everywhere. The abstract studies which your young head is stuffed with are only called this because they abstract your mind from reality. Look the devil straight in the eye and if it *is* the devil then say so and don't go running off to Kant or Hegel for an explanation.'

The zoologist stopped for a moment and then went on, 'Twice two are four and a stone's a stone. Tomorrow there's going to be a duel. It's all very well for us to say how stupid and ridiculous it is, that duels have outlived their time, that the nobleman's duel is essentially no different from a drunken tavern brawl. All the same, we won't wait, we'll go off and fight. That means there's a power which is stronger than all our discussions on the subject. We cry out that war is robbery, barbarity, horror, fratricide and we faint at the sight of blood. But the French or the Germans only have to insult us and immediately our spirits soar, we cheer passionately and throw ourselves on the enemy. You'll invoke God's blessing on our guns while our valour will arouse universal and genuine elation. Once again, that means there's a power, if not loftier, then at least stronger than us and our philosophy. We are as powerless to stop it as that cloud over there coming in from the sea. Don't be hypocritical, don't stick your tongue out at it behind its back and don't say, "Oh, it's stupid, it's out of date, it doesn't agree with the Scriptures!" Look it straight in the eye and acknowledge that it's reasonable and in the rightful order of things. And when for example it wishes to destroy some feeble, scrofulous, depraved tribe, don't hinder it with all your medical remedies and quotations from imperfectly understood Gospels. Leskov has a highly virtuous character called Danila, who feeds a leper he found outside the town and keeps him warm in the name of love and Christ. If this Danila had really loved people, he would have hauled that leper as far away from the town as he could and thrown him into a ditch. Then he would have gone off to lend a hand to the healthy. Christ preached the love that is sensible, meaningful and useful, that's what I hope.'

'Get on with you!' the deacon laughed. 'You don't believe in Christ, so why do you mention him so much?'

'No, I do believe in him. But in my own special way, not yours. Oh, deacon, deacon,' the zoologist said, laughing, as he put his arm round the deacon and gaily added, 'Well, what now? Are you going to that duel tomorrow?'

'My cloth doesn't allow it, or I would come.'

'What do you mean *cloth*?'

'I'm in holy orders, by God's grace.'

'Oh, deacon, deacon!' von Koren repeated, laughing. 'I love talking to you.'

'You say you have faith,' the deacon said. 'But what is it? Now, I have an uncle, just an ordinary parish priest, whose faith is such that when he goes into the fields to pray for rain during a drought, he takes his umbrella and a leather coat to avoid a soaking on the way home. There's faith for you! When he speaks of Christ there's a halo over his head and all the peasant men and women sob their hearts out. He would have made that cloud stop and put any of your powers to flight. Yes . . . faith moves mountains.'

The deacon burst out laughing and slapped the zoologist on the shoulder. 'And so,' he went on, 'that's what you're teaching the whole time, plumbing the depths of the ocean, sorting out the weak from the strong, writing pamphlets and challenging people to duels. But everything stays where it was. You wait, though, one old man only has to whisper a word in the name of the Holy Spirit – or some new Muhammad to come galloping out of Arabia, scimitar in hand – and everything will be turned upside down, leaving not one stone standing on another in Europe.'

'But that's a load of rot, deacon!'

'Faith without actions is dead and actions without faith are even worse, a sheer waste of time, nothing more.'

The doctor appeared on the front. Seeing the deacon and the zoologist he went up to them.

'Everything's arranged, it seems,' he said, gasping for breath. 'Govorovsky and Boyko will be seconds. They'll be here at five tomorrow morning. What a lot of clouds!' he said, looking at the sky. 'Can't see a thing. We're in for a shower any minute now.'

'I hope you're coming with us,' von Koren asked.

'No, God forbid. I'm just plain exhausted. Ustimovich is going instead. I've already spoken to him.'

Far over the sea lightning flashed and there were hollow peals of thunder.

'It's so close before a storm!' von Koren said. 'I'll wager you've already been round to cry on Layevsky's shoulder.'

'Why should I go there?' the doctor replied, taken aback. 'Well, what next!'

Before sunset he had walked up and down the boulevard and street several times, hoping to meet Layevsky. He was ashamed of his outburst and of that sudden benevolent impulse that had followed. He wanted to apologize to Layevsky in jocular vein – to give him a little ticking-off, to calm him down and to tell him that duelling was a relic of medieval barbarism, but that Providence itself had shown them that duelling was a means of reconciliation. The next day the two of them, both fine, highly intelligent men, would – after exchanging shots – come to appreciate each other's integrity and become friends.

'But why should I go to see him?' Samoylenko repeated. 'I didn't insult him, he insulted me. Tell me, if you don't mind, why did he attack me? Have I ever done him any harm? I merely went into the drawing-room and suddenly, without rhyme or reason, he called me a spy! A fine thing! Tell me, what started it? What did you say to him?'

'I told him that his situation was hopeless. And I was right. Only honest people and crooks can escape from *any* situation, but anyone wanting to be crooked and honest at one and the same time will never find a way out. However, it's eleven already, gentlemen, and we have to be up early tomorrow.'

There was a sudden gust of wind. It raised clouds of dust on the sea front, whirled them round and drowned the sound of the sea with its howling.

'A squall!' the deacon said. 'Let's go, or I'll have my eyes full of dust.'

When they had gone, Samoylenko sighed and said, gripping his hat, 'I probably won't sleep now.'

'Don't worry,' the zoologist laughed. 'You can relax, the duel will come to nothing. Layevsky will magnanimously fire into the air – he can't do anything else – and most likely I shan't fire at all. To find myself in court because of that Layevsky, wasting my time because of him – the game's not worth the candle. By the way, what's the penalty for duelling?'

'Arrest, and should your opponent die, up to three years in prison.'

'The Peter and Paul?'

'No, a military prison, I think.'

'That young puppy should be taught a lesson!'

Lightning flashed on the sea behind them and for a brief moment lit up the roofs of the houses and the mountains. Near the boulevard the friends parted. When the doctor had disappeared in the darkness and his footsteps had already begun to die away, von Koren shouted after him, 'I'm scared the weather might spoil things tomorrow.'

'It might well do that. Let's hope it does!'

'Good night.'

'What? What did you say?'

It was difficult to hear anything against the roaring wind and sea, and the thunderclaps.

'Oh, nothing!' shouted the zoologist, and hurried home.

XVII

... a crowd of oppressive thoughts
Throngs my anguished mind; silently
Before me, Memory unfolds its long scroll;
And with loathing, reading the chronicle of my life,
I tremble and curse, and shed bitter tears,
But I do not wash away these sad lines.

PUSHKIN

Whether he was killed in the morning or made to look a fool – that is, allowed to go on living – it was all finished now. That dishonoured woman might kill herself in despair and shame, or she might drag out her wretched existence – either way she too was finished.

These were Layevsky's thoughts as he sat late that evening at his table, rubbing his hands together as always. The window suddenly banged open, the strong wind burst into the room and the papers flew off the table. Layevsky shut the window and bent down to pick them up. He experienced a new kind of sensation, a kind of awkwardness which he had never known before and his movements seemed foreign to him. He walked about gingerly, thrusting his elbows to each side, twitching his shoulders. When he sat down at the table he started rubbing his hands again. His body had lost its suppleness.

Letters should be written to close relatives the day before one is going to die and Layevsky remembered this. He took his pen and wrote 'Dear Mother!' with trembling hand.

He wanted to ask his mother, in the name of all-merciful God in whom she believed, to shelter and give the warmth of her affection to that unfortunate, lonely, impoverished and weak woman whom he had dishonoured, to forget and forgive everything, and at least partly expiate her son's terrible sin by her sacrifice. But then he remembered how his mother, a plump, heavily built old lady in a lace cap, used to go from house to garden in the morning, followed by her companion with a lapdog. He remembered how she would bully her gardener and servants in that imperious voice of hers and how proud and arrogant her face was. All this he remembered and he crossed out what he had written.

The lightning flashed vividly in all three windows, followed by a deafening roll of thunder – indistinct at first, but then crashing and crackling so violently that the window panes rattled. Layevsky stood up, went over to the window, and pressed his forehead to the glass. Outside, a mighty, beautiful storm was raging. On the distant horizon lightning constantly darted out of the clouds on to the sea in white ribbons, illuminating the towering black waves for miles around. To the left and right, and probably over the house as well, the lightning flashed.

'A thunderstorm!' Layevsky whispered, feeling an urge to pray to someone or something, even if only to the lightning or the clouds. 'What a lovely storm!'

He remembered how once when he was a child a storm had made him run bareheaded into the garden with two fair-headed blue-eyed girls chasing after him, how they were all soaked by the rain. They laughed with delight, but then came a violent thunderclap and the girls trustfully snuggled up close to him as he crossed himself and hurriedly started reciting, 'Holy, holy, holy.' Oh, where have you gone, in what ocean have you foundered, first glimmerings of beautiful, innocent life? No longer did he fear thunderstorms, he had no love for nature, he had no God, and all those trustful girls he had once known had long since been ruined by himself and his friends. Never had he planted one sapling, never had he grown one blade of grass in his garden at home and never in his life had he spared a single fly even, but had only wrecked, ruined, and told lies, lies, lies . . .

'Is there anything in my past life except vice?' he asked himself, trying to cling to some bright memory, as a man falling over a precipice clutches at bushes.

And the High School? The University? It was all a deception. He had been a bad student and had forgotten what he had been taught. And what of his service to the community? That was deception as well, since he had never done any work and received a salary for doing nothing, so his 'service' was nothing more than disgraceful embezzlement of government funds which goes unpunished in court.

He had no need for the truth and had never sought it. Under the spell of vice and deception, his conscience had either slept or remained silent. Like an alien or someone hired from another planet, he had done nothing to help people in their everyday life, was indifferent to their sufferings, ideas, religion, knowledge, searchings, strivings; never had he spoken a kind word to anyone, never had he written one line that was not cheap or worthless, never had he done a thing for others. Instead, he had eaten their food, drunk their wine, seduced their wives, copied their ideas. And to justify his despicable, parasitical life in his own eyes and theirs, he had always tried to give the impression of being a nobler, superior kind of being. Lies, lies, lies ... He clearly recalled what he had witnessed that evening at Myuridov's and he felt unbearably sick with loathing and anguish. Kirilin and Achmianov were repulsive, but they were after all carrying on what *he* had begun. They were his accomplices and pupils. He had taken a young weak woman, who had trusted him more than her own brother, away from her husband, her circle of friends, her native land, and had brought her to this place, to endure stifling heat, fever, boredom. Day after day she had come to mirror his idleness, loose living and lying in herself – her feeble, dull, wretched life consisted of this, and only this. Later on, when he had had enough of her, he began to hate her, but was not man enough to drop her, and so he redoubled his efforts to entangle her in a web of lies ... The people here added the finishing touches.

Layevsky first sat at the table, then went over to the window again. Then he would snuff the candle and light it again. He cursed himself out loud, wept, complained, asked for forgiveness. Several times he ran despairingly over to the table and wrote, 'Mother!'

Apart from his mother, he had no blood relatives or close friends at all. But how could his mother help him? And where was she? He felt like running to Nadezhda, falling at her feet, kissing her hands and feet and begging her to forgive him. But she was his victim and he feared her, just as though she were dead.

'My life is ruined!' he muttered, rubbing his hands. 'For God's sake, why am I still alive!'

He had cast down his dim star from the sky, it had faded and its trail merged with the darkness of night. Never would it return to the heavens again, as life is given only once and is never repeated. If he were able now to bring back all those days and years that had passed he would replace all the lies they held with the truth, all the idleness with work, all the boredom with joy; he would return innocence to those he had robbed of it, and he would have found God and justice. But this was as impossible as putting that fading star back in the sky and the hopelessness of ever achieving this reduced him to despair.

When the storm had passed he sat by the open window and calmly considered what was going to happen to him. Von Koren would kill him, most likely. That man's lucid, cold outlook admitted the extermination of the weak and the useless. And if this frame of mind deserted him at the critical moment, he could call on the hatred and revulsion Layevsky aroused in him. But if he missed, or merely wounded him, just to make a laughing-stock of his odious opponent, or if he fired into the air, what could he do then? Where could he go?

'Should I go to St Petersburg?' Layevsky asked himself. 'But that would mean starting that damnable old life all over again. Whoever seeks salvation by going somewhere else, like a bird of passage, will find nothing, since things will be the same wherever he goes. Should I seek salvation among people? But from whom and how? Samoylenko's kindness and goodness of heart will do as little to save me as that deacon's laughing at everything or von Koren's hatred. Salvation must be sought in oneself alone, and if I fail there's no point in wasting any more time. I will have to kill myself, that's all ...'

He heard the sound of a carriage. It was already growing light. The carriage passed, turned and with wheels crunching over the damp sand came to a stop by the house. Two people were sitting in it.

'Wait a moment, I'm coming!' Layevsky told them through the window. 'I haven't slept. Surely it's not time already?'

'Yes, it's four o'clock. By the time we get there ...'

Layevsky put on his coat and cap, stuffed some cigarettes into his pocket and stopped to think for a moment. There was still something he had to do, it seemed. In the street the seconds were quietly chatting, the horses snorted. These early morning sounds, on a damp day, when everyone was asleep and dawn was breaking, filled Layevsky with a feeling of despondency that was just like an evil omen. He stood thinking for a little while and then went into the bedroom.

Nadezhda was lying stretched full length on the bed with a rug up to her head. She lay so still that she looked like an Egyptian mummy – her head in particular. Silently watching her, Layevsky inwardly prayed for her to forgive him and he thought that if heaven was not an empty place, if God really did exist, then he would stay with her. But if God did not exist, then she might as well perish, as she would have nothing to live for.

Suddenly she started and sat up in bed. She raised her pale face, gave Layevsky a horrified look and asked, 'Is that you? Is the storm over?'

'Yes.'

She remembered what had happened, came to her senses, placed both hands on her head and trembled all over.

'I feel so miserable!' she said. 'If only you knew how miserable I feel!' She screwed her eyes up and continued, 'I was expecting you to kill me, or drive me out into the rain and the storm, but you seem to be hesitating, hesitating.'

Impulsively, he gave her a violent embrace, showered her knees and hands with kisses. After she had murmured something, shuddering as she recollected the past events, he smoothed her hair and as he gazed into her face he came to realize that this unhappy, depraved woman was the only person in his life who was near and dear to him and who could not be replaced.

When he left the house and sat in the carriage he felt he wanted to come back alive.

XVIII

The deacon got up, dressed, took his thick, knotty walking-stick, and quietly slipped out of the house. It was dark and at first he could not even see his white stick as he walked down the street. Not a star was in the sky and it looked like rain again. There was a smell of moist sand and sea.

'I hope I'm not attacked by Chechens,' the deacon thought as he listened to the lonely, ringing sound of his stick as it clattered on the road in the silence of the night.

When he was out of the town he began to make out both the road and his stick. Here and there in the black sky there were dim patches of light and before long a single star peeped out and timidly winked. The deacon was walking along a high rocky cliff-top, from which he could not see the sea down below; invisible waves lazily, heavily, broke on the beach and seemed to be sighing in pain. And how slowly they rolled in! One wave broke on the beach and the deacon counted eight paces before the next arrived; six paces later came a third wave. The world was probably like this when nothing was visible, with only the lazy, sleepy sound of the sea in the darkness; and he was conscious of that infinitely remote, unimaginable time when God hovered over the void.

The deacon felt nervous, thinking that God might punish him for associating with unbelievers and because he was even going to watch a duel, which would be trivial, bloodless and ludicrous. In any case, it was a pagan spectacle and it was quite unbecoming for a member of the clergy to be present at such an event. He stopped and wondered if he should go back. But a keen, restless curiosity overcame his doubts and he continued on his way.

He comforted himself by saying, 'Although they are unbelievers, they are still good people and will be saved.'

Then he lit a cigarette and said out loud, 'They're bound to be saved.'

What criterion was needed to assess people's virtues, so as to arrive at a fair judgement? The deacon remembered his enemy, an inspector at the school for sons of the clergy, who believed in God, never fought duels, lived a chaste life, but who once gave the deacon some bread with sand in it and who had once almost torn his ear off. If human life had turned out to be so inane that everyone respected that cruel, dishonest inspector who stole government flour and prayed in school for his health and salvation – how could *he* be justified in steering clear of people like Layevsky and von Koren just because they were unbelievers?

The deacon tried to solve this problem, but he remembered how comical Samoylenko had looked yesterday and this disrupted his train of thought. What a good laugh they would have later on! The deacon imagined himself sitting among the bushes watching them and when von Koren started boasting over lunch he could have a good laugh as he told him every single detail of the duel.

'How do you know all that?' the zoologist would ask. 'That's a good question,' he would reply. 'I was at home, but I *know*.'

It would be great fun to pen a comical description of the duel. His father-in-law would be amused when he read it – he was the type who would go hungry, as long as someone told him or sent him a story that was funny.

The Yellow River valley opened out before him. The rain had made the river wider and angrier, and it no longer grumbled but roared instead. Dawn began to break. The dull grey sky, those clouds scurrying towards the west to catch up with a bank of storm clouds, the mountains girdled with mist, the wet trees – all this struck the deacon as ugly and evil-looking. He washed himself in a stream, said his morning prayers and conceived a sudden longing for the tea and hot buns filled with sour cream served every morning at his father-in-law's table. He thought of the deaconess and that piece *Lost Hope* she played on the piano. What kind of person was she really? In just one week he had been introduced, engaged and married to her. He had lived with her less than a month, then he was sent here, so that up to now he hadn't had a chance to find out what sort of person she was. All the same, it was rather boring without her. 'I ought to drop her a few lines,' he thought.

The flag over the inn was soaked with rain and hung limply. And the inn's wet roof made it seem darker and lower than before. A bullock cart stood by the door. Kerbalay, two Abkhazians and a young Tartar girl in wide trousers (probably Kerbalay's wife or daughter) were carrying sacks filled with something from the inn and laying them on maize straw in the cart. Two asses were standing near the cart, heads bowed. When the sacks were loaded, the Abkhazians and the Tartar girl started covering them over with straw and Kerbalay hastily began to harness the asses. 'Contraband, most likely,' the deacon thought.

Here was the uprooted tree with its dry needles and over there a black patch where the bonfire had been. He recalled every detail of the picnic, the fire, the Abkhazians' songs, those sweet dreams of becoming a bishop and the church procession. The rain had turned the Black River even blacker and wider. The deacon cautiously crossed the rickety bridge which was now washed by the crests of the turbid waves and clambered up the short ladder into the drying-room.

'That man has a wonderful brain!' he thought as he stretched out on the straw and thought of von Koren. 'A wonderful brain, God bless him! Only he does have a cruel streak . . .'

Why did von Koren hate Layevsky, and why did Layevsky hate him? Why were they going to fight a duel? Had they known the poverty the deacon had suffered from early childhood; had they been brought up among ignorant, soulless, grasping people who begrudged them every scrap of food, who were rough and uncouth, who spat on the floor and belched during dinner and prayers; had they not been spoilt since childhood by living in comfort among a select circle of friends – how they would cling to each other, how eagerly they would overlook each other's faults and truly value what was best in every one of them! But there are so few even superficially decent people in the world! True, Layevsky was wild, dissolute, strange, but at least even he wouldn't steal, spit loudly on the floor or tell his wife, 'You like to guzzle all right, but you won't do any work.' *He* would never whip his child with horse reins or feed his servants with stinking salt beef. Surely all that was enough to earn him some sort of indulgence? What's more, wasn't *he* the first to suffer from his own shortcomings, like a sick person suffers from his own wounds? Instead of an absurd searching for degeneracy, decline, inherited failings and the rest of it in each other, just because they were bored, and for lack of understanding, wouldn't they do better to set their sights lower and direct their hatred and anger where entire streets reverberated with barbaric ignorance, greed, reproaches, filth, abuse, women's screams . . .?

The sound of a carriage broke the deacon's train of thought. He peered through the doorway and saw a barouche with three men in it – Layevsky, Sheshkovsky and the local postmaster.

'Stop!' Sheshkovsky said.

All three climbed out of the carriage and surveyed one another.

'They haven't arrived yet,' Sheshkovsky said, wiping the mud off. 'All right, then. Until proceedings commence, let's find a suitable spot. It's impossible to move here.'

They went upstream and were soon out of sight. The Tartar coachman went inside the carriage, laid his head to one side and fell asleep. After waiting about ten minutes the deacon came out of the shed, took his black hat off so as not to be seen and made his way along the river bank, squatting in the bushes and maize and looking around. Heavy raindrops fell on him from the trees and bushes, and the grass and maize were wet.

'How degrading!' he muttered, lifting his wet, muddy skirts. 'I wouldn't have come if I'd known.'

Soon he heard voices and saw people. Layevsky, stooping, and with his hands in his sleeves, was swiftly pacing back and forth across the small clearing. His seconds stood right by the river bank rolling cigarettes.

'Most peculiar . . .' thought the deacon, not recognizing Layevsky's walk. 'Just like an old man.'

'How rude of them!' the postmaster said, looking at his watch. 'Perhaps those smart alecs think it's clever to be late, but if you ask me, they're behaving like pigs.'

Sheshkovsky, a fat man with a black beard, pricked his ears up and said, 'They're coming!'

XIX

'I've never seen anything like that before! How magnificent!' von Koren said as he appeared in the clearing and held out both hands to the east. 'Just look at those green rays!'

In the east two green rays stretched out from behind the mountains and they were truly beautiful. The sun was rising.

'Good morning!' the zoologist continued, nodding to Layevsky's seconds. 'I hope I'm not late.'

He was followed by his seconds, Boyko and Govorovsky, two very young officers of identical height, in white tunics, and the thin, unsociable Dr Ustimovich, who was carrying a bundle of some sort in one hand, while he kept the other behind him. Putting the bundle on the ground, without a word of greeting to anyone, he placed his other arm behind his back and paced backwards and forwards across the clearing.

Layevsky experienced the weariness and awkwardness of a man who perhaps was soon going to die and therefore was the centre of attention. He wanted to have the killing over and done with, as soon as possible, or to be taken home. It was the first time in his life he had seen the sunrise. The early morning, the green rays, the damp and those men in wet jackboots were no part of his life at all, he had no need of them, and they had a cramping effect. None of this had the least connection with the night he had just lived through, with his trains of thought and feelings of guilt, and consequently he would gladly have left without waiting for the duel.

Von Koren was visibly excited and tried to hide this by pretending he was interested in those green rays. The seconds were embarrassed, exchanging glances as if to ask why they were there and what they had to do.

'I don't think there's any point in going on further, gentlemen,' Sheshkovsky said. 'It's fine here.'

'Yes, certainly,' von Koren agreed.

Silence followed. Ustimovich suddenly halted, turned sharply towards Layevsky and breathed into his face as he said in an undertone, 'Most likely they haven't managed to inform you of my terms. Each side pays me fifteen roubles and in the event of the death of one of the parties the survivor will pay the whole thirty.'

Layevsky knew this man from before, but only now did he have the first clear view of his lacklustre eyes, wiry moustache and his gaunt, wasted neck. This was a usurer, not a doctor! His breath smelt unpleasantly of beef.

'There are some peculiar people in this world,' Layevsky thought as he answered, 'All right.'

The doctor nodded and strode off again. It was obvious he did not need money at all, but had simply demanded it out of hatred. Everyone felt it was high time they began or finished what had been put in motion, but they did neither, merely walked around or stood smoking.

The young officers who were attending a duel for the first time and who now felt very sceptical about a contest between two civilians, which was quite unnecessary in their opinion, carefully inspected their tunics and smoothed down their sleeves. Sheshkovsky went over to them and said softly, 'Gentlemen, we must make every effort to stop this duel. We must reconcile them.' He blushed and went on, 'Yesterday Kirilin called on me to complain that Layevsky had caught him with Nadezhda, and *all that*.'

'Yes, we know,' Boyko said.

'Well, just have a look ... Layevsky's hands are shaking, and all that. He can't even pick his pistol up. Fighting him would be as inhuman as fighting a drunk or someone with typhus. If they can't be reconciled, gentlemen, then perhaps we should postpone the duel ... It's all damned stupid, I don't think I can even look.'

'You'd better have a word with von Koren.'

'I don't know the rules of duelling, blast it, and I don't want to know. Perhaps he'll think Layevsky's got cold feet and sent me over. He can think what he likes, however. I'll talk to him.'

Hesitantly and limping slightly, as though he had pins and needles in his foot, Sheshkovsky went towards von Koren and he looked the very embodiment of laziness as he sauntered over, clearing his throat. 'There is something I must tell you, sir,' he began, closely studying the floral pattern on the zoologist's shirt. 'It's confidential ... I don't know the rules of duelling, damn it, and I don't want to know, so I'm not speaking as a second, and all that, but as a man, that's all.'

'Yes. Well what?'

'When seconds propose a reconciliation they are usually ignored as it's considered a formality. Pride, and all that. But I most humbly beg you to take a look at Ivan Layevsky. He's not normal today, he's not in his right mind, in a manner of speaking he's just pathetic. He's had a terrible misfortune. I cannot stand scandal' (here Sheshkovsky blushed and took a look round) 'but I have to tell you this because of the duel. Yesterday evening he found his lady friend at Myuridov's with a ... certain gentleman.'

'How shocking!' the zoologist muttered. He went pale, frowned and spat noisily. 'Ugh!'

His lower lip quivered. He walked away from Sheshkovsky, not wishing to hear any more and once again, as if he had accidentally eaten something bitter, spat loudly. For the first time that morning he gave Layevsky a hateful look. His excitement and embarrassment passed and he shook his head and said in a loud voice,

'Gentlemen, I ask you, why are we waiting? Why don't we begin?'

Sheshkovsky exchanged glances with the officers and shrugged his shoulders. 'Gentlemen!' he said out loud, without addressing anyone in particular, 'Gentlemen! We suggest you settle your differences!'

'Let's get the formalities over with,' von Koren said. 'We've already discussed a reconciliation. What's next on the agenda? Now, let's get a move on, gentlemen, there's no time to waste.'

'All the same, we insist you make it up,' Sheshkovsky said, in the guilty tone of someone forced to get involved in other people's business. Blushing and placing his hand over his heart he continued, 'Gentlemen, we cannot find any causal connection between the insult and the duel. Insults which we sometimes inflict on each other out of human frailty have nothing to do with duels. You are educated, university men and naturally you see duels as an outmoded, empty formality, and all that. We see it like that too, otherwise we wouldn't have come, since we cannot allow people to shoot at each other in our presence, and all that.' Sheshkovsky wiped the sweat from his brow and went on, 'Please settle your differences, gentlemen, shake hands and let's all go home and have a drink on it. Honestly, gentlemen!'

Von Koren said nothing. When Layevsky saw them looking at him he said, 'I've nothing against Nicholas von Koren. If he thinks I'm the guilty party, then I'm prepared to apologize.'

Von Koren took offence at this. 'Obviously, gentlemen,' he said, 'you would like to see Mr Layevsky return home as the chivalrous knight, but I cannot afford either him or you that pleasure. And there was no need to get up at the crack of dawn and ride six miles out of town just for a friendly drink and bite to eat, and to be told duels are outmoded formalities. Duels are duels and we should not make them out to be even more stupid and artificial than they actually are. I wish to fight!'

Silence followed. Officer Boyko took two pistols from a box, one was handed to von Koren and the other to Layevsky. Then followed a state of confusion which amused the zoologist and the seconds for a while. It turned out that not one of the whole assembled company had ever attended a duel before and no one knew precisely how they should stand, or what the seconds should say or do. But then Boyko remembered and he smiled as he began to explain.

'Gentlemen, who remembers Lermontov's description?' von Koren asked, laughing. 'And in Turgenev, Bazarov had a duel with someone or other ...'

'Why bring all that up now?' Ustimovich asked impatiently as he halted. 'Just measure out your distances, that's all.'

He took three steps as if to show how measuring should be done. Boyko counted out the paces, while his fellow officer bared his sword and scratched the ground at the extreme ends to mark the barrier.

Amid general silence the two opponents took up their positions.

'Moles!' the deacon recalled as he sat in the bushes.

Sheshkovsky said something, Boyko explained something further, but Layevsky did not hear; rather, he probably heard but did not understand. When the moment arrived he cocked the cold heavy pistol and pointed it upwards. He had forgotten to unbutton his coat and felt terribly cramped around the shoulders and armpits, and he raised his arm so awkwardly the sleeve seemed to be made of metal. He remembered the hatred he had felt yesterday for that swarthy forehead and curly hair and reflected that even then, when his hatred and anger were at boiling-point, he could never have fired at a man. Afraid the bullet might accidentally hit von Koren, he raised his pistol higher and higher, feeling that this terribly ostentatious show of magnanimity was tactless and not at all magnanimous; but he was incapable of acting in any other way. As he watched the pale, mocking face of von Koren, who was evidently convinced from the start that his opponent would fire into the air, Layevsky thought that it would be all over any moment, thank God, and that he only had to squeeze the trigger a little harder ...

The pistol recoiled violently against his shoulder, a shot rang out and back came the echo from the mountains.

Von Koren cocked his pistol and looked towards Ustimovich, who was still striding back and forwards, hands behind his back, oblivious of everything.

'Doctor,' the zoologist said, 'please be so good as to stop going up and down like a pendulum. You're giving me spots before the eyes!'

The doctor stopped. Von Koren began taking aim at Layevsky.

'It's all over now!' Layevsky thought.

The barrel which was directed right at his face, the hatred and scorn in von Koren's whole bearing and posture, the murder that was about to be committed by a decent man in broad daylight in the presence of other decent men, the silence, that strange power that compelled Layevsky to stand firm and not run away – how mysterious, incomprehensible and terrifying all this was!

The time von Koren took to aim seemed longer to Layevsky than the whole night. He looked imploringly at the seconds; their faces were pale and they did not move.

'Hurry up and fire!' Layevsky thought, sensing that his pale, trembling, pathetic face must arouse even deeper loathing in von Koren.

'I'll kill him right now,' von Koren thought, aiming at the forehead and already feeling the trigger. 'Yes, of course I will . . .'

'He's going to kill him!' a desperate cry came from somewhere quite close.

At once the shot rang out. When they saw Layevsky still standing in the same place everyone looked where the cry had come from – and they saw the deacon.

Pale-faced, soaked, covered in mud, his wet hair clinging to his forehead and cheeks, the deacon was standing in the maize on the far bank, smiling peculiarly and waving his wet hat. Sheshkovsky laughed for joy, burst into tears and walked to one side.

XX

Shortly afterwards von Koren and the deacon met near the bridge. The deacon was disturbed, breathing heavily and avoiding people's eyes. He was ashamed of being so scared, and of his wet, muddy clothes.

'I thought you wanted to kill him,' he muttered. 'How alien to human nature! How extremely unnatural!'

'But where on earth did you come from?' the zoologist asked.

'Don't ask!' the deacon said, waving his arm. 'The devil's to blame, he tempted me here. So off I went and I nearly died of fright in the maize. But now, thank God, thank God ... I'm very pleased with you,' the deacon muttered. 'And Grandpa Tarantula will be pleased too ... What a laugh, eh, what a laugh! But I beg of you, most earnestly, not to breathe a word to a soul that I was here or I'll get it in the neck from the authorities. They'll say a deacon acted as second.'

'Gentlemen!' said von Koren. 'The deacon requests you not to tell anyone you saw him here. It could have unpleasant consequences for him.'

'How alien to human nature!' the deacon sighed. 'Please be generous and forgive me – but from the way you looked I thought you were definitely going to kill him.'

'I was strongly tempted to have finished with that scoundrel,' von Koren said, 'but your shout put me off, and I missed. I'm just not used to all this repulsive procedure, it's worn me out, deacon. I feel terribly weak. Let's drive back now.'

'No, please permit me to walk. I must dry myself out, I'm soaked and frozen stiff.'

'Well, please yourself,' the exhausted zoologist said wearily as he climbed into the carriage and closed his eyes. 'As you like.'

While they were walking round the carriages and taking their seats, Kerbalay stood by the roadside, clasped his stomach with both hands, made a low bow and showed his teeth. He thought that the gentlemen had come to enjoy the beauties of nature and to drink tea, and he could not fathom why they were getting back into their carriages. The procession moved off in complete silence; only the deacon stayed behind at the inn.

'Me come to inn, me drink tea,' he said to Kerbalay. 'Me want eat.'

Kerbalay knew Russian well, but the deacon thought that the Tartar would understand broken Russian better.

'You make fried egg, you serve cheese ...'

'Come on, come on, Father,' Kerbalay said, bowing. 'I'll give you everything . . . There's cheese and wine . . . Eat what you like.'

'What's Tartar for "God"?' the deacon asked as he entered the inn.

'Your God, my God – just the same,' Kerbalay said, not understanding. 'God same for everyone, only people different. Some are Russians, some Turks, some English, there's all kinds of different people, but God is one.'

'All right then. If all nations worship the same God, then why do you Muslims treat Christians as your eternal enemies?'

'Why you angry?' Kerbalay asked, clutching his belly with both hands. 'You're priest, me Muslim, you say "I want to eat" and I give you food . . . Only the rich man make difference which your God, which my God. But it's all the same for the poor man. Please eat.'

While this theological discussion was in progress at the inn, Layevsky was driving home and he realized how terrifying it had been travelling at dawn, when the road, rocks and mountains were wet and dark, and an unknown future had held the terrors of a seemingly bottomless abyss. But now the raindrops hanging from the grass and stones sparkled like diamonds in the sun, nature smiled joyfully and that terrifying future was left behind. He looked at Sheshkovsky's gloomy, tear-stained face, at the two barouches in front with von Koren, his seconds and the doctor in them and it seemed they were all returning from a cemetery where they had buried some dreadful bore who had been a thorn in everyone's side.

'It's all over,' he thought, reflecting on his past and gingerly running his fingers over his neck.

On the right side of his neck, near the collar, a small swelling had come up as long and wide as his little finger and it was so painful it seemed someone had passed a hot iron over it. This was the bruise from the bullet.

And then, when he arrived home, a long, strange, sweet day stretched out in front of him, as vague as oblivion. As though released from prison or hospital, he scrutinized long-familiar objects and was astonished that tables, windows, chairs, light and sea brought him a keen, childlike joy that he had not known for such a long time.

Nadezhda, pale and terribly thin, did not understand his gentle voice and strange walk. She hurried to tell him all that had happened to her. He probably couldn't hear her properly, she thought, and didn't understand her – if he knew everything he would curse and kill her. But he listened, stroked her face and hair, looked into her eyes and said, 'I've no one besides you.'

Afterwards they sat for a long time in the front garden, snuggling close to one another, saying nothing. Or they would give voice to their dreams of the happy life that lay ahead, speaking in brief, broken sentences, and he felt that never before had he spoken so long and so eloquently.

XXI

More then three months passed.

The day of von Koren's departure arrived. From early morning there had been a cold, heavy rain, a north-easterly had blown up and a strong sea was running. In that kind of weather, people said, a steamer would have difficulty in getting into the roadstead. According to the timetable, it should have arrived at ten in the morning, but when he went down to the quay at noon and after lunch, von Koren could make out nothing through his binoculars except grey waves and rain veiling the horizon.

By the end of the day the rain had stopped and the wind dropped appreciably. Von Koren had already reconciled himself to the fact that he would not be leaving that day and sat down to a game of chess with Samoylenko. But after dark the batman reported that lights had been sighted out at sea and that a flare had been seen.

Von Koren began to hurry. He slung a knapsack over his shoulders, kissed Samoylenko and the deacon, went round all the rooms for no reason at all, said good-bye to his batman and cook, and went out into the street feeling as if he had left something behind at the doctor's or at his flat. He walked at Samoylenko's side, the deacon following with a chest and the batman bringing up the rear with two suitcases. Only Samoylenko and the batman could make out the tiny, dim lights at sea, the others peered into the darkness without seeing a thing. The steamer anchored far from the shore.

'Come on now, quicker!' von Koren said, hurrying along. 'I don't want to miss it!'

Passing the little three-windowed house into which Layevsky had moved soon after the duel, von Koren could not resist taking a look through one of the windows. Layevsky was sitting writing, hunched up at a table, his back to the window.

'Well, I'm amazed!' the zoologist said quietly. 'Just look how he's pulled himself together!'

'Yes, you may well be amazed,' Samoylenko sighed. 'He sits like that from morn till night, just sits and works. He wants to pay off his debts. But he's living worse than a pauper, my dear chap!'

About half a minute passed in silence. The zoologist, the doctor and the deacon stood at the window, all watching Layevsky.

'So the poor devil didn't manage to get away,' Samoylenko said. 'Do you remember how hard he tried?'

'Yes, he's really pulled himself together,' von Koren repeated. 'His marriage, this daylong sweating and slaving for a crust of bread, that new look on his face, his walk even – it's all so extraordinary, words just fail me.' The zoologist grabbed Samoylenko's sleeve and went on in an emotional voice, 'Please tell him and his wife that I left this place full of admiration and that he has my very best wishes ... and please ask him, if that's possible, not to bear any grudges. He knows me very well. He knows that had I foreseen the change in him at the time, I might have become his best friend.'

'Go in and say good-bye.'

'No, that would be embarrassing.'

'But why? God knows, you might never see him again.'

The zoologist pondered for a moment and said, 'That's true.'

Samoylenko softly tapped on the window. Layevsky shuddered and turned round.

'Ivan, Nicholas von Koren wants to say good-bye,' Samoylenko said. 'He's just leaving.'

Layevsky got up from the table and went into the hall to open the door. Samoylenko, von Koren and the deacon went in.

'I've just dropped in for a moment,' the zoologist began as he took off his galoshes in the hall, already regretting that he had bowed to sentiment and called uninvited. 'I feel I'm intruding,' he thought; 'it's silly.'

'Forgive me for disturbing you,' he said, following Layevsky into his room, 'but I'm on my way now and I felt I had to come and see you. God knows if we'll ever meet again.'

'Delighted ... Please come in ...' Layevsky said, clumsily putting chairs in front of his guests as though wanting to bar their way. He stopped in the middle of the room, rubbing his hands.

'I should have left the others in the street,' von Koren thought.

'Don't think too badly of me, Layevsky,' he said firmly. 'Of course, one can't forget the past, it's too sad and I haven't come to apologize or to try and assure you I wasn't to blame. I acted in all sincerity and have since stuck to my convictions. It's true, and I'm delighted to see it, that I was mistaken about you, the best of us can take a tumble – that's only human destiny. If you don't trip up on the main things, you'll stumble over the small. No one knows the real truth of the matter.'

'Yes, no one knows the truth ...' Layevsky said.

'Well, good-bye ... Good luck and God be with you.'

Von Koren offered Layevsky his hand; he shook it and bowed.

'Don't think too badly of me,' von Koren said. 'Remember me to the wife and tell her I was very sorry I didn't manage to say good-bye.'

'She's here.'

Layevsky went to the door and spoke into the next room.

'Nadezhda, Nicholas von Koren wishes to say good-bye.'

Nadezhda came in. She stopped by the door and timidly surveyed the visitors. Her face was frightened and guilty and she held her hands to her sides, like a schoolgirl being told off.

'I'm leaving now, Nadezhda,' von Koren said, 'and I've come to say good-bye.'

Hesitantly she held her hand out to him, while Layevsky bowed.

'What a pathetic pair!' von Koren thought. 'They don't have an easy life.'

'I'll be in Moscow and St Petersburg,' he said. 'Is there anything I can send you?'

'But what?' Nadezhda said and exchanged anxious glances with her husband. 'I can't think of anything ...'

'No, there's nothing,' Layevsky said, rubbing his hands. 'Give them our regards.'

Von Koren did not know what else he could or should say, but when he first came in he had contemplated saying a great deal of uplifting, kindly, significant things. Silently he shook Layevsky's and his wife's hands and went away feeling heavy at heart.

'What people!' the deacon whispered as he followed the others. 'Heavens, what people! "Verily the Lord's right hand hath sown this vine ... Oh Lord, one hath conquered thousands, the other tens of thousands".' Solemnly he continued, 'Von Koren, you should know that today you overcame mankind's most powerful enemy – pride!'

'That's enough, deacon! What sort of conquerors do you think Layevsky and I are? Conquerors look down like eagles from their heights, but he's pathetic, timid, downtrodden and he bows like a Chinese dummy ... I feel very sad.'

They heard footsteps behind them. Layevsky wanted to see von Koren off and was trying to catch them up. The batman stood on the quayside with the two suitcases and a little way off were four oarsmen.

'It's really blowing hard ... brrrrr!' Samoylenko said. 'There must be a real gale out there. Oh dear! You've picked a fine time to leave, Nicholas!'

'I'm not scared of seasickness.'

'I don't mean that. I only hope those idiots don't have you in the water. You should have taken the agent's boat. Where is the agent's boat?' he shouted to the oarsmen.

'It's gone, General.'

'And the Customs boat?'

'She's gone too.'

'But why didn't you tell me?' Samoylenko said furiously. 'Block-heads!'

'It doesn't matter, don't let it upset you,' von Koren said. 'Well, good-bye, God protect you.'

Samoylenko embraced von Koren and made the sign of the cross over him three times.

'Now don't forget us, Nicholas ... write ... we'll expect you in the spring.'

'Good-bye, deacon,' von Koren said, shaking his hand. 'Thanks for your company and all the excellent conversations. Think about the expedition.'

'Yes, even to the very ends of the earth!' the deacon laughed. 'I didn't say no, did I?'

Von Koren recognized Layevsky in the dark and silently offered him his hand. The oarsmen were already down below holding the boat which banged against the wooden piles, although the pier offered protection from the main swell. Von Koren went down the ladder, leapt into the boat and sat by the rudder.

'Do write!' Samoylenko shouted. 'And look after yourself!'

'No one knows the real truth,' Layevsky thought, raising his collar and stuffing his hands into his sleeves.

The boat jauntily rounded the quay and went out into the open sea. It disappeared among the waves, then immediately rose up from a deep trough to the crest of a high wave, so that the men and even the oars were visible. For every eighteen feet the boat moved forward, she was thrown back twelve.

'Write!' Samoylenko shouted. 'What the hell possessed you to travel in this weather!'

'Yes, no one knows the real truth . . .' Layevsky thought, dejectedly surveying the restless, dark sea.

'The boat's tossed back,' he thought; 'it makes two movements forward and one back, but the oarsmen don't give up, they swing the oars tirelessly and have no fear of the high waves. The boat moves on and on, now it's disappeared from view. In half an hour the rowers will be able to see the ship's lights clearly and within an hour they'll be alongside the ladder. Life is like that . . . As they search for truth people take two paces forward and one back. Suffering, mistakes and life's tedium throw them back, but thirst for the truth and stubborn willpower drive them on and on. And who knows? Perhaps they'll arrive at the real truth in the end.'

'Good-bye!' shouted Samoylenko.

'No sight or sound of them now,' the deacon said. 'Safe journey!'

It began to drizzle.

My Wife

I

I received the following letter:

Dear Mr Asorin,

Not very far from you – in the village of Pyostrovo, to be precise – there are some deplorable things going on which I consider it my duty to report to you. All the villagers sold their huts, all they possessed, and went off to settle in Tomsk province, but they never got there and came back home. Of course, everything that was theirs has all gone now and belongs to others. There are three or four families living in one hut, which adds up to at least fifteen of either sex, not counting small children. What it all boils down to is this: there's no food, they're starving, and there's a mass epidemic of spotted or famine fever. Literally everyone is ill. The district nurse tells me: 'You go into a hut and what do you see? They're all ill, all of them are delirious, some roar with laughter, others are going raving mad. There's a terrible stench, no one to give them water or to fetch any for them, and all they have to eat is frostbitten potatoes.' What can the district nurse and Sable (our local doctor) do when they need food rather than medicine and there isn't any? The council says it can't help, since these people are not on their register any more and are listed under Tomsk. And there's no money either.

Informing you of this and knowing how humane you are, I beg you not to refuse urgent help.

A well-wisher.

The district nurse herself or that doctor with the animal's name had obviously written this. Daily involvement over many years has convinced local doctors and district nurses that they are absolutely powerless to do anything in these matters. Yet they receive their salaries from people who have to live on frozen potatoes and still they think they have the right to decide if I'm humane or not.

Alarmed by this anonymous letter, by peasants coming to my servants' kitchen every morning and begging on their knees for something to eat, by peasants breaking down the wall of my barn at night and stealing twenty sacks of rye, and by the all-pervasive mood of depression encouraged by conversations, newspapers and the dreadful weather – with all this to worry me I was working sluggishly and fruitlessly. I was writing a 'History of Railways' and this meant reading piles of Russian and foreign books, pamphlets and magazine articles. I had to click away at my abacus, thumb through logarithm tables, think, write – and then read, click and think all over again. But hardly had I picked up a book and tried to concentrate than my ideas became all muddled up. I would screw up my eyes and leave my desk with a sigh and wander through the spacious rooms of my deserted country house. When I was bored with walking I would stop by my study window. If I looked beyond the wide courtyard, the pond and bare young birches, across the broad open fields covered with fresh snow that was now thawing, I could make out, on a hill on the horizon, a cluster of brown huts from which a muddy black path led down in an irregular stripe across the white fields. This was Pyostrovo, the village mentioned by my anonymous correspondent. Had it not been for those cawing rooks, heralds of rain or snow, winging their way over pond and field, had it not been for that knocking in the carpenter's shed, then this little world, the subject of so much fuss now, would have seemed like the Dead Sea, so quiet, still, lifeless and gloomy was everything all around.

I was too worried to concentrate on my work. I didn't know the reason for it and liked to think it was disillusionment. In actual fact I had left my job at the Ministry of Transport and come out here, to the country, to live a peaceful life and to do some work on sociology. This was a long-cherished dream. But now I had to say farewell to the quiet life and to literature, to give it all up and devote myself solely to peasants. There was no alternative, since besides myself there was positively no one else in the whole province to help the victims of the famine – of that I was convinced. I was surrounded by uneducated, backward, thick-skinned people. The majority were dishonest — those who *were* honest tended to be unbalanced and superficial, like my wife for example. One couldn't rely on such people and to abandon the peasants to their fate was out of the question. So I was compelled to submit to the inevitable and carry the rescue operation on my own shoulders.

The first thing I did was donate five thousand roubles to the famine fund. But this only served to increase my worries, not relieve them. As I stood by the window, or paced up and down my rooms, a new problem began to torment me: how could I best use the money? To organize the purchase of food, to go from hut to hut handing it out was more than one man could manage on his own, not to mention the risk I'd be running of hurrying things and giving twice as much to those who had sufficient or more than they needed to those who were starving. I had no faith in bureaucracy: those administrative officials and tax-assessors were all young and I distrusted them, as I did all modern young people of my day with their materialism and lack of ideals. The rural and parish councils and in general all those county offices didn't inspire me with the least desire to call on their help. I knew very well that these institutions had their teeth into local government funds, that their mouths were forever gaping wide, ready to feed on even richer spoils.

I thought of inviting the local squires over and suggesting that some kind of committee or centre be set up in my house as a collection point for all donations, and where distribution of funds for the whole area could be organized. Such an organization, which would facilitate frequent meetings and a broad, flexible method of control, accorded perfectly with my views on the matter. But I had visions of cold buffets, dinners, suppers, of all the fuss, timewasting, idle chatter and bad taste that this motley provincial crew was bound to bring into my house, so I hastily abandoned the idea.

As for my own servants, they were the very last people on whom I could count for help. Of my late father's family (once large and very busy) only Mademoiselle Marie my governess (or Miss Marya as she was called now) remained, and she was of no consequence whatsoever. This neat, tiny old lady of seventy, who looked like a china doll in her light grey dress and bonnet with white ribbons, was always sitting in the drawing-room reading a book. Whenever I passed her she knew why I was so deep in thought.

'But what do you expect, Paul?' she would ask. 'I told you before what would happen, just look at our own servants.'

My second family – I mean Natalie my wife – lived on the ground floor, occupying every room. She ate, slept and received visitors down below, completely unconcerned as to how I ate, slept or whom I entertained. Ours was an uncomplicated relationship, free of stress, but cold, empty and dreary as one commonly finds with two people who have drifted so far apart that they still can be complete strangers, although they live under the same roof. Nothing remained of that passionate, turbulent love – now sweet, now bitter as wormwood – that Natalie had once stirred in me. And gone were those earlier outbursts, those heated exchanges, reproaches, complaints, explosions of hatred which had usually ended with my wife going abroad or back to her family, and with my sending her money – just a little at a time to wound her pride all the more. (My proud, conceited wife and her relatives live at my expense; and however much she would have liked it, my wife is in no position to refuse money – this gave me great pleasure and was the sole consolation in my misery.) And now, when we happened to meet in the corridor downstairs or in the courtyard, I would bow, while she answered with a friendly smile. We would discuss the weather, the fact that it was time to fix the double window-frames for the winter, or how someone had driven a carriage over the dam with bells ringing. And at the same time her expression told me: 'I'm faithful and I don't blacken the good name you set so much store by. And you're sensible and don't bother me – that makes us quits.'

I tried to convince myself that my love had died long ago and that I was too absorbed in my work to give any serious thought to my relationship with my wife. But alas, these were only thoughts. When she was speaking out loud down below I would listen intently, although I never managed to distinguish a single word. When she played the piano downstairs I would stand up and listen. When her carriage or horse were brought round, I'd go over to the window and wait for her to come out of the house. I'd watch her climb into her carriage or mount her horse and then ride out of the yard. I would feel something jar inside me and I was afraid the look on my face might give me away. I would watch her go and then wait for her return in the hope I might catch another glimpse of her face, shoulders, coat, hat. I was bored and depressed and felt an infinite regret for something. I had an urge to walk through her rooms while she was out and I wished that the problem, which neither myself nor my wife had managed to solve (our temperaments differed so much) would quickly resolve itself naturally, of its own accord. By that I mean to say, if only that beautiful twenty-seven year old woman would hurry up and grow old, and if only my head would go grey or bald and do it as soon as possible!

One lunch-time Vladimir my estate-manager informed me that the villagers of Pyostrovo had set about stripping the thatch off their roofs to feed their cattle. Miss Marya gave me a frightened, puzzled look.

'What can I do?' I told her. 'I can't cope with everything on my own and I've never felt so lonely as I do now. I'd give anything to find just one reliable man in the whole district.'

'Why don't you ask Ivan Bragin?' Marya said.

'Of course!' I said gleefully. 'That's a good idea! *C'est raison*.'

I sang as I went back to my study to write to Bragin, '*C'est raison, c'est raison* . . .'

II

The sole survivor of that mass of friends who, about twenty-five or thirty-five years ago, had drunk or eaten in my house, come in their party clothes, fallen in love, married, bored everyone with their talk of wonderful hounds and horses, was Ivan Bragin. At one time he had been a very active, talkative, boisterous, amorous person, renowned for his radicalism and peculiar facial expression that not only women, but men, found charming. But since then he had aged a great deal, run to fat and was doddering on without the radicalism or the facial charm. He arrived the day after he received my letter, in the evening, when the samovar had just been brought into the dining-room and little Miss Marya was slicing a lemon.

'Delighted to see you, my friend!' I said, gaily greeting him. 'But you're stouter than ever!'

'Not stout – just swollen,' he replied. 'I've been stung by some bees.'

With the familiarity of one able to laugh at his own corpulence, he put both arms round my waist, laid his large soft head on my chest (his hair was combed down over the forehead, Ukrainian style), and broke into a shrill, senile laugh.

'You're getting younger every day!' he said in between peals of laughter. 'I don't know what dye you use for your head and beard, but you might let me have some.' Wheezing and panting he embraced me and kissed me on the cheek.

'You must let me have some,' he repeated. 'You're not forty yet, are you, old chap?'

'Oho, I'm forty-six!' I laughed.

Ivan Bragin smelt of tallow and cooking, which suited him. His large, bloated clumsy body was tightly held by a long, high-waisted frock-coat, like a coachman's tunic, with hooks and eyes instead of buttons. It would have been strange if he had smelt of eau-de-Cologne, for example. In that long, unshaven, blue-grey double chin, with bristles like burdock, in his bulging eyes, that wheezing, his whole clumsy, unkempt figure, his voice, laughter and speech, it was difficult to recognize the well-built, interesting old prattler who had once made the local husbands jealous.

'I really do need your help, my friend,' I said when we were sitting over tea in the dining-room. 'I want to organize relief for the famine victims and I don't know how to go about it. Perhaps you'll be kind enough to let me have some advice.'

'Yes, yes, yes,' Bragin sighed. 'Quite so, quite so . . .'

'I wouldn't have troubled you, but honestly, I've absolutely no one to turn to except you, my dear chap. You know what they're like round here.'

'Quite so, quite so . . . Yes . . .'

We were going to have a serious, very businesslike meeting, I thought, in which anyone could take part, irrespective of position or personal relations, so why not invite Natalie?

'*Tres faciunt collegium,*' I said breezily. 'What about inviting Natalie? What do you think?' Then I turned to the maid and said, 'Fenya, ask Mrs Asorin to come up, right away if possible. Tell her it's urgent.'

A little later Natalie came in. I rose to greet her: 'Sorry to trouble you, Natalie,' I said, 'we're discussing something very important and we just had the happy idea of asking you for advice, which we're sure you won't refuse us. Please sit down.'

Bragin kissed Natalie's hand and she kissed his head. When we were all seated round the table he gave her a tearful, blissful look, leant over and kissed her hand again. She was dressed in black, had taken great pains with her hair and smelt of fresh perfume. Evidently she was going out to visit someone or she was expecting a guest. As she entered the dining-room she offered me her hand and in a simple, friendly way smiled at me just as warmly as she had to Bragin, which pleased me. But she kept twiddling her fingers and throwing herself back quite sharply in her chair as she spoke. Her jerky speech and her movements irritated me and reminded me of her native Odessa, where the local society, both male and female, had at one time wearied me with its bad taste.

'I want to help the starving peasants,' I said, and after a brief pause went on, 'Of course, money is all-important, but restricting ourselves to financial aid and being satisfied with that is the same as buying one's way out of the main problems. Help in the form of money should be given, but we must, before we do anything else, organize it correctly and treat it as a serious matter. Let's think it over, my friends, and do something.'

Natalie gave me a quizzical look and shrugged her shoulders as if to ask: 'What do I know about these things?'

'Yes, yes, famine . . .' Bragin muttered. 'Indeed . . . yes . . .'

'The situation is serious,' I said, 'and help is needed most urgently. And I suggest that urgency must take pride of place among the principles we are going to work out. As they say in the army: size it up, move sharply and attack!'

'Yes, move sharply,' Bragin muttered drowsily, limply, as though dozing off. 'But there's nothing we can do. The crops have failed, you can't change that. So you won't be able to win through by any amount of sizing up or charging into battle. It's the elements . . . You can't go against God and fate . . .'

'Agreed. But wasn't man given a brain to combat the elements?'

'What's that? Oh, yes. Quite so, quite so . . . Yes.'

Bragin sneezed into his handkerchief, brightened up and looked at me and my wife as if he had just woken up.

'My crops have failed as well,' he laughed shrilly and gave a crafty wink, as if it really was very funny. 'No money, no food, and my place is swarming with workmen, like Count Sheremetyev's. I'd like to throw them out on their ears, but I feel too sorry for them.'

Natalie laughed and started questioning Bragin about his domestic affairs. Her presence gave me such pleasure as I had not known for a long time and I was too frightened to look at her in case I might somehow betray my secret feelings. Our relationship was such that these feelings might have appeared unexpected and comical. My wife laughed and talked to Bragin, quite unembarrassed that she was in *my* part of the house and that I wasn't laughing.

'So, my friends, what are we going to do?' I asked, waiting for a pause. 'First of all, I think we should start a subscription. You and I, Natalie, will write to our friends in St Petersburg and Odessa for donations. When we have some cash in the kitty we'll buy food and cattle fodder. And you, Bragin, will see to the distribution of funds. Counting on your innate tact and efficiency, we for our part would merely make so bold as to express our wish that, before distributing relief, you will acquaint yourself on the spot with all the details of the matter in hand. In addition — and this is crucial — you will make sure the food is given only to the really needy, and not to drunkards, idlers or the well-off.'

'Yes, yes, yes,' Bragin muttered. 'Quite so, quite so.'

'Well, we won't get far with this drivelling old wreck,' I thought, irritated.

'Blow those famine victims, I'm fed up with them,' Bragin went on, sucking a lemon peel. 'They've always got their backs up. The starving are peeved with those who have food. And those with food have a grudge against the starving. Yes . . . Hunger makes a man mad, stupid and wild. Hunger is no joke. A hungry man will swear and steal — and do something even worse perhaps . . . You must understand that.'

Bragin choked over his tea, coughed, and then shook all over with squeaky, suffocating laughter.

'Now that puts me in mind of a little story,' he said, trying to wave away with both arms the laughter and coughing which prevented him from speaking. 'Listen to this. About three years after the serfs were freed there was a famine in two districts and along came dear old Fyodor, of blessed memory, and asked me over to his place. "Let's go, let's go," he kept nagging. Well, why not? So we upped and went. It was getting towards evening and snowing a bit. It was night by the time we got to his farm. Suddenly there was a loud bang from the forest, then another. Bang! "Damn and blast you!" I said. I leapt from the sledge to have a look. Someone was coming at me in the dark, wallowing up to his knees in snow. I gripped his shoulder with one hand and knocked the gun out of his hands. Then another pops up, so I clumped him on the back of the head. He grunted and down he flopped into the snow, nose first. I was strong in those days, quite a bruiser. I polished two of them off and then I saw Fyodor sitting astride a third. We didn't let the three young devils go, tied their hands behind their backs so they couldn't do themselves or us an injury and we took the idiots into the kitchen. We were right mad with them, but ashamed to look them in the eye. They were peasants whom we knew, a decent bunch and we felt sorry for them. Scared out of their lives they were. One was crying and begging us to forgive him, another stared like a wild animal and swore. The third knelt down to pray. I told Fyodor, "Now, don't be too angry, let the devils go!" He gave them food, a sack of flour each and sent them packing, telling them to go to hell. That's how it happened. God rest his soul! He understood, he didn't hold it against them. But there were those who did – and the people they ruined! Yes ... After that affair at the Klochkovo Inn alone eleven men were carted off to the penal battalions. Yes ... And the same thing's happening again. Last Thursday Anisin the detective spent the night at my place and he was telling me about some landowner ... Yes ... One night they broke through the wall of his barn and came out with twenty sacks of rye. In the morning, when the landowner found out about these criminal activities, off he fires a telegram to the Governor, then another to the Public Prosecutor, a third to the local magistrate, a fourth to the detective. You know how scared people are of busybodies ... The authorities got the wind up and there was a right old hullabaloo. They searched two villages.'

'Now come on, Bragin,' I said. '*I* was robbed of the twenty sacks of rye, *I* cabled the Governor, *I* cabled St Petersburg as well. But this wasn't because I'm a busybody, as you like to put it, nor because I felt any resentment. I always look at the principle of the thing first. Whether a thief is hungry or stuffed with food makes no difference in the eyes of the law.'

'Yes, yes,' Bragin blurted out, taken aback. 'Of course, quite ... yes.'

Natalie blushed. 'There are *some* people ...,' she said and then stopped. She was trying her hardest to appear indifferent, but she couldn't stop herself looking into my eyes with the hatred I knew so well. 'There are some people,' she went on, 'for whom hunger and suffering are merely something they can vent their own nasty, petty natures on.' I shrugged my shoulders in embarrassment. 'If I may generalize,' she continued, 'there are some people who are absolutely insensitive, without any feelings for others and who yet cannot resist involving themselves in other people's misery and interfering because they're afraid these other people might be able to do without them. They're so conceited, nothing is sacred to them ...'

'There are some people,' I said softly, 'who have the character of angels, yet they express their lofty thoughts in such a way you can't tell them from Odessa street-traders.'

A rather unfortunate remark, I must admit.

My wife looked at me as if it cost her an immense effort of will to keep quiet. Her sudden outburst, followed by her ill-timed eloquence about my wish to help the starving, were uncalled for, to say the least. When I invited her to come upstairs, I had expected her to take quite a different attitude to myself and the things I had in mind. I cannot lay my finger on exactly what I was expecting, but my feeling of expectancy had pleasantly exhilarated me. Now I realized that any further talk about the starving would be tedious and perhaps rather stupid.

'Yes,' Bragin muttered irrelevantly. 'You know, that merchant Burov's worth four hundred thousand, perhaps more. I told him: "Come on, Ivan, can't you stump up two hundred thousand for the starving? You're going to die anyway and you can't take it with you." He took great umbrage at this. But he has to die one day, hasn't he? Death's no joke.'

Once again there was silence.

'So, that leaves only one thing,' I sighed: 'to do what I can on my own. One man can't achieve much against the many. All right then, I'll just keep soldiering on by myself. Perhaps I'll have more success with my war on want than my war on apathy.'

'They're waiting for me downstairs,' said Natalie. She got up from the table and turned to Bragin. 'You'll come down, just for a moment, won't you? I won't say good-bye just yet.' And she left.

Bragin was already drinking his seventh glass of tea, puffing and panting, smacking his lips, sucking at his moustache and lemon rind in turn. Drowsily and limply he muttered something, but I was not listening – I was waiting for him to leave. At last, with a look that seemed to say all he had come for was a glass of tea, he got up and began to make his farewell.

'Now, you haven't given me any advice at all.'

'What? I'm a fat, silly old fool,' he replied. 'My advice is useless. You're worrying for nothing ... I really don't know why you worry so much. Stop worrying, my dear chap.' Then he whispered affectionately and sincerely, as if trying to comfort a child, 'Really, it's all right!'

'What do you mean, *all right*? Peasants are stripping roofs and it's rumoured typhus is going around.'

'Well, what of it? Next year there'll be a good crop, there'll be new roofs, and if we die from typhus others will survive us. Everyone has to die anyway – if not now, then later. So don't worry, old boy!'

'I can't help worrying,' I said irritably.

We stood in the dimly lit hall. Bragin suddenly grabbed my elbow and looked at me for about thirty seconds, as if about to tell me something that was apparently most important.

'Paul!' he said softly, and his fat, lifeless face and dark eyes suddenly lit up with that peculiar expression for which he had once been famous, and which really was enchanting. 'Paul, let me tell you as a friend. Please try and change your nature. It's hard going with you! Oh, extremely hard going, my dear chap!'

He stared me in the face. That fine expression faded, the eyes grew dim. 'Oh, yes, yes ... please forgive an old man ... I've been talking a load of old rot!'

As he lumbered down the stairs, holding his arms out to balance himself and displaying his massive fat back and red neck, he looked rather ugly, like some sort of crab.

'You should go away, my dear sir,' he murmured, 'to St Petersburg or abroad ... Why do you have to live here, wasting the best years of your life? You're young, healthy, rich ... Yes ... Oh, if I were younger you wouldn't see me for dust!'

III

My wife's outburst put me in mind of our life together. At one time, after every flare-up, we used to feel an irresistible attraction for one another and we would come together, igniting all the dynamite that had been accumulating inside us in the meantime. And now, after Bragin's departure, I had a strong urge to see my wife. I felt like going downstairs and telling her that her behaviour over tea had insulted me, that she was cruel, small-minded and that her Philistine mind was incapable of grasping what I was saying or doing. I walked up and down my room for a long time trying to think what I could say to her and guessing her reply.

In the evening, after Bragin had gone, I experienced a particularly irritating form of that anxiety which had been haunting me over the past few days. I could neither sit nor stand, only walk, walk, choosing only the lighted rooms and staying closest to the one where Miss Marya was sitting. This feeling was very similar to one I had once had on the North Sea during a storm, when everyone was afraid the ship might capsize, because it carried no cargo or ballast. That evening I realized my anxiety was not disillusionment, as I had formerly thought, but something different – exactly *what* I did not understand; and this irritated me even more.

'I'll go to her room,' I decided. 'I'll think of some excuse.'

ANTON CHEKHOV

I went downstairs and strolled over the carpet in the vestibule
and hall. Bragin was on the drawing-room couch, muttering and
drinking tea again. My wife was standing opposite, holding the back
of an armchair. Her face wore that calm, sweet, dutiful expression
with which one listens to holy idiots and fools, when trivial words
and mutterings are supposed to conceal some special, hidden meaning. I thought that there was something morbid, nun-like in my
wife's expression, and her low-pitched, half-dark, very well-heated
rooms with their antique furniture, birds asleep in cages and the
smell of geraniums, reminded me of the quarters of a Mother
Superior or some devout old lady who was a general's wife.

I entered the drawing-room. My wife showed neither surprise
nor embarrassment and gave me a stern, calm look as if she knew
I would be coming.

'Excuse me,' I said quietly. 'I'm very pleased you haven't gone,
Bragin. I forgot to ask you upstairs if you knew the first names
of the chairman of our rural council.'

'Andrey Stanislavovich. That's it . . .'

'*Merci*,' I said, taking a notebook from my pocket and jotting
it down.

A silence followed, during which my wife and Bragin were probably waiting for me to go. My wife did not believe that I could
need the chairman of the rural council – I could read it in her eyes.

'So, I'll be off then, my dear lady,' Bragin muttered after I had
paced the length of the drawing-room once or twice and sat down
by the fireplace.

'No,' Natalie said hurriedly, touching his hand. 'Another quarter
of an hour, I beg you.'

Obviously she did not want to be left alone with me, without
witnesses.

'All right then,' I thought, 'I'll wait quarter of an hour too.'

'Oh, it's snowing!' I said, getting up and looking out of the window. 'What excellent snow! A shame I don't hunt, Bragin,' I added,
pacing up and down. 'I can imagine the enjoyment chasing after
wolves and hares over snow like that!'

My wife stood still, following my movements out of the corner
of her eye, without turning her head. From the way she was looking

it seemed she suspected me of having a sharp knife or revolver tucked away in my pocket.

'Bragin, you must take me hunting some time!' I said in a gentle voice. 'I'd be very, very grateful.'

Just then a visitor entered the drawing-room. It was a gentleman I did not know, about forty, tall, thickset, with a large fair beard and small eyes. From his creased, baggy clothes and his manners I took him for a sacristan or teacher, but my wife introduced him as Dr Sable.

'Delighted to meet you!' the doctor said in a loud, high-pitched voice, firmly shaking my hand and giving a naive smile. 'Delighted.'

He sat down at the table, took a glass of tea and asked in his loud voice: 'Do you have any rum or brandy, by any chance?' Turning to the maid he said, 'Be a nice girl, Olga, have a look in the cupboard. I'm frozen stiff.'

I sat by the fireside again, watching, listening, and now and again contributing a few words to the general conversation. My wife smiled warmly at the visitors and kept her eyes glued on me as though I were some wild animal. My presence was a burden to her, and this aroused my jealousy, irritation and a stubborn desire to hurt her. This wife, these cosy rooms, that inglenook – these are mine, I thought, and have been mine for ages, so why should some doddering old Bragin or Sable have more right to them than me? Now I no longer see my wife through a window, but close by, in her usual domestic surroundings, those same surroundings which I am deprived of now that I'm getting on in years. Despite her hatred for me, I yearn for her, just as I once used to pine for nanny when I was a child. I feel that now, with old age creeping on, my love for her is purer, nobler than before – this is why I want to go up to her and bring my heel hard down on her toe, to cause her pain, and to smile while I'm doing it.

'Monsieur Racoon,' I said, turning to the doctor, 'how many hospitals are there in this district?'

'The name's Sable,' my wife corrected.

'Two, sir,' Sable replied.

'And how many mortalities are there per hospital per annum?'

'Paul, I must have a word with you,' my wife said.

She excused herself to her guests and went into the next room.
I got up and followed.

'Go upstairs to your room. Immediately!' she said.

'Where are your manners?' I said.

'Up to your room. *Immediately!*' she snapped, looking into my
face with loathing.

She was so close that had I bent down just a little my beard would
have touched her face.

'What's the matter?' I asked. 'What have I done wrong all of
a sudden?'

Her chin quivered. She hurriedly dried her eyes, glanced at herself
in the mirror.

'It's the same old story all over again,' she whispered. 'Of course
you won't go. Well, please yourself. I'm going, you can stay.'

We went back to the drawing-room, she with a determined look,
while I shrugged my shoulders and tried to sneer. Some other visitors
had arrived: an elderly lady and a young man in spectacles. Without
welcoming the new arrivals or saying good-bye to the old, I went
to my room.

After what happened over tea in my room and now with the
events downstairs, I saw quite clearly that our 'domestic saga', which
we had already begun to forget over the past two years, had renewed
itself for some absurd, silly reason; that neither I nor my wife could
stop ourselves now; and that a day or so after this outburst of loathing – as far as I could judge from previous experience – something
shocking was bound to happen, which would make a complete
shambles of our lives. As I began to pace my rooms, I thought that
we hadn't grown any cooler or calmer over the last two years. And
tears would flow again, there would be shouting, curses, suitcases,
journeys abroad and then the persistent, morbid fear that she would
bring down disgrace on my head with some dandified Italian or
Russian ladies' man. Once again I would refuse her a passport and
once again there would be letters, utter loneliness, longing for her
and then, in five years' time, old age, grey hair ... I paced up and
down imagining the impossible, how that beautiful woman, more
buxom now, would embrace some man I didn't know. Convinced
by now that this was bound to happen, I asked myself despairingly:

why hadn't I given her a divorce during one of our very first quarrels? Why hadn't she made a clean break with me for good at the time? In that case I wouldn't have felt this present longing for her and I would have been free from hatred, anxiety, living out my life working peacefully, with nothing to brood upon ...

A carriage with two lamps drove into the courtyard, followed by a broad sledge drawn by three horses. My wife was giving a party, no doubt.

Until midnight everything was quiet downstairs and I could hear nothing, but after that chairs were shifted around and crockery clattered: they must be having supper. Then I could hear chairs being moved again and a noise came through the floor. It seemed they were all cheering. Miss Marya was already asleep and there was no one but me on the entire upper floor. From the dining-room walls portraits of my ancestors – vicious nobodies – looked down on me, while the reflection of my lamp in the study window winked unpleasantly. Feeling jealous and envious of what was going on downstairs, I strained my ears.

'I'm the master here,' I thought, 'and I could kick that entire venerable company out this minute if I wanted to.' But I knew that was nonsense, that I couldn't kick anyone out and that the word 'master' meant nothing. It's possible to call oneself master, husband, man of substance and status to one's heart's content and still not know the meaning of the words.

After supper someone began to sing in a tenor voice downstairs.

'Well then, nothing out of the ordinary has happened, has it?' I tried to reassure myself. 'So why am I so worked up? I won't go down and see her tomorrow, that's all and that will be the end of our quarrel.'

At a quarter past one I went off to bed. 'Have the downstairs guests left?' I asked Aleksey as he helped me undress.

'Yes, sir, they've all gone.'

'What were they cheering about?'

'Mr Makhonov has donated a thousand sacks of flour and a thousand roubles for the famine victims. And an old lady, I don't know her name, has promised to set up a soup kitchen for a hundred and fifty on her estate. God be praised, sir. Mrs Asorin's decided that all the ladies and gentlemen will meet every Friday.'

'Do you mean here, downstairs?'

'Yes, sir. Before supper they read a paper which said that since August Mrs Asorin has collected eight thousand roubles in cash, besides food. God be praised, sir ... As I understand it, sir, if the lady takes the trouble to save her soul, then she'll collect a lot, sir. There's some rich people round here.'

When I'd dismissed Aleksey, put the light out and pulled the blankets over my head I asked myself: 'Why do I worry so much? What power is drawing me to the hungry, like a moth to the flame? I don't even know them, do I? I don't understand them, I've never seen them and I don't like them. So why should I worry about them?'

Suddenly I crossed myself beneath the eiderdown. 'But what a woman!' I told myself, thinking of my wife. 'Holds whole committee meetings in my house and doesn't even tell me! Why is she hiding it from me? Why this conspiracy? What have I done to them?'

Bragin was right, I ought to go away.

Next day I awoke firmly resolved to leave as soon as possible. Yesterday's events – that conversation over tea, my wife, Sable, the supper, my fears – had exhausted me and I was cheered by the thought that I might soon find release from surroundings that kept reminding me of them. While I was drinking my coffee Vladimir Prokhorych, my manager, read me a long report on various matters. He kept the best bit till last.

'They've found the thieves who stole our rye,' he informed me, smiling. 'Yesterday the detective arrested three peasants in Pyostrovo.'

'Clear off!' I shouted, absolutely furious, and for no apparent reason seized a basket of sponge-cakes and flung it on the floor.

IV

After lunch I rubbed my hands and wondered if I ought to go and tell my wife I was leaving. But what was the point? Who cared? Nobody, I told myself. But why *not* tell her, especially as it would give her nothing but pleasure? Besides, it wouldn't have been altogether tactful of me to leave without a word, after yesterday's quarrel. She might think I was scared of her and perhaps the idea that she had driven me out of my own house might lie heavy on her conscience. Moreover, it wouldn't do any harm if I told her I was donating five thousand, if I gave her some advice on organization and if I warned her that, in such a complex and responsible undertaking, her lack of experience could have the direst consequences. In short, I longed to see my wife and even while I was thinking up various pretexts for calling on her, I had already firmly made up my mind that this was what I was going to do.

When I went to her room it was still light and the lamps hadn't been lit yet. She was sitting in her workroom, which formed a passage between drawing-room and bedroom, and she was writing something rapidly, bent low over the table. She shuddered when she saw me, went away from the table and stood as if trying to shield her papers from me.

'Excuse me, I've just popped in for a minute,' I said, and for some reason felt embarrassed. 'I just happened to hear, Natalie, that you're organizing relief for the famine victims.'

'Yes, I am,' she replied. 'But that's my business.'

'Yes, it is your business,' I replied quietly. 'I'm pleased, as it suits my intentions perfectly. I'm asking permission to take part.'

'I'm sorry, but I can't allow it,' she replied, looking to one side.

'Why not, Natalie?' I asked gently. 'Why not? I'm well-fed too and I want to help the starving.'

'I don't know what it's got to do with you,' she said with a supercilious laugh, shrugging one shoulder. 'No one asked you.'

'But no one asked you either and yet you've set up a whole committee in *my* house!' I said.

'I *was* asked, but no one will ever ask you, mark my words! Go and take your help where no one knows you.'

'For God's sake, don't take that tone with me.'

I tried to be gentle with her and summoned up all my strength so as not to lose my temper. During the first few minutes it was extremely pleasant being near my wife. I felt I was in the presence of something gentle and homely, youthful, feminine, exceedingly elegant – exactly what was missing on my own floor of the house, as well as in my life in general. She was wearing a pink flannel housecoat, which made her look remarkably young and lent smoothness to her swift, occasionally jerky movements. Her fine black hair, the mere sight of which had once filled me with passion, was hanging loose from sitting hunched up for so long and looked untidy. But in my eyes this made it only richer and more voluptuous. However, all this is a rather vulgar way of describing it. Before me stood an ordinary woman, not very pretty perhaps and lacking in refinement, but she was my wife, with whom I had once lived and with whom I would still be living to this day, but for her unfortunate character. She was the only person in the whole world whom I loved. And now, as I was about to leave and I knew that I wouldn't see her through my window any more, even though she seemed so uncompromising, cold and aloof as she answered me with that superior, contemptuous smile – in spite of all these things I still found her captivating. I was proud of her and had to admit that leaving her would be terrible, quite out of the question.

'Paul,' she said after a little while, 'for two years we haven't got in each other's way and we've lived in peace. So why this sudden urge to bring back the past?' She raised her voice, her face flushed and her eyes blazed with hate as she went on, 'Yesterday you came to insult and humiliate me, but please restrain yourself, don't do it, Paul! Tomorrow I'll apply for a passport, and I'll go away, away, away! I'll go into a convent, a widows' home, an almshouse . . .'

'What about a lunatic asylum!?' I shouted, losing my temper.

'Even a lunatic asylum!' With eyes flashing she continued, 'That would be the best thing, the best! When I was in Pyostrovo today I felt jealous of the starving and sick women, because they didn't have to live with someone like you. They are honest and free, but as for me – I'm a parasite, thanks to you, wasting away in idleness, eating your food, spending your money, and I'm paying for this with my freedom and a kind of faithfulness that is no use to anyone. Since you won't give me a passport, I have to protect your good name, which simply doesn't exist.'

I had to keep silent. Gritting my teeth I quickly went into the drawing-room, but returned immediately. 'I beg you most earnestly, no more of these gatherings, plots and conspiratorial dens in *my* house! I only let people I already know into this house and if all that rabble of yours wants to dabble in philanthropy, then let them go somewhere else. I won't have people cheering for joy in my house in the middle of the night because they can exploit a neurotic like you.'

Pale-faced, my wife swiftly crossed the room, wringing her hands and groaning as if she had toothache. I flung my arms up and went into the dining-room. I was choking with rage and at the same time trembling with fear I might lose my temper and do or say something I would regret for the rest of my life. And I tightly clenched my fists, thinking this would help me control myself.

After a glass of water I calmed down a little and went back to my wife. She was in the same pose as before, as though shielding the table and papers from me. Tears slowly trickled down her cold, pale face. I remained silent for a moment. Then I told her bitterly, but not angrily: 'How little you understand me! How unjust you are! I swear that my motives for coming to see you were pure, I only wanted to do some good!'

'Paul,' she said, crossing her hands on her breast, and her face assumed that suffering, pleading expression of a frightened, weeping child begging not to be punished, 'I know very well you'll refuse, but I'm asking all the same. Force yourself, do a good deed for once in your life. I implore you to leave this place! That's the only thing you can do to help the starving. If you leave I'll forgive you everything, everything!'

'There's no need to insult me, Natalie,' I sighed, suddenly feeling a strange surge of humility. 'I've already decided to leave, but I shan't go before I've done something for the famine victims. It's my duty.'

'Oh,' she said softly, with an impatient frown. 'You can build an excellent railway or bridge, but you can't help the starving. Get that into your head.'

'Really? Yesterday you reproached me for my indifference, for having no compassion. How well you know me!' I laughed. 'You believe in God. Well, as God is my witness, I worry day and night ...'

'I can see you're worried, but that has nothing to do with hunger or compassion. You're worried because starving peasants can do without you and because the Rural Council and the helpers in general don't need you to guide them!'

I paused for a moment to stifle my irritation and said, 'I came here to talk business with you. Sit down. *Please* sit down.' She did not sit down. 'Please sit down, I beg you!' I repeated and pointed to a chair. She sat down. I sat too and pondered for a moment. 'Now, please think about this seriously,' I said. 'Listen ... You're motivated by love for your fellow men and you've taken upon yourself the task of organizing famine relief. Of course, I've no objection to that, you have my full sympathy and I'm ready to cooperate in any way I can, however things are between us. But for all your qualities of mind and heart, yes ... and heart,' I repeated, 'I can't allow such a difficult, complex and responsible matter as famine relief to rest in your hands alone. You are a woman, you are inexperienced, ignorant of life and you are too trusting and effusive. You have surrounded yourself with helpers whom you don't know at all. I'm not exaggerating if I say that, under the aforesaid circumstances, your activities are bound to entail two distressing consequences. Firstly, the district will be left without any aid at all. Secondly, you will have to pay for your mistakes and those of your helpers not only from your own pocket, but with your reputation. All right, I'll cover the losses and omissions, but who will restore your good name? When the rumour starts spreading – in consequence of your incompetence and negligence – that you, and therefore I, have made two hundred thousand out of it, will your helpers still rally to your support?' She did not reply. 'As you say, not from vanity,' I continued, 'but purely because I neither wish the starving to be left without any help nor you to lose your good name, I consider it my moral duty to intervene.'

'Make it short,' my wife said.

'You will be so good as to show me how much you've received to date, and how much has been spent. Subsequently, you will account to me daily for every new receipt, whether in cash or kind, and for each new outlay. You will also give me a list of your helpers, Natalie. They may be quite respectable people – I don't doubt that. All the same, we must keep a check.' She did not reply. I rose and walked up and down. 'Let's make a start, then,' I said, sitting down at her table.

'Are you serious?' she asked, looking at me bewildered and frightened.

'Natalie, be reasonable,' I pleaded, as I could see from her face that she wanted to protest. 'I beg you, have complete confidence in my experience and integrity!'

'I still don't understand what you want!'

'Show me how much you've collected and how much you've spent up to now.'

'I have no secrets, anyone can see. Take a look.'

Five school exercise-books lay on the table, a few sheets of paper covered with scribbling, a map of the district and lots of scraps of paper of different sizes. It was getting dark and I lit a candle.

'I'm sorry, I can't see anything yet,' I said, turning over the pages in the exercise-books. 'Where's the register of monies received?'

'You can find that in the subscription lists.'

'Yes, but you really should have a register!' I said, smiling at her naivety. 'Where are the letters that came with the donations in cash and kind? *Pardon*, may I offer a small piece of practical advice, Natalie? It's essential you keep those letters. You must number each one and enter it in a special register. You should do that with your personal letters as well. However, I'll see to all that myself.'

'See to it then,' she said. 'See to it.'

I was very pleased with myself. Fascinated by the lively, interesting work in hand, by that small table, by those innocent exercise-books and the delights that working with my wife held in store for me, I was afraid she might suddenly try and stop me and ruin everything with some sudden eruption. Therefore I hurried and tried hard not to attach any importance to her trembling lips and those fearful, confused, sideways glances of a small, trapped animal.

'Now listen, Natalie,' I said, without looking at her. 'Let me take all these papers and exercise-books upstairs. I'll have a good look through them, find out what's there and give you my opinion to-morrow.'

'Do you have any more of these papers?' I asked, folding the exercise-books and leaflets into bundles.

'Take them, take the lot!' my wife said, helping me to fold the papers into bundles. Large tears trickled down her face. 'Take the lot! They're all I had left in life ... Take my last possessions away from me ...'

'Oh, Natalie, Natalie!' I sighed reproachfully.

Elbowing me in the chest and brushing my face with her hair she pulled out the table drawer and began throwing the papers towards me across the table haphazardly. As she did this, coins poured over my knees and onto the floor. 'Take it all,' she said hoarsely.

When she had thrown all the papers out she went away and collapsed onto the couch, clutching her head with both hands. I picked up the money, put it back in the drawer and locked it so the servants wouldn't be tempted. Then I gathered a whole armful of papers and went to my room. As I passed my wife I stopped.

'You're such a child, Natalie. Really!' I said, glancing at her back and trembling shoulders. 'Listen to me: when you realize what a serious and responsible matter this is you'll be the first to thank me. I swear it.'

Back in my room I did not hurry through the papers. The exercise-books were not bound, the pages were not numbered. The entries were in different hands, and evidently anyone who happened to come along had been able to tinker with those books. In the lists of donations in kind, the value of goods had not been entered. But of course, rye, which now stands at one rouble fifteen copecks, could go up to two roubles fifteen copecks in two months' time, couldn't it? A fine way to open an account! Next I found 'thirty-two roubles given to A. M. Sable'. When, and for what, were they given? Where was the receipt? There was nothing, and I couldn't make head or tail of anything. In the event of legal action, these papers would serve only to obscure the whole matter.

'How naive she is!' I wondered. 'Such a child!' I felt both angry and amused.

V

My wife had already collected eight thousand roubles, which together with my five made thirteen all told. Very good for a start.

The business which so interested and worried me was at last under my control. I was doing what others didn't want to do, or couldn't. I was fulfilling my duty, organizing famine relief along correct, serious lines.

Everything seemed to be working out according to my intentions and wishes, but why was I still plagued with anxiety? I spent four hours looking through my wife's papers, clarifying their meaning and correcting mistakes; but instead of peace of mind I felt as if some stranger were behind me, running his rough hand over my back. What did I need, then? The organization for famine relief was in reliable hands now, the hungry would be fed – what else did I want?

For some reason that easy, four-hour stint had so exhausted me I could neither bend forwards when I sat down, nor write. Now and again a dull moaning came from down below – this was my wife sobbing. The ever-docile, drowsy, sanctimonious Aleksey kept coming over to the table to see to the candles and he gave me some rather peculiar looks.

'No, I *must* leave!' I finally decided, absolutely exhausted. 'I must escape from all these magnificent happenings here! I'll go tomorrow.'

I gathered the papers and exercise-books together and went down to my wife's room. Terribly weary, completely worn out, I pressed the papers and books to my chest with both arms, crossed my bedroom, saw my suitcases – and at that moment the sound of crying came drifting from down below.

'You hold a high rank, don't you?' someone seemed to be whispering into my ear. 'Very nice. But you're a bastard all the same.'

'It's all such nonsense, such utter nonsense!' I murmured to myself as I went downstairs. 'Absolute nonsense. And it's rubbish to say I'm motivated by pride or vanity. How small-minded! I'm not going to get a medal for helping the famine victims, or be appointed departmental director, am I? Utter nonsense! And anyway, what kind of place is the countryside for showing off?'

I was tired, dreadfully tired. 'That's all very nice,' someone whispered in my ear, 'but you're a bastard all the same.' For some reason I recalled a line from some old poem I once knew as a child: 'Being good brings such delight!'

My wife was lying in the same position on the couch: face downwards, her head clutched in both hands. She was crying. The maid was standing at her side and she looked frightened, bewildered. I sent her away, put the papers together on the table and pondered for a moment.

'This is your office, then, Natalie,' I said. 'Everything's fine, everything's marvellous and I'm very pleased. I'm leaving tomorrow.'

She was still crying. I went into the drawing-room and sat there in the dark. My wife's sighing and sobbing seemed to be accusing me, so to justify myself I recalled our whole quarrel, starting with my unfortunate idea of inviting my wife to a consultation and ending with those exercise-books and tears. This was a quite normal outbreak of conjugal hatred, ugly and senseless, like so many that had taken place after our wedding. But what did the famine victims have to do with it? How could they have fallen foul of us? It was as though we had happened to run into a church as we chased one another and started fighting before the altar.

'Natalie, *please*,' I said quietly from the drawing-room. 'That's enough!'

To stop her crying and put an end to this agonizing situation I had to go to my wife, comfort and caress her, or offer an apology. But how could I make her believe me? How could I convince this captive wild duckling, full of hatred for me, that I was fond of it and sympathized with its sufferings? I had never really known my wife and therefore never knew what to say to her or how to express it. I knew her very well from the outside and showed appreciation where it was due. But as for her spiritual and moral world, her intellect, general attitude to life, her frequent changes of mood, her eyes full of hatred, her arrogance, her wide reading that astonished me at times or that nun-like expression, for example, that she had assumed yesterday – all these things were an unknown quantity to me, a mystery. When we clashed I tried to determine what kind of person she really was, but my psychology could not extend beyond such definitions as 'flighty', 'frivolous', 'unhappy', and 'typical woman's mentality', and this seemed to be quite adequate. But now, while she was weeping, I had a passionate desire to know more.

The crying stopped and I went to my wife. She was sitting on the couch, propping her head on both hands and thoughtfully gazing into the fire without moving.

'I'm leaving tomorrow morning,' I said. She did not reply. I crossed the room and sighed. 'Natalie,' I said, 'when you asked me to leave, you told me: I forgive you everything, everything … So you consider me the guilty one. Please, give me an account of what I've done wrong, in calm, brief terms.'

'I'm exhausted. It can wait till later …' my wife said.

'How am I to blame?' I went on. 'What have I done? You're young, beautiful, you want to live, while I'm almost twice your age and you detest me. But that's not my fault, is it? I didn't force you to marry me. Well, all right, if you want to be free then go, I give you your freedom. Go, you can love anyone you like … And I'll give you a divorce.'

'I don't need that,' she said. 'You know I loved you before and always thought of myself as older than you. All that doesn't mean very much … You're to blame, not because you're older and I'm younger, or because I could love another if I were free, but because you're a self-centred, misanthropic pain in the neck.'

'Perhaps I am, I don't know,' I said.

'Please leave me now. You want to go on tormenting me till morning, but I'm warning you, I've no strength left and I can't give you an answer. You promised you would go away and for that I'm truly grateful. I ask for nothing more.'

My wife wanted me to go upstairs, but it was not easy for me. I was weak and shrank at the thought of my large, uncomfortable, dreary rooms. Whenever I had pain as a child I would snuggle up to my mother or nanny, and when I buried my face in the folds of a warm dress I felt I was hiding from it. And now, in the same way, it somehow seemed that I could escape from my worries only in this little room close to my wife. I sat down and shielded my eyes from the light with my hand. It was quiet.

'So, you wanted to know how you are to blame?' my wife asked after a long silence, looking at me with eyes red and shining from tears. 'You've had an excellent education and upbringing, you're very honest, fair, with high principles, but the net result of all this is that wherever you are, you create an incredibly stuffy, oppressive atmosphere around you, something extremely offensive and humiliating. You are perfectly honest, therefore you hate the whole world. You hate people who have faith, because faith is an expression of immaturity and ignorance, and at the same time you hate those who don't believe, for having no faith or ideals. You hate old men for their backwardness and conservatism, and you hate the young for their free-thinking. The interests of the common people and Russia are dear to you, and therefore you hate the peasants, since you suspect every one of them of being a thief or robber. You hate everyone. You are a just man, you always stand up for law and order, so therefore you're always mixed up in lawsuits with peasants and neighbours. You had twenty sacks of rye stolen and out of love of good order you complained to the Governor and to all the authorities about the peasants, and then you reported the local authorities to St Petersburg.

'In the interests of law and order!' my wife continued and burst out laughing. 'On the basis of law and in the interests of morality, you refuse me a passport. It's a nice brand of morality or system of law which lays down that a young, healthy, self-respecting woman should spend her life in idleness, anguish, perpetual fear, for which she is repaid with food and lodging from a man she doesn't love. You know the law backwards, you are exceedingly honest and just, you respect marriage and the foundations of family life, but all this boils down to is that throughout your life you haven't performed a single good deed and everyone hates you, you're at loggerheads with everyone, and out of seven years of marriage you haven't even spent seven months with your wife. You haven't *had* a wife, I haven't had a husband. It's impossible to live with a man like you, I've no more strength. During the early years I was scared of you, now I'm ashamed of you ... So the best years have been wasted ... Doing battle with you has ruined my whole personality: I've become brusque, rude, jumpy, mistrustful ... Oh, what's the use of talking!? As if you wanted to know! Now go away, blow you!'

My wife lay on the couch, deep in thought. 'Oh, what a wonderful, enviable life we could have had together!' she said quietly, gazing pensively at the fire. 'What a life! But we can't bring it back now.'

Whoever has spent the winter in the country and is familiar with those long, tedious, quiet evenings when even the dogs are too bored to bark and the clocks seem to be languishing, so tired they are of ticking; whoever has been troubled on such evenings by twinges of conscience and has hectically rushed around here, there and everywhere trying first to pacify it, then to unravel its secrets – he will appreciate what entertainment and pleasure the sound of a woman's voice echoing in a cosy little room gave me as I was told what a bad person I was. I did not understand what my conscience desired, but my wife interpreted for me the meaning of my uneasiness – as a woman would, but lucidly all the same. How often before, in moments of extreme anxiety, I would hazard a guess that the key to the whole mystery lay not with famine victims, but in my being not the right sort of man.

My wife made a great effort, rose to her feet and came over to me. 'Paul,' she said, smiling sadly. 'Forgive me, but I don't believe you. You won't go. But I'm asking you once more.' She pointed at her papers. 'You may call this self-deception, say that I'm an illogical woman, that it's a mistake – you can still call it anything you like, but don't interfere. It's all I have left in life.' She turned away and fell silent for a moment. 'Before this I had nothing. I wasted my youth doing battle with you. Now that I've become involved in work I've come alive again, I'm happy. I feel I've found a means of justifying my existence.'

'Natalie, you're a fine, idealistic woman,' I said, looking at my wife delightedly, 'and everything you do or say is beautiful and clever.' I walked up and down the room to hide my feelings. 'Natalie,' I continued a minute later, 'before I leave I'm asking you, as a special favour, to help me do something for the starving!'

'But what can I do?' she said, shrugging her shoulders. 'I could let you have the subscription list.' She rummaged in her papers and found the list. 'Donate some money,' she said, and I could tell from her tone of voice that she didn't attach serious importance to the list. 'There's no other way you can help.'

I took the list and wrote: 'Five thousand roubles, ANONYMOUS.'

There was something wrong, false, arrogant about that 'Anonymous', but I realized this only when I saw my wife blush violently and hastily push the list into a pile of papers. We were both ashamed. I felt that I must immediately make up for my clumsiness, at all costs, otherwise I would feel ashamed afterwards in the train and then in St Petersburg. But how? What should I say?

'Your work has my blessing, Natalie,' I said sincerely, 'and I wish you every success. But may I give you a parting word of advice? Natalie, be more careful with Sable and your helpers in general, don't confide in them. I'm not saying they're dishonest, but they're not gentlemen. They're lacking in ideas, they have no ideals or beliefs, they have no purpose in life or firm principles, and all that matters to them is money. Money, money, money!' I sighed. 'They let others do the dirty work and in this respect the better educated they are, the more they can jeopardize your work.'

My wife went over to the couch and lay down. 'Ideas, ideals,' she murmured limply and reluctantly. 'Ideals, ideas, the purpose of life, principles . . . You always used these words when you wanted to humiliate or insult someone, to say something nasty. Now isn't that just like you! If a person with your views and attitude to people were allowed to get anywhere near our work, that would mean ruining it from the start. It's time you realized that.' She sighed and was silent for a moment. 'It's your coarseness of nature, Paul,' she said. 'You're highly educated, well-bred, but basically you're an absolute barbarian! This is because you live like a real misanthrope, buried away and shut off from the world. You don't mix at all, you read nothing but books on engineering. But there are nice people, good books! Oh, yes . . . but I'm worn out and tired of talking. I must get some sleep.'

'Well, I'll go away then, Natalie,' I said.

'Yes, yes . . . *Merci*.'

I stood there for a moment and then I went up to my room. An hour later – at half past one – I came downstairs again with a candle to talk to my wife. I didn't know what to say to her, but I sensed it had to be something of supreme importance. She wasn't in her workroom, her bedroom door was closed.

'Natalie, are you asleep?' I asked softly.

There was no answer. I stood at the door, sighed, and went into the drawing-room. There I sat on the couch, snuffed my candle and stayed in the dark until dawn.

VI

I left for the station at ten in the morning. There was no frost, but heavy sleet was falling and there was a damp, unpleasant wind.

We drove past the pond, then the birch-grove and started to climb the hill which was visible from my window. I turned round for one last look at my home, but I could see nothing in the sleet. A little further on dark huts loomed up as though in a fog. It was Pyostrovo.

'If ever I go mad, Pyostrovo will be to blame,' I thought. 'It's persecuting me.'

We drove down the street. All the roofs were undamaged, not one had been stripped, therefore my manager must have been lying. A boy was pulling a little girl and a baby along in a toboggan while another boy, about three years old, his head muffled like an old woman's and wearing enormous mittens, laughed as he tried to catch flying snowflakes on his tongue. Then a cart with brushwood came towards us, with a peasant walking beside it, and it was impossible to make out if he was naturally white-haired or if it was the snow on his beard. He recognized my coachman, smiled to him and said something, while to me he automatically doffed his cap. Dogs came running out of yards and looked inquisitively at my horses. Everything was quiet, natural and simple. The migrant villagers had returned. There was no food, in the huts 'some were roaring with laughter, others had gone raving mad', but it was all so natural that it was hard to believe any of it had really happened. There were no distraught faces, no voices crying out for help, no weeping, no cursing, only tranquillity and life taking its normal course all around, with children, toboggans, dogs with tails in the air ... The children weren't worrying, nor was the peasant we'd passed, so why was *I* so worried?

Looking at the smiling peasant, the boy with those huge mittens, at the huts, and remembering my wife, I understood now that no disaster could defeat these people. It seemed there was already the scent of victory in the air, I was proud and ready to shout out loud that I too was on their side. But the horses took me out of the village into the open fields, the snow whirled, the wind roared, and

I was alone with my thoughts. Out of the millions who were working for the public good, life had rejected me, an unwanted, useless, rotten citizen. I was a nuisance, a small part of the peasants' tribulations myself. Defeated and rejected, I was rushing to the station to escape from it, to hide myself away in a hotel on the Great Morskoy Street in St Petersburg.

An hour later we arrived at the station. A porter with a badge and my coachman carried my suitcases into the ladies' waiting-room. Soaked through from the snow, his coat tails tucked inside his belt and wearing felt boots, my coachman Nikanor was pleased I was leaving, gave me a friendly smile and said, 'Pleasant journey, Your Excellency. Good luck to you.'

Incidentally, everyone calls me 'Your Excellency', although I'm a mere collegiate assessor*. The porter said the train hadn't left the last station yet and there was a delay. I went outside and wandered aimlessly over to the water-tower, barely able to drag one foot after the other and with a heavy head after a sleepless night. There wasn't a soul about.

'Why am I going?' I asked myself. 'What's in store for me there? Friends whom I'd already run away from before, loneliness, restaurant meals, noise, electric light which hurts my eyes ... Where am I going and why? Why am I going?'

Somehow it was strange leaving without saying a thing to my wife. I felt I'd left her in the dark: when I went I should have told her she was right. I really am a bad person.

As I turned away from the water-tower, the stationmaster (about whom I'd already complained twice to his superiors) appeared in the doorway. His frock-coat collar was turned up and he shrank from the wind and the snow as he came over to me and touched the peak of his cap with two fingers. With an expression that was full of panic, loathing and feigned respect all at once he told me the train would be twenty minutes late and asked if I would like to wait in the warm.

'No, thank you,' I replied, 'I may not be travelling. Tell my coachman to wait, I want to think about it.'

* A middle-ranking official in the Civil Service, equivalent to colonel.

I walked up and down the platform wondering whether to go or not. When the train drew in I decided not to go. All I could expect at home was my wife's bewilderment and taunts perhaps, that dreary upper storey and all my worries, but at my age this was still easier to put up with, something that was closer to me, than travelling two whole days with strangers to St Petersburg, where I would be aware, every minute of the day, that my life was quite useless to anyone, that it was drawing to its close. No, it was better to go back, however bad things were. I left the station. It would have been absurd returning in broad daylight to a house where everyone had so rejoiced in my departure. I could pass the rest of the day, until evening, with one of the neighbours. But with whom? I thought for a moment, and then I remembered Bragin.

'Let's go to Bragin's,' I told the coachman as I got into the sledge.

'That's a long way,' Nikanor sighed. 'A good eighteen miles, I dare say. Might even be twenty.'

'*Please*, my dear man,' I said in a tone that suggested Nikanor had the right to disobey. 'Let's go, please!'

Sceptically Nikanor shook his head and slowly told me that Yeoman or Goldfinch should really have been put between the shafts, and not Circassian. Undecided, as though expecting me to change my mind, he took the reins in his mittens, reflected for a moment and then flourished his whip.

'A whole trail of inconsistencies,' I thought, hiding my face from the snow. 'I must be out of my mind. Oh well, it can't be helped ...'

At one point on the very high, precipitous slope, Nikanor carefully kept the horses in check until halfway down, but then they suddenly broke loose and bolted off at terrifying speed. He shuddered, raised his elbows and shouted in a wild, frantic voice I had never heard him use before, 'Hey, let's take the general for a ride! If you get winded the master'll buy new ones, my beauties! Hey, look out there, we'll run you over!'

Only now, as the breakneck speed we were travelling at took my breath away, did I see that he was terribly drunk. He must have had a few at the station. Ice cracked at the bottom of the gully and a heavy lump of snow, caked with dung, flew up from the road and struck me a painful blow in the face. The runaway horses streaked uphill just as fast and before I managed to call out to Nikanor, my troika was already flying over level ground in an old fir forest, where the tall trees stretched their bristly white paws out to me from all directions.

'I'm insane, my coachman's drunk,' I thought. 'How very nice!'

I found Bragin at home. He laughed so much he had a coughing fit, laid his head on my chest and greeted me with the same old remark, 'You look younger every day. I don't know what dye you use for your hair and beard, but I'd like some.'

'I've come to repay your call,' I lied. 'Don't be too hard on me, I'm from St Petersburg, with my own funny ideas. I like to keep the account straight.'

'Delighted, my dear chap! I'm a bit childish these days, I like good form!'

I could tell from his voice and blissfully smiling face that he was deeply flattered by my visit. Two peasant women took my coat in the hall and a peasant in a red shirt hung it on a peg. I went with Bragin into his little study and saw two barefooted little girls sitting on the floor looking at a picture-book. Seeing us, they leapt up and ran off, and immediately afterwards a tall, thin, bespectacled old woman curtsyed solemnly to me, picked up a cushion from the couch and the picture-book from the floor and went out. An incessant whispering and scuffling of bare feet came from the adjoining room.

'I'm expecting the doctor for lunch today,' Bragin said. 'He promised to come straight from surgery. Yes. Every Wednesday he comes for lunch, God grant him good health!' He leant over and kissed me on the neck. 'So, you've come, my dear chap, that means you can't be angry,' he whispered, wheezing. 'No, don't be angry. I ask only one thing of God before I die, that's to live decently, in peace and harmony with everyone.'

'You don't mind if I put my feet up?' I said, feeling so terribly tired I couldn't be my usual self. I settled back on the couch and put my feet up on an armchair. After the snow and wind my face was burning and my whole body seemed to be soaking in warmth, and this had an enervating effect.

'It's very nice here,' I went on, 'so warm, soft, cosy ... And there are goose quills,' I laughed, glancing at the writing-table. '*And a sand-box ...*'

'What? Oh, yes, yes ... The writing-table and this little mahogany cupboard were made for my father by Gleb Butyga, a self-taught cabinet-maker, one of General Zhukov's serfs. Yes ... A real craftsman in his field.'

Languidly, in the voice of a man falling asleep, he began to tell me about Butyga the cabinet-maker and I listened. Then Bragin went into the next room to show me his astonishingly beautiful and inexpensive rosewood chest of drawers. He tapped it with one finger, then drew my attention to a tiled stove with designs one doesn't see anywhere these days. And he tapped that as well. The chest of drawers, the tiled stove, the armchairs, the pictures worked in wool and silk on canvas in their sturdy, ugly frames – all of this imparted an atmosphere of satiety and geniality. When one thinks that all these objects were still in exactly the same places, in exactly the same order, from the time I was a little boy and used to come to parties here with my mother, it becomes hard to believe that they could ever cease to exist.

I wondered at the enormous difference between Butyga and myself. Butyga, for whom solidity and durability came before anything else, regarded human longevity as particularly important and never gave a thought to death – probably hardly thought it possible. On the other hand, while I had built iron and stone bridges that would last for thousands of years, I could not help thinking, 'They won't last long. What's the point of them? If some intelligent art historian happened to come across Butyga's cupboard and my bridge, in the passage of time, he would say, "These two men were remarkable, each in his own way. Butyga loved people and would never acknowledge that they could die and decompose, and this explains why he always had an immortal man in mind when he made his furniture. But Asorin the engineer loved neither people nor life. Even in happy moments of creativity the thought of death, dissolution and the finite did not repel him. So take a look and you'll see how insignificant, limited, tentative and pathetic those lines are ..."'

'I keep only these rooms heated,' Bragin muttered as he showed me over the place. 'Since the wife died and my son was killed in the war, I've kept the main rooms locked. Yes ... as you see ...'

He unlocked one door and I saw a large room with four columns, an old piano, and a heap of peas on the floor. It smelt cold and musty.

'There are some garden benches in the next room ...' Bragin said. 'We've no one to dance the mazurka here any more, so I keep it locked.'

We heard a noise: it was Dr Sable arriving. As he rubbed his hands from the cold and smoothed his wet beard I managed to see that, firstly, he was bored with life and therefore pleased to see me and Bragin; and secondly, what a simple-minded, naive man he was. He looked at me as if I were absolutely delighted and fascinated to see him.

'Haven't slept for two nights,' he said, looking at me ingenuously and combing his beard. 'Spent the first with a woman in labour, the other at a peasant's where the bedbugs bit me all night long. I could damned well do with some sleep!'

Convinced, by all appearances, that his presence could not fail to bring me the purest pleasure, he took me by the arm and led me into the drawing-room. His naive eyes, his crumpled frock-coat, his cheap tie and the smell of iodoform produced an unpleasant impression. I felt I was lowering myself by associating with him. When we sat at the table he poured me some vodka which I drank with a helpless smile. Then he put a slice of ham on my plate and, obediently, I ate it.

'Repetitio est mater studiorum,' Sable said, hurriedly draining a second glass. 'You know, the sheer joy of seeing nice people has woken me up. I've become a peasant, a country oaf, I'm just like a savage living out here in the wilds. But for all that I'm still an educated man and, I'm telling you, quite honestly it's miserable without friends around me!'

For the cold dish, white sucking-pig with horse-radish and sour cream was served; then a rich, boiling-hot cabbage soup with pork and buckwheat gruel, from which the steam rose in a column. The doctor carried on talking and I was soon convinced that here was a feeble, disorganized, unhappy man. Three glasses went to his head and he grew unnaturally lively, grunting and smacking his lips as he crammed himself with food. Now he honoured me Italian style, dubbing me *Eccelenza*. Evidently convinced (I could tell from the way he innocently looked at me) that I must be absolutely delighted to see and listen to him, he told me he had long been separated from his wife, that he allowed her three quarters of his salary, that she was living in town with his children – a boy and a girl whom he adored – and that he was in love with another woman, a lady of culture and a landowner's widow. But he rarely visited her, since he was busy from morning till night and had no time at all to spare.

'The whole day I'm either at the hospital or doing my rounds,' he told me, 'and on my word of honour, *Eccelenza*, not only do I never have the time to call on the woman I love, I never even get round to reading a book. I haven't read anything for ten years! Ten years, *Eccelenza*! As for my material needs, just ask Bragin. Sometimes I don't even have enough money to buy any tobacco.'

'But there's your moral satisfaction,' I said.

'What?' he asked, screwing up one eye. 'Come on, let's have a good drink.'

I listened to the doctor and, as was my habit, I applied my usual criteria to him – materialist, idealist, money, herd instinct, etc. But not one yardstick was anywhere near the mark. And the strange thing was, if I just listened and looked at him I could understand him perfectly, but as soon as I tried to categorize him he became extraordinarily complex, involved, inscrutable – for all his candour and frankness. Could this man, I asked myself, be capable of embezzlement, of abusing confidence, of being a sponger? The question that once had seemed so serious and significant, now struck me as naive, petty and crude.

Pie was served and then (with long intervals for imbibing fruit liqueurs) we had pigeon stew, a kind of fried giblets, roast sucking-pig, duck, partridge, cauliflower, fruit dumplings, curds and whey, jelly – and pancakes and jam to round it all off. At first I ate with great appetite – especially the cabbage soup and gruel – but then I chewed and swallowed like a machine, smiling helplessly and tasting nothing. The boiling soup and heat of the room made my face burn. Bragin and Sable were red-faced as well.

'To your wife's health!' Sable said. 'She likes me. Tell her that her "physician-in-ordinary" sends his regards.'

'Heavens, she's a capable woman,' Bragin sighed. 'Without any fuss, effort or worry she's made herself the leading light in the district, running practically everything and everyone's buzzing round her – the doctor, magistrates and the ladies. If you're the right kind of person, you can do those things without even trying. Oh yes ... Apple trees don't have to worry about the apples growing, they just do.'

'People who are indifferent to others don't have worries,' I said.

'What? Oh, yes, yes,' Bragin muttered, not quite catching what I said. 'That's true. One should be indifferent. Well, that's precisely it. Do the right thing in the eyes of the Lord and your fellow human beings and all the rest can go to hell.'

'*Eccelenza,*' Sable said solemnly. 'Just look at nature all around us. If you stick your nose or ear outside your collar, the frost will nip them off. Stay just one hour in the fields and you'll be buried by snow. The countryside hasn't changed since the Middle Ages, it hasn't changed one bit. There's still the same barbarians and savages roaming around. All we have now is fires, famine, and a battle against nature on all fronts. Now, what was I on about? Oh, yes. If you put your thinking-cap on and try to make head or tail of all this shambles, if you'll pardon the expression, it's no life at all. A theatre fire, rather! Whoever falls down or cries out in panic or rushes around is the worst enemy of good order. So be sure to stand up straight, be on your guard and don't turn a hair. There's no time for snivelling and messing about with trivialities. If you're fighting the elements, then combat them with other elements. Be firm and unyielding as a rock.'

He turned to Bragin, laughed and said, 'Isn't that right, Grandpa? I'm like an old woman, a wet rag, a bellyacher, and I don't like bellyaching! I can't stand petty emotions! One man grouses, another's a coward, another will pop in here right now and tell you, "Hey, you! Stuffed yourself with a ten-course meal – and you can talk about the starving!" It's so petty and stupid! Another will take *you* to task, *Eccelenza*, because you're rich. Forgive me, *Eccelenza*,' he continued in a loud voice, laying his hand over his heart, 'but giving our detective all that work, getting him to hunt your burglars day and night – that's a rotten thing to do, if I may say so! I've had a drop too much, that's why I'm telling you this. But do you see, it's pretty shabby of you!'

'Who asked him to trouble himself? I don't follow,' I said, getting up. Suddenly I felt intolerably ashamed and humiliated and I started walking round the table. 'Who asked him to exert himself? It wasn't me, damn him!'

'He arrested three men and let them go. They turned out to be the wrong ones.' Sable laughed. 'It's a sad state of affairs!'

'But *I* didn't ask him to go to any trouble,' I said, on the verge of weeping with annoyance. 'What's the point? What's the point of any of it? Well, let's suppose I was wrong and let's suppose I acted badly, why must people still try to put me even more in the wrong?'

'Well, well, well!' Sable said, trying to calm me down. 'Come on! I only said this because I've drunk too much. My tongue is my worst enemy. Well now,' he sighed, 'we've eaten, drunk liqueurs, now it's time to turn in.'

He got up from the table, kissed Bragin on the head and left the dining-room, staggering and replete. Bragin and myself sat smoking in silence.

'As for me, my dear chap, I never sleep after dinner,' Bragin said, 'but you go and lie down in the lounge, please!'

I accepted the invitation. Long broad sofas, firm and solid – Butyga the cabinet-maker's work – stood along the walls of that dimly lit, well-heated so-called 'sofa-room' or lounge. They were piled high with soft white bedding, probably made up by the old woman in spectacles. Without coat or boots, Sable was already sleeping on one of them, his face towards the back. Another sofa was waiting for me. I took off my coat and boots and, surrendering to fatigue, to the spirit of Butyga that reigned over that quiet lounge and to the gentle, friendly snores of Sable, I obediently lay down.

Right away I dreamt of my wife, her room, the stationmaster with his face full of loathing, the heaps of snow and the theatre fire ... I dreamt of those peasants who had stolen twenty sacks of rye from my barn ... 'Anyway, a good thing the detective let them go,' I said.

Awakened by the sound of my own voice, I looked for a moment in bewilderment at Sable's broad back, his waistcoat clasp and his thick heels, then I lay down again and fell asleep.

When I woke up for the second time it was dark. Sable was sleeping. Now I felt rested and wanted to go home without delay. I dressed and left the 'sofa-room'. Bragin was in his study, sitting quite still in an armchair and staring at some fixed object. Clearly he had been in this state of paralysis the whole time I had been asleep.

'Good!' I said, yawning. 'I feel as if I've woken up after Carnival Week. I shall come here more often from now on. Tell me, has my wife ever eaten here?'

'Ye-es,' Bragin muttered, making an effort to stir himself. 'Last Saturday she had lunch here. Yes ... she's very fond of me.'

After a pause I said, 'Bragin, you remember telling me that I have a rotten nature and that you find me hard going? Well, how can I change my character?'

'Don't really know, my dear chap ... I'm just a silly old dodderer. I can't advise you ... No ... But I told you that, because I'm very fond of you and your wife, and I was fond of your father too. Yes ... I'll soon be dead so why should I hold anything back or lie to you? So, as I say, I'm very fond of you but I don't respect you. No, I don't have any respect for you.' He turned towards me and whispered between gasps, 'It's impossible to respect you, dear fellow. To look at, you seem genuine enough. In appearance and bearing you're like President Carnot of France – I saw a picture of him in a magazine the other day. Yes ... You have a noble turn of speech, you're clever, you're highly placed, you've left us all way behind, but, my dear chap, you haven't got a soul ... There's no strength in it ... No.'

'In short, I'm a barbarian,' I laughed. 'But what about my wife? Tell me something about my wife. You know her better.'

I wanted to discuss my wife, but Sable came in and stopped us. 'I've had a sleep and a wash,' he said, giving me an innocent look. 'Just some tea with rum and I'll be off.'

VII

It was after seven in the evening. Besides Bragin, the peasant women, the old woman in spectacles, the little girls and the male peasant accompanied us from the hall to the front porch, showering us with incantations and sundry good wishes, while some people with lanterns were standing or wandering in the dark by the horses, telling our coachmen the best way to go and wishing us a good journey. The horses, sledge and people were all white.

'Where are all these people from?' I asked when my three-horse team and the doctor's pair were ambling out of the courtyard.

'They're all serfs of his,' Sable said. 'Emancipation hasn't reached here yet. Some of the old servants are just living out the rest of their lives, and there's various orphans as well who've nowhere to go. Some of them forced themselves on him and he can't budge them. He's a real queer fish!'

Once again we rode rapidly along, once more we heard drunken Nikanor's peculiar voice. The wind and inescapable snow everywhere drove into eyes, mouth, into every fold of one's fur coat.

'God, what a ride!' I thought as my sleigh-bells rang out with the doctor's, the wind whistled, the coachmen whooped. With all this mad din around me I recalled every detail of that strange wild day, unique in my life, and I felt as if I really had gone out of my mind or become a different person. It was as though I were already a stranger to the man I had been until yesterday.

The doctor rode behind and kept up a loud conversation with his coachman. At times he caught me up, drove alongside offering me cigarettes and asking for matches with the same naive assurance that all this must be giving me unbounded pleasure. After drawing level he suddenly stood right up in his sledge, waved his coat sleeves (which were almost twice as long as his arms) and shouted, 'Whip 'em, Vaska. Show those thousand-rouble horses your paces! Hey, my kittens!'

To the sound of Sable and Vaska's loud, mocking laughter, the doctor's kittens tore on ahead. My Nikanor took offence and held our horses back, but as soon as the doctor's sleigh-bells were out of earshot, he raised his elbows with a whoop and my team dashed off like mad in hot pursuit. We drove into some village. Lights and silhouettes of huts flashed by and someone shouted, 'Blast them devils!'

We must have galloped a mile and a half, but still that street stretched on and on, seemingly endless. When we drew level with the doctor and slowed down a little he asked for matches.

'How can anyone feed this street!' he said. 'And there's another five just like it, sir.' Then he shouted, 'Stop! Stop! Turn off at the pub! We must warm ourselves up and rest the horses.'

We stopped at the pub.

'In my "diocese" there are lots of villages like this,' the doctor said, opening the heavy door with its squeaking block and pulley and letting me go in first. 'Seems as if there's no end to these streets when you look at them in broad daylight and there are the side-streets too. All you can do is just scratch your head about it, that's all.'

We entered the 'lounge' bar, where there was a strong smell of tablecloths. When he saw us come in, a sleepy peasant in a waist-coat and with his shirt outside his trousers jumped up from a bench. Sable ordered beer, myself tea.

'It's hard to know what to do,' Sable said. 'Your wife has faith and I admire and respect her, but I'm no true believer. As long as we treat the common people as mere objects for charity – for orphanages or nursing-homes – we'll only be cheating, dodging the real issue and deceiving ourselves. Our dealings with them must be businesslike, with expediency, knowledge and fairness as our starting-points. All his life my Vaska worked as labourer for me. His crops have failed now, he's hungry and sick. If I pay him fifteen copecks a day now, that means I'm trying to turn him into the ordinary labourer he was before – that's to say, I'm putting my own interests first. And yet I can still call these fifteen copecks help, relief, good work. Look at it like this. If you reckon seven copecks a head and five to a family, then we need three hundred and fifty roubles a day to feed a thousand families, at the most modest estimate. Our basic business obligations towards a thousand families are deter-mined by this figure. For all that, we don't give them three hundred and fifty roubles a day, only ten, and we call this assistance, relief. And because of this we think your wife and all of us are exceptionally

nice people – and hats off to philanthropy! So that's it, old chap!
Oh, if only we didn't talk about philanthropy and did more cal-
culating and reasoning, if only we took our responsibilities more
conscientiously! Just consider how many humane, sensitive people
there are among us who in all sincerity go running around farms
with subscription lists, but who don't pay their tailors or cooks!
There's no logic in our lives, that's what! Just no logic!'

We fell silent for a moment. I made a mental calculation and
said, 'I'll provide food for a thousand families for two hundred days.
Come and have a talk about it tomorrow.'

I was pleased at having expressed myself so simply, and glad that
Sable gave me an even simpler reply: 'Agreed.'

We paid the bill and left.

'I like these muddles,' Sable said as he climbed into his sledge.
'*Eccelenza*, give me a match, I've left mine at the pub.'

An hour later his pair had lagged behind and no longer could
I hear his sleigh-bells through the roar of the blizzard. When I
arrived home I paced up and down my rooms trying to assess my
position and obtain as clear a picture of it as possible. I hadn't prepared
one word or sentence for my wife. My brain was not functioning.
Failing to think of anything, I went downstairs to my wife. She
was standing in her room, in that same pink housecoat, in the same
pose, as though shielding her papers from me. Her face expressed
bewilderment and scorn. Obviously, she had found out about my
return and was prepared not to cry, not to ask for anything or
defend herself as she had done the day before, but to laugh at me
instead, give me contemptuous answers and to act decisively. Her
face seemed to be saying, 'If that's what you want, then good-bye.'

'Natalie, I didn't go away,' I said, 'but it's no deception on my
part. I've gone out of my mind, I've grown old, I'm sick, I've become
another man. All right, think what you like ... I've recoiled with
horror from my former self, with horror, and I despise it and I'm
ashamed of it. But the new man inside me since yesterday won't
let me leave. Don't drive me away, Natalie!'

She stared into my face, believed what I said and the anxiety
shone in her eyes. Enchanted by her presence, warmed by the heat
of her room I held out my hand and muttered deliriously, 'I'm telling

you, there's no one near and dear to me besides you. I missed you every minute of the day and only my pigheaded vanity has prevented me from admitting it. We cannot bring back the past, when we lived as man and wife, and there's no need even to try. But make me your servant, take all my property and give it to whoever you like. I'm not worried, Natalie, I'm content . . . I'm not worried.'

My wife stared me inquisitively in the face, then suddenly she gave a faint cry, burst into tears and ran into the next room. I went upstairs.

An hour later I was at my table writing my 'History of Railways' and the famine victims didn't interfere with my work. I don't feel worried any more. Those ugly scenes I saw when recently making a tour of the huts in Pyostrovo with my wife and Sable, the vicious rumours, the mistakes of those around me, my approaching old age – none of this worries me. In the same way that in war, flying shells and bullets don't stop soldiers from talking about their affairs, from eating, and mending their boots, so the starving don't stop me sleeping peacefully and getting on with my own business. Work is in full swing in my house, in the yard, and far and wide – Dr Sable calls it an 'orgy of charity'. My wife often comes and sees me, casting a worried look over my rooms as though searching for something else to give to the starving, so that she can find 'justification for her existence'. And I can see that, thanks to her, we'll soon have nothing left and we'll be poor. But it doesn't bother me and I smile cheerfully at her. What's going to come of all this, I just don't know.

Murder

I

They were celebrating vespers at Progonnaya Station. A crowd of railwaymen, their wives and children, with some woodcutters and sawyers working nearby along the line, were standing before the great icon brightly painted on a gold background. All of them stood in silence, spellbound by the glittering light and the howling blizzard which had blown up all of a sudden, although it was the eve of Annunciation Day. The old priest from Vedenyapino was officiating and the singers were the precentor, and Matvey Terekhov.

Matvey's face glowed with joy; and as he sang he craned his neck, as though he wanted to fly up into the sky. He sang tenor and read the canon in the same sweet, persuasive tenor voice. While they were singing 'Song of Archangels' he waved his hand like a choirmaster and produced some extremely complicated sounds in his effort to harmonize with the old layreader's hollow bass. One could see from his face that he was thoroughly enjoying himself. But then the service ended, the congregation quietly left, the place became dark and empty again, and that silence descended which is found only at lonely stations in the open country or in forests when nothing can be heard except the moaning of the wind, all one feels is emptiness all around and the wretchedness of life slowly slipping by.

Matvey lived near the station, at his cousin's inn. But he did not feel like going home and sat at the counter in the refreshment-room talking in a low voice. 'We had our own choir at the tile-works. And I must say, although we were just simple workmen, we were great singers. It was marvellous. We were often invited into town and when Ivan the suffragan bishop took the service at Trinity Church the cathedral choir sang in the right-hand stalls, while we were on the left. But people in the town complained we sang too long and said that lot from the tile-works were dragging things out.

They were right, St Andrew's Vigil and the Te Deum began before seven and didn't finish till after ten, so very often it was gone midnight before we were back at the works.'

Matvey sighed. 'Really marvellous it was, Sergey, really marvellous. But I don't get much joy living here in the old house. The nearest church is three miles away, I can't manage that in my state of health and there's no choir. And you can't get a moment's peace with our family, just one long racket all day, with swearing, filth, everyone eating from the same bowl like peasants, and cockroaches in the soup. If God had blessed me with good health I'd have cleared off ages ago, Sergey.'

Matvey Terekhov was not old – about forty-five – but he had an unhealthy look. His face was covered in wrinkles and his thin, weedy beard was already completely white, which made him seem a lot older. He spoke cautiously, in a feeble voice, clasped his chest when he coughed – then he had the uneasy, worried look of a true hypochondriac. He would never say what exactly was wrong, but he loved telling a long story about straining himself lifting a heavy box once at the tile-works, giving himself a 'rumpture', as he put it, which forced him to leave his job there and go back home. But what a 'rumpture' was, he could not explain.

'I must say, I don't like that cousin of mine,' he continued, pouring himself some tea. 'He's older than me, it's wrong to say things against him, and I'm a God-fearing man. But I just can't stand him. He's a proud, stern man, always swearing and tormenting the life out of his relatives and workmen, and he doesn't go to confession. Last Sunday I asked him, all nice and friendly, "Let's go to the service at Pakhomo, cousin," and he replies: "Not me, the priest there plays cards." And he didn't come here today either, he says the priest at Vedenyapino smokes and drinks vodka. He just hates the clergy! He says his own offices, and matins, and vespers, and his sister's his lay reader. While he's saying his "We beseech Thee, oh Lord", she's screeching away like a turkey-hen with her "Lord have mercy". Right sinful, that's what it is. Every day I tell him, "Come to your senses, Cousin Yakov! Repent, Cousin!", but he just ignores me.'

Sergey the buffet-attendant poured out five glasses of tea and carried them to the ladies' waiting-room on a tray. A moment later they could hear someone shouting, 'Is that the way to serve tea, you pig? You don't know your job!' It was the stationmaster. A timid muttering followed, then more shouting, angry and brusque: 'Clear off!'

The buffet-attendant returned looking very put out. 'Time was when I waited on counts and princes,' he said softly, 'but now I don't know how to serve tea, do you see? Swearing at me in front of a priest and ladies!'

Sergey the buffet-attendant once had money and managed the refreshment-room at a main-line junction in a county town. In those days he used to wear coat and tails, and a gold watch. But then he fell on bad times, all his money wasted on fancy equipment and his staff robbing him. Gradually sinking deeper and deeper into debt, he moved to a station that was not so busy. There his wife ran off with all the silver. He moved to a third station, which was even worse – they did not serve hot meals there. Then he went to a fourth. After numerous moves, sinking lower and lower the whole time, he finally ended up at Progonnaya, where he only sold tea and cheap vodka, and where the only food he served was hard-boiled eggs and tough sausage that smelt of tar: he himself thought it was a joke, calling it 'bandsmen's food'. He was completely bald on top, had bulging blue eyes and thick, fluffy whiskers which he was always combing, peering at himself in a small hand-mirror. He was perpetually tormented by memories and just could not get used to 'bandsmen's sausage', to the stationmaster's insults and the haggling peasants – in his opinion haggling was just as improper in a station refreshment-room as in a chemist's. He was ashamed of being so poverty-stricken and degraded, and this feeling of shame was his chief worry in life.

'Spring's late this year,' Matvey said, listening hard. 'And it's a good thing. I don't like the spring, it's very muddy, Sergey. In books they write about the spring, birds singing and the sun setting, but what's so nice about it? A bird's a bird, that's all. I like good company, so I can hear what people have to say, I like chatting about religion or singing something nice in the choir. But I've no time for all them nightingales and nice little flowers!'

He went on again about the tile-works and the choir, but Sergey was deeply offended, would not calm down and kept shrugging his shoulders and muttering. Matvey said good night and went home.

It was not freezing – it was thawing on the roofs – yet it was snowing hard. The snow swiftly whirled through the air and white clouds chased each other along the railway track. Dimly lit by a moon that lay hidden high up in the clouds, the oak-grove lining both sides of the track kept up a constant roar. How terrifying trees can be when they are shaken by a violent storm! Matvey walked along the road by the track, covering his face and hands. The wind shoved him in the back. Suddenly he caught sight of a small, wretched-looking horse, plastered with snow; a sledge scraped the bare cobbles of the road and a peasant, his muffled head as white as his horse, cracked a whip. Matvey looked round, but the sledge and peasant had already vanished as if in a dream, and he quickened his pace, suddenly feeling scared – of what, he did not know.

He reached the level crossing and the dark hut where the keeper lived. The barrier was raised and all around were massive snowdrifts and clouds of snow whirling like witches at a sabbath. The track was crossed here by an old road, once a main trunk route and still called the highway. On the right, just by the level crossing and on the road, was Terekhov's inn, an old coaching-house. A small light always glimmered there at night.

When Matvey arrived home the whole house, even the hall, smelled strongly of incense. Cousin Yakov was still celebrating vespers. In the corner of the 'chapel' where the service was being held, facing the door, stood an icon-case filled with old-fashioned family icons, all in gilt, and both walls to right and left were covered with icons in the old and new style, some in cases, some without. On the table, draped with a cloth that touched the floor, was an icon of the Annunciation, as well as a cross made from cypress-wood, and a censer. Candles were burning. Near the table stood a lectern. As he passed the chapel, Matvey stopped to look through the door. Yakov was reading at the lectern and worshipping with him was Yakov's sister Aglaya, a tall, skinny old woman in a dark blue dress and white kerchief. Yakov's daughter Dashutka was there as well – she was an ugly girl of about eighteen, covered in freckles. As usual, she was barefoot and wearing the dress in which she watered the cattle in the evenings.

'Glory to Thee who has shown us the light!' chanted Yakov as he bowed low.

Aglaya propped her chin on her hand and, without hurrying, sang in a thin, shrill voice. From the room above came vague voices: they sounded sinister and seemed to be issuing threats. After the fire of long ago no one had lived on the upper storey; the windows were boarded up and empty bottles were scattered about on the floor between the wooden beams. The wind banged and howled up there and it sounded as though someone was running around and stumbling over the beams.

Half of the ground floor was taken up by the inn and the Terekhovs lived in the other, so when drunken visitors called at the inn they could hear every word from their living-room. Matvey lived next to the kitchen in a room with a large stove, where they had baked the bread every day when the coaching-inn had been there. Dashutka, without her own room, had her little space here, behind the stove. At night a cricket was always chirping and mice scurried about.

Matvey lit a candle and started reading a book he had borrowed from the railway policeman. While he sat reading, the prayers finished and everyone went to bed, Dashutka included. She immediately started snoring but soon woke up and said, yawning, 'Uncle Matvey, you shouldn't waste candles.'

'It's my own,' Matvey replied. 'I bought it myself.'

Dashutka tossed and turned for a while, then fell asleep again. Matvey stayed up for a long time, as he did not feel sleepy, and when he had finished the last page he took a pencil from a trunk and wrote in the book: 'I, Matvey Terekhov, have read this book and I find it the best of all those read by me, in which I hereby impress me grettitude to Kuzma Zhukov, senior officer of the railway police, owner of the aforesaid priceless book.'

He considered it only polite to make inscriptions in other people's books.

II

When Annunciation Day arrived, after they had seen the mail train off, Matvey sat in the refreshment-room drinking tea with lemon, and talking. The buffet-attendant and Constable Zhukov were listening.

'Let me tell you,' Matvey was saying, 'even when I was a nipper I was all for relidgun. When I was only twelve I was already reading the Acts and the Epistles in church and this was a great comfort to my parents. And every summer I used to go on a pilgrimage with Mother, God rest her soul. Other boys used to sing songs or go after crayfish, but I stayed with Mother. The older folk thought well of me and I was pleased, because I was such a well-behaved boy. And after I'd gone off to the tile-works with Mother's blessing I'd sing tenor in our choir, in my spare time, never enjoyed anything so much. Of course, I didn't touch vodka, or smoke, and I kept myself clean. As you know, the Devil don't like that way of life and took it into his head to ruin me and he began to cloud my mind, just as he's doing to Cousin Yakov. The first thing I did was vow to fast on Mondays and not to eat meat on any day, and it wasn't long before I went a bit soft in the head. The Holy Fathers say you must have cold dry food in the first week in Lent, up to the Saturday, but it's no sin for the weak or them that toil to have a cup of tea even. Not a crumb passed my lips until the Sunday. And the whole of Lent I didn't take a scrap of butter, and on Wednesdays and Fridays I didn't eat anything at all. It was the same during the minor fasts. At St Peter's Fast my mates at the works had their fish soup, but I would just suck a dry biscuit. Some folk are stronger than others, of course, but I didn't find it too hard on fast days, and in fact the harder you try, the easier it is. You only get hungry during the first few days, but then you take it in your stride, it gets easier and easier and by the end of the week it's not hard at all and all you have is that numb feeling in your legs, as though you were walking on clouds. And what's more, I imposed all sorts of penances on myself – I'd get up at night and prostrate myself, drag heavy stones around and walk barefoot in the snow. And I'd wear irons.

'But a little later, when I was at confession, the idea suddenly dawned on me: that priest's married, he doesn't keep the fasts and he smokes. Then why should he hear me confess, what authority did he have to pardon my sins, with him more of a sinner than me? I even kept away from vegetable oil, but he'd have his sturgeon all right, I dare say. I went to another priest, but as luck would have it I landed myself with a real fatty in a silk cassock that rustled like a lady's dress – and he smelt of tobacco too. I went to a monastery to prepare for communion, but I was ill at ease there too, it struck me the monks didn't keep to their rules. After that I couldn't find any kind of church service to my liking. In one place they rushed it or sang the wrong hymns, in another the lay reader spoke through his nose. And there was once a time – God forgive me, sinner that I am – when I'd stand in the church seething with rage, and that's no way to pray. And it seemed to me that the congregation weren't crossing themselves properly or listening right. Whoever I looked at seemed to be a drunkard, fast-breaker, smoker, fornicator, card-player. Only *I* kept the Commandments. The Devil didn't sleep and things got even worse. I didn't sing in the choir any more and didn't go to church. I didn't think the church was good enough for a godly man like me. I was a fallen angel, swollen-headed beyond belief. Then I tried to start my own church. I rented a poky little room from a deaf woman a long way out of town, by the cemetery, and I set up a chapel – like my cousin's, but I had proper candlesticks and a real censer. In this chapel I abided by the rules of Mount Athos, that's to say, matins always began at midnight, and on the eve of the twelve great festivals vespers went on for ten, sometimes twelve hours even. According to their rules monks could sit while the Psalms and Parables were read, but I wanted to go one better, so I stood up the whole time. I wept and sighed as I read and sang, dragging everything out and lifting my arms up. And I went straight from prayers to work, without any sleep, and I'd still be praying while I worked.

'Well now, people in town started saying, "Matvey's a saint, Matvey heals the sick and insane." Of course, I never healed anyone, but everyone knows when you have any kind of schisms or heresy you just can't keep the women away, they're like flies round a jam-pot. Some women and old maids started calling on me, threw themselves at my feet, kissed my hand and shouted that I was a saint and so on. One of them even saw a halo round my head. It grew cramped in my chapel, so I took a larger room and it was absolute bedlam! The Devil really had his claws into me and his accursed hooves blotted the true light from my eyes. And we all seemed possessed by the Devil. I'd read, and the old girls and maids would sing. After going without food or drink for long periods, after being on their feet for twenty-four hours or more they'd suddenly get the shakes, as if they'd caught a fever. Then one would cry out, then another – it was terrifying! And I was shaking all over too, like a cat on hot bricks and I didn't know why. There we were, all jumping about! It's very odd, I must say, when you are jumping away and swinging your arms, and you can't stop yourself. After this there was shouting and screaming, and we all danced and kept chasing each other till we dropped. This was how, in one of these frenzied fits, I became a fornicator.'

The policeman burst out laughing, but became serious when he saw no one else was.

'It's like the Molokans,' he said. 'I've read they're all that way inclined in the Caucasus.'

'But I was not struck by lightning,' Matvey went on, crossing himself before the icon and moving his lips. 'My mother must have prayed in heaven for me. When everyone in town thought me a saint and even fine ladies and gents started visiting me on the sly for comfort, I chanced to go and see the boss, Mr Osip, to ask him to forgive me, as it was Forgiveness Day. Well, he put the latch on the door and there we were, the two of us face to face. He gave me a real ticking-off. I should mention that Mr Osip's got no education, but he's no fool and everyone feared and respected him, because he led a strict and holy life and was a real hard worker. He'd been mayor and churchwarden for twenty years, I think, and he did a lot of good. He laid gravel on the New Moscow Road and had the church painted – the pillars were done up to look like malkalite.

'So he shuts the door. "I've been after you for a long time, you damned so-and-so," he says. "Think you're a saint, do you? No, you're no saint, but an apostate, a heretic and a scoundrel!" On and on he went, can't say it the way he did, all smooth and clever like in books, enough to make you weep, it was. He carried on for two hours. His words struck home and my eyes were opened. I listened and listened – and I just sobbed my heart out! And he said, "Be like normal men, eat, drink, dress and pray like everyone else. Doing more than you ought is the work of the Devil. Those irons of yours are the Devil's, your fasts are from the Devil and your chapel's a Devil's chapel. It's all pride."

'Next day – the first Monday in Lent – God willed me to fall ill. I'd strained myself and was taken to hospital. I suffered something cruel I did, wept bitter tears and trembled. I thought I'd go straight from hospital to hell, and it nearly finished me off. About six months I lay suffering in bed and when they let me out the first thing I did was take proper communion and I became a human being again.

'Mr Osip let me go home. "Now don't forget, Matvey," he ordered, "doing more than you should is the Devil's work." So now I eat and drink and pray like everyone else. If I meet an old priest who smells of tobacco or spirits I daren't condemn him, as priests are normal human beings too. But the moment I hear some holy man's set himself up in the town or country and doesn't eat for weeks, keeping to his own rules, then I know for sure who's at the bottom of it all. Well, my dear sirs, all that happened to me once. And now I'm just like Mr Osip, I order my cousin and his sister around, I reproach them, but mine is a voice crying in the wilderness. God didn't grant me the gift.'

Matvey's story evidently made no impression at all. Sergey said nothing and began clearing food from the counter, while the police constable observed how rich Matvey's cousin Yakov was: 'He's worth at least thirty thousand.'

Constable Zhukov was red-haired, full-faced (his cheeks quivered as he walked), healthy and well-fed. When his superiors weren't around he usually sprawled in his chair, his legs crossed. He would rock to and fro as he spoke, nonchalantly whistling, with a smug, sated expression as if he had just had dinner. He had plenty of money and always spoke of it as if he were an expert on the subject. He was a commission agent and whenever people had an estate, a horse or a second-hand carriage to sell they would come to him.

'Yes, he could be worth thirty thousand,' Sergey agreed. 'Your grandpa had a large fortune,' he added, turning to Matvey. 'Really enormous! Then everything went to your father and uncle. Your father died young and your uncle got the lot, and then Yakov of course. While you were going round churches and monasteries with your mother and singing in the factory choir, there were some here who weren't standing idle.'

'Your share's about fifteen thousand,' the policeman said, rocking in his chair. 'The inn's jointly owned by you, so's the capital. Yes. If I'd been in your shoes I'd have sued them long ago. Of course, I'd have taken him to court, but while it was being sorted out I'd have got him to one side and given him a right good bash in the mug.'

Yakov was not liked, because people with queer beliefs tend to upset others, even those who are indifferent to religion. And in any case the policeman did not like him, as he too dealt in horses and second-hand carriages.

'You won't sue your cousin because you've plenty of money of your own,' the buffet-attendant told Matvey, giving him an envious look. 'It's all right for those what has means, but I'll probably be stuck here in this job until I die.'

Matvey tried to assure them that he had no money at all, but Sergey was not listening any more. Memories of his past life, of the daily insults he had suffered, came flooding over him. His bald head sweated, he went red in the face and blinked.

'Oh, this damned life!' he exclaimed, deeply annoyed, and threw a piece of sausage on the floor.

III

The coaching-inn was said to have been built back in Alexander I's reign by a widow, Avdotya Terekhov, who had settled there with her son. Travellers passing in mail coaches, especially on moonlit nights, would feel depressed and strangely uneasy at the sight of that dark yard with its lean-to shed and perpetually locked gates.

It was as if the place were the haunt of sorcerers or robbers. Drivers would look back and urge on their horses every time they went past. People never liked staying overnight there, as the innkeepers were always unfriendly and charged exorbitant prices. The yard was muddy even in summer and huge fat pigs wallowed in the muck; horses – the Terekhovs were dealers – wandered around loose, often becoming restive; then they would race out of the yard and tear like mad down the road, frightening women pilgrims. In those days there was a lot of traffic. Long trains of loaded wagons would pass through and there were incidents, like the one about thirty years ago for example, when some angry wagoners had lost their tempers, started a fight and murdered a passing merchant. A crooked cross still stands about a quarter of a mile from the inn. Mail troikas with bells and landowners' heavy *dormeuses* would drive by, and herds of bellowing cattle passed in clouds of dust.

When they first built the railway, there had been only a halt here, simply called a passing-point. Then about ten years later the present Progonnaya Station was built. The traffic along the old post-road almost vanished; now it was used only by local landowners and peasants, and in spring and autumn gangs of workmen crowded along it on foot. The coaching-inn became just an ordinary tavern. The top floor was damaged by fire, the roof went yellow with rust, the lean-to shed gradually collapsed, but enormous fat pigs – pink and revolting – still wallowed in the mud in the yard. As before, horses would sometimes tear out of the yard and race furiously down the road with tails streaming. At the inn they sold tea, hay, oats, flour, as well as vodka or beer for consumption on or off the premises. They were a little tight-lipped about the alcohol they sold, however, since they had never been licensed.

The Terekhovs had always been renowned for their piety and had even earned the nickname 'Pillars of the Faith'. But perhaps because they lived like bears, keeping to themselves, avoiding company and thinking out things for themselves, they were prone to wild dreaming, religious wavering, and almost every generation had its own approach to religion and matters of faith.

Grandma Avdotya, who had built the coaching-inn, was an Old Believer, but her son and two grandsons (Matvey and Yakov's fathers) worshipped at the Orthodox Church, entertained the clergy and prayed to the new icons just as reverently as to the old. In his old age her son gave up meat and took a vow of silence, considering any kind of talk at all a sin, while the grandsons were odd in not taking the Scriptures at their face value – they were always seeking some hidden meaning, maintaining that every holy word must hold some secret. Avdotya's great-grandson Matvey had struggled against lack of faith since he was a young boy and this was very nearly his undoing. Yakov, the other great-grandson, was Orthodox, but he suddenly stopped going to church when his wife died, and worshipped at home. Aglaya followed his bad example, stayed away from church and did not let Dashutka go either. It was said that when Aglaya was a young girl she used to go to Flagellant meetings at Vedenyapino and that she was still a secret member of the sect, which was why she went around in a white kerchief.

Yakov Terekhov was ten years older than Matvey. He was a handsome old man, tall, with a broad grey beard that nearly reached his waist and bushy eyebrows that lent his face a grim, even malevolent expression. He wore a long coat of good cloth, or a black sheepskin jacket and always tried to dress neatly and decently. Even in fine weather he wore galoshes. He stayed away from church because, in his opinion, they did not observe the rites properly and because the priests drank wine at the wrong times and smoked. Every day he read and sang the service at home with Aglaya. During matins at Vedenyapino they did not read the canon, omitted vespers – even on high holidays – whereas he read through the prescribed portion at home, not hurrying or leaving out one line. In his spare time he would read aloud from the lives of the saints. And in his everyday life he stuck close to the rules. For example, if wine was permitted on a certain day during Lent 'because of the long vigil', he would invariably have a drink, even if he did not feel like one.

He did not read, sing or burn incense in the hope that God might shower his blessings down on him, but for form's sake. Man cannot live without faith, and faith must be correctly expressed, from year to year and from day to day according to established formulae which laid down that man should address God each morning and evening with the exact words and thoughts appropriate to that particular day or hour. His life, and therefore his method of prayer, must be pleasing to God and so he should read and sing each day only what pleased God, that is, what was laid down by Church law. Therefore the first chapter of St John should be read only on Easter Sunday, and from Easter Sunday till Ascension Day certain hymns must not be sung. Awareness of this procedure and its importance gave Yakov Terekhov great pleasure during hours of prayer. When he was forced to depart from his routine – having to fetch goods from town or go to the bank – then his conscience tormented him and this made him feel wretched.

When Cousin Matvey unexpectedly arrived from the tile-works, making the inn his home, he started breaking the rules right from the start. He did not wish to pray with the others, had his meals and tea at the wrong times, got up late and drank milk on Wednesdays and Fridays because of his poor health. Almost every day, at prayer-time, he would go into the chapel and shout: 'Listen to reason, Cousin! Repent, Cousin!' This would make Yakov see red and Aglaya lose her temper and start swearing. Or Matvey would sneak into the chapel at night and softly say: 'Cousin, your prayer is not pleasing to the Lord, as it is said, "First make peace with thy brother and then bring thy gifts." But you're nothing but a money-lender and a vodka trader. Repent!'

In Matvey's words Yakov could see only the usual lame excuse made by empty, sloppy people who always talk about 'love thy neighbour', 'be reconciled with thy brother' and the rest of it just to avoid fasting, praying and reading sacred books, and who turn their noses up at profit and interest because they don't like hard work. Indeed, it's far easier being poor, not to save up – much easier than being rich.

For all this, he felt worried and could not worship as he used to. No sooner did he enter the chapel and open his book than he began to feel apprehensive – any moment his cousin might come in and interrupt him. And in fact Matvey would soon appear and shout in a trembling voice, 'Come to your senses, Cousin! Repent, Cousin!' His sister would start cursing and Yakov would lose his temper and shout, 'Clear out of my house!'

Matvey told him, 'This house belongs to all of us.'

Yakov would return to his reading and singing but was never able to calm himself and he would suddenly start day-dreaming over his book without even noticing it. Although he thought his cousin's words were nonsense, why had *he* recently taken to thinking that it was hard for the rich to enter the Kingdom of Heaven, that he had done very nicely out of that stolen horse he had bought two years ago, that a drunk had died at the inn from too much vodka, in his wife's lifetime? ...

Now he slept very badly, lightly at night and he heard Matvey, who could not sleep either, sighing as he pined for his tile-works. And as he tossed and turned Yakov recalled that stolen horse, the drunkard, what the Gospels said about camels.

He was beginning to have doubts again, it seemed. And although it was already the end of March, it snowed every day, as if on purpose; the forest roared as though it were winter and it seemed impossible that spring would ever come. This kind of weather made everyone bored, quarrelsome and hateful, and when the wind howled above the ceiling at night it seemed someone was living up there in the empty storey. And then doubts gradually flooded his mind, his head burnt and he did not want to sleep.

IV

On the morning of the Monday in Passion Week, Matvey was in his room and could hear Dashutka saying to Aglaya, 'A few days ago Uncle Matvey was telling me I don't need to fast.'

Matvey remembered the whole conversation he'd had with Dashutka the previous day and suddenly felt insulted.

'That's a sinful way to speak, girl,' he said in the moaning voice of a sick man. 'There has to be fasting. Our Lord Himself fasted forty days. I was just trying to tell you even fasting won't help the wicked.'

'Just hark at him with his tile-work sermons, trying to teach us to be good,' scoffed Aglaya as she washed the floor (she normally washed the floors on weekdays and lost her temper with everyone in the process). 'We know how they fast at the tile-works! Just ask that old uncle of yours about his little darling, how him and that filthy bitch guzzled milk in Lent. Likes preaching to others all right but forgets that slut quick enough. Ask him who he left the money with. Who?'

Matvey took pains to hide the fact, as though it were a festering sore, that when he'd been frisking about and making merry with those old women and young girls at prayer meetings he had had an affair with a woman from the town, who bore him a child. Before he went home he gave her everything he had saved up at the tile-works and borrowed the money for his fare from the boss. And now he had only a few roubles for tea and candles. Later on his 'darling' informed him that the baby had died, and wrote to ask what she should do with the money. The workman brought the letter from the station but Aglaya intercepted it and read it, and every day after that kept reproaching Matvey about his 'darling'.

'Mere chicken-feed, only nine hundred roubles!' Aglaya continued. 'Gave nine hundred to a stranger, that bitch, that factory tart! Damn you!' She flew off the handle and shrieked, 'Nothing to say for yourself then? I could tear you to pieces, you spineless wretch! Nine hundred roubles, like chicken-feed! You should have left it to Dashutka, she's your own flesh and blood. Or sent it to the poor orphans' home in Belyov. Why couldn't she choke, that cow of yours, blast her! Bloody bitch, damn her eyes! May she rot in hell!'

Yakov called her, as it was time to begin lauds. She washed, put on a white kerchief and now went quietly and meekly to her beloved brother in the chapel. When she spoke to Matvey or served tea to peasants at the inn she was a skinny, sharp-eyed old hag, but in chapel she looked pure and radiant. Making elaborate curtsies, coyly pursing her lips even, she looked so much younger.

As always during Lent, Yakov began to read the offices in a soft, mournful voice. After a little while he stopped to savour the calm that reigned over the whole house. Then he started reading again, deriving great pleasure from it. He clasped his hands as if to pray, turned his eyes up, shook his head and sighed.

Suddenly he heard some voices. Sergey and the policeman had come to visit Matvey. Yakov felt awkward reading out loud and singing with strangers in the house and now the sound of voices made him read slowly, in a whisper. In the chapel they could hear what the buffet-attendant was saying:

'The Tartar at Shchepovo is selling his business for fifteen hundred. He'll accept five hundred now and we can draw up a bill of exchange for the rest. So please, Matvey Terekhov, help me out and lend me the five hundred. I'll pay you two per cent a month interest.'

Matvey was staggered and said, 'But what money? What money have *I* got?'

'Two per cent a month would be a godsend for you,' the policeman explained. 'But if the money's left lying around here, it'll only be food for moths and that'll do you no good at all.'

The visitors left and silence fell. But Yakov had hardly returned to his reading and singing than a voice came through the door: 'Cousin, give me a horse, I want to go to Vedenyapino.'

It was Matvey. Yakov felt uneasy again. 'But which one?' he asked after a moment's thought. 'The workman's taking the bay to cart a pig and I'm off to Shuteykino on the stallion as soon as I'm finished here.'

'My dear cousin, why are you allowed to do what you want with the horses while I'm not?' Matvey asked angrily.

'Because I'm not going on a joyride, they're needed for a job.'

'The property belongs to all of us, that means horses as well. You must understand that, Cousin.'

Silence fell. Yakov did not go back to his devotions, but waited for Matvey to go away from the door.

'Cousin,' Matvey said, 'I'm a sick man, I don't want any part of the estate. You can keep it, I don't care, but just let me have enough to live on seeing as I'm so poorly. Give it to me and I'll go away.'

Yakov did not reply. He dearly wanted to be rid of Matvey, but he could not let him have any money, since it was all tied up in the business. Among the whole Terekhov clan there had never been a single case of cousins sharing – that meant going broke.

Yakov still said nothing, waiting for Matvey to leave and he kept looking at his sister, frightened she might interfere and start another quarrel like they'd had that morning. When Matvey had gone at last he went back to his reading, but he took no enjoyment in it. His head was heavy from all those prostrations, his eyes were dim and he found the sound of his own soft, mournful voice most monotonous. When he was depressed like this at night he ascribed it to lack of sleep, but during the day it scared him and he began to think devils were sitting on his head and shoulders.

After he somehow finished reading the offices he left for Shuteykino, feeling disgruntled and irritable. In the autumn, navvies had dug a boundary ditch near Progonnaya and run up a bill for eighteen roubles at the inn: now he had to catch their foreman in Shuteykino and get his money. The thaw and snowstorms had ruined the road. It was dark, full of potholes and already breaking up in places. The snow was lying lower than the road level, along the verges, so that it was like driving along a narrow embankment. Giving way to oncoming traffic was quite a job. The sky had been overcast since morning and a moist wind was blowing . . .

A long train of sledges was coming towards him – some women were carting bricks – so Yakov had to turn off the road. His horse sank up to its belly in the snow, his one-man sledge tilted to the right. He bent over to the left to stop himself falling off and sat that way while the sledge slowly moved past. Through the wind he could hear the sledges creaking, the skinny horses panting, and the women saying: 'There goes His Grace.' One of them looked pityingly at his horse and said quickly, 'Looks like the snow'll last until St George's Day. We're fair worn out!'

Yakov sat uncomfortably hunched, screwing up his eyes in the wind as horses and red bricks went by. Perhaps it was because he felt cramped and had a pain in his side that he suddenly began to feel annoyed; the purpose of his journey struck him as unimportant and he concluded that he could send his man to Shuteykino tomorrow. Once again, as on the last sleepless night, he recalled the words about the camel and then all sorts of memories came to mind – the peasant who sold him the stolen horse, the drunkard, the women who pawned their samovars with him. Of course, every trader was out for all he could get, but he was tired of it and wanted to go as far away as he could from that mode of life. The thought that he would have to read vespers that evening depressed him. The wind that lashed him right in the face and rustled in his collar seemed to be whispering all these thoughts to him, carrying them from the wide white fields ... As he looked at these fields he had known from childhood, Yakov remembered having had just the same feelings of apprehension, just the same worries as a young man, when he was assailed by serious doubts and his faith began to waver.

It was frightening being all alone in the open fields and he turned back and slowly followed the sledge train. The women laughed and said, 'His Grace's turned back.'

As it was Lent, no cooking was done at home and they did not use the samovar, which made the day seem very long. Yakov had long ago stabled the horse and sent flour to the station. Once or twice he had started reading the Psalms, but it was a long time till evening. Aglaya had already washed down the floors and for something to do was tidying her trunk. The inside of its lid had bottle labels stuck all over it. Hungry and depressed, Matvey sat reading or went over to the Dutch stove, where he stood a long time inspecting the tiles, which made him think of the works. Dashutka slept, but soon woke up again and went off to water the cattle. As she was drawing water from the well, the rope broke and the bucket fell into the water. The workman hunted around for a hook to haul it out with, and Dashutka followed him over the muddy snow, her bare feet as red as a goose's. She kept repeating, 'It's *dippy* there!' – she wanted to say the water in the well was too deep for the hook, but the man did not understand. Evidently she had got on his nerves as he suddenly turned round and swore at her. Yakov happened to come out into the yard just then and heard Dashutka quickly reply with a stream of choice obscenities she could only have picked up from drunken peasants at the inn. He shouted at her and even became quite frightened: 'What's that, you shameless bitch? What kind of language is that?'

She gave her father a stupid, puzzled look, not understanding why such words were forbidden. He wanted to give her a good telling-off, but she seemed so barbarous, so ignorant. For the very first time since she had been with him he realized that she believed in nothing. His whole way of life – the forests, snow, drunken peasants, swearing – struck him as just as wild and barbarous as the girl, so instead of telling her off he merely waved his arm and went back to his room.

Just then the policeman and Sergey came back to see Matvey again. Yakov recalled that these people had no faith either – this didn't worry them in the least and his life seemed strange, mad and hopeless, a real dog's life in fact. He paced up and down the yard bareheaded, then he went out into the road and walked up and down with fists clenched (at that moment the snow began to fall in large flakes) and his beard streamed in the wind. He kept shaking his head as something seemed to be weighing down on his head and shoulders – it was just as though devils were sitting on them. It was not he who was wandering about, so he thought, but some huge and terrifying wild beast, and it seemed he only had to shout for his voice to roar through the fields and woods, terrifying everyone . . .

V

When he returned to the house, the policeman had gone and the buffet-attendant was sitting in Matvey's room working with his abacus. Earlier he had been in the habit of calling at the inn almost every day. Then he would go and see Yakov, but now it was Matvey. He was always busy with his abacus, and then his face would be tense and sweaty; or he would ask for money, or stroke his whiskers and tell how he had once made punch for some officers at a main-line station and had personally served the sturgeon soup at regimental dinners. His sole interest in life was catering, his sole topic of conversation food, cutlery and wines. Once, wanting to say something pleasant, he had told a young mother feeding her baby, 'A mother's breast is milk-bar for baby!'

As he worked away at the abacus in Matvey's room he asked for money, saying he could not live at Progonnaya any more and as if about to burst into tears he asked, 'Oh, where can I go now? Please tell me where I can go?'

Then Matvey came into the kitchen and started peeling some boiled potatoes he had probably put by the day before. It was quiet and Yakov thought that the buffet-attendant had gone. It was high time for vespers. He called Aglaya and, thinking no one was at home, began singing in a loud, uninhibited voice. He sang and read, but in his mind he recited something quite different, 'Lord forgive me! Lord save me!'

And without stopping he performed a series of low bows, as though he wanted to tire himself out, shaking his head the whole time so that Aglaya looked at him in astonishment. He was scared Matvey might come in – he was convinced he would and neither his prayers nor his many prostrations were enough to suppress his feeling of anger towards him.

Matvey opened the door extremely quietly and entered the chapel. 'What a sin, what a sin!' he sighed reproachfully. 'Repent! Come to your senses, Cousin!'

Yakov dashed out of the chapel, fists clenched, without looking at him, in case he was tempted to hit him. He felt he was a huge terrible beast again – the same feeling he'd had a little while before on the road – and he crossed the hall into the grey, dirty part of the inn, thick with haze and smoke, where peasants usually drank their tea. For some time he paced up and down, treading so heavily that the china on the shelves rattled and the tables shook. Now he realized quite clearly that he was no longer satisfied with the way he believed and he could no longer carry on praying as before. He must repent, come to his senses, see reason, live and worship somehow differently. But how was he to worship? Perhaps all this was only the Devil trying to confuse him and he really needed to do none of these things? ... What would happen? What should he do? Who could teach him? How helpless he felt! He stopped, clutched his head and started to think, but could not take stock of everything in peace, since Matvey was so near. And he quickly returned to the living-quarters.

Matvey was sitting in the kitchen eating from a bowl of potatoes which he had in front of him. Aglaya and Dashutka were sitting in the kitchen too, by the stove, facing each other and winding yarn. An ironing-board had been set up between the stove and the table where Matvey was sitting; on it was a cold flat-iron.

'Cousin Aglaya,' asked Matvey, 'give me some oil, please!'

'But no one has oil in Lent!' Aglaya said.

'I'm not a monk, Cousin Aglaya, I'm an ordinary man. Being so poorly I'm even allowed milk, let alone oil.'

'You factory lot think you can do just what you like!'

Aglaya reached for a bottle of vegetable oil from the shelf and banged it angrily in front of Matvey with a spiteful grin, obviously delighted to see he was such a sinner.

'I'm telling you, you're not allowed any oil!' Yakov shouted.

Aglaya and Dashutka shuddered, but Matvey poured some oil into his bowl and went on eating as though he had not heard.

'I'm telling you that you mustn't have oil!' Yakov shouted even louder. He went red, suddenly seized the bowl, held it above his head and dashed it on the floor as hard as he could; the pieces went flying.

'Don't you dare say anything!' he shouted furiously, although Matvey did not say one word. 'Don't you dare!' he repeated and thumped his fist on the table.

Matvey went pale and got up. 'Cousin!' he said, still chewing. 'Come to your senses, Cousin!'

'Get out of my house this minute!' Yakov shouted. Matvey's wrinkled face, his voice, the crumbs in his moustache revolted him. 'I'm telling you to get out!'

'Cousin, calm down! Your pride is the Devil's work!'

'Shut up!' Yakov said, stamping his feet. 'Clear off, you devil!'

'If you really want to know,' Matvey kept on shouting, beginning to lose his temper now, 'you're an apostate and heretic. Accursed demons have blotted out the true light from your eyes, your prayers don't satisfy God. Repent, before it's too late! A sinner's death is terrible! Repent, Cousin!'

Yakov grabbed him by the shoulders and dragged him away from the table. Matvey turned even paler. Terrified out of his wits he muttered, 'What's all this? What's going on?'

As he struggled and fought to free himself from Yakov's grip, Matvey accidentally caught hold of his shirt near the neck and tore the collar. But Aglaya thought he wanted to hit Yakov, screamed, seized the bottle of oil and brought it down with all her strength on the crown of this hateful cousin's head. Matvey staggered and in an instant his face became calm, indifferent. Yakov breathed heavily. He was very excited and took great pleasure in hearing the bottle grunt like a living thing as it made contact with Matvey's head. He held him up and several times (this he remembered very clearly later) directed Aglaya's attention to the iron. Only when the blood was streaming through his hands, when he heard Dashutka's loud sobbing, when the ironing-board had crashed to the ground with Matvey slumped over it did his anger subside and he realized what had happened.

'Let him die, that factory ram!' Aglaya said with loathing, still holding on to the iron. Her white, blood-spattered kerchief had slipped down to her shoulders and her grey hair fell loose. 'Serves him right!'

It was a terrible sight. Dashutka was sitting on the floor by the stove with yarn in her hands, sobbing and prostrating herself, making a kind of munching sound each time she bowed. But nothing terrified Yakov so much as the bloodstained boiled potatoes, and he was afraid of treading on them. And there was something even more terrifying, which oppressed him like a dreadful nightmare and which seemed to pose the greatest threat and did not register at first. Sergey the buffet-attendant was standing in the doorway holding his abacus. He was very pale and looked in horror at the scene in the kitchen. Only after he had turned, dashed through the hall and then outside did Yakov realize who it was, and he went after him.

He pondered everything as he walked along, rubbing snow on his hands. The thought flashed through his mind that the workman had asked if he could spend the night at home and had long since left for his village. The day before they had killed a pig and large patches of blood lay on the snow and the sledge. Even one side of the well-head was spattered with blood. Consequently, even if all Yakov's family were up to their eyes in blood, no one would have suspected a thing. The thought of concealing the murder was torment enough, but the idea of a policeman turning up whistling and sneering from the station, that peasants would come and bind Yakov and Aglaya's hands tightly together and haul them off triumphantly to the largest village in the district, then to the town -- this was the most agonizing thing of all. Everyone would point at them on the way and scoff: 'Their Graces've been nabbed!'

Yakov wanted to put off the evil day somehow so that he could suffer the disgrace some time later, not now.

'I can lend you a thousand roubles ...' he said, catching up with Sergey. 'Won't do any good telling anyone, no good at all ... We can't bring him back from the dead anyway.'

He could hardly keep up with the buffet-attendant, who never looked round and was quickening his pace.

'I could lend you fifteen hundred,' he added.

He stopped for breath, but Sergey kept going at the same pace, possibly scared *he* might be next. Only when he had passed the level crossing and was half way along the road to the station did he take a brief look back and slow down. Red and green lamps were already shining at the station and along the line; the wind had slackened, but it was still snowing hard and the road had turned white again. Then, almost at the station, Sergey stopped, thought for a moment, and then determinedly retraced his steps. It was growing dark.

'I'll take the whole fifteen hundred then, Mr Yakov,' he said softly, trembling all over. 'Yes, I'll take 'em!'

VI

Yakov Terekhov's money was held at the town bank or lent out on mortgage. He kept a little petty cash in the house for immediate business expenses. He went into the kitchen and groped around for the tin of matches, and from the blue, sulphurous flame was able to take a close look at Matvey, still lying in the same place by the table, but draped in a white sheet now, so that only his boots showed. A cricket was chirping. Aglaya and Dashutka weren't in any of the living-rooms, but sat behind the counter in the tea-room silently winding yarn. Yakov Terekhov went to his room with a lamp and pulled out the small chest in which he kept the petty cash from under the bed. There happened to be 420 roubles in small notes and thirty-five in silver. The notes had an unpleasant, oppressive smell. Stuffing the money into his cap he went into the yard and out through the gate. He looked to each side as he went, but there was no sign of the buffet-attendant.

'Hallo!' Yakov shouted.

Right by the level crossing a dark figure detached itself from the swing barrier and approached him hesitantly. Yakov recogr⁀ ⌐d the buffet-attendant.

'Why can't you stay put?' he asked irritably. 'Here you are, just short of five hundred . . . there's no more in the house.'

'Fine . . . much obliged,' Sergey muttered as he greedily snatched the money and stuffed it in his pockets. Even though it was dark he was clearly shaking all over.

'But don't worry yourself, Mr Yakov . . . Why should *I* let on? All I did was come here and then go away. As they say, hear no evil . . .' Then he sighed and added, 'It's a lousy, rotten life!'

They stood in silence for a moment, without looking at each other.

'All for nothing, God knows how . . .' the buffet-attendant said trembling. 'There I was doing me adding when suddenly I hear a noise . . . I look through the door and see you all having a row over some oil . . . Where is he now?'

'Lying in the kitchen.'

'You should ditch the body somewhere . . . Don't hang about!'

Without saying a word Yakov went with him as far as the station, then went back home and harnessed the horse to take Matvey to Limarovo – he had decided to take him to the forest there and leave him on the road. Afterwards he would tell everyone that Matvey had gone off to Vedenyapino and had not returned. They would all think he had been murdered by some people on the way. He knew that no one would be fooled by that story, but he felt that being on the move, doing things and keeping himself busy was less of an ordeal than just sitting around waiting. He called Dashutka and the two of them took Matvey away, while Aglaya stayed behind to clean up the kitchen.

When Yakov and Dashutka were on the way back they had to stop at the level crossing, as the barrier was down. A long goods train passed through, drawn by two panting engines which threw sheaves of crimson fire from their funnels. The engine in front gave a piercing whistle at the crossing when it was in view of the station.

'What a noise, goes right through you . . .' Dashutka said.

The train at last passed through and the keeper slowly raised the barrier. 'Is that you, Yakov?' he asked. 'They say it's lucky not recognizing someone.'

When they were back in the house they had to get some sleep. Aglaya and Dashutka made up a bed on the tea-room floor and lay side by side, while Yakov settled down on the counter. They did not pray before going to sleep, nor did they light the icon-lamps. All three of them lay awake till morning, but they did not say one word and all night long felt someone was moving around in the empty storey above.

Two days later the district police officer and an examining magistrate came from town, searched Matvey's room and then the whole place. Yakov was questioned first and he testified that Matvey had left that Monday evening for Vedenyapino to prepare for communion in the church there, so he must have been murdered on the way by some sawyers working along the track. But when the magistrate asked why it was that Matvey had been found on the road, while his cap turned up at home – would he really have gone to Vedenyapino without it? – and why hadn't they found a single drop of blood near him in the snow on the road considering his head was smashed in and his face and chest were black with blood, Yakov became confused, lost his head and replied, 'Don't know sir.'

Yakov's worst fears were realized: the railway policeman arrived, a local constable smoked in the chapel, and Aglaya attacked him with a torrent of abuse and was rude to the inspector. And later, when Yakov and Aglaya were being taken away, peasants thronged the gate and called out, 'They've nabbed His Grace!' Everyone seemed glad.

The railway policeman said outright, under cross-examination, that Yakov and Aglaya had murdered Matvey to avoid having to share the property with him and if none of it had turned up when they were searching the place, then obviously Yakov and Aglaya had used it. Dashutka was questioned as well. She said Uncle Matvey quarrelled with Aunt Aglaya every day, that they almost came to blows over the money. Uncle must have been rich, she said, to have given a 'lady friend' a present of nine hundred roubles.

Dashutka was left on her own at the inn. No one came for tea or vodka and she would either tidy up or drink mead and eat buns. But a few days later the level crossing keeper was questioned and he testified that he had seen Yakov and Dashutka driving back late on Monday evening from Limarovo. Dashutka was arrested as well, taken to town and put in prison. It soon transpired, from what Aglaya said, that Sergey had been there at the time of the murder. They searched his room and found the money in a strange place – a felt boot under the stove, all in small change. There was three hundred in one-rouble notes alone. He swore he had earned it from the business and that he hadn't been to the inn for over a year; but witnesses testified that he was poor and that recently he had been particularly short of cash. They said he had been coming to the inn every day to borrow from Matvey. The railway policeman told how, on the day of the murder, he himself had gone twice to the inn with the buffet-attendant to help him raise a loan. Incidentally, people remembered that on the Monday evening Sergey had not been there to meet the combined goods and passenger train, but had wandered off somewhere. So he was arrested too and sent to town.

The trial took place eleven months later. Yakov Terekhov had aged terribly, grown thinner and spoke in the subdued voice of a sick man. He felt weak and pathetic and that he was shorter than anyone else, and pangs of conscience and religious doubts that constantly preyed on him in prison too seemed to have aged and emaciated his spirit as much as his body. When his absence from church was brought up the judge asked, 'Are you a dissenter?'; to which he replied, 'Don't know, sir.'

By now his faith had completely deserted him. He knew nothing, understood nothing and his former religion repelled him and struck him as irrational and barbarous. Aglaya was still on the warpath and still swore at poor departed Matvey, blaming him for all her misfortunes. Instead of whiskers, Sergey grew a beard now. In the courtroom he sweated and blushed and was plainly ashamed of his grey prison coat and of having to sit in the dock with common peasants. Clumsily, he tried to defend himself, and in his efforts to prove that he had not visited the inn for a whole year, argued with all the witnesses, which made him a general laughing-stock. Dashutka had put on weight while she was in prison. She did not understand any of the questions she was asked in court and only managed to reply that while Uncle Matvey was being killed she had been scared stiff, but that she had felt all right afterwards.

All four were found guilty of murder for gain. Yakov Terekhov was sentenced to twenty years' hard labour, Aglaya to thirteen, Sergey to ten and Dashutka to six.

VII

Late one evening a foreign steamer anchored in the Dué Roads and asked for coal. The captain was requested to wait until morning, but he wasn't disposed to wait one hour even, and said that should the weather break during the night he risked having to leave without any coal at all. In the Tartary Straits the weather can deteriorate very sharply – in a matter of half an hour – and then the Sakhalin coast becomes extremely dangerous. The wind was freshening already and quite a swell was running.

A convict gang was ordered out to the coalpits from the Voyevoda prison – the gloomiest and most forbidding prison on the island. The convicts were to load coal onto barges which a steam launch would tow to the steamer anchored about half a mile out. There they would have to transfer the load (back-breaking work), with the launch smashing against the ship and the men hardly able to stand for seasickness. Turned out of bed only a short time before, the convicts went along the shore half asleep, stumbling in the dark and clanking their chains. To the left they could barely make out a high, incredibly gloomy cliff, while to the right was pitch-black, unrelieved darkness and the long, drawn-out, monotonous groaning of the sea. Only when a warder lit his pipe, casting a brief light on a guard with a rifle and two or three rough-looking convicts standing nearby, or when he went close to the water with his lantern, could the white crests of the nearest waves be seen.

In this party was Yakov, who had been nicknamed 'Old Shaggy' on account of his long beard. No one ever called him Mr Yakov now, he was simply plain Yakov. Now his stock stood very low, for three months after reaching the penal settlement he had become terribly, unbearably homesick, yielded to temptation and ran away. But he was soon caught, given a life sentence and forty lashes. Subsequently he was flogged twice more for losing prison clothing, although in both cases the clothing had been stolen from him. He had begun to feel homesick the moment he was on the way to Odessa. The convict train had stopped during the night at Progonnaya and Yakov had pressed against the window, trying to make out the old place, but it was too dark to see anything.

There was no one he could talk to about home. His sister Aglaya had been sent to a prison on the other side of Siberia and he did not know where she was now. Dashutka was on Sakhalin but had been given to some ex-convict, to live with him in some remote settlement. There was no news of her at all; but once a settler who came to the Voyevoda prison told Yakov that Dashutka had three children. Sergey was not far away, working in some official's house in Dué, but one could not be sure of meeting him, since he was too stuck-up to associate with rank-and-file convicts.

The gang reached the pithead and the convicts took their positions on the quayside. The news went round that the weather was getting too bad for loading and the steamer appeared to be about to weigh anchor.

Three lights were visible. One was moving – this was the steam launch that had gone out to the ship and which was apparently returning now to report if there would be any work or not. Shivering from the autumn cold and the damp sea air, and wrapped tight in his short, torn sheepskin coat, Yakov stared unblinking in the direction of his native land. Ever since his life had begun in prison with others who had been brought there – Russians, Ukrainians, Tartars, Georgians, Chinese, Finns, gypsies and Jews – ever since he had listened to what they had to say and seen them suffer, he had once again begun to pray to God. He felt that at last he had discovered the true faith that his entire family had thirsted for from the time of Grandma Avdotya, had sought for so long without ever finding it. Now he knew all this and he understood where God was and how he could serve Him. But one thing he did not understand – why one man's destiny should differ so much from another's. Why had that simple faith, God's gift to other men, cost him so dear? What was the reason for all those horrible sufferings which made his arms and legs twitch like a drunkard's and which would clearly give him no respite until his dying day? He peered hard into the gloom and thought he could make out, over thousands of miles of pitch darkness, his homeland, his native province, his district, Progonnaya; he thought he could see the ignorance, savagery, heartlessness, the blind, harsh, bestial indifference of those he had left behind. His eyes were blurred with tears, but still he peered into the distance where the steamer's pale lights faintly glimmered. And his heart ached with longing for his native land, and he felt an urge to *live*, to go back home and tell them all about his new-found faith. If only he could save just one man from ruin – and be free of suffering for just one day!

The launch arrived and the warder announced in a loud voice that the job was off. 'Back!' he ordered. 'Stand to attention!'

He could hear the anchor chain being stowed on board the ship. A strong biting wind was blowing now and somewhere, high up on the steep cliffs, the trees were creaking. Most probably a storm was getting up.

The Black Monk

I

Andrey Kovrin, MA, was exhausted, his nerves were shattered. He did not take any medical treatment but mentioned his condition in passing to a doctor friend over a bottle of wine, and was advised to spend the spring and summer in the country. And as it happened he received just then a long letter from Tanya Pesotskaya, inviting him to come and stay at Borisovka. So he decided he really must get away.

At first – this was in April – he went to his own estate Kovrinka, where he lived on his own for three weeks. Then after waiting until the roads were passable, he drove off in a carriage to see his former guardian and mentor Pesotsky the horticulturalist, who was famous throughout Russia. It was no more than about fifty miles from Kovrinka to Pesotsky's place at Borisovka and it was pure joy travelling along the soft road in spring, in a comfortable sprung carriage.

Pesotsky's house was huge, with columns, peeling plaster lions, and a footman in coat and tails at the entrance. The gloomy, severe, old-fashioned park was strictly laid out in English style, stretched almost half a mile from the house to the river, and ended in a precipitous clayey bank where pines grew, their exposed roots resembling shaggy paws. Down below, the water glinted uninvitingly, sandpipers flew past squeaking plaintively, and it was generally the kind of place to make you want to sit down and write a ballad. But near the house itself, in the courtyard and the orchard, which took up about eighty acres, including the nursery beds, it was cheerful and lively, even in bad weather. Nowhere, except at Pesotsky's, had Kovrin seen such wonderful roses, lilies, camellias, so many different tulips, with colours ranging from white to soot-black, such a profusion of flowers. It was only the beginning of spring and the real splendours of the flowerbeds were still hidden in the hothouses. But the flowers in bloom along the paths – and here and there in the beds – were enough to make you feel that you were in the very kingdom of tender hues as you strolled in the garden, especially early in the morning, when dew sparkled on every petal.

The ornamental section of the garden, which Pesotsky disparagingly called 'sheer nonsense', had seemed like a fairyland to Kovrin as a child. The oddities, elaborate monstrosities and travesties of nature that were to be seen here! There were trellised fruit-trees, a pear-tree shaped like a Lombardy poplar, globe-shaped oaks and limes, an apple-tree umbrella, arches, initials, candelabra, and even an '1862' made from plums – this was the year Pesotsky first took up horticulture. Here also were fine, graceful saplings with straight, firm stems like palm-trees, and only after a very close look could you tell that they were gooseberries or blackcurrants. But what most of all made the garden a cheerful, lively place was the constant activity. From dawn to dusk gardeners with wheelbarrows, hoes and watering-cans swarmed like ants near the trees and bushes, on the paths and flowerbeds.

Kovrin arrived at the Pesotskys' after nine in the evening. He found Tanya and her father Yegor in a terribly worried state. The clear, starry sky and the thermometer foretold frost towards morning, but the head gardener Ivan Karlych had gone off to town and there was no one left they could rely on.

During supper, they talked only of this morning frost and decided that Tanya would not go to bed, but would go round the orchard after midnight to check if everything was all right, while Yegor would get up at three, even earlier perhaps. Kovrin sat with Tanya the whole evening and after midnight went with her into the garden. It was cold and there was a strong smell of burning. In the big orchard, called 'commercial' as it brought Yegor Pesotsky several thousand roubles profit every year, a dense, black, acrid smoke was spreading over the ground and enveloping the trees, saving all those thousands from the frost. Here the trees were planted like draughts pieces, in straight, even rows, like columns of soldiers. This strict, pedantic regularity, plus the fact that all the trees were exactly the same height, all of them having absolutely identical crowns and trunks, made a monotonous, even boring picture. Kovrin and Tanya walked between the rows, where bonfires of manure, straw and all kind of refuse were smouldering, and every now and then they met workers drifting through the smoke like shadows. Only cherries, plums and certain varieties of apple were in bloom, but the whole orchard was drowning in smoke. Kovrin breathed a deep breath only when they reached the nurseries.

'When I was a child the smoke used to make me sneeze,' he said, shrugging his shoulders, 'but I still don't understand why this smoke saves the plants from frost.'

'Smoke is a substitute for clouds when the sky is clear . . .' Tanya said.

'But what use are *they*?'

'You don't normally get a frost when it's dull and overcast.'

'That's right!'

He laughed and took her arm. Her broad, very serious face, chill from the cold, with its fine black eyebrows, the raised coat collar which cramped her movements, her whole slim, graceful body, her dress tucked up from the dew – all this moved him deeply.

'Heavens, how you've grown up!' he said. 'Last time I left here, five years ago, you were still a child. You were so thin, long-legged, bareheaded, with that short little dress you used to wear. And I teased you and called you a heron . . . How time changes everything!'

'Yes, five years!' Tanya sighed. 'A lot of water has flowed under the bridge since then. Tell me, Andrey, in all honesty,' she said in an animated voice, peering into his face, 'have you grown tired of us? But why am I asking you this? You're a man, you live your own interesting life, you're an eminent person . . . Becoming like strangers to each other is really so natural! Anyway, Andrey, I want you to treat us as your family, we have a right to that.'

'But I do, Tanya.'

'Word of honour?'

'Yes, word of honour.'

'You were surprised before that we had so many of your photos. You must know Father idolizes you. At times I think he loves you more than me. He's proud of you. You are a scholar, a remarkable person, you've made a dazzling career for yourself and he's convinced this is because he brought you up. I let him think this, I don't see why I should stop him.'

Dawn was breaking – this was particularly evident from the clarity with which puffs of smoke and the tree tops were outlined now in the air. Nightingales were singing and the cries of quails came from the fields.

'But it's time for bed,' Tanya said. 'Besides that, it's cold.' She took his arm. 'Thanks for coming, Andrey. Our friends aren't very interesting, not that we have many. All we have is the garden, garden, garden, nothing else.' She laughed. 'First-class, second-class, Oporto, rennets and winter apples, budding, grafting. Our whole life has gone into this garden, I dream of nothing but apple- and pear-trees. Of course, it's all very nice and useful, but sometimes I want something else, to break the monotony. I remember the times you came for the holidays, or just for a short visit, how the house became somehow fresher and brighter then, as though the covers had been taken off the chandeliers and furniture. I was a little girl then, but I did understand.'

She spoke for a long time and with great feeling. Suddenly Kovrin was struck by the idea that he might even conceive an affection for this small, fragile, loquacious creature during the course of the summer, become attracted to her and fall in love. In their situation that would be so natural and possible! He was both touched and amused by the thought. He leant down towards that dear, worried face and softly sang:

'Onegin, I will not hide it,
I love Tatyana madly ...'

Yegor Pesotsky was up already when they returned to the house. Kovrin did not feel like sleeping, got into conversation with the old man and went back to the garden with him. Yegor Pesotsky was a tall, broad-shouldered man, with a large paunch. Although he suffered from short breath, he always walked so fast it was hard keeping up with him. He had an extremely worried look and was always hurrying off somewhere as if all would be lost should he be just one minute late.

'It's a peculiar thing, my dear boy,' he began, then paused for breath. 'As you see, it's freezing down on the ground, but just you hold a thermometer on a stick about twelve feet above it and you'll find it's warm there ... Why is it?'

'I honestly don't know,' Kovrin said, laughing.

'Hm ... one can't know everything of course ... However capacious your brain is, it won't accommodate everything, Philosophy's more your line, isn't it?'

'I give lectures on psychology, but my main interest is philosophy.'

'And you're not bored?'

'On the contrary, it's my life.'

'Well, God bless you ...' Yegor Pesotsky murmured, thoughtfully stroking his grey side-whiskers. 'God bless you ... I'm very pleased for you ... very pleased, dear boy.'

But suddenly he pricked up his ears, pulled a horrified face, ran to one side and soon disappeared in the clouds of smoke behind the trees.

'Who tied a horse to that apple-tree?' the despairing, heart-rending cry rang out. 'What swine, what scum dared to tie a horse to an apple-tree? Good Lord! They've ruined, frozen, polluted, mucked everything up! The garden's ruined! Ruined! Oh, God!'

He went back to Kovrin, looking exhausted, outraged. 'What can you do with this confounded riff-raff?' he said tearfully, flinging his arms out helplessly. 'Last night Stepka was carting manure and tied his horse to the apple-tree. He twisted the reins so hellishly tight, damn him, that the bark's rubbed off. How could he do it? I had words with him, but the idiot just stood gaping. Hanging's too good for him!'

After he had calmed down he put his arms round Kovrin and kissed him on the cheek. 'Well, God bless, God bless ...' he muttered. 'I'm very pleased you came. I can't say how glad I am ... Thanks.'

Then, at the same rapid pace and with that same worried look, he toured the whole garden, showing his former ward all the conservatories, greenhouses, cold frames, and the two apiaries he called the 'wonder of the century'.

As they walked along, the sun rose, filling the garden with a bright light. It grew warm. Anticipating a fine, cheerful, long day, Kovrin recalled that in fact it was only the beginning of May and that the whole summer lay ahead – just as bright, cheerful and long, and suddenly there welled up within him that feeling of radiant, joyous youth he had known in his childhood, when he had run around this garden. And he embraced the old man in turn and kissed him tenderly. Both of them, deeply moved, went into the house and drank tea from old-fashioned porcelain cups, with cream and rich pastries. These little things again reminded Kovrin of his childhood and youth. The beautiful present, the freshly awakened impressions of the past, blended together: they had a somewhat inhibiting effect, but none the less gave him a feeling of well-being.

He waited for Tanya to wake up, drank coffee with her, went for a stroll, and then returned to his room and sat down to work. He read attentively, took notes, now and again looking up at the open window or the fresh flowers that stood, still moist with dew, in vases on the table, then lowering his eyes on his book again; it seemed every vein in his body was pulsating and throbbing with pleasure.

II

In the country he continued to lead the same nervous, restless life as in town. He read and wrote a great deal, studied Italian, and on his strolls took pleasure in the thought that he would soon be back at work again. Everyone was amazed he slept so little. If he chanced to doze off during the day for half an hour, he could not sleep at all later and would emerge from a night of insomnia vigorous and cheerful, as if nothing was wrong.

He talked a lot, drank wine and smoked expensive cigars. Young ladies who lived nearby called on the Pesotskys almost every day and played the piano and sang with Tanya. Sometimes a young gentleman from the neighbourhood, an excellent violinist, would call. Kovrin would listen so hungrily to the playing and singing it tired him out, and the exhaustion was plainly visible from the way his eyelids seemed to stick together and his head dropped to one side.

One evening, after tea, he was sitting on the balcony reading. At the same time Tanya, who sang soprano, together with one of the young ladies – a contralto – and the young violinist, were practising Brag's famous *Serenade*. Kovrin listened hard to the words (they were Russian) but could not understand them at all. Finally, after putting his book aside and listening very closely, he did understand:

a young girl, with a morbid imagination, was in her garden one night and heard some mysterious sounds, so beautiful and strange, she had to admit that their harmony was something divine, incomprehensible to mere mortals as it soared up again into the heavens whence it came. Kovrin began to feel sleepy. He rose to his feet, wearily walked up and down the drawing-room, then the ballroom. When the singing stopped, he took Tanya by the arm and went out onto the balcony with her.

'Since early this morning I haven't been able to get a certain legend out of my mind,' he said. 'I can't remember if I read it somewhere or if I heard it, but it's really quite strange – doesn't appear to make any sense at all. I should say from the start that it's not distinguished for its clarity. A thousand years ago a certain monk, dressed in black, was walking across a desert – somewhere in Syria or Arabia ... A few miles from where he was walking a fisherman saw another black monk slowly moving across the surface of a lake. This second monk was a mirage. Now forget the laws of optics, which the legend apparently doesn't acknowledge and listen to what happened next. The mirage produced another one. This second mirage produced a third, so that the image of the black monk began to be transmitted endlessly from one layer of the atmosphere to the other. He was sighted in Africa, then Spain, India, the far North ... He finally left the earth's atmosphere and now wanders through the whole universe, never meeting the conditions which would make it possible for him to fade away. Perhaps he'll be seen somewhere on Mars now, or on some star in the Southern Cross. But, my dear, the essence, the real crux of the legend is this: precisely one thousand years after that monk first walked across the desert, the mirage will return to the earth's atmosphere and appear to people. And it seems these thousand years are almost up. According to the legend, we can expect the black monk any day now.'

'A strange mirage,' said Tanya, who did not care for the legend.

'But the most amazing thing is,' Kovrin said, laughing, 'I just can't remember what prompted me to think of it. Did I read it somewhere? Did I hear about it? Perhaps the black monk was only a dream? I swear to God, I can't remember. But I'm intrigued by this legend. I've been thinking about it all day.'

Leaving Tanya to her guests, he went out of the house and strolled by the flowerbeds, deep in thought. The sun was setting. The freshly watered flowers gave off a moist, irritating scent. In the house the singing had started again; from the distance the violin sounded like a human voice. Kovrin racked his brains trying to remember where he had read or heard about that legend as he walked unhurriedly towards the park, reaching the river before he knew where he was.

He descended the path that ran down a steep bank, past bare roots, to the water, where he disturbed some sandpipers and frightened two ducks away. Here and there on the gloomy pines gleamed the last rays of the setting sun, but evening had already come over the surface of the river. Kovrin crossed the foot-bridge to the other side. Before him lay a broad field full of young rye not yet in ear. There was no human habitation, not a living soul out there, and it seemed the path would lead him to that same unknown, mysterious spot where the sun had just set and where the evening glow spread its flames so magnificently over all that wide expanse.

'So much space, freedom, peace here!' Kovrin thought as he walked along the path. 'The whole world seems to be looking at me, has gone silent, and is waiting for me to understand it.'

But just then some ripples spread across the rye and a gentle evening breeze lightly caressed his bare head. A moment later there was another gust, stronger this time, and the rye rustled and he could hear the dull murmur of the pines behind him. Kovrin stood motionless in astonishment. On the horizon a tall black column was rising up into the sky, like a whirlwind or tornado. Its outlines were blurred, but he could see at once that it was not standing still, but moving at terrifying speed straight towards him – and the nearer it came, the smaller and clearer it grew. Kovrin leapt aside into the rye to make way – and he was only just in time ... A monk in black vestments, grey-haired and with black eyebrows, his arms across his chest, flashed past; his bare feet did not touch the ground. After he had raced on another six yards he looked round at Kovrin, nodded and gave him a friendly, but artful, smile. What a pale, terribly pale, thin face though! Growing larger again, he flew across the river, struck the clayey bank and the pines without making a sound, passed straight through and disappeared into thin air.

'So, there it is ...' murmured Kovrin. 'That shows there's truth in the legend.'

Without trying to find an explanation for this strange apparition and satisfied that he had managed to get such a close look, not only at the black vestments, but even at the monk's face and eyes, he went back to the house feeling pleasantly excited.

People were strolling peacefully in the park and garden, the musicians were playing in the house, so only he had seen the monk. He had a strong urge to tell Tanya and Yegor Pesotsky about everything, but he realized they would surely think the story crazy and be scared stiff. Better keep quiet about it. He laughed out loud, sang, danced a mazurka; he was in high spirits and everyone – Tanya, her guests – found that he really had a radiant, inspired look about him that evening, that he was most interesting.

III

After supper, when the guests had left, he went to his room and lay on the couch. He wanted to think about the monk, but a moment later, in came Tanya.

'Here, Andrey, read Father's articles,' she said, handing him a bundle of pamphlets and offprints. 'They're wonderful, he's an excellent writer.'

'I wouldn't say that!' Yegor Pesotsky said, forcing a laugh as he followed her into the room; he felt embarrassed. 'Don't listen to her, please! Don't read them! But if you need something to make you sleep, then go ahead. They're an excellent soporific!'

'In my opinion they're magnificent,' Tanya said with great conviction. 'Read them, Andrey, and persuade Father to write more often. He could write a whole course in horticulture.'

Yegor Pesotsky gave a forced laugh, blushed and started speaking in the way shy authors usually do. In the end he gave in. 'In that case, read Gaucher's article first, then these short ones in Russian,' he muttered, turning over the pamphlets with trembling hands. 'Otherwise you won't understand a thing. Before you read my objections, you must know what it is I'm objecting to. However, it's rubbish ... boring. What's more, I think it's time for bed.'

Tanya went out. Yegor Pesotsky sat beside Kovrin on the couch and sighed deeply. 'Yes, my dear boy,' he began after a short silence. 'Yes, my dear Master of Arts. Here I am writing articles and exhibiting at shows and winning medals ... They say Pesotsky has "apples as big as your head" and that he made his fortune with his orchard. Pesotsky is monarch of all he surveys, in short. But, you may ask, what's the point of it all? The garden is really beautiful, a show-garden in fact. It's not so much a garden as a complete institution, of the greatest importance to the State, a step, so to speak, towards a new era in Russian economics and industry. But what's the point of it? What's the use?'

'It speaks for itself.'

'That's not what I mean. I'd like to know, what will happen to the garden when I die? It won't be kept up to its present standard for more than one month. The secret of my success isn't that it's a big garden, with lots of gardeners, but because I love the work – do you follow? Perhaps I love it better than myself. I work from dawn till dusk. The grafting, pruning, planting – I do them all myself. When people start helping me, I get jealous and irritated until I'm downright rude to them. The whole secret is *love*, and by that I mean the keen eye and head of the master looking after his own place, the feeling that comes over you when you've gone visiting for an hour and you just sit still. But your heart's not there, you're miles away – afraid something might be going wrong in the garden. And when I die who'll look after it? Who'll do the work? The head gardener? The ordinary gardeners? What do you think? So let me tell you, dear boy, the principal enemy in our work isn't hares, cock-chafers or frost, but the man who doesn't care.'

'And Tanya?' laughed Kovrin. 'She couldn't possibly do more harm than a hare. She loves the work, she understands it.'

'Yes, she loves and understands it. If the garden passes into *her* hands after my death and she takes charge, I could hope for nothing better. But supposing she marries, God forbid?' Yegor Pesotsky whispered and gave Kovrin a frightened look. 'This is my point! She'll marry, have children and then she'll have no time to think about the garden. But my main worry is her marrying some young whipper-snapper who'll grow greedy, rent the garden out to some market-woman and it'll all go to rack and ruin within a year! In this kind of business women are like the plague!'

Pesotsky sighed and was silent for a few minutes. 'Perhaps it's just egotism, but I'm telling you quite frankly: I don't want Tanya to marry. I'm afraid! There's that young fop who comes here scraping his fiddle. I know Tanya won't marry him, I know that very well, but I just can't stand the sight of him. On the whole I'm quite a crank, dear boy. I admit it.' Pesotsky got up and paced the room excitedly; it was plain he wanted to say something very important, but he couldn't bring himself to.

'I'm extremely fond of you and I'll be open with you,' he said at last, stuffing his hands into his pockets. 'I'm usually quite straight-forward when it comes to certain ticklish questions and I'm telling you exactly what I think – I can't stand these so-called "innermost thoughts". I'm telling you straight: you're the only man I wouldn't mind marrying my daughter. You're clever, you have feelings and you wouldn't let my beloved work perish. But the main reason is – I love you like a son . . . and I'm proud of you. If Tanya and yourself became fond of each other, well then, I'd be very glad, happy even. I'm telling you straight, without frills, as an honest man.'

Kovrin burst out laughing. Pesotsky opened the door to go out and stopped on the threshold. 'If Tanya gave you a son I'd make a gardener out of him,' he said thoughtfully. 'However, that's an idle dream . . . Good night.'

Left alone, Kovrin settled himself more comfortably on the couch and started on the articles. One bore the title *Intermedial Cultivation*, another *A few Observations on Mr Z's Remarks on Double-Trenching in New Gardens*, and another *More about Grafting Dormant Buds*; and there were other titles like that. But what a restless, uneven tone, what highly charged, almost pathological fervour! Here was an article with apparently the most inoffensive title and unexceptionable subject – the winter dessert apple. But Pesotsky first weighed in with an *audiatur altera pars*★ and ended with *sapienti sat*†, interpolating these dicta with a whole torrent of venomous animadversions apropos the 'learned ignorance of our self-appointed gentlemen-

★ 'Let the other side be heard.'
† 'Enough for a wise man.'

horticulturalists who look down on nature from their Olympian heights'; or Gaucher, 'whose reputation was made by ignoramuses and dilettantes'. These remarks were followed by the totally irrelevant, forced, sham regret for the fact that it was no longer legal to birch peasants who stole fruit and damaged trees in the process.

'It's a fine, pleasant, healthy occupation, but even here it's passion and warfare,' Kovrin thought. 'Probably, it's because intellectuals are neurotic and over-sensitive everywhere, in all walks of life. Perhaps it can't be avoided.'

He thought of Tanya who liked Pesotsky's articles so much. She was not tall, was pale and thin, with protruding collar-bones; her dark, clever, staring eyes were always peering, seeking something. She walked just like her father, taking short, quick steps. Very talkative, she loved to argue and would accompany the most trivial phrase with highly expressive mimicry and gesticulations. She was probably highly strung.

Kovrin read on, but he understood nothing and gave up. That same, agreeable feeling of excitement he had had when dancing his mazurka and listening to the music made him weary now and stirred a multitude of thoughts. He stood up and started walking round the room, thinking about the black monk. It occurred to him that if he alone had seen that strange, supernatural apparition, then he must be ill and a prey to hallucinations. This thought frightened him, but not for long.

'In fact I feel fine. I'm not harming anyone. So that means there's nothing bad in these hallucinations,' he thought and felt fine again.

He sat on the couch and clasped his head to hold in check that incomprehensible feeling of joy which filled his whole being; then he paced up and down again and started to work. But the ideas he found in the book left him unsatisfied. He wanted something gigantic, immense, staggering. Towards dawn he undressed and reluctantly got into bed. After all, he had to sleep!

When he heard Pesotsky's footsteps receding into the garden, Kovrin rang the bell and told the servant to bring him some wine. After enjoying a few glasses of claret his senses grew dim and he fell asleep.

IV

Pesotsky and Tanya had frequent quarrels and said nasty things to each other. One morning, after a squabble about something, Tanya burst into tears and went to her room. She didn't appear for lunch, or tea. At first Pesotsky walked around solemnly and pompously, as if he wanted to make it known that he considered justice and order more important than anything else in the world. But he could not keep up the pose for long and lost heart. Sadly he wandered through the park, sighing the whole time, 'Ah, Good Lord, Good Lord!' and he did not eat a thing for dinner. Finally, full of guilt and remorse, he knocked on the locked door and called out timidly, 'Tanya! Tanya?'

A weak voice, drained by tears, but still determined, replied from behind the door, 'Leave me alone, I beg you.'

The anguish of the master and mistress was reflected all over the house, even in the gardeners. Kovrin was immersed in his interesting work, but in the end he too felt bored and embarrassed. Trying to dispel the prevailing unpleasant atmosphere, he decided to intervene and towards evening knocked at Tanya's door. She let him in.

'Come now, you should be ashamed!' he joked, looking in amazement at Tanya's tear-stained, mournful face that was covered in red blotches. 'Surely it's not as bad as all that? Now, now!'

'If you only knew how he torments me!' she said and copious, bitter tears welled from her large eyes. 'He's tormented the life out of me,' she went on, wringing her hands. 'I didn't say *anything* to him ... nothing at all. I only said we don't need to keep on extra workers when ... when we can engage day-labourers if we want to. You know, our gardeners have been standing idle for a whole week. That's all I said, but he shouted and said many insulting, deeply offensive things. Why?'

'Now, that's enough, enough,' Kovrin said, smoothing her hair. 'You've had your quarrel and a good cry, and that's enough. You must stop being angry now, it's not good ... especially as he loves you so very much.'

'He's ruined my whole life,' Tanya continued, sobbing. 'All I hear is insults and abuse ... He thinks there's no place for me in this house. Agreed. He's right. I'll leave this place tomorrow, get a job as a telegraphist ... That's what I'll do.'

'Come now, there's no need to cry, Tanya. Please don't, my dear ... You're both quick-tempered, easily upset, and you're both to blame. Come on, I'll make peace between you.'

Kovrin spoke with feeling, convincingly, but she kept on crying, her shoulders twitching and her hands clenched as if something really terrible had happened to her. He felt all the more sorry for her because, although her grief was nothing serious, she was suffering deeply. How little it took to make this creature unhappy all day long, for her whole life perhaps! As he comforted Tanya, Kovrin thought that he wouldn't find two people who loved him so much as Tanya and her father in a month of Sundays. Having lost his father and mother as a small child, but for these two, probably, he would never have known true affection until his dying day. He would never have known that simple, disinterested love that is felt only for those who are very close, for blood relations. And he felt that this weeping, trembling girl's nerves were reacting to his own half-sick, overwrought nerves like iron to a magnet. He could never have loved a healthy, strong, rosy-cheeked woman, but that pale, weak, unhappy Tanya attracted him.

And he gladly stroked her hair and shoulders, pressed her hands and wiped away the tears ... Finally she stopped crying. For a long time she complained about her father and her hard, intolerable life in that house, imploring Kovrin to see things as she did. Then gradually, she began to smile and said sighing that God had given her *such* a bad character. In the end she laughed out loud, called herself a fool and ran out of the room.

Shortly afterwards, when Kovrin went into the garden, Pesotsky and Tanya were strolling side by side along the path as if nothing had happened. They were both eating rye bread with salt, as they were hungry.

Pleased with his success as peacemaker, Kovrin went into the park. As he sat pondering on a bench he heard the clatter of carriages and a woman's laughter – guests had arrived. As the shadows of evening fell across the garden he heard the vague sounds of a violin, voices singing, which reminded him of the black monk. Where, in what country or on what planet was that optical absurdity wandering now?

Hardly had he recalled that legend, conjuring up the dark spectre he had seen in the rye field when quite silently, without the slightest rustling, a man of medium height, his grey head uncovered, all in black, barefoot like a beggar, his black eyebrows sharply defined on his deathly white face, slipped out from behind the pine trees just opposite. Nodding his head welcomingly, this beggar or pilgrim silently came over to the bench and Kovrin could see it was the black monk. For a minute they both eyed each other – Kovrin in amazement, the monk in a friendly way, with that same rather crafty look.

'You're just a mirage,' Kovrin murmured. 'Why are you here, sitting still like that? It doesn't tally with the legend.'

'Never mind,' the monk answered softly after a brief pause, turning his face towards him. 'The legend, myself, the mirage are all products of your overheated imagination. I'm an apparition ...'

'That means you don't exist?' Kovrin asked.

'Think what you like,' the monk said with a weak smile. 'I exist in your imagination, and your imagination is part of nature, so I exist in nature too.'

'You have a very aged, clever and extremely expressive face, as if you really have lived more than a thousand years,' Kovrin said. 'I didn't know my imagination could create such phenomena. But why are you looking at me so rapturously? Do you like me?'

'Yes. You're one of the few who are rightly called God's Chosen. You serve Eternal Truth. Your ideas, intentions, your amazing erudition, your whole life – all bear the divine, heavenly stamp, since they are devoted to the Rational and the Beautiful, that is, to the Eternal.'

'You mentioned "Eternal Truth" ... But is that within men's reach, do they need it if there's no such thing as eternal life?'

'There *is* eternal life,' the monk said.

'Do you believe in immortality?'

'Yes, of course. A great, bright future awaits you human beings. And the more men there are like you on earth, the quicker will this future come about. Without men like you serving the highest principles, living intelligently and freely, humanity would be worthless. In the normal course of events it would have to wait a long time for its life upon earth to come to an end. But you will lead it into the Kingdom of Eternal Truth a few thousand years ahead of time – this is your noble service. You are the embodiment of God's blessing which has come to dwell among men.'

'But what is the purpose of eternal life?' asked Kovrin.

'Like any other kind of life – pleasure. True pleasure is knowledge, and eternal life will afford innumerable and inexhaustible sources of knowledge: this is the meaning of the saying, "In my Father's house are many mansions."'

'If you only knew how enjoyable it is listening to you!' Kovrin said, rubbing his hands with pleasure.

'I'm very pleased.'

'But I know one thing: when you've gone I'll start worrying whether you really do exist. You're a phantom, a hallucination. Does that mean I'm mentally ill, insane?'

'Even if that were so, why let it bother you? You're ill from overworking, you've worn yourself out. I'm trying to say that you've sacrificed your health for an idea and it won't be long before you sacrifice your very life to it. What could be better? All noble spirits blessed with gifts from on high have this as their aim.'

'If I *know* that I'm mentally ill, how can I have any faith in myself?'

'But how do you know that men of genius, in whom the whole world puts its faith, haven't seen ghosts too? Nowadays scientists say genius is akin to madness. My friend, only the mediocre, the common herd are healthy and normal. Thoughts about an age of neurosis, overwork, degeneracy and so on can seriously worry only those for whom the purpose of life lies in the present – that is, the common herd.'

'The Romans used to speak of *mens sana in corpore sano*.'

'Not all that the Greeks and Romans said is true. Heightened awareness, excitement, ecstasy – everything that distinguishes prophets, poets, martyrs to an idea, from ordinary people is hostile to man's animal side – I mean, his physical health. I repeat: if you want to be healthy and normal, go and join the herd.'

'It's strange the way you repeat things I think of myself very often,'

ANTON CHEKHOV

Kovrin said. 'It's as though you spied out and eavesdropped on my most secret thoughts. But let's not talk about me. What do you mean by Eternal Truth?'

The monk did not answer. Kovrin looked at him and could not make out his face – its features had become hazy and indistinct. Then the monk's head and arms began to disappear. His torso merged with the bench and the twilight shadows, and he vanished completely.

'The hallucination's over!' Kovrin said laughing. 'A pity!'

He went back to the house happy and cheerful. The monk's few words had flattered not his pride, but his very soul, his whole being. To be one of the Chosen, to serve Eternal Truth, to stand in the ranks of those who, a thousand years ahead of time, would make men worthy of the Kingdom of God, thereby saving them from several thousand years of needless struggle, sin and suffering, to surrender, to surrender everything – youth, strength, health – to an idea, to be ready to die for the common weal – what a noble, blissful destiny! The memory of his pure, chaste, hardworking past flashed through his mind; he remembered what he had learned, what he had taught others, and he decided that the monk had not been exaggerating.

As he went through the park he met Tanya. She was wearing a different dress now.

'So you're here,' she said. 'We've all been looking for you, looking everywhere . . . But what's the matter?' she asked in surprise, studying his radiant, glowing face. 'How strange you are, Andrey.'

'I'm contented, Tanya,' Kovrin said as he put his hands on her shoulders. 'I'm more than contented, I'm happy! Tanya, dear Tanya, you're such a likeable person! Dear Tanya, I'm so glad, so glad!'

He kissed both her hands passionately and went on, 'I've just experienced some bright, wonderful, divine moments. But I can't tell you everything, because you'd call me mad or disbelieve me. Let's talk about you. Dear, wonderful Tanya! I love you. I'm *used* to loving you now. Having you near me, meeting you ten times a day has become a spiritual necessity. I don't know how I will cope when I go home.'

'Well!' Tanya laughed. 'You'll forget about us in a couple of days. We're small fry and you're a great man.'

'No, let's be serious!' he said. 'I shall take you with me, Tanya. Will you say yes? Will you come with me? Will you be mine?'

'Well!' Tanya said and felt like laughing again. But she could not and her face came out in red blotches. Her breath came faster and she quickly went away, not towards the house, but further into the park. 'I hadn't given it any thought ... I hadn't thought ...' she said, wringing her hands despairingly.

But Kovrin kept following her, still speaking with that same radiant, rapturous expression on his face, 'I want a love which will completely transport me, and only *you* can give me that love, Tanya! I'm happy, so happy!'

Quite stunned, she stooped, shrank and suddenly seemed to have aged ten years. But he found her beautiful and shouted out in delight, 'How beautiful she is!'

V

When he heard from Kovrin that not only were they enamoured of each other, but that there was even going to be a wedding, Pesotsky paced up and down for a long time, trying to conceal his excitement. His hands started shaking, his neck swelled up and turned crimson. He ordered his racing drozhky to be harnessed and drove off somewhere. When Tanya saw him whipping the horses and pulling his cap almost onto his ears, she realized the kind of mood he was in, locked herself in her room and cried all day long.

The peaches and plums in the hothouses were already ripe. The packing and despatch of this delicate, temperamental cargo required a great deal of care, labour and trouble. Because of the very hot, dry summer, each tree needed watering, which involved a great deal of the gardeners' time. Swarms of caterpillars appeared, which the gardeners – even Pesotsky and Tanya – squashed with their bare fingers, much to Kovrin's disgust. Besides this, they had to take orders for fruit and trees for the autumn and conduct an extensive correspondence. And at the most critical time, when no one seemed to have a moment to spare, the harvesting started and this took half the work-force away from the garden. Extremely sunburnt, worn-out and in a dreadful mood, Pesotsky would tear off into the garden, then out into the fields, shouting that they were tearing him to pieces and that he was going to put a bullet in his head.

And now there were rows about the trousseau, to which the Pesotskys attached no little importance. The snipping of scissors, the rattle of sewing-machines, the fumes from the hot-irons, the tantrums of the dressmaker – a nervous, touchy woman – had everyone's head in a whirl in that household. And as ill luck would have it, guests turned up every day and had to be amused, fed, even put up for the night. But all this toil passed by unnoticed, as though in a mist. Tanya felt as if she had been caught quite unawares by love and happiness, although, from the age of fourteen, she had been somehow sure that Kovrin would marry her, and no one else. She was amazed, bewildered and could not believe what had happened. One moment she would feel such joy that she wanted to fly up into the clouds and offer prayers to God; another time she would suddenly remember that she would have to leave her little nest and part from her father in August; on another occasion the thought would come to her, God knows from where, that she was an insignificant, trivial sort of woman, unworthy of a great man like Kovrin, and she would go to her room, lock the door and cry bitterly for several hours. When they had visitors she would suddenly find Kovrin extremely handsome and think that all the women were in love with him and jealous of her. And her heart would fill with rapturous pride, as if she had conquered the whole world. But he only had to give some young woman a welcoming smile and she would tremble with jealousy, go to her room – and there would be tears again. These new feelings took complete hold of her, she helped her father as though she were a machine and was blind to peaches, caterpillars, workers, oblivious of how swiftly the time was passing.

Almost exactly the same thing was happening to Pesotsky. He worked from morning till night, was always hurrying off somewhere, would boil over and lose his temper, but all this in some kind of magical half-sleep. He seemed to be two different persons at once: one was the real Pesotsky, listening to the head gardener Ivan Karlych's reports of things going wrong, flaring up and clutching his head in despair; the other was not the real Pesotsky, a half-intoxicated person who would suddenly break off a conversation about business in the middle of a sentence, tap the head gardener on the shoulder and mutter, 'Whatever you say, good stock matters. His mother was an amazing, noble, brilliant woman. It was a pleasure looking at her kind, bright, pure face, the face of an angel. She was excellent at drawing, wrote poetry, spoke five languages, sang ... The poor woman, God rest her soul, died of consumption.'

The unreal Pesotsky would continue after a brief silence, 'When he was a boy, growing up in my house, he had the same angelic, bright, kind face. And his look, his movements and his conversation were like his mother's – gentle and refined. And as for his intellect, he always staggered us with his intellect. By the way, he didn't become an MA for nothing, oh no! But you wait and see, Ivan Karlych, what he'll be like in ten years' time! There'll be no touching him!'

But at this point the real Pesotsky would suddenly take charge, pull a terrifying face, clutch his head and shout, 'The swines! They've polluted, fouled, frozen everything solid! The garden's ruined! It's finished!'

But Kovrin kept on working with his former enthusiasm and did not notice all the commotion around him. Love only added fuel to the flames. After every meeting with Tanya he would return to his room feeling happy, exultant and would pick up a book or manuscript with the same passion with which he had just kissed Tanya and declared his love. What the black monk had told him about God's Chosen, Eternal Truth, humanity's glittering future and so on lent his work a special, remarkable significance and filled his heart with pride and awareness of his own outstanding qualities. Once or twice a week he met the black monk in the park or in the house, had a talk with him, but it did not frighten him. On the contrary, it delighted him, as he was now firmly convinced that these kinds of visions visited only the select few, only outstanding men who had dedicated themselves to an idea.

One day the monk appeared at dinner time and sat by the window in the dining-room. Kovrin was overjoyed and deftly started a conversation with Pesotsky on a topic that the monk would very likely find interesting. The black visitor listened and nodded his head amiably. Pesotsky and Tanya listened too, cheerfully smiling and without suspecting that Kovrin was speaking not to them, but to his hallucination.

The Fast of the Assumption came unnoticed and soon afterwards the wedding-day, which, as Pesotsky insisted, was celebrated with 'a great splash', that is to say, with senseless festivities that went on for two whole days. They got through three thousand roubles' worth of food and drink, but with that miserable hired band, the riotous toasts and scurrying servants, the noise and the crush, they did not appreciate the expensive wines, nor the startling delicacies that had been ordered from Moscow.

VI

One long winter's night Kovrin was reading a French novel in bed. Poor Tanya, who suffered from headaches in the evening as she wasn't used to town life, had long been asleep and was muttering something incoherent.

Three o'clock struck. Kovrin snuffed the candle and lay down. He remained with eyes closed for a long time, but he could not sleep, possibly because the bedroom was very hot and Tanya was talking in her sleep. At half past four he lit the candle again and this time he saw the black monk sitting in the armchair near the bed.

'Good evening,' the monk said. After a brief pause he asked, 'What are you thinking about now?'

'Fame,' Kovrin answered. 'I've just been reading a French novel about a young scholar who does stupid things and who's wasting away because of his longing for fame. This longing is something I can't understand.'

'That's because you're intelligent. You're indifferent to fame, it's a toy that doesn't interest you.'

'Yes, that's true.'

'Fame doesn't tempt you. What is flattering, or amusing, or edifying in having your name carved on a tombstone only for it to be rubbed off by time, gilding as well? Fortunately there are too many of you for humanity's weak memory to retain your names.'

'I understand that,' Kovrin agreed. 'And why should they be remembered? But let's talk about something else. Happiness, for example. What is happiness?'

When the clock struck five he was sitting on the bed, his feet dangling over the carpet. He turned to the monk and said, 'In antiquity, a certain happy man grew scared of his own good fortune in the end, it was so immense. So, to propitiate the Gods, he sacrificed his favourite ring. Do you know that I myself, like Polycrates, am getting rather uneasy about my own good fortune? It seems strange that from morning to night I feel only joy, it fills my whole being and stifles all other feelings. As for sorrow, sadness or boredom, I just don't know what they are. Here I am, unable to sleep, suffering from insomnia, but I'm not bored. Seriously, I'm beginning to wonder what it all means.'

'But why?' the monk said in astonishment. 'Is joy something supernatural? Shouldn't it be looked on as man's normal state? The higher man's intellectual and moral development, the freer he is and the more pleasure life gives him. Socrates, Diogenes and Marcus Aurelius experienced joy, not sadness. And the Apostle says, "Rejoice ever more." So rejoice and be happy.'

'But supposing the Gods suddenly became angry?' Kovrin said jokingly and burst out laughing. 'If they were to take my comforts away and make me freeze and starve I don't think I would like that.'

Meanwhile Tanya had woken up and she looked at her husband in horror and bewilderment. He was talking to the armchair, laughing and gesticulating. His eyes shone and there was something peculiar in his laughter.

'Andrey, who are you talking to?' she asked, clutching the hand he had held out to the monk. 'Andrey, who is it?'

'What? Who?' Kovrin said, taken aback. 'Well, to *him* ... He's sitting over there,' he said, pointing at the black monk.

'There's no one here ... no one! Andrey, you're ill!' Tanya embraced her husband and pressed herself against him, as if to protect him from ghosts and covered his eyes with her hand. 'You're ill!' she sobbed, shaking all over. 'Forgive me, my dearest, but for some time now I've noticed something's wrong with you. You're sick in your mind, Andrey ...'

Her trembling infected him as well. He looked once more at the armchair, which was empty now and felt a sudden weakness in his arms and legs. This frightened him and he started to dress.

'It's nothing, Tanya, nothing,' he muttered, trembling. 'But to tell the truth, I am a little unwell ... it's time I admitted it.'

'I noticed it some time ago ... and Papa did too,' she said, trying to hold back her sobs. 'You talk to yourself, you smile so strangely ... you're not sleeping. Oh, good God, good God, save us!' she said in horror. 'But don't be afraid, Andrey dear, don't be afraid. For God's sake don't be afraid ...'

She began to dress too. Only now, as he looked at her, did Kovrin fully realize how dangerous his position was, only now did he understand the meaning of the black monk and his talks with him. He was quite convinced now that he was insane.

Both of them got dressed, without understanding why, and went into the ballroom, she first and he following. And there stood Pesotsky (he was staying with them and had been awakened by the sobbing) in his dressing-gown, with a candle in his hand.

'Don't be afraid, Andrey,' Tanya said, shaking as though in a fever. 'Don't be afraid ... Papa, it will pass ... it will pass ...'

Kovrin could not speak, he was so upset. He wanted to tell his father-in-law, just for a joke, 'Please congratulate me, I think I've gone mad ...', but all he could do was move his lips and smile bitterly.

At nine in the morning they put his greatcoat and furs on, wrapped a shawl round him and took him in a carriage to the doctor's. He began a course of treatment.

VII

Summer had come and the doctor ordered him into the country. Kovrin was better now, had stopped seeing the black monk and it only remained for him to get his strength back. Living with his father-in-law in the country, he drank a lot of milk, worked only two hours a day, and did not drink or smoke.

On the eve of Elijah's Day evening service was held in the house. When the lay reader handed the priest the censer, the enormous old ballroom smelt like a graveyard. Kovrin grew bored. He went out into the garden, wandered about without noticing the gorgeous flowers, sat down on a bench, and then strolled through the park. When he reached the river he went down the slope and stood looking thoughtfully at the water. The gloomy pines with their shaggy roots which had seen him here the previous year looking so young, joyful and lively, no longer talked in whispers, but stood motionless and dumb, as though they did not recognize him. And in fact his hair had been cut short, it was no longer beautiful, he walked sluggishly and his face had grown fuller and paler since the previous summer.

He crossed the foot-bridge to the other side. Where rye had been growing last year were rows of reaped oats. The sun had already set and a broad red glow burned on the horizon, a sign that it would be windy next day. It was quiet. Looking hard in the direction where the black monk had first appeared last year, Kovrin stood for about twenty minutes until the evening glow began to fade.

When he returned to the house, feeling listless and dissatisfied, the service was over. Pesotsky and Tanya were sitting on the terrace steps drinking tea. They were discussing something, but suddenly became silent when they saw Kovrin, and he guessed from their expressions that they had been talking about him.

'Well, I think it's time for your milk,' Tanya told her husband.

'No, it's not,' he answered, sitting on the lowest step. 'Drink it yourself, I don't want any.'

Tanya anxiously exchanged glances with her father and said quietly, 'But you yourself said the milk does you a lot of good!'

'Yes, a lot of good!' Kovrin replied, grinning. 'I congratulate you – since Friday I've put on another pound.' He firmly clasped his head and said in an anguished voice, 'Why, why did you try to cure me? All those bromides, idleness, warm baths, supervision, the cowardly fear with every mouthful, every step. All this will finally turn me into a complete idiot. I was going out of my mind, I had megalomania, but I was bright and cheerful, even happy. I was interesting and original. Now I've grown more rational and stable, but I'm just like everyone else, a nobody. Life bores me ... Oh, how cruelly you've treated me! I did have hallucinations, but did they harm anyone? Who did they harm, that's what I'd like to know?'

'God knows what you're talking about!' Pesotsky sighed. 'It's downright boring listening to you.'

'Then don't listen.'

Kovrin found other people's presence, especially Pesotsky's, irritating and he would answer him drily, coldly, rudely even; and he could not look at him without a feeling of hatred and mockery, which embarrassed Pesotsky, who would cough guiltily, although he didn't feel he was in the least to blame. Unable to understand why their friendly, loving relationship had changed so suddenly, Tanya pressed close to her father and looked him anxiously in the eye. She wanted to understand, but she could not, and she could only see that with every day relations were getting worse, that her father had aged considerably recently, while her husband had become irritable, moody, quarrelsome and uninteresting. No longer could she laugh and sing, she ate nothing at mealtimes, and lay awake whole nights expecting something terrible. She went through such torture that once she lay in a faint from lunch until the evening. During the service she thought that her father was crying and now, when the three of them sat on the terrace, she endeavoured not to think about it.

'How fortunate Buddha, Muhammad or Shakespeare were in not being treated by kind-hearted relatives for ecstasy and inspiration!' Kovrin said. 'If Muhammad had taken potassium bromide for his nerves, had worked only two hours a day and drunk milk, then that remarkable man would have left as much to posterity as his dog. In the long run doctors and kind relatives will turn humanity into a lot of morons. Mediocrity will pass for genius and civilization will perish. If only you knew,' Kovrin added with annoyance, 'how grateful I am to you!'

He was absolutely infuriated and quickly got up and went into the house, in case he said too much. It was quiet and the smell of tobacco flowers and jalap drifted in from the garden through the open windows. Green patches of moonlight lay on the floor in the huge dark ballroom and on the grand piano. Kovrin recalled the joys of the previous summer, when there was that same smell of jalap, and the moon had shone through the windows. Trying to recapture that mood he hurried to his study, lit a strong cigar and told a servant to bring him some wine. But the cigar left a bitter, disgusting taste and the wine tasted differently from last year: these were the effects of having given up the habit. The cigar and two mouthfuls of wine made his head go round, he had palpitations, for which he had to take potassium bromide.

Before she went to bed Tanya told him, 'Father adores you. You're cross with him about something and this is killing him. Just look, he's ageing by the hour, not by the day. I beg you, Andrey, for God's sake, for the sake of your late father, for the sake of my peace of mind, *please* be nice to him!'

'I can't and I won't!'

'But why not?' Tanya asked, trembling all over. 'Tell me, why not?'

'Because I don't like him, that's all,' Kovrin said nonchalantly, with a shrug of the shoulders. 'But let's not talk about him, he's *your* father.'

'I just can't understand, I really can't!' Tanya said, clutching her temples and staring fixedly at something. 'Something incomprehensible and horrible is going on in this house. You've changed, you're not your normal self. A clever, remarkable man like you losing your temper over trifles, getting mixed up in petty squabbles ... These little things worry you and sometimes I'm simply amazed, I just can't believe it's really you.' Then she continued, frightened of her own words and kissing his hands, 'Now, now, don't be angry, don't be angry. You are a clever man, and a good man. You will be fair to father, he's so kind.'

'He's not kind, only smug. Music-hall clowns like your father, bounteous old cranks, with their well-fed, smug faces, used to touch and amuse me once in stories, farces and in real life. But now I find them repugnant. They're egotists to the marrow. What I find most disgusting is their being so well fed, with that optimism that comes from a full belly. They're just like oxen or wild pigs.'

Tanya sat on the bed and lay her head on the pillow. 'This is sheer torture,' she said and from her voice it was plain that she was utterly exhausted and that she found it hard to speak. 'Not a single moment's peace since winter ... It's so terrible. Oh God, I feel shocking!'

'Yes, of course I'm the monster and you and your daddy are the sweet innocents. Of course!'

His face seemed ugly and unpleasant to Tanya. Hatred and that mocking expression did not suit him. And she had in fact noticed before that there was something lacking in his face, as if that had changed too since his hair was cut short. She wanted to say something to hurt him, but immediately she became aware of this hostile feeling she grew frightened and left the bedroom.

VIII

Kovrin was awarded a professorship. His inaugural lecture was fixed for 2 December and a notice announcing it was put up in the university corridor. But on the appointed day he cabled the dean, informing him he was not well enough to lecture.

He had a haemorrhage in the throat. He would spit blood, but twice a month there was considerable loss of blood, which left him extremely weak and drowsy. The illness did not frighten him particularly, since he knew his late mother had lived with exactly the same disease for ten years or more. And the doctors assured him it was not dangerous, and merely advised him not to get excited, lead a regular life and to talk as little as possible.

In January the lecture was again cancelled for the same reason and in February it was too late to start the course, which had to be postponed until the following year.

He no longer lived with Tanya, but with another woman two years older than he was and who cared for him as though he were a child. His state of mind was calm, submissive. He eagerly gave in to her and when Barbara (his mistress's name) decided to take him to the Crimea he agreed, although he expected no good to come from the trip.

They reached Sevastopol one evening and rested at a hotel before going on to Yalta the next day. They were both exhausted from the journey. Barbara drank some tea, went to bed and soon fell asleep. But Kovrin did not go to bed. Before he had left home – an hour before setting off for the station – he had received a letter from Tanya and had decided not to open it. It was now in one of his coat pockets and the thought of it had a disagreeable, unsettling effect on him. In the very depths of his heart he now considered his marriage to Tanya had been a mistake, and was pleased he had finally broken with her. The memory of that woman who had ended up as a walking skeleton and in whom everything seemed to have died – except for those large, clever, staring eyes – this memory aroused only pity in him and annoyance with himself. The writing on the envelope reminded him how unjust and cruel he had been two years ago, how he had taken revenge on others for his spiritual emptiness, his boredom, his loneliness, his dissatisfaction with life.

In this respect he remembered how he had once torn his dissertation and all the articles written during his illness into shreds and thrown them out of the window, the scraps of paper fluttering in the breeze, catching on trees and flowers. In every line he saw strange, utterly unfounded claims, enthusiasm run riot, audacity and megalomania, which had made him feel as if he were reading a description of his own vices. But when the last notebook had been torn up and had flown through the window, he felt for some reason bitterly annoyed; he had gone to his wife and told her many unpleasant things. God, how he had tormented her! Once, when he wanted to hurt his wife, he told her that her father had played a most distasteful role in their romance, having asked him if he would marry her. Pesotsky happened to hear this and rushed into the room speechless from despair; all he could do was stamp his feet and make a strange bellowing noise, as if he had lost the power of speech, while Tanya looked at her father, gave a heart-rending shriek and fainted. It was an ugly scene.

All this came to mind at the sight of the familiar handwriting. Kovrin went out onto the balcony. The weather was warm and calm, and he could smell the sea. The magnificent bay reflected the moon and the lights, and its colour was hard to describe. It was a delicate, soft blending of dark-blue and green; in places the water was like blue vitriol, in others the moonlight seemed to have taken on material substance and filled the bay instead of water. But what a harmony of colour, what a peaceful, calm and ennobling mood reigned over all!

The windows were most probably open in the room below,

beneath the balcony, as he could hear women's voices and laughter quite distinctly. Someone was having a party, it seemed.

Kovrin forced himself to open the letter, returned to his room and read: 'Father has just died. I owe that to you, as you killed him. Our garden is going to rack and ruin — strangers are running it — that's to say, what poor father feared so much has come about. I owe this to you as well. I hate you with all my heart and hope you'll soon be dead. Oh, how I'm suffering! An unbearable pain is burning inside me. May you be damned! I took you for an outstanding man, for a genius, I loved you, but you turned out a madman . . .'

Kovrin could not read any more, tore the letter up and threw it away. He was seized by a feeling of anxiety that was very close to terror. Barbara was sleeping behind a screen and he could hear her breathing. From the ground floor came women's voices and laughter, but he felt that besides himself there wasn't a living soul in the whole hotel. He was terrified because the unhappy, broken-hearted Tanya had cursed him in her letter and had wished for his death. He glanced at the door, as if fearing that the unknown force which had wrought such havoc in his life and in the lives of those near and dear over the last two years might come into the room and take possession of him again.

He knew from experience that the best cure for shattered nerves is work. One should sit down at a table and force oneself at all costs to concentrate on one idea, no matter what. From his red briefcase he took out a notebook in which he had sketched out a plan for a short work he had considered compiling in case he was bored doing nothing in the Crimea. He sat at the table and started work on the plan and it seemed his calm, resigned, detached state of mind was returning. The notebook and plan even stimulated him to meditate on the world's vanity. He thought how much life demands in return for those insignificant or very ordinary blessings that it can bestow. For example, to receive a university chair in one's late thirties, to be a run-of-the-mill professor, expounding in turgid, boring, ponderous language commonplace ideas that were not even original, in brief, to achieve the status of a third-rate scholar he, Kovrin, had had to study fifteen years — working day and night —

suffer severe mental illness, experience a broken marriage and do any number of stupid, unjust things that were best forgotten. Kovrin realized quite clearly now that he was a nobody and eagerly accepted the fact since, in his opinion, every man should be content with what he is.

The plan would have calmed his nerves, but the sight of the shiny white pieces of letter on the floor stopped him concentrating. He got up from the table, picked up the pieces and threw them out of the window, but a light breeze blew in from the sea and scattered them over the window-sill. Once again he was gripped by that restless feeling, akin to panic, and he began to think that there was no one else besides him in the whole hotel . . . He went out onto the balcony. The bay, which seemed to be alive, looked at him with its many sky-blue, dark-blue, turquoise and flame-coloured eyes and beckoned him. It was truly hot and humid, and a bathe would not have come amiss. A violin began to play on the ground floor, under his balcony, and two female voices softly sang a song he knew. It was about some young girl, sick in her mind, who heard mysterious sounds one night in her garden and thought it must be a truly divine harmony, incomprehensible to us mortals . . . Kovrin caught his breath, he felt twinges of sadness in his heart and a wonderful, sweet, long-forgotten gladness quivered in his heart.

A tall black column like a whirlwind or tornado appeared on the far side of the bay. With terrifying speed it moved over the water towards the hotel, growing smaller and darker as it approached, and Kovrin barely had time to move out of its path . . . Barefoot, arms folded over chest, with a bare grey head and black eyebrows, the monk floated past and stopped in the middle of the room.

'Why didn't you trust me?' he asked reproachfully, looking affectionately at Kovrin. 'If you had trusted me then, when I told you that you were a genius, you wouldn't have spent these two years so miserably, so unprofitably.'

Kovrin believed now that he was one of God's Chosen, and a genius, and he vividly recollected all his previous conversations with the black monk; he wanted to speak, but the blood welled out of his throat onto his chest. Not knowing what to do, he drew his hands over his chest and his shirt cuffs became soaked with blood.

He wanted to call Barbara, who was sleeping behind the screen and with a great effort murmured, 'Tanya!'

He fell on the floor, lifted himself on his arms and called again, 'Tanya!'

He called on Tanya, on the great garden with its gorgeous flowers sprinkled with dew, he called on the park, the pines with their shaggy roots, the rye-field, his wonderful learning, his youth, his daring, his joy; he called on life, which had been so beautiful. On the floor near his face, he saw a large pool of blood and was too weak now to say one word, but an ineffable, boundless happiness flooded his whole being. Beneath the balcony they were playing a serenade, and at the same time the black monk whispered to him that he was a genius and that he was dying only because his weak human body had lost its balance and could no longer serve to house a genius. When Barbara woke and came out from behind the screen Kovrin was dead and a blissful smile was frozen on his face.

Terror

My Friend's Story

Dmitry Silin had taken his degree at university and worked as a civil servant in St Petersburg, but when he was thirty he gave up his job to take up farming. Although this did not go at all badly, I felt that it wasn't his true vocation and that he would have done better to go back to St Petersburg. Sunburnt, grey with dust and exhausted by work, he would meet me near his gate or at the entrance and then would struggle to keep awake over supper, until his wife bundled him off to bed like a baby. At other times he would conquer his drowsiness and start expounding his lofty ideas in his gentle, sincere, almost pleading voice, and then I no longer saw him as a farmer or agriculturalist, but as a tormented man. I could see quite clearly that he didn't need his farming – all he wanted was to get through the day without any disaster.

I loved visiting him and sometimes I used to stay two or three days at a time. I liked his house, his park, his large orchard, his little river, and his rather languid, over-elaborate yet clear-sighted attitude to life. I must have liked him as a person too, though I can't vouch for that, since I still cannot properly interpret my feelings at the time.

He was clever, kind, quite interesting and sincere, but I well remember feeling upset and embarrassed whenever he revealed his innermost thoughts to me, telling me what great friends we were. There was something uncomfortable, oppressive in his fondness for me and I would have much preferred to be simply on ordinary, friendly terms.

The fact is, I was extremely attracted by his wife Marya. I wasn't actually in love with her, but I liked her face, her eyes, her voice, the way she walked. I would miss her when I hadn't seen her for some time and there was no one whose image I would so eagerly

ANTON CHEKHOV

conjure up as that beautiful, refined young woman's. I had no definite
designs on her, nor did I harbour any romantic illusions, but whenever we were alone I somehow remembered that her husband considered me his friend, and this made me feel most awkward. I loved
listening when she played my favourite piano pieces or when she
told me something interesting, and at the same time, when I thought
how she loved her husband, that he was my very good friend, that
she looked upon me as *his* friend, it would spoil my mood and I
would feel listless, embarrassed, bored. She would notice these
changes in me and usually say, 'You're bored without your friend.
I must call him in from the fields.'

When Silin arrived she would say, 'Well, your friend's here now,
that should make you happy.'

This state of affairs went on for about eighteen months. One
Sunday in July, for want of something better to do, Silin and I drove
out to the large village of Klushino to buy food for supper. While
we were shopping, the sun began to go down and evening came – an
evening I shall probably never forget for the rest of my life. After
buying some cheese that looked like soap and petrified sausage smelling of tar we went over to the inn in search of beer. Our coachman
drove off to the smithy to have the horses shod and we told him
we would wait for him by the church. As we wandered around,
talking and laughing at our purchases, we were shadowed by a man
with the silent, mysterious look of a detective, known in the district
by the rather peculiar nickname of 'Forty Martyrs'. This Forty
Martyrs was none other than Gabriel (or simply Gavryushka)
Severov, for a short while employed by me as footman, before I
dismissed him for drunkenness. He had worked for Dmitry Silin
as well and had been sacked for the same weakness. He was a violent
drunkard and his entire life had been just as drink-sodden and dissipated
as the man himself. His father had been a priest and his mother a
gentlewoman, so he had been born into the privileged classes. But
however closely I scrutinized his gaunt, submissive, always sweaty
face, his greying reddish beard, his pathetic tattered jacket and the
red shirt he wore outside his trousers, I could never find the least
trace of what is commonly called privilege. He considered himself
educated and said that he had studied at a church school, but hadn't

finished the course, having been expelled for smoking. Then he sang in the bishop's choir, and lived for two years in a monastery, from which he was also expelled – not for smoking, this time, but for his 'weakness'. He had trudged over two whole provinces, made certain applications to the local church authorities and various government offices and had appeared four times in court. Finally he became bogged down in our district, working as footman, forester, keeper of hounds, and church caretaker. He had married a widowed cook of loose morals and had finally sunk into this sea of drudgery and grown so used to its filth and squabbling that even he talked rather sceptically about his privileged origin, as if it were a myth. At the time I am writing of, he was wandering about jobless, passing himself off as a farrier and huntsman, while his wife vanished without trace.

We left the inn and walked over to the church, where we sat in the porch waiting for our coachman. Forty Martyrs was standing a short way off, pressing his hand to his mouth so that he could cough respectfully into it, should the need arise. It was dark now. There was a strong smell of evening dampness and the moon was about to rise. Right above us there were two clouds in the clear, starry sky, one large, the other smaller, just like mother and child. All alone, they were scurrying after each other towards the dying sunset glow.

'What a marvellous evening,' Silin said.

'Exceptional ...' Forty Martyrs agreed, respectfully coughing in his hand. 'Whatever made you come here, Mr Silin?' he asked in an ingratiating voice, evidently wanting to draw us into conversation.

Silin didn't reply. Forty Martyrs gave a deep sigh and said softly, without looking at us, 'I'm suffering only for something for which I must answer to God Almighty. Of course, I'm really finished, no good at nothing. Believe me, I've got nothing to eat, I'm worse off than a dog ... Forgive me for saying so, Mr Silin!'

Silin did not listen and sat reflecting with his head propped on his fists. The church stood on a high bank at the end of the street and through the churchyard railings could be seen a river, water-meadows on the far side and the crimson glow of a bonfire, around which dark figures and horses were moving. And beyond the fire were more lights – this was a hamlet ... they were singing there.

A mist was rising above the river and over the meadow in patches. Tall, thin wisps of thick, milky-white mist drifted over the river, veiling the reflection of the stars and clinging to the willows. Their shapes were ever-changing and some appeared to be embracing, some were bowing, while others held up arms draped in broad, priestly sleeves and seemed to be praying. They must very likely have put Silin in mind of ghosts and departed spirits, as he turned his face to me and asked with a sad smile, 'My dear chap, can you tell me why, when we want to tell some terrifying, mysterious, fantastic story, we don't draw on life for our subject-matter, but invariably on the world of ghosts, on beyond the grave?'

'What we *don't* understand – that's what scares us.'

'But we don't really understand life, do we? Tell me if we understand this life any better than the world beyond?'

Silin sat so close to me I could feel his breath on my cheek. In the evening gloom his pale, thin face seemed even paler and his dark beard blacker than soot. His eyes were sad, sincere and rather frightened, as if he were going to tell me something terrifying. He looked me in the eye and continued in that habitually pleading voice of his, 'Both this life and the next are equally incomprehensible and frightening. Anyone who's afraid of ghosts should be afraid of me too, and of these lights, and the sky, since all these things – if you think hard about it – are just as incomprehensible and fantastic as visitors from the world beyond. Prince Hamlet did not kill himself, because he feared "in that sleep of death what dreams may come". I like his celebrated soliloquy, but to be honest, it never really moved me. Speaking to you as a friend, I must tell you that sometimes, in moments of anguish, I have imagined my last hours on earth and my fancy has conjured up thousands of the grimmest apparitions. I've managed to work myself into an agony of exaltation, of night-marish proportions. But I can assure you I found reality even more terrifying. There's no denying that ghosts *are* frightening, but so is life. I don't understand life and it scares me, my dear friend. Perhaps I'm sick, perhaps I've gone off the rails. It seems to a normal, healthy man that he understands everything he sees or hears, but I've lost my grip on this "seems" and day after day I poison myself with fear. There's an illness, fear of open spaces: mine is fear of life. When I lie on the grass and look for a long time at a small insect that was born only yesterday and understands nothing, I think its life must be just one never-ending horror, and in this insect I can see myself.'

'But what exactly are you afraid of?' I asked.

'Everything. By nature I'm not very deep, I don't interest myself very much in questions like the world hereafter or the destiny of mankind, and I'm not the kind of man who likes to soar into the clouds. What I'm most afraid of is ordinary, everyday existence, which no one can escape. I can't tell the true from the false when I act and this worries me. I realize that the conditions I live in and my upbringing have imprisoned me in a closed circle of lies, that my whole life is nothing but worrying every day how to deceive others and myself without noticing it. The thought that I shan't escape from this tissue of lies until the day I die really frightens the life out of me. I do something one day, and the next I have no idea why I did it. I entered government service in St Petersburg, became frightened, so I came here to farm and got scared again ... I realize we know very little, that's why we make mistakes every day. We're unjust, slander people or torment the life out of them, waste all our energy on futile trash which only makes our lives harder. And this scares me. I just don't see how anyone can need it. I don't understand people, my friend, and I'm scared of them. Just looking at peasants terrifies me and I have no idea for what higher purpose they suffer so much, or what they are living for. If life is only for pleasure, then they're superfluous, no use to anyone. But if the purpose of life is poverty, complete and utter ignorance, then I don't see what use this torment can be to anyone. I don't understand anyone or anything.' Silin pointed to Forty Martyrs and said, 'Just see if *you* can decipher that character over there! Have a good think about him!'

When he saw both of us looking at him, Forty Martyrs respectfully coughed into his fist and said, 'I was always a loyal servant to good masters, but it was drinking spirits what really finished me. If you could find room in your hearts for a miserable wretch like me and give me a job, I'd swear before God not to touch them, I would. And I never go back on my word!'

The church caretaker passed by, gave us a puzzled look and started pulling the bell-rope. Slowly, with long drawn-out peals that rudely shattered the evening calm, the bell tolled ten.

'Why, it's ten already!' Silin said. 'Time we were off. Yes, my dear friend,' he sighed, 'if only you knew how scared I am of my own, ordinary, everyday thoughts, which, on the face of it, don't appear to hold any terrors. I plunge myself into my work to stop myself thinking and try to tire myself out, so I can get a good night's sleep. Children, a wife, are nothing special for other men, but I find them such a burden, my dear friend!' He rubbed his face, cleared his throat and laughed. 'If only I could tell you what a stupid role I've played in my life-time!' he said. 'Everyone tells me I have a nice wife, lovely children, and that I'm a good family man. They think I'm very happy and they envy me. Well, as we've gone this far I might as well let you into a secret – my happy family life is really only a tragic mistake and it frightens me too.'

A strained smile made his pale face look ugly. He put his arm round my waist and continued in an undertone, 'You're a real friend, I trust you and have deep respect for you. Friendship is sent from above so that we can unburden our hearts and find refuge from those mysteries that prey on our nerves. Please let me take advantage of your affection and tell you the whole truth. My family life, which you find so delightful, is my crowning misfortune and what scares me most. I made a peculiar, stupid marriage. I should tell you that before our marriage I was madly in love with Marya and courted her for two years. I proposed five times and she refused me, as she felt nothing for me. The sixth time, when I was burning with passion and went down on my knees to ask for her hand like someone begging for charity, she consented ... "I don't love you," she told me, "but I will be faithful ..." Rapturously, I accepted this condition. I knew what it meant at the time, but I swear by God that I don't know what it means any more. "I don't love you, but I will be faithful" – what *does* it mean? It's all so obscure, so hazy ... I love her now as much as I did on our wedding-day, but she seems as indifferent as ever and she's probably glad when I'm not here. I don't know for certain whether she loves me or not, I just don't know. But after all, we live under the same roof, call each other "dear", sleep together, have children, hold our property in both names, don't we?

What does it all mean? What's the point of it all? Can you make anything of it, my dear friend? It's sheer torture! Because I don't understand anything about our relationship, first I hate her, then myself, then the two of us together. My mind's a perfect jumble, I torture myself and I'm growing more stupid by the day. And as if to spite me she looks prettier every day, she's becoming quite stunning ... I think she has marvellous hair and she smiles like no other woman. I love her, yet I know my love is hopeless. Hopeless love for a woman who has already borne you two children! What do you make of that? Isn't it enough to terrify anyone? Isn't it more frightening than all those ghosts of yours?'

He was just in the mood to carry on like this for some time, but fortunately the coachman called us: the horses were ready. As we climbed into our carriage, Forty Martyrs doffed his cap, helped us to our seat and his expression indicated he had long been waiting for this chance to touch our precious bodies.

'Mr Silin, may I come and see you?' he asked, blinking violently, his head cocked to one side. 'Please have pity, for God's sake! I'm dying of hunger!'

'Oh, all right then,' Silin said. 'You can come for three days, we'll see how it goes after that.'

Forty Martyrs was overjoyed and exclaimed, 'Oh, yes sir! I'll be along later today, sir.'

It was about four miles to the house. Pleased that he had at last unburdened himself to his friend, Silin kept his arm around my waist all the way back. His voice was no longer full of woe and apprehension, and cheerfully he explained that if things had been happy at home he would have returned to St Petersburg to do some academic work. The prevailing mood, he said, which had driven so many gifted young people into the countryside, was very much to be regretted. Russia had abundant rye and wheat, but no civilized persons at all. Healthy and gifted young people should take up science, the arts and politics. Anything else was wasteful. He loved philosophizing like this and regretted having to leave me early next morning, as he had to go to a timber sale.

I felt awkward and dispirited and I sensed I was deceiving him. At the same time the feeling was a pleasant one. As I looked at the huge, crimson rising moon, I pictured that tall, shapely, pale-faced blonde, always so elegantly dressed and smelling of some special scent, rather like musk, and the thought that she didn't love her husband cheered me up a little.

When we reached home we sat down to supper. Marya laughingly regaled us with the food we had bought. I found that she really did have remarkable hair, that she smiled like no other woman. As I watched her, I wanted every movement and glance to tell me she didn't love her husband, and that seemed to be the case.

Silin was soon struggling against sleep. He sat with us for about ten minutes after supper, then he said, 'Please do what you like, but I have to be up at three, so you'll have to excuse me.'

He kissed his wife tenderly, firmly and gratefully shook my hand and made me promise to visit them next week without fail. To avoid oversleeping he went off to spend the night in one of the outbuildings.

Marya always went to bed late — in St Petersburg style — and I was now rather glad of it.

'Well,' I began when we were alone. 'Well now, please play something for me.'

I didn't want any music, but I didn't know how to start a conversation. She sat down at the piano and played — I can't remember what it was. I sat close by, looking at her plump white arms and trying to read her cold, indifferent face. But just then something made her smile and she looked at me.

'It's boring for you without your friend,' she said.

I laughed. 'Once a month would have been enough to keep up the friendship, but here I am more than once a week.'

Having said that I stood up and paced the room excitedly. She stood up as well and went over to the fireplace. 'What do you mean by that?' she asked, raising her big, bright eyes at me. I didn't reply.

'What you said isn't true,' she went on after a moment's reflection. 'You only come here because of Dmitry. Well, I'm glad. It's not often one sees such friendship these days.'

'Well!' I thought and not knowing what to say asked, 'Would you care for a stroll in the garden?'

'No.'

I went out on to the terrace. My scalp tingled and I felt chill with excitement. Now I was convinced that our conversation would be absolutely trivial and that we wouldn't manage to say anything special to each other. But the thing I had never even dared dream of was bound to happen that night – that was certain. It just had to be then – or never.

'What marvellous weather!' I said in a loud voice.

'I really don't care about the weather,' came the reply.

I went into the drawing-room. Marya was still standing by the fireplace, her hands behind her back, thinking and looking away.

'Why don't you care?' I asked.

'Because I'm bored. You're bored only when you're without your friend, but I'm always bored. However ... that wouldn't interest you.'

I stood at the piano, struck a few chords and waited to hear what she would say next.

'Please, don't stand on ceremony,' she said, glaring at me as if about to cry with annoyance. 'If you're tired, then go to bed. Don't think because you're Dmitry's friend you have to be bored by his wife. I don't want any sacrifices, please go.'

Of course, I didn't. She went out onto the terrace, while I stayed in the drawing-room turning over the pages in the music-book for about five minutes. Then I went out too. We stood side by side in the shadow of the curtains and the steps below were flooded in moonlight. The black shadows of trees lay across flower-beds and on the yellow sand of the paths.

'I shall have to leave tomorrow too,' I said.

'Of course, you can't stay if my husband's not here,' she said mockingly. 'I can imagine how miserable you would be if you fell in love! Just wait, one day I'll suddenly throw my arms round your neck ... then I'll be able to watch the horrified expression on your face as you run away. It should be interesting.'

There was anger in her words and her pale face, but her eyes were full of the most tender, passionate love. Now I looked on this beautiful creature as my very own and for the first time I noticed that she had marvellous golden eyebrows, such as I had never seen before. The thought that I could take her in my arms there and then, fondle her, touch her wonderful hair, suddenly seemed so fantastic that I laughed and closed my eyes.

'It's late, though,' she said. 'Have a restful night.'

'I don't want a restful night,' I said, laughing, as I followed her into the drawing-room. 'To hell with tonight if it turns out restful!'

Squeezing her hands as I led her to the door, I could tell from her face that she understood me and that she was pleased I had understood her.

I went to my room. Dmitry's cap was lying near the books on the table and this reminded me of our friendship. Taking my walking-stick, I went out into the garden. The mist was rising and those tall, thin spectres I had seen not long before on the river were drifting near trees and bushes and embracing them. What a pity I could not speak to them!

Every leaf, every dew-drop was sharply outlined in the exceptionally clear air, everything was smiling at me in the sleepy silence. As I passed the green benches the words from some play of Shakespeare's came to mind:

How sweet the moonlight sleeps upon this bank!

There was a small hillock in the garden. I climbed it and sat down. An overwhelming feeling of enchantment took hold of me. I knew for sure that soon I would embrace her, press against that voluptuous body and kiss those golden eyebrows, but I didn't want to believe it: I wanted to tease myself and I was sorry she had yielded so easily and hadn't made me suffer.

But then, suddenly, I heard heavy footsteps. A man of medium height appeared on the path and immediately I recognized Forty Martyrs. He sat on the bench with a deep sigh, crossed himself three times and lay down. A minute later he stood up and lay on his other side. He could not sleep for the gnats and the night dampness. 'What a life!' he muttered. 'What a wretched, harsh life!'

Looking at his thin, bent body and listening to his deep, hoarse sighs reminded me of another unhappy, wretched life, confessed to me that same day, and I was appalled at my own blissfully happy state. I climbed down the hillock and went back to the house.

'My friend finds life terrifying,' I thought, 'so I mustn't stand on ceremony with it – I must wreck it, grasp everything I can get before life crushes *me*.'

Marya was standing on the terrace. Silently I put my arms around her and hungrily kissed her eyebrows, temples, neck ...

In my room she told me that she had loved me for a long time, more than a year. She swore that she loved me, wept and begged me to take her away with me. Every now and then I led her over to the window, so that I could see her face in the moonlight. She was like a beautiful dream and I rushed to hold her tight to convince myself that it was all really happening. It had been a long time since I had known such ecstasy ... But for all that, somewhere in the depths of my heart, I felt discomforted, uneasy. There was something just as awkward, unwished-for, oppressive in the love she felt for me as in Dmitry's friendship. This was love on the grand scale, all very serious, with the usual tears and vows, but I didn't want anything serious – I wanted no tears, or vows, or talks about the future: all I wanted was for this moonlit night to flash through our lives like a bright meteor – that would be enough.

On the stroke of three she left me, and as I was standing in the doorway watching her go, Silin suddenly appeared at the end of the corridor. On seeing him she shuddered, made way, and her whole body expressed revulsion. He smiled rather strangely, coughed and came into my room.

'I left my cap here yesterday,' he said, without looking at me.

He found it, put it on with both hands; then he looked at my embarrassed face, my slippers and said in a strange hoarse voice that wasn't like his at all, 'I'm probably fated never to understand anything. If you can make head or tail of anything then I must congratulate you. Everything's black as pitch to me.'

He went out, coughing. Afterwards I watched him through the window harnessing the horses by the stables. His hands were shaking, he was hurrying and he kept looking back at the house. Most likely, he was frightened. When he climbed into his carriage and struck the horses there was a strange, persecuted look on his face.

I left soon after. The sun was already rising and yesterday's mist clung timidly to the bushes and hillocks. Forty Martyrs had already managed to get a drink somewhere and was sitting on the box talking drunken nonsense.

'I'm a free man!' he shouted at the horses. 'Whoa, my beauties! *I* was born a real gent, if you want to know!'

I could not get Silin's terror out of my mind and it infected me as well. I thought about all that had happened and I could make nothing of it. I watched the crows, and their flight struck me as strange and terrifying.

'Why *did* I do it?' I asked myself in bewilderment and desperation. 'Why did things turn out that way, and not differently? To whom, and for what, was it necessary for his wife to fall so seriously in love with me and for him to come to my room for his cap? And what did his cap have to do with it?'

That day I left for St Petersburg and I have never seen Dmitry Silin and his wife since. People say they're still living together.

The Two Volodyas

'Let me go, *I* want to drive. I'm going to sit next to the driver,' Sophia shouted. 'Driver, wait. I'm coming up on to the box to sit next to you.'

She stood on the sledge while her husband Volodya Nikitych and her childhood friend Volodya Mikhaylovich held her by the arm in case she fell. Away sped the troika.

'I said you shouldn't have given her brandy,' Volodya Nikitych whispered irritably to his companion. 'You're a fine one!'

From past experience the Colonel knew that when women like his wife Sophia had been in riotous, rather inebriated high spirits he could normally expect fits of hysterical laughter and tears to follow. He was afraid that once they got home he would have to run around with the cold compresses and medicine instead of being able to go to bed.

'Whoa!' Sophia shouted. 'I want to drive.'

She was really very gay and in an exultant mood. For two months after her wedding she had been tormented by the thought that she had married Colonel Yagich for his money or, as they say, *par dépit*. That same evening, in the out-of-town restaurant, she finally became convinced that she loved him passionately. In spite of his fifty-four years, he was so trim, sprightly and athletic, and he told puns and joined in the gypsy girls' songs with such charm. It is true that nowadays old men are a thousand times more interesting than young ones, as though age and youth had changed places. The Colonel was two years older than her father, but was that important if, to be quite honest, he was infinitely stronger, more energetic and livelier than she was, even though she was only twenty-three?

'Oh, my darling!' she thought. 'My wonderful man!'

In the restaurant she had come to the conclusion too that not a spark remained of her old feelings. To her childhood friend Volodya, whom only yesterday she had loved to distraction, she now felt completely indifferent. The whole evening he had struck her as a lifeless, sleepy, boring nobody and the habitual coolness with which he avoided paying restaurant bills exasperated her so much this time that she very nearly told him, 'You should have stayed at home if you're so poor.' The Colonel footed the bill.

Perhaps it was the trees, telegraph poles and snowdrifts all flashing past that aroused the most varied thoughts. She reflected that the meal had cost one hundred and twenty roubles – with a hundred for the gypsies – and that the next day, if she so wished, she could throw a thousand roubles away, whereas two months ago, before the wedding, she did not have three roubles to call her own and she had to turn to her father for every little thing. How her life had changed!

Her thoughts were in a muddle and she remembered how, when she was about ten, Colonel Yagich, her husband now, had made advances to her aunt and how everyone in the house had said that he had ruined her. In fact, her aunt often came down to dinner with tear-stained eyes and was always going away somewhere; people said the poor woman was suffering terribly. In those days he was very handsome and had extraordinary success with women; the whole town knew him and he was said to visit his admirers every day, like a doctor doing his rounds. Even now, despite his grey hair, wrinkles and spectacles, his thin face looked handsome, especially in profile.

Sophia's father was an army doctor and had once served in Yagich's regiment. Volodya senior's father had also been an army doctor and had once served in the same regiment as her own father and Yagich. Despite some highly involved and frantic amorous adventures, Volodya junior had been an excellent student. He graduated with honours from university, had decided to specialize in foreign literature and was said to be writing his thesis. He lived in the barracks with his doctor father and he had no money of his own, although he was now thirty. When they were children, Sophia and he had lived in different flats, but in the same building, and he often came to play with her; together they had dancing and French lessons. But when he grew up into a well-built, exceedingly good-looking young man, she began to be shy of him. Then she fell madly in love with him and was still in love until shortly before she married Yagich. He too had extraordinary success with women, from the age of fourteen almost, and the ladies who deceived their husbands with him exonerated themselves by saying Volodya was 'so little'. Not long before, he was said to be living in digs close to the University and every time you knocked, his footsteps could be heard on the other side of the door and then the whispered apology: *'Pardon, je ne suis pas seul.'* Yagich was delighted with him, gave him his blessing for the future as Derzhavin had blessed Pushkin,[*] and was evidently very fond of him. For hours on end they would silently play billiards or piquet, and if Yagich went off somewhere in a troika, he would take Volodya with him; only Yagich shared the secret of his thesis. In earlier days, when the Colonel was younger, they were often rivals, but were never jealous of one another. When they were in company, which they frequented together, Yagich was called 'Big Volodya' and his friend 'Little Volodya'.

Besides Big Volodya and Little Volodya, and Sophia, there was someone else in the sledge, Margarita – or Rita as everyone called her – Mrs Yagich's cousin. She was a spinster, in her thirties, very pale, with black eyebrows, pince-nez, who chain-smoked even when it was freezing; there was always ash on her lap and chest. She spoke through her nose and drawled; she was cold and unemotional, could drink any quantity of liqueur or brandy without getting drunk and told stories abounding in *doubles entendres* in a dull, tasteless way. At home she read the learned reviews all day long, scattering ash all over them; or she would eat crystallized apples.

'Sophia, don't play the fool,' she drawled; 'it's really so stupid.'

When the town gates came into view the troika slowed down; they caught glimpses of people and houses, and Sophia quietened down, snuggled against her husband and gave herself up to her thoughts. And now gloomy thoughts began to mingle with her happy, carefree fantasies. The man opposite knew that she had loved him (so she thought), and of course he believed the reports that she

[*] The aged poet Derzhavin had blessed Pushkin as a schoolboy when he recited his celebratory poem before him at Tsarskoye Selo.

had married the Colonel *par dépit*. Not once had she confessed her love and she did not want him to know. She had concealed her feelings, but his expression clearly showed that he understood her perfectly, and so her pride suffered. But most humiliating of all about her situation was the fact that Little Volodya had suddenly started paying attention to her after her marriage, which had never happened before. He would sit with her for hours on end, in silence, or telling her some nonsense; and now in the sledge he was gently touching her leg or squeezing her hand, without saying a word. Evidently, all he wanted was for her to get married. No less obviously, he did not think much of her and she interested him only in a certain way, as an immoral, disreputable woman. And this mingling of triumphant love for her husband and injured pride was the reason for her behaving so irresponsibly, prompting her to sit on the box and shout and whistle ...

Just as they were passing the convent the great twenty-ton bell started clanging away. Rita crossed herself.

'Our Olga is in that convent,' Sophia said, crossing herself and shuddering.

'Why did she become a nun?' the Colonel asked.

'*Par dépit*,' Rita answered angrily, obviously hinting at Sophia's marriage to Yagich. 'This *par dépit* is all the rage now. It's a challenge to the whole of society. She was a proper good-time girl, a terrible flirt, all she liked was dances and dancing partners. And then suddenly we have all this! She took us all by surprise!'

'That's not true,' Little Volodya said, lowering the collar of his fur coat and revealing his handsome face. 'This wasn't a case of *par dépit*, but something really terrible. Her brother Dmitry was sentenced to hard labour in Siberia and no one knows where he is now. The mother died of grief.' He raised his collar again. 'And Olga did the right thing,' he added dully. 'Living as a ward, and with a treasure like our Sophia, what's more – that's enough food for thought!'

Sophia noted the contempt in his voice and wanted to say something very nasty in reply, but she said nothing. Once more euphoria gripped her. She stood up and shouted tearfully, 'I want to go to morning service. Driver, turn back! I want to see Olga!'

They turned back. The convent bell had a dull peal and Sophia felt there was something in it reminding her of Olga and her life. Bells rang out from other churches. When the driver had brought the troika to a halt, Sophia leapt from the sledge and rushed unescorted to the gates.

'Please don't be long!' her husband shouted. 'It's late.'

She went through the dark gates, then along the path leading to the main church; the light snow crunched under her feet and the tolling of the bells sounded right over her head now and seemed to penetrate her whole being. First she came to the church door, the three steps down, then the porch, with paintings of the saints on both sides; there was a smell of juniper and incense. Then came another door, which a dark figure opened, bowing very low ... In the church the service had not yet begun. One of the nuns was in front of the icon-screen lighting candles in their holders, another was lighting a chandelier. Here and there, close to the columns and side-chapels, were motionless, black figures. 'They'll be standing in exactly the same places till morning,' Sophia thought and the whole place struck her as dark, cold, depressing – more depressing than a graveyard. Feeling bored, she glanced at the motionless, frozen figures and suddenly her heart sank. Somehow she recognized one of the nuns – short, with thin shoulders and a black shawl on her head – as Olga, although when she had entered the convent she had been plump and taller, she thought. Deeply disturbed for some reason, Sophia hesitantly walked over to the lay sister, looked over her shoulder into her face and saw it *was* Olga.

'Olga!' she said, clasping her hands and too excited to say anything else. 'Olga!'

The nun recognized her immediately, raised her eyebrows in astonishment and her pale, freshly washed face (even, it seemed, her white kerchief visible under her shawl) glowed with joy.

'God has performed a miracle,' she said and also clasped her thin, pale little hands.

Sophia firmly embraced her and kissed her, frightened as she did so that her breath might smell of drink.

'We were just passing and we thought of you,' she said breathlessly, as though she had just completed a fast walk. 'Heavens, how pale you are! I'm ... I'm very pleased to see you. Well, how are you? Bored?' Sophia looked round at the other nuns and now she lowered her voice: 'So much has happened ... you know I married Volodya Yagich. You must remember him ... I'm very happy.'

'Well, thank the Lord for that! And is your father well?'

'Yes, he often remembers you. But you must come and see us during the holidays, Olga. Will you do that?'

'Yes, I'll come,' Olga said smiling. 'I'll come the day after to-morrow.'

Without even knowing why, Sophia burst into tears and cried in silence for a whole minute. Then she dried her eyes and said, 'Rita will be very sorry she didn't see you. She's with us too. And Little Volodya. They're at the gate. How pleased they would be to see you! Come out and see them, the service hasn't started yet.'

'All right,' Olga agreed. She crossed herself three times and walked out with Sophia.

'So, you said you're happy, Sophia,' she said after they were past the gates.

'Very.'

'Well, thank God.'

When Big Volodya and Little Volodya saw the nun they got off the sledge and greeted her respectfully. They were visibly moved by her pale face and her nun's black habit, and they were both pleased that she remembered them and had come to greet them. Sophia wrapped her in a rug and covered her with one flap of her fur coat to protect her from the cold. Her recent tears had lightened and cleansed her soul and she was glad that the noisy, riotous and essentially immoral night had unexpectedly come to such a pure and quiet conclusion. Then to keep Olga by her side longer, she suggested, 'Let's take her for a ride! Olga, get in. Just a little one.'

The men expected the nun to refuse – religious people don't go around in troikas – but to their amazement she agreed and got in. When the troika hurtled off towards the town gates, no one said a word; their only concern was to make her warm and comfortable. Each one of them thought about the difference in her from before. Her face was impassive, somewhat expressionless, cold, pale, trans-parent, as though water flowed in her veins instead of blood. Two or three years ago she had been buxom and rosy-cheeked, had talked about eligible bachelors and laughed loud at the least thing.

The troika turned round at the town gate. Ten minutes later they were back at the convent and Olga climbed out. The bells were ringing a series of chimes.

'God be with you,' Olga said, giving a low, nun-like bow.

'So you will come then, Olga?'

'Of course I will.'

She quickly left and soon disappeared through the dark gateway. After the troika had moved on everyone somehow felt very sad. No one said a word. Sophia felt weak all over and her heart sank. Making a nun get into a sledge and go for a ride with that drunken crowd struck her now as stupid, tactless and almost sacrilegious. The desire for self-deception vanished with her tipsiness and now she clearly realized that she did not and could not love her husband, it was all nothing but silly nonsense. She had married for money because, as her ex-schoolgirl friends put it, he was 'madly rich', because she was terrified of becoming an old maid, like Rita, because her doctor father got on her nerves and because she wanted to annoy Little Volodya. Had she guessed when she was contemplating marriage that it would turn out to be so nasty, painful and ugly, she would never have agreed to it, not for anything in the world. But the damage was done now, she had to accept things.

They arrived home. As she lay in her warm, soft bed and covered herself with a blanket, Sophia recalled the dark porch, the smell of incense, the figures by the columns, and she was distressed at the thought that these figures would still be standing there, quite motionless, all the time she was sleeping. Early morning service would be interminably long, and after that there would be the hours, then Mass, then more prayers ...

'But surely God exists? He certainly exists and I must certainly die. Therefore, sooner or later, I must think of my soul, eternal life, like Olga does. Olga is saved now, she has solved all her problems for herself ... But what if there is *no* God? Then her life has been wasted. But how has it been wasted? Why?'

A minute later another thought entered her head, 'God exists, death will certainly come. I should be thinking of my soul. If Olga could see her death this very minute she would not be afraid. She's ready. But the most important thing is, she's solved the riddle of existence for herself. God exists ... yes. But isn't there another way out apart from becoming a nun? *That* means renouncing life, destroying it ...' Sophia became rather scared and hid her head under the pillow. 'I mustn't think about it,' she whispered, 'I mustn't.'

Yagich was walking up and down in the next room, his spurs softly jingling; he was deep in thought. Sophia thought that this man was near and dear to her only in one thing – he was called Volodya too. She sat on her bed and tenderly called, 'Volodya!'

'What do you want?' her husband replied.

'Nothing.'

She lay down again. There were bells tolling – from that same convent, perhaps – and once again she recalled the porch and the dark figures. Thoughts of God and inescapable death wandered through her mind; she pulled the blanket over her head to drown the sound of the bells. She expected, before old age and death came, that her life would drag on for such a terribly long time, and from one day to the next she would have to cope with the nearness of someone she did not love, and who had come into the room just at that moment and was getting into bed; and she would have to suppress that hopeless love for another – someone who was so young, so charming and apparently so unusual. She looked at her husband and wanted to say good night, but she suddenly burst into tears instead. She felt annoyed with herself.

'Well, we're off again,' Yagich said.

She did calm down, but not until later, towards ten in the morning. She had stopped crying and shaking all over; she developed a severe headache, however. Yagich was hurrying, getting ready for late Mass and in the next room he was grumbling at the batman helping him dress. He came into the bedroom once, his spurs softly jingling, took something, and when he came in a second time he was wearing epaulettes and decorations; he limped slightly from rheumatism. He gave Sophia the impression he was a beast of prey, prowling and looking round.

Then she heard him on the telephone. 'Please put me through to the Vasilyevsky Barracks,' he said. A minute later he went on, 'Is that

Vasilyevsky Barracks? Please ask Dr Salimovich to come to the phone.' Then, a minute later, 'Who am I speaking to? Volodya? Fine. My dear chap, please ask your father to come over right away, my wife is terribly off colour after what happened yesterday. What's that? He's out? Hm ... thanks ... Yes, I'd be much obliged. *Merci*.'

Yagich came into the bedroom for the third time, bent over his wife, made the sign of the cross over her, let her kiss his hand (women who loved him would kiss his hand, he was used to this), and said he would be back for dinner. And he left.

Towards noon the maid announced Little Volodya. Swaying from weariness and her headache, Sophia quickly put on her stunning new lilac, fur-trimmed négligé and hurriedly tidied her hair. In her heart she felt inexpressibly tender and trembled for joy – and for fear he might leave. She wanted just one look at him.

Little Volodya was paying her a visit in formal dress – tailcoat and white tie. When Sophia came into the drawing-room he kissed her hand, said how deeply sorry he was to see her so unwell. When they had sat down he praised her négligé.

'Seeing Olga last night has upset me,' she said. 'At first it was painful for me, but now I envy her. She is like an immovable rock, it's impossible to budge her. But was there really no other way out for her, Volodya? Can burying oneself alive really solve life's problems? You'd call that death, not life, wouldn't you?' At the mention of Olga, Little Volodya's face showed deep emotion. 'Now look, Volodya, you're a clever man,' Sophia said; 'teach me to be like her. Of course, I'm a non-believer and I couldn't become a nun. But couldn't I do something that would be just as good? I find life hard enough.' After a brief silence she continued, 'Teach me ... tell me something that will convince me. Just one word.'

'One word? Okay. Ta-ra-ra-boomdeay.'

'Volodya, why do you despise me?' she asked excitedly. 'You speak to me in some special – if you'll forgive the expression – fancy language that one doesn't use with friends and respectable women. You're a successful scholar, you love your studies, but why do you never tell me about them? Why? Aren't I good enough?'

Little Volodya frowned irritably and said, 'Why this sudden passion for scholarship? Perhaps you want us to have a constitution? Or perhaps sturgeon with horse-radish?'

'Oh, have it your way then. I'm a mediocre, worthless, unprincipled, stupid woman ... I've made thousands, thousands of mistakes. I'm not right in the head, a loose woman, and for that I deserve contempt. But you're ten years older than me, Volodya, aren't you? And my husband is thirty years older. You watched me grow up and if you'd wanted to, you could have made me anything you wanted, an angel even. But you ...' (here her voice shook) 'treat me dreadfully. Yagich was an old man when he married me, and you ...'

'Well, enough of that. Enough,' Volodya said, drawing closer to her and kissing both her hands. 'We'll leave the Schopenhauers to philosophize and argue about anything they like, but now we're going to kiss these sweet little hands.'

'You despise me and if only you knew the suffering it causes me,' she said hesitantly, knowing beforehand that he would not believe her. 'If you only knew how I want to improve myself, to start a new life! It fills me with joy just thinking about it,' she murmured and actually shed a few joyous tears. 'To be a good, honest, decent person, not to lie, to have a purpose in life.'

'Stop it please! You don't have to put on an act for me, I don't like it,' Volodya said, looking peevish. 'Heavens, you'd think we were at the theatre! Let's behave like normal human beings!'

To prevent him from leaving in a temper she began to make excuses, forced herself to smile – to please him – mentioned Olga again and that she wanted to solve the riddle of her existence, to become a real human being.

'Ta-ra-ra-boomdeay,' he chanted softly. 'Ta-ra-ra-boomdeay!'

And then quite suddenly he clasped her waist. Barely conscious of what she was doing she put her hands on his shoulders and for a whole minute looked rapturously at his clever, sarcastic face, his forehead, eyes, handsome beard ...

'You've known for a long time that I love you,' she confessed with an agonized blush and she felt that even her lips had twisted in a paroxysm of shame. 'I love you. So why do you torment me?'

She closed her eyes and kissed him firmly on the lips. For a long time – a whole minute perhaps – she just could not bring herself to end this kiss, although she knew very well that she was behaving badly, that he might tell her off, or that a servant might come in . . .

Half an hour later, when he had got what he wanted, he sat in the dining-room eating a snack while she knelt before him, staring hungrily into his face. He told her she was like a small dog waiting for someone to toss it a piece of ham. Then he sat her on one knee, rocked her like a child and sang, 'Ta-ra-ra-boomdeay . . . Ta-ra-ra-boomdeay!'

When he was about to leave she asked him passionately, 'When? Later on? Where?' And she held out both hands to his mouth, as if wanting to catch his reply in them.

'It's not really convenient today,' he said after a moment's thought. 'Perhaps tomorrow, though.'

And they parted. Before lunch Sophia went off to the convent to see Olga, but was told that she was reading the Psalter for someone who had died. From the convent she went to her father's and drove aimlessly up and down the main streets and side-streets until evening. While she was riding, for some reason she kept remembering that aunt with the tear-stained eyes, who was fretting her life away.

That night they all went riding on troikas again and heard the gypsies in that out-of-town restaurant. And when they were once again passing the convent Sophia thought of Olga and became terrified at the thought that there was no escape for girls and women in her circle, except perpetual troika-rides or entering a convent to mortify the flesh . . .

The following day she had a lovers' rendezvous once again. She went for solitary cab-rides around town and thought of her aunt.

A week later Little Volodya dropped her. Then life reverted to normal and was just as boring, dreary – and sometimes just as excruciating as it had ever been. The Colonel and Little Volodya had long billiards and piquet sessions, Rita told her tasteless anecdotes in the same lifeless fashion, Sophia kept driving in cabs and asking her husband to take her for troika-rides.

Almost every day she called at the convent, boring Olga with her complaints of intolerable suffering; she cried and felt that she had brought something impure, pathetic and shabby into the cell. Olga, however, as if repeating a well-learned lesson parrot-fashion, told her that there was nothing to worry about, that it would all pass and that God would forgive her.

FOR THE BEST IN PAPERBACKS, LOOK FOR THE

In every corner of the world, on every subject under the sun, Penguin represents quality and variety – the very best in publishing today.

For complete information about books available from Penguin – including Puffins, Penguin Classics and Arkana – and how to order them, write to us at the appropriate address below. Please note that for copyright reasons the selection of books varies from country to country.

In the United Kingdom: Please write to *Dept E.P., Penguin Books Ltd, Harmondsworth, Middlesex, UB7 0DA.*

If you have any difficulty in obtaining a title, please send your order with the correct money, plus ten per cent for postage and packaging, to *PO Box No 11, West Drayton, Middlesex*

In the United States: Please write to *Dept BA, Penguin, 299 Murray Hill Parkway, East Rutherford, New Jersey 07073*

In Canada: Please write to *Penguin Books Canada Ltd, 2801 John Street, Markham, Ontario L3R 1B4*

In Australia: Please write to the *Marketing Department, Penguin Books Australia Ltd, P.O. Box 257, Ringwood, Victoria 3134*

In New Zealand: Please write to the *Marketing Department, Penguin Books (NZ) Ltd, Private Bag, Takapuna, Auckland 9*

In India: Please write to *Penguin Overseas Ltd, 706 Eros Apartments, 56 Nehru Place, New Delhi, 110019*

In the Netherlands: Please write to *Penguin Books Netherlands B.V., Postbus 195, NL–1380AD Weesp*

In West Germany: Please write to *Penguin Books Ltd, Friedrichstrasse 10–12, D–6000 Frankfurt/Main 1*

In Spain: Please write to *Longman Penguin España, Calle San Nicolas 15, E–28013 Madrid*

In Italy: Please write to *Penguin Italia s.r.l., Via Como 4, I-20096 Pioltello (Milano)*

In France: Please write to *Penguin Books Ltd, 39 Rue de Montmorency, F-75003 Paris*

In Japan: Please write to *Longman Penguin Japan Co Ltd, Yamaguchi Building, 2–12–9 Kanda Jimbocho, Chiyoda-Ku, Tokyo 101*

FOR THE BEST IN PAPERBACKS, LOOK FOR THE

PENGUIN CLASSICS

Anton Chekhov	**The Duel and Other Stories**
	The Kiss and Other Stories
	Lady with Lapdog and Other Stories
	Plays (The Cherry Orchard/Ivanov/The Seagull/
	Uncle Vanya/The Bear/The Proposal/A
	Jubilee/Three Sisters)
	The Party and Other Stories
Fyodor Dostoyevsky	**The Brothers Karamazov**
	Crime and Punishment
	The Devils
	The Gambler/Bobok/A Nasty Story
	The House of the Dead
	The Idiot
	Notes From Underground and **The Double**
Nikolai Gogol	**Dead Souls**
	Diary of a Madman and Other Stories
Maxim Gorky	**My Apprenticeship**
	My Childhood
	My Universities
Mikhail Lermontov	**A Hero of Our Time**
Alexander Pushkin	**Eugene Onegin**
Leo Tolstoy	**Anna Karenin**
	Childhood/Boyhood/Youth
	The Cossacks/The Death of Ivan Ilyich/Happy
	Ever After
	The Kreutzer Sonata and Other Stories
	Master and Man and Other Stories
	Resurrection
	The Sebastopol Sketches
	War and Peace
Ivan Turgenev	**Fathers and Sons**
	First Love
	A Month in the Country
	On the Eve
	Rudin

FOR THE BEST IN PAPERBACKS, LOOK FOR THE

PENGUIN CLASSICS

Honoré de Balzac	**The Black Sheep**
	The Chouans
	Cousin Bette
	Eugénie Grandet
	Lost Illusions
	Old Goriot
	Ursule Mirouet
Corneille	**The Cid/Cinna/The Theatrical Illusion**
Alphonse Daudet	**Letters from My Windmill**
René Descartes	**Discourse on Method and Other Writings**
Denis Diderot	**Jacques the Fatalist**
Gustave Flaubert	**Madame Bovary**
	Sentimental Education
	Three Tales
Marie de France	**Lais**
Jean Froissart	**The Chronicles**
Théophile Gautier	**Mademoiselle de Maupin**
Edmond and Jules de Goncourt	**Germinie Lacerteux**
La Fontaine	**Selected Fables**
Guy de Maupassant	**Bel-Ami**
	Pierre and Jean
	Selected Short Stories
	A Woman's Life

FOR THE BEST IN PAPERBACKS, LOOK FOR THE 🐧

PENGUIN CLASSICS

Molière	The Misanthrope/The Sicilian/Tartuffe/A Doctor in Spite of Himself/The Imaginary Invalid
	The Miser/The Would-be Gentleman/That Scoundrel Scapin/Love's the Best Doctor/Don Juan
Michel de Montaigne	Essays
Marguerite de Navarre	The Heptameron
Blaise Pascal	Pensées
Marcel Proust	Against Saint-Beuve
Rabelais	The Histories of Gargantua and Pantagruel
Racine	Andromache/Britannicus/Berenice
	Iphigenia/Phaedra/Athaliah
Arthur Rimbaud	Collected Poems
Jean-Jacques Rousseau	The Confessions
	A Discourse on Equality
	The Social Contract
Jacques Saint-Pierre	Paul and Virginia
Madame de Sevigné	Selected Letters
Voltaire	Candide
	Philosophical Dictionary
Émile Zola	La Bête Humaine
	Germinal
	Nana
	Thérèse Raquin

FOR THE BEST IN PAPERBACKS, LOOK FOR THE

PENGUIN CLASSICS

Horatio Alger, Jr.	**Ragged Dick** and **Struggling Upward**
Phineas T. Barnum	**Struggles and Triumphs**
Ambrose Bierce	**The Enlarged Devil's Dictionary**
Charles Brockden Brown	**Edgar Huntly**
George W. Cable	**The Grandissimes**
Kate Chopin	**The Awakening and Selected Stories**
James Fenimore Cooper	**The Deerslayer**
	The Pioneers
	The Prairie
Stephen Crane	**The Red Badge of Courage**
Richard Henry Dana, Jr.	**Two Years Before the Mast**
Frederick Douglass	**Narrative of the Life of Frederick Douglass, An American Slave**
Theodore Dreiser	**Sister Carrie**
Ralph Waldo Emerson	**Selected Essays**
Joel Chandler Harris	**Uncle Remus**
Nathaniel Hawthorne	**Blithedale Romance**
	The House of the Seven Gables
	The Scarlet Letter and Selected Tales
William Dean Howells	**The Rise of Silas Lapham**
Washington Irving	**The Sketch Book of Geoffrey Crayon**
Alice James	**The Diary of Alice James**

FOR THE BEST IN PAPERBACKS, LOOK FOR THE 🐧

PENGUIN CLASSICS

FOR THE BEST IN PAPERBACKS, LOOK FOR THE 🐧

PENGUIN CLASSICS

FOR THE BEST IN PAPERBACKS, LOOK FOR THE

PENGUIN CLASSICS

Carl von Clausewitz	On War
Friedrich Engels	The Origins of the Family, Private Property and the State
Wolfram von Eschenbach	Parzival
	Willehalm
Goethe	Elective Affinities
	Faust
	Italian Journey 1786–88
	The Sorrows of Young Werther
Jacob and Wilhelm Grimm	Selected Tales
E. T. A. Hoffmann	Tales of Hoffmann
Henrik Ibsen	The Doll's House/The League of Youth/The Lady from the Sea
	Ghosts/A Public Enemy/When We Dead Wake
	Hedda Gabler/The Pillars of the Community/The Wild Duck
	The Master Builder/Rosmersholm/Little Eyolf/John Gabriel Borkman
	Peer Gynt
Søren Kierkegaard	Fear and Trembling
	The Sickness Unto Death
Friedrich Nietzsche	Beyond Good and Evil
	Ecce Homo
	A Nietzsche Reader
	Thus Spoke Zarathustra
	Twilight of the Idols and The Anti-Christ
Friedrich Schiller	The Robbers and Wallenstein
Arthur Schopenhauer	Essays and Aphorisms
Gottfried von Strassburg	Tristan
August Strindberg	Inferno and From an Occult Diary

BY THE SAME AUTHOR

THE KISS AND OTHER STORIES

Translated and Introduced by Ronald Wilks

The ten stories in this selection were written between 1887 and 1902 when Chekhov had reached his maturity as a short-story writer. They show him as a master of compression and as a probing analyst, unmasking the mediocrity, lack of ideals and spiritual and physical inertia of his generation. In these grim pictures of peasant life and telling portraits of men and women enmeshed in trivialities, in the finely observed, suffocating atmosphere of provincial towns with their pompous officials, frustrated, self-seeking wives and spineless husbands, Chekhov does not expound any system of morality but leaves readers to draw what conclusions they will.

PLAYS

Translated by Elisaveta Fen

One of a generation on the brink of a tremendous social upheaval, Anton Chekhov (1860–1904) paints in his plays an essentially tragic picture of Russian society. The plays in this volume – *Ivanov, The Cherry Orchard, The Seagull, Uncle Vania* and *Three Sisters*, together with three one-act 'jests' – all display Chekhov's overwhelming sense of the tedium and futility of everyday life. Yet his representation of human relationships is infinitely sympathetic, and each play contains at least one character who expresses Chekhov's hope for a brighter future.

Also published

LADY WITH LAPDOG AND OTHER STORIES